PENGUIN BOOKS

ANA OF CALIFORNIA

Andi Teran is from El Paso, Texas. Her nonfiction has been published by *Vanity Fair*, *Monocle*, and the *Paris Review Daily*. She currently resides in Los Angeles. *Ana of California* is her first novel.

ANA
of
CALIFORNIA

ANDI TERAN

PENGUIN BOOKS

PENGUIN BOOKS

Published by the Penguin Group
Penguin Group (USA) LLC
375 Hudson Street
New York, New York 10014

USA | Canada | UK | Ireland | Australia | New Zealand | India | South Africa | China
penguin.com
A Penguin Random House Company

First published in Penguin Books 2015

LIBRARY OF CONGRESS CATALOGING-IN-PUBLICATION DATA
Teran, Andi.
Ana of California : a novel / Andi Teran.
pages cm
ISBN 978-0-14-312649-2
1. Teenage girls—Family relationships—Fiction. 2. Foster children—Fiction.
3. California—Fiction.
I. Title
PS3620.E73A85 2015
813'.6—dc23   2014042525

Printed in the United States of America
1 3 5 7 9 10 8 6 4 2

Set in ITC Esprit Std
Designed by Sabrina Bowers

TO ALBERT AND BARBARA,
AND FOR CELIA

In between two tall mountains
there's a place they call Lonesome.
Don't see why they call it Lonesome;
I'm never lonesome now I live there.

—CONNIE CONVERSE, "TALKIN' LIKE YOU (TWO TALL MOUNTAINS)"

ACKNOWLEDGMENTS

Thank you to Pamela Ribon for setting this entire adventure in motion. Many thanks to everyone at Penguin, especially Pete Harris, Patrick Nolan, Claire Abramowitz, and to my editor, Emily Murdock Baker, for the encouragement and guidance. Thank you to Alexis Hurley and InkWell for the incredible support and that second glass of wine.

Love and thank you to my family and friends: to Nicholas Almanza, Carrie Teran, Margie Copeland Ruth, Margaret and Graham Millar, and to Lucy Robertson and the Heirlooms; to Faye and Ellery Casell for being my rainbow in a happy tree; to Elizabeth Hanks, Emily Ryan Lerner, and Katie Orphan, aka the ladies of Sweater Weather Underground, for their feedback; to Chelsea Fairless and Sam Buffa for their expertise; and to Rebecca Davis, Alex Diaz, Julie Sagalowsky Diaz, Christina Gregory, Deirdre Corley, Alex Garinger, Shannon Wier McMillan, Matt Mullin, and Amy Dickson Noland for their kind ears and loving support.

This book is dedicated to my parents and to my grandma, who are an enormous inspiration to me. Thank you forever. And, most of all, thank you to Hamish Robertson for absolutely everything tied in a blue ribbon wrapped around my heart. You are the reason.

ANA
of
CALIFORNIA

CHAPTER ONE

She was out of beginnings, this she knew.

Ana ran her hands through her knotted hair, wondering when she'd last washed it. She'd been up for more than twenty-four hours, and there was still ketchup on her shirt.

"This is the fifth home you've been expelled from in the last ten years."

"To be fair, it was only four. I was at the Mitchell house twice."

"Well, this time it's . . . a situation."

Ana stared at the wall behind the desk. She'd seen the corkboard many times before and had studied the photographs of Mrs. Saucedo's children over the years. She'd watched them grow older, lose teeth, win ribbons, and pose for class photos. There was always a birthday card or thank-you note pushpinned to the board. Today it was a small California license plate bearing the word MOM.

"I know it's been hard, but we need to find a solution,"

Mrs. Saucedo said, adjusting her glasses. "I'd like us to work together on this."

Ana let her eyes roam around the room. The walls were still a pale industrial green, and there was a fake tree in the corner, the same one with the rubber branches that would never grow. She remembered the first time she saw the tree and how it had been strung with lights and ornaments. There were reindeer, paper stars, and angels made of tin. One branch was weighed down by a heavy gourd, the middle hollowed out to hold figurines of a man and a woman staring down at a baby, a glittered star hanging above them. She remembered how she wanted to climb inside the gourd and live there forever.

"*Feliz Navidad*," Ana said, still staring at the tree. "Those were the first words you said to me."

Mrs. Saucedo looked down at her desk. Everything was in its place save for Ana's file, which was thick and open to a photo of a little girl in a pink puffy coat.

"I remember," she said.

"It was cold, not like today."

"Yes, it was."

"It was the first time I ever wished for snow—not that it would ever happen."

Ana shifted in the chair. The armrests were worn and rough under her fingertips.

"Would you like to talk about what happened that night?" Mrs. Saucedo asked, knowing Ana never did.

This time, though, Ana did want to talk about it. She remembered everything, every detail. Back then, it was referred to as "an accident," and also, "the incident," but Ana chose to name it as you would a melodramatic poem or story—"With Sorrow and Black Doves." She was the only one who had seen what had happened the night she was brought in to child services, and every time she entered Mrs. Saucedo's small office, the memories of The Night That Started It All returned harsh and fast. She'd managed to shut them away year after year, but there, in that windowless room, the images flickered in the periphery.

"You don't have to if you don't want to," Mrs. Saucedo said, keeping her voice soft and slow, trying to catch Ana's eyes, which remained fixed on the tree.

If there was anyone she could talk to it was Mrs. Lupe Saucedo, the nice lady behind the desk who genuinely cared about her well-being—even after all these years. Though she hadn't felt it physically since they'd met almost a decade ago, Mrs. Saucedo's warmth remained. She remembered how the woman's arms had embraced her that day and how the scent of roses and clean cotton still tickled her nose. Mrs. Saucedo had whispered to her back then too.

" '*Ya me canso de llorar y no amanece.*' "

"You're not crying and you do have hope." Mrs. Saucedo sighed. "Please, this isn't a telenovela. Like I've told you many times before, the drama does you no favors."

"It's a line from a song, not a comment on my psychological state."

"Well, I'm glad to hear you still speaking Spanish. I think your grandma would be proud."

Almost as a reflex, Ana's hands squeezed the armrests of the chair. She kept her eyes focused anywhere but on Mrs. Saucedo's face and concentrated instead on her own breathing. She wanted to speak but feared giving in to her tears, so she dipped her chin to her chest.

What she wanted to tell Mrs. Saucedo was that the line had been from her grandma's—her *abuela*'s—favorite song, and that she had memorized every word. She wanted to explain that if there had been music playing on the day of the incident, it would have been this very song. She imagined the voice of a banshee swooping in to replace the screaming, how a trumpet might have substituted for blasts, and how she wished the plucking of an acoustic guitar had kept her company in the aftermath of silence, a melancholy soundtrack for the newly alone.

"I don't speak it as much as I should," Ana said, instead tucking her hands between her knees, which wouldn't stop bouncing.

"You understand I have nowhere left to send you, yes? We talked about three strikes less than a year ago, and since then you've gone from the group home to another failed foster situation. This is it—no more homes, no more chances," Mrs. Saucedo said. "It might help to talk about what happened that night, talk about your abuela, and talk about what we can do to get you to where she'd want you to be."

"If it's all right with you, I'd rather talk about what's been going on the past few months."

Mrs. Saucedo had heard complaints about foster parents before. She anticipated an elaborate explanation, knowing Ana's flair for the dramatic. In her younger years, Ana's stories were wildly embellished but had since boiled down to silent defiance after being removed from her third foster home.

"I spoke with Ms. Fenton."

"I'm desperate to hear what she had to say."

"I think you know exactly what she said."

"If you had any idea how we've been treated all summer . . ."

"Ana . . ."

"—And how the rules were completely . . ."

"It's not your place to step in."

"But it wasn't right, and someone needed to do something because no one ever does."

"I understand the conditions were not the best," Mrs. Saucedo said, trying not to raise her voice. "And for that I apologize. But Ms. Fenton is a longtime foster mother, and despite the strict household, it is not your job to tell her how to discipline the other children."

"So, I'm just supposed to sit there and let two little kids go without any food for the second day in a row? I'm supposed to kick back while the so-called mother of the house eats the freezer and shelves clean just to prove a stupid point? It's Ludicrous, capital L."

"I don't understand."

"She doesn't give any of us lunch or dinner—like zero food—anytime she feels we're doing something wrong, which is pretty much all the time. She got angry that I gave an ice cream sandwich to the kids to share, and I get that it was the last one in the freezer and everything, but it was all we had. And she took it out on them. It's not the first time it's happened, either."

"Ms. Fenton relayed to me that you were combative and inappropriate, and while I disagree wholeheartedly with her methods, I do not condone your response to them."

"Believe me, I can skip a ton of meals, but the kids? She takes their toys away and never lets them play, as if their lives weren't completely messed up already, as if we weren't starving enough. So, yeah, something needed to be done. Sorry but not sorry."

"I was unaware this was going on," Mrs. Saucedo said, taking a breath. "I understand your point, but staging a death scene isn't funny and you know it."

Mrs. Saucedo thought she detected a smile. Ana sometimes smiled when she was uncomfortable, rarely when she was proud or defiant. It was a habit that often led to miscommunication.

"That's not what we were doing," Ana said, sitting up and looking at Mrs. Saucedo for the first time. "Like I said, there was nothing in the cupboards and only ketchup in the fridge, so I told the kids to imagine they were eating hamburgers. I squirted ketchup in their mouths, and we pretended we were so full we couldn't get up from the floor. It was just a stupid game . . . something I made up to take their minds off things."

Mrs. Saucedo had a hard time believing that had been the extent of it.

"Haven't you been going to the recreation center for lunch?" she asked, remembering Ana and her foster siblings were part of the Summer Food Program. "Hasn't Ms. Fenton been making sure that you go?"

"She didn't let us out of the house a few times this week because she was angry that I stayed late at the library. Sometimes when she gets angry, she punishes all of us and says we're 'putting her in a mood.' It's a mood I like to call completely insane."

Mrs. Saucedo kept her eyes on Ana.

"I'm not making this up."

"I never said you were."

"Really, Mrs. S., she's the most deplorable woman. I don't mean to call you out or criticize the way things are done around here or anything, but the way you guys pick foster parents sucks. I know it was stupid to leave, and I know I've done it a few times before, but after she refused to feed us again, after so many days with no lunch, and after we were forced to sit on the couch while she inhaled a bag of Cheetos without offering us any and then told everyone it was all my fault—you have to understand why I had to get out of there. But I wasn't making a run for it, I swear. I was going to get something for everyone to eat."

Ana chewed her bottom lip and kept her hands folded in her lap. She looked down at her ripped jeans, focusing on the misshapen hearts and stars drawn all over her exposed kneecaps, the remnants of an afternoon spent playing "art school" with her foster brother and sister, the two she knew she'd probably never see again.

"Not to elaborate, but she made us do all the housework too. Honestly, I don't mind, but if there was toothpaste on the mirror, or if I didn't iron all the wrinkles out of her shirts, she would take it out on all of us. I tried to be nice, to do extra work. I tried to ignore the way her disgusting boyfriend used to stare at my T-shirt as if invited by a logo emblazoned across my chest, and I tried to do everything you've always told me to do."

"You don't have to say anything else," Mrs. Saucedo said.

"But I shouldn't have left like that . . . I get it."

"No, you shouldn't have. Nor should you have called Ms. Fenton what you called her, regardless of how she treated you."

Ana had heard the sound of the screen door slam behind her as she ran out of the house. Her throat was raw and the imprint of small hands still warmed her palms. She remembered running through the gravel in the front yard and all the way down the block, ignoring the heat of the sidewalk seeping into her sneakers. She couldn't remember how far she'd gone or why she'd neglected to say good-bye, knowing, even then, that she wouldn't be allowed to return. She had promised she'd never leave her foster siblings there—that she'd never leave them period—but she'd broken that promise again, in the same way it had always been broken to her.

"You're almost sixteen," Mrs. Saucedo said. "You are old enough and smart enough to know how and when to rise above a situation. I know you were looking after the others, but the person you need to look after most is yourself."

Mrs. Saucedo studied Ana's face, which was tense; her eyes focused on clasped hands, one thumb picking at the other. She'd seen this look before.

"What's the matter?"

"I know you don't want me to get into it, but I should probably tell you that she brought up my mother."

"What did she say?"

"That I'm going to end up just like her."

Mrs. Saucedo took a breath. "Is that all she said?"

"No."

"I want you to tell me exactly what she said."

It wasn't the first time Ana's file had been used against her, if the file even allowed her to be assigned to a foster home in the first place. No one wanted to deal with a child who had been marked as difficult or traumatized.

"She said I'm going to end up in jail, where I quote un-quote 'belong,' if a bullet doesn't find me first. It's not like I haven't heard it before."

"You know that's not true."

"Isn't it?" Ana said, hands gripping a bouncing knee.

"Your parents knew what they were involved in, and the

rest . . . None of it was your fault," Mrs. Saucedo said, removing her glasses and placing them on top of Ana's file. "We've talked about how to deal with difficulty, how to temper your emotions, but we've never talked about why they flare up every time you settle in to a new place. We're either going to talk about it now and figure out the next steps or I'm going to have to make a decision without your input."

"Just put me in another foster home. I can start over again."

"That's not an option."

"What if I lived with you? I can do all the housework. You can put me in the garage or something, and I'll babysit your kids until school starts—really, I can help out. I'll be quiet, and you won't even see me."

Mrs. Saucedo closed her eyes for a moment. She thought back to her training and reflected on her decades of experience. She reminded herself not to show any anger or sign of frustration, so she inhaled deeply, and even though it was discouraged, she thought about her own children.

"You won't even know I'm there. I'm good at washing dishes and fixing things. And I don't need to eat much. I can go days without food, done it many times before. And I know a million bedtime stories that my abuela told me, ones I'm sure your kids haven't heard before. It'll just be until I'm sixteen—not like forever or anything."

Mrs. Saucedo moved closer to Ana, who turned her body toward the door.

"I'm not crying," Ana said. "My eye itches. And I'm just sick of this."

"I know."

"Honestly, I didn't mean to freak out and run. I'm trying to do the right thing."

"I know you are, but that's not the problem."

"Please don't send me back to the group home."

Ana wiped her face. She told herself that if her eyes met Mrs. Saucedo's again, she might drown.

"I'll do anything," Ana said. "Just please don't send me back there."

She felt her voice slip and knew she'd never be able to catch it. Every breath seemed heavier and harder to swallow. She'd been to a group home before Ms. Fenton's; in fact, it was the last time she'd sat in Mrs. Saucedo's office arguing against another situation that had remained woefully unchecked. Ana could barely remember the faces of those who had surrounded her back then, though she could recite every word they said. Her memory flashed to the bathroom, the group of girls standing behind her as she tried not to make eye contact in the mirror. They were older and greater in number, swift and quiet in their attack. She was shoved from behind first and punched once or twice—she couldn't remember—before her head hit the floor. There were multiple feet near her face, that she remembered, and she'd kept her eyes focused on the chipped tile where there was a clump of her own hair.

"Take a breath," Mrs. Saucedo said and slid a box of tissues across the desk. Ana Cortez had cried in her office on only two occasions. The first time, Mrs. Saucedo had put her arms around Ana's small, rigid shoulders, which refused to soften, unlike those of her own daughters. This time, Mrs. Saucedo remained still, willing herself not to do or say anything she couldn't promise.

"I'm serious about working for you," Ana repeated. "I can sleep on the floor. You won't even know I'm here. I'll do all your filing, whatever job you want me to do."

"Funny enough, I think a job is exactly what you need."

In all the years that Lupe Saucedo had thought about Ana Cortez—and she'd thought about her more often than she'd anticipated—she had never truly known what to do. Ana was six years old when she was brought in the first time on an unseasonably cold Southern California night wearing dirty shorts and a pink coat. Unlike other children brought in under similar situations, Ana was talkative and had been known around the Ramona Houses as *La Boca*. The police officers had said she had told them her name was "*Fantasma,*" and when Mrs. Saucedo asked the young Ana why she wanted to call herself "ghost," the girl had looked her in the eye and said she had made her parents disappear. It was the only time Lupe ever considered bringing a child home.

She'd been relieved when Ana's grandmother arrived, heaving with worry. She watched as the slight woman swooped the little girl into her arms and they both held on to each other and cried. It was a rare happy ending that lasted for just more than a year. Ana was back in her office the following spring, her hair drawn up in colorful ribbons that clashed with the bandages peeking out from the neck of her dress. Where she'd been surprisingly chatty the first time around despite the grim circumstances, she had remained relatively mute following the death of her grandmother.

Year after year, every time the slightly older Ana sat across from her, hair longer, frame slighter, Mrs. Saucedo felt a ghost was still with her. There were times she'd be shopping in the grocery store, her own kids in tow, and she'd catch the gaze of a child in someone else's cart. They'd be the same eyes—deep, placid, and reflective—wanting of so much and so little in a single glance that Mrs. Saucedo would feel a chill pass through her.

"Put me anywhere you want then," Ana said. "Doesn't matter. Like you said, I'm almost sixteen, right? So put me in a group house, and I'll put myself on the streets. I know how to take care of myself."

"I have something more interesting in mind," Mrs. Saucedo said, opening an e-mail.

"Let me guess . . . juvie? That's the next logical step, right?"

"We've yet to discuss the possibility of emancipation," she explained. "Do you understand what that means?"

"I can live on my own if I want?"

"It's not as simple as that. You'll have to work at a job. Upon completion of that job, your employers will decide— along with me as well as a judge—whether you can formally emancipate yourself. Think of it like speeding ahead to eighteen only with better options. You and I both know living on the streets isn't easy, especially here."

"What kind of job are we talking about?"

Mrs. Saucedo swiveled around the computer. On the screen was a photograph of a gray house with a red door, impressive but not imposing. There were white steps leading up to a wraparound porch with two chairs and several wooden boxes overflowing with wildflowers. The entire house was surrounded by lush fields of green.

"It's a one-month trial. If the work goes well, you'll stay through Labor Day and go to school there. If it doesn't, you come back to a group home and school here."

"Where's there?"

"Have you ever been to a farm?" Mrs. Saucedo asked.

"Not really my kind of thing."

"Well, I'm afraid this is your only choice."

Ana stared at the house in the photo, which was set back against towering trees. She hadn't noticed it at first, but there was a woman standing off to the side. It was hard to make out her face, but she was captured smiling and in mid-wave.

"Have you ever been outside of Los Angeles?" Mrs. Saucedo asked.

"No," Ana answered. "I've never even been to the beach."

"Ever been on an airplane?"

"Nope."

"Never wanted to travel?"

"Sure, but c'mon, Mrs. S., let's get real . . ."

"Let's," Mrs. Saucedo said. She shut Ana's file and leaned across the desk. "Grab your backpack."

CHAPTER TWO

Nothing irritated Abbie Garber more than unexpected visitors during the summer harvest. Everyone in Hadley knew that for her it was a sacred time devoted to picking, packing, pruning, and preserving while managing the staff and overseeing produce season. What this meant for Abbie—proprietress of all products stamped GARBER FARM—was a gentle dose of mania. The last thing she wanted was to finish the day feeling even the slightest bit behind.

"Emmett!" Abbie shouted out the screen door. "If that woman is here to bother Manny about the tractor, I will sharpen my shears on her Beemer's bumper!"

Abbie broke her own rule by letting the screen door slam shut. She walked toward one of the curtained windows at the front of the house, checking her reflection in the hall mirror along the way.

She took a breath before peeling back the linen curtain. Just beyond the wooden fence, on the perimeter of the fields, stood her close but not-so-close neighbor Minerva F. Shaw, chatting with the farm's field manager, Manny, who leaned against his tractor stroking an overgrown mustache and looking the opposite of amused. While it was true the F stood for "Fellowes," in memory of Minerva's long-dead first husband, why she kept the initial after she married her second late husband, Bob Shaw, had remained a mystery. Abbie didn't care to know the reason why, especially because she'd always given the F a different meaning; she just wanted Minerva to mind her own business.

"I'm going to give you five seconds, Minerva Fellowes Shaw," Abbie said, turning to the pair of armchairs flanking the fireplace in the corner of the room. "And if you're still standing there when I pull back this curtain again, so help you, I will unleash the dogs."

In actuality, Garber Farm had only one dog, Dolly, a retriever mix who favored lounging on the porch or barking at the wind to any sort of farm duties. Still, Minerva Shaw's repeated visits on matters of tractor noise, fence placement, and anything that was no business of her own enraged Abbie's proud sensibilities enough for her to imagine a pack of wild dogs once and for all chasing her meddlesome neighbor away.

There had been a time when Garber Farm housed a whole menagerie of animals. Abbie and her brother, Emmett, had enjoyed growing up on the idyllic Northern California farm, its fields vast, lush, and undulating up and down the hillside in shades of brilliant green. Their hands had helped their mother roll out pie dough and make preserves each season when they weren't helping their father plant every crop. And though the siblings spent most of their lives together, Abbie had left home in her teen years, following the unexpected death of their mother.

Emmett Garber had lived in Hadley all of his life, sharing several of those years happily working and living above the barn with his beloved wife, Josie. But in the year of the codling moth, when the whole of the county had suffered nature's winged misfortune, Emmett Garber Sr. had died too, leaving the farm and all its dealings to both Emmett and Abbie equally. Though they both hadn't lived at the farm together in more than a decade, they came back together to take their rightful place as inheritors of the soil.

It was a turbulent time, especially for Emmett, but coming back to Garber Farm had been a blessing for Abbie. Mired in a troubled marriage with a man more devoted to his guitar, Abbie had been searching for a way to let him and a life in the city go. Following her father's death, she packed a single suitcase, donned her great-grandmother's old straw hat, which had been languishing in the back of her tiny closet for years, and left the ramshackle San Francisco apartment she'd worked so hard to love.

Though Emmett and Abbie had settled comfortably into farm life, there were times when the wind danced through the buckeyes or a majestic hawk circled overhead, and each one of them would feel a lump sliding down their throats. Abbie worked late into the night, making jam and a wide variety of pickles with names like Fab Figs or Beauteous Beets. On lonelier evenings, typically in the colder months or when Emmett had retreated to his haven in the barn, she would pore over recipe books or read online forums on the best way to make cider or tackle all-natural pest control.

Emmett preferred to harness himself to the land. He was

up every morning before dawn, tending to the more grueling workings of the farm; in truth, he preferred the silence in those early hours. Josie would awaken with him at the same time every morning. There would always be a cup of coffee and freshly baked muffin on their small breakfast table, and when he returned from inspecting the crops and opening the fence for the morning staff, he'd stride over the hill, sunrise illuminating the tiny barn, and Josie would wave to him from the window. These days, he took his breakfast with Dolly on the porch or back in the barn. Rarely did Abbie join him outside. It had been almost a year since Josie's unexpected departure, an event that rendered both siblings speechless. Their mutual affection for her reached back to a shared childhood. Abbie often watched through the window as Emmett stared out into the horizon, streaks of gray speckling his shadow of a beard, his cowboy hat drawn low.

Garber Farm was their life, and it wasn't an easy one. Emmett and Abbie felt a duty to preserve the legacy of the farm, one of the only small organic farms still in existence around Hadley. After all, Garbers had been farming this land for a hundred years. In order to stay afloat, they'd had to move beyond selling at the local farmers' markets. Their wide variety of vegetables and herbs was legendary, and more crops meant more work. Abbie had also taken to making seasonal batches of infused oil to sell along with pickles, preserves, and her award-winning hard cider, all adapted from her mother's or grandmother's recipes. Still, even in a successful year, they never had the margin the bigger corporate farms enjoyed.

They knew something needed to change. Emmett's solution was to retreat to the barn and brood, but Abbie figured a younger, more robust extra hand was what they needed to shake things up. She worried about her brother and his melancholy ways and thought having a young person to live with them and take along on weekly deliveries might help clear out the cobwebs. It wouldn't hurt to have some help in the kitchen either.

After much debate, they settled on the idea of a farm intern who would work for school credit. Emmett reached out to Hadley High and Abbie posted a notice on the advertising board at Moon Pharm General Store. But the results were the same: the town's local boys were either on the football field, tending to their own family business after school, or, as Hadley's oldest and wisest resident, Alder Kinman, put it, "Sodding off in the forest with the rest of the jugs and thugs. Wouldn't you?"

Despite Emmett's initial protestations, Abbie contacted the local foster system. In the same way that she pursued the rest of her "harebrained ideas"—Emmett's words and often her father's too—Abbie went ahead with the paperwork, background checks, and home visit anyway, which occurred while Emmett was coming in from the fields. She knew the only way to change her brother's mind was to never give him any option in the first place, and he signed off on the matter hoping that would be the end of it. Abbie was surprised when the system matched her with a young woman from Los Angeles, less than a week after her approval came through. It was a "special case," they had said, and one in which there was no option to dispute the gender. Emmett would grumble, but he'd get used to it. And Abbie relished the idea of female company. She reassured Emmett that the "foster student" was up for the challenge of farm work, and he never asked any more than that, not that she intended to elaborate.

The last person she wanted to explain all this to was

Minerva Shaw. It was only a matter of time before the news was all over Main Street anyway. Any bit of news became Minerva's sole duty to share. She was the self-appointed chief of Hadley's gossip police.

"No need to get everyone talking yet," Abbie thought before opening the door and stepping onto the front porch. Minerva made her way up the stone-lined front path, hips swinging, her red heels awkwardly clacking up the wooden steps.

"I must say, I just had the most astonishing conversation with your brother." Minerva trilled through coral-colored lips.

"Hello to you too," Abbie answered.

"Likewise, dear." Minerva removed her oversize sunglasses and tucked them into her pink leather handbag.

"He mumbled something about going to the airport . . . something about someone of the male persuasion coming to see you?"

"We do have visitors from time to time."

Minerva pursed her lips and squinted as if inspecting a dappled onion. "Not to be a nuisance, but I'm just checking that all is well with you, my dear. I wouldn't want some cold-blooded killer swooping into your single-occupied farmhouse while the menfolk are away. As much as I love your brother, his silence is quite the concern since you-know-who vacated the premises."

"We're fine, Minerva," Abbie said. "Honestly, there hasn't been a murder in Hadley since the gold rush."

"Of course you are," Minerva said with a wink. "Well, enough with this idle chatter. I stopped by for some pickled carrots. I'd love to serve some with the wine and cheese tonight . . . maybe a bottle of cider too? I have a full house this weekend."

"I think that can be arranged," Abbie said as they headed inside.

Minerva could never bring herself to tell Abbie how much she loved the farmhouse, especially the kitchen, which was all white with wooden countertops and glass-fronted cabinets that showed off the Garber family's collection of mismatched Victorian china. A picture window above the sink looked out over the back garden, which was meticulously laid out with rows of herbs, lettuces, beans, and heirloom tomatoes, the perimeter bursting with wildflowers. A thin shelf built across the middle of the window displayed small bud vases and mason jars full of clipped rosemary and scarlet zinnias.

Abbie's touch was all over the kitchen. There were vintage tea towels near the sunken sink and a large green tin with BREAD painted across it in bold letters. Tucked into the corners of the countertops were well-used cookbooks leaning up against glass containers full of flour, sugar, and assorted baking goods. Along the walls hung antique plates and framed wildflower prints. There was flair to the kitchen beyond its warm, vanilla-scented spell, and it never failed to render Minerva Shaw speechless.

"I've got only a few jars of carrots left but plenty of cider," Abbie bellowed from her cavernous pantry. "But we'll be back into full swing in the coming weeks. I can do two carrots for fifteen and bottles of cider for seven each."

"Wonderful," Minerva said. Her eyes swept across the kitchen, taking in the rustic table in the corner. "Sweet peach? You've laid out the table with your mother's napkins and those plates with the scratched roses. You weren't expecting me to stay for dinner, were you?"

Abbie emerged from the pantry with bottles in hand.

"Definitely not. Why?"

"Well, dear, because the table is set for three," Minerva said. She draped her fingertips across her chest, her head tipped and primed for information.

"As I said, we're expecting company tonight."

"You seem to be going through a lot of trouble for this mystery guest. Let me guess . . . an old Garber relative?" Minerva inquired. "Perhaps a certain faraway customer to which you or Emmett has become . . . close?"

Minerva always had a way of emphasizing the solitude the Garber siblings shared. She also had a habit of going out of her way to introduce any bachelor types drastically above and below Abbie's age range if she happened to run into Abbie in town. Abbie knew she meant well, but it was amusing.

"Yes, they'll be here for an extended stay," Abbie offered.

"How exciting!"

"It's been difficult knowing exactly what to prepare, seeing as how my guest is coming from quite a ways away," Abbie said.

Minerva's eyes widened as she cleared her throat.

"I have a lot to do to prepare," Abbie said. She set the box of rattling jars on the counter and smoothed down her well-worn shirt.

"Yes, of course," Minerva said, backing away from the table. She dug into her purse and pulled out an overflowing leopard-print wallet. She handed over the cash and looked down at the box on the counter, then back up at Abbie again.

Abbie smiled and picked up the box, carrying it out onto the porch, and noticed Minerva had parked her BMW all the way down the road.

"Please tell Teresa and the gals at the inn I send my regards," Abbie said, setting the box in Minerva's unwilling arms.

She walked to the door before turning back around on the threshold.

"And Minerva?"

"Yes?"

"If you don't see me around town this weekend, or happen to drive by and notice the curtains drawn, don't be alarmed. I'll most likely be entertaining an adolescent murderer."

"No need for sarcasm, my dear," said Minerva, theatrically balancing the box and tottering down the walkway. "An unexpected savage might be just what you need!"

CHAPTER THREE

Emmett Garber took the usual route. It was his favorite time of day—namely, anytime he found himself alone in the old pickup truck. He rolled down the windows, turned up the music, and accelerated down the farm road.

When Abbie first mentioned the idea of taking on an extra hand, Emmett envisioned an intern from the university up north. Class credit was just as desirable as a wage, he thought, and a young man with farming prospects would be glad of the experience. He'd been college age when his father enlisted his help on the farm.

"The world needs more men in the field," his father had said. "Nothing more noble than tying yourself to tradition and terrain."

Emmett had been offered two choices on his eighteenth birthday: life on the farm or time in the military, and he'd chosen the former.

He'd been content enough, if a little lonely. It was the

summer Abbie left the farm that Emmett first noticed Josie, Abbie's childhood best friend. She'd been there all along really. But one night at a bonfire down on the beach with a bunch of other kids, he found himself sitting next to her and realizing they'd never actually had a conversation. Without Abbie around to protest her best friend's dating her older brother, it wasn't long before Josie was once again a permanent fixture around Garber Farm.

Emmett moved out of the farmhouse and into the barn. Farm life took on a different meaning now that he had someone to share it with. He and Josie were married on a windy, cloudy day as the meadowlarks sang. It was a small ceremony, with just a few people in attendance, including Abbie as the slightly bewildered maid of honor. But it was the first time Emmett Garber remembered welcoming the seasons of his future.

"Our future," he had told Josie. "For what is mine is yours, forever."

"Forever's a helluva long time, son," his father had said. "Sometimes *way* too long."

But an eternity without Josie seemed almost worse. It was easier for Emmett to remember the bitterness of the end, still too painful to remember the warmth of the beginning. Whatever he chose to remember, the circumstances remained the same: he was still here and she was still gone. The farm and Abbie were all that was left.

"What kind of grown man lives alone with his goddamned sister?"

Emmett said this to Neil Young, whom he always envisioned riding shotgun. Neil was a good listener. He didn't always answer, but sometimes he did, so Emmett turned the music up and sailed toward the oncoming shore.

"*A maid. A man needs a maid.*"

"Indeed," Emmett thought to himself.

"*It's hard to make that change . . .*" Neil sang.

"Right again," Emmett said.

He turned the truck down Roseberry Lane, away from the sandy coastline. He drove past familiar flat green farmland dotted here and there with cottages, errant tractors, and worn dairy silos dwarfed by their redwood neighbors.

The cars began to multiply as he drove closer to civilization, closer to the populated area where learning and logging had lured both the hippie and the money-hungry pioneer. Though most of Emmett's friends had moved away, he was never interested in life outside of Hadley. He'd never seen the point. Everything he'd ever wanted was a stone's skip away from the farm; the wider world never tugged at his chin like it did for Abbie.

Emmett sped up as he approached the airport and parked in front. The small parking lot was surprisingly empty given that there was an incoming flight. He shoved his hand into his coat pocket and pulled out the torn paper with the flight number and name of the kid, whoever he was, whatever he looked like—Abbie hadn't elaborated—to make sure he'd arrived at the appropriate time.

"Cortez," he read aloud with a shake of his head, wondering if Neil had reached into his pocket and scrawled it himself.

"*Cortez . . . the Killer.*"

Ana sat chewing the skin around her nails. It wasn't as if she'd never been left somewhere before. She chose the most visible seat nearest to the doors of the airport entrance, reminding herself not to panic, and calmly took in her surroundings.

"So much wood," she thought of the wall-to-wall paneling. "Like a lumberjack's cabin."

The airport lobby couldn't have been more different from the vast steel blankness and harried blur of LAX. There was a deer head mounted on one wall, for instance, and only a handful of travelers milling about. One man seemed to be looking for someone in particular, scrutinizing each passenger in turn. He got the attention of the lone security guard, the very same one who had approached Ana earlier with crossed arms and pursed lips.

"I'm looking for a kid, about sixteen, name of Cortez. He was supposed to be in on the flight from L.A.," Emmett told the security guard, who didn't seem the slightest bit interested.

"Yeah, buddy, that flight's been in for over half an hour."

"See any teenage boys wandering around?"

"Nope. But there's a girl . . ."

"Boy, Cortez something. My sister didn't give me the last name. Typical."

"You sure you're not looking for a girl? Because there's a kid been taking up the whole front bank of chairs over there. Says she's working on a farm for the summer, but you and I both know that's code in these parts."

Emmett looked over at the lone figure sitting near the door. It was most definitely a girl, somewhat diminutive, though hard to tell under the oversize army jacket she was hiding underneath. He continued staring, hoping his eyes were playing tricks. She caught him looking and sat up straighter.

"That's her," the guard said, pointing in Ana's direction. "Has to be. Seems like trouble if you ask me."

"Surely this couldn't be my ride," Ana thought. Mrs. Saucedo said to expect a single woman named Abigail Garber who'd most likely be thrilled to see her, and not this puzzled-looking man. Ana grabbed her backpack and clutched it to her chest.

"Cortez?" the lumberjack said as he ambled over.

"Yeah, I mean, yes, I'm Ana Cortez."

"Where'd you fly in from?"

"L.A.—the Los Angeles International Airport," she corrected herself. "Are you Abigail Garber?"

"Do I look like Abigail Garber?"

"Well, I wouldn't want to presume. People have all kinds of crazy names these days. Not that it's a crazy name."

"You're waiting for Abigail Garber, correct?"

"I am. Sir."

Ana held her bag tighter. Emmett nodded his head and clenched his teeth, unable to hide his frustration.

"Do you have some sort of paperwork or verification?" he asked.

"I don't have a driver's license if that's what you're asking, but I do have an ID card."

"No, I mean papers telling me your . . . specifics."

"No offense," Ana said, "but I was told by Mrs. Lupe Saucedo from Los Angeles County Support Child Services that I was to wait for an Abigail Garber to pick me up and not to leave with anyone else."

"I'm Emmett Garber, Abbie's brother."

"Do *you* have paperwork or verification?"

"This is ridiculous," Emmett said. "If your name is Cortez and you're waiting for Abigail Garber to take you to Garber Farm, then I'm your ride."

Ana remained still, her eyes focused and unblinking,

making it difficult for Emmett to hold her gaze. He cleared his throat and pulled a well-worn leather wallet out of his back pocket.

"The mustache is a beard now," he said, handing over his license.

"I can see that. It's distinguished. Like a regal lumberjack."

"You think I look like a lumberjack?"

"Honestly, I don't really have a frame of reference."

"May I?" Emmett reached for Ana's backpack but she held it close.

"If you don't mind, sir, I'd like to hold on to it."

"Call me Emmett, not sir," he said, taking back his license and walking toward the doors. "Let's go."

Ana had no choice but to follow.

They sat in silence as the old Chevy choked its way down the highway. Emmett gripped the wheel and chewed his cheeks. Ana stared out the window. She didn't have the same queasy feeling she'd felt in the past when situations became sticky, but she knew better than to drop her guard. She kept one eye on the towering trees, the other on the driver's reflection in the window. It wasn't as if she didn't know self-defense—with or without the army knife they confiscated back at the airport in L.A.—but she liked reminding herself to remain alert, as if some familiar person was sitting next to her whispering it into her ear.

Emmett shot his hand toward the stereo, then hesitated and placed it back on the wheel. Ana edged closer to the door and slid the hand covertly hiding underneath the backpack on her lap nearer to the latch. The truck was feeling crowded—mentally, at least. Emmett had already made up his mind back at the airport, but felt it important to reiterate to his brain that the Cortez girl would not be staying. He went over the conversation he'd undoubtedly have with Abbie later. She would be the one to break the news, seeing as how she was the one who got this all wrong in the first place. Until then, he thought it best to keep the journey back to Hadley breezy yet conversationally minimal.

"Music," Emmett announced, switching the stereo on, thinking that at least with Neil there'd be a third person in the truck.

Tall trees darkened the highway as they wound through the state park. Ana marveled at the roadside restaurants barely glowing with lamplight and the gas stations selling dream catchers and giant chainsaw-carved bears. She inhaled the cool mountain air trickling in through the crack in the window, letting it cool her nerves.

"Dark velvet," she said.

"Excuse me?"

"It looks and smells like dark velvet out there—kind of smooth and earthy yet soft with a hint of something undetectable that'll suffocate you out if you inhale too much. I have a strong nose."

"Looks like it."

"Does it? You're not the first person to point that out, but I appreciate your honesty and interest in facial aesthetics. My abuela said my nose is a mark of strength, like María Félix's, and that I'll grow into it one day. I'm not offended or anything; I think some of the greatest faces are marked by a distinguished nose."

"I meant that it sounds like you have a strong sense of smell."

"Oh."

"Who's your abuela?"

"My grandma."

"I see."

"She's dead."

Sunlight zigzagged across the dashboard as the truck crept out of the density of the forest and coasted down the hill into a canyon dotted with pine trees.

"Holy—" Ana exhaled. "This view is insane!"

"Yep."

"Everything's concrete where I come from. Strip malls, buildings, metal fences, that kind of thing. But this . . . this is unreal. Magnificent even."

"Mm-hm."

"But I'm sure you're used to it in a way that makes it harder to see its beauty. Like if you stared out at the same building every day and never noticed the new plant in the window across the street. We become blind to what waves right in front of us sometimes. I'm not suggesting you're blind or anything, it's more that—"

"You're trying to fill the air?"

"Am I talking too much? I'll shut up. It's just, I've never seen anything like this before."

The truck rattled as the road began to snake in and around the oncoming hills. Emmett turned the music up.

"It's kind of funny you put this on," Ana continued, raising her voice over the volume. "I mean it's totally apt."

"What is?" Emmett said, turning it back down again, but only slightly.

"He says he's been to Hollywood and Redwood, then he says, '*I crossed the ocean for a heart of gold . . .*' I didn't cross the ocean, but I did see it for the first time from the airplane.

I've been to Hollywood Boulevard a bunch of times, and now I'm here in the redwoods. Neil's kind of nailin' it right now."

"You know Neil Young?"

"Not personally or anything, but I met this guy in the library who I'm pretty sure lived there during the day. He was always camped out at one of the music stations and suggested I check out Neil, so I did and started to get into the lyrics. We would talk about bands sometimes—Ronnie, I mean, the guy in the library—or sometimes he'd talk about crazy stuff, like Vietnam, and I'd just listen. This guy had a ton of sensational stories, volumes. Anyway, *Harvest* is way better than *After the Gold Rush*, which we both found to be a little whiny."

"*After the Gold Rush* is a masterpiece."

"But it's like Neil's struggling to find air when he's singing, right? Like he's trying to find his voice or something, and there are way too many other voices throwing themselves around. Also? Not enough harmonicas. But if we're singling out songs, 'Birds' is kind of beautiful if you deafen yourself to the lyrics, which seem maudlin, even for Neil."

Emmett snorted, or laughed; it was hard to tell.

"You went to the library to listen to Neil Young?"

"I went there because it's quiet, but also for the free music and books. I mean it's a library. That's what you do there."

"I don't go to libraries."

"Well, you're missing out."

"Not really much of a reader."

"Or a music critic."

Emmett turned the music back up as the truck rattled along. They descended into a valley lined with dry creek beds and withered ferns. It reminded Ana of the empty river in L.A., all cracked and concrete with a few weeds that refused to stop growing.

"Look, I know you're going to send me back," she said.

Emmett remained mum.

"It doesn't take a genius of perception to read the signs, so don't feel weird. You can just turn around and take me back to the airport or I can hitch it back to L.A. You're not the first person to send me back almost immediately, probably won't be the last, so no hard feelings. I'm used to it."

Emmett inhaled audibly.

"Honestly, I don't really want to work on a farm anyway," she continued. "I said yes to this whole thing only because I didn't want to go back into the system or get shuttled off to another group home, which, trust me, is like a step up from prison, or what I imagine prison is like, not that I've ever been, but who knows, it's probably my destiny. I'm fully aware that my mouth gets me into trouble, and you're completely right about me filling the air—it's a nervous habit—but I did try to make conversation about music, which you clearly have some sort of interest in, judging by all the CD cases on the floor. It's kind of cool that you still listen to them and that you have Creedence because 'Have You Ever Seen the Rain?' is one of the most profoundly depressing songs of all time, especially if you're a dude living or not living alone in a library in East L.A. But that's just me. I'm not a music critic either."

Emmett remained silent. Neil sang something about dominoes.

"I don't know what you were expecting, but Abbie, your sister, sounded nice from what Mrs. Saucedo told me, and I saw a photo of your farm, which seems truly spectacular.

What I'm trying to say is I appreciate your flying me all the way up here, and I totally get it. The ride through all of this was worth it, even for the day, just to see trees that look taller than the buildings in downtown L.A. But, like I said, I can find my own way back."

"It's too late to take you back. At least, today it is," Emmett said.

"I understand."

"You're here for only a month anyway," he said out loud, wondering why he said it, because he'd already decided Ana wouldn't be staying.

"I was told it might be for longer, but as usual it's not my place to decide."

"Why don't you put on some other music," Emmett said, wanting to change the subject. "Pick something."

Ana eased her backpack onto the floor and fished through the CDs swimming at her feet.

"You've got a lot of Fleetwood Mac," she said.

"Those aren't mine. You can play anything you want except for those," Emmett said, rolling down his window, airing out the front seat with early evening breeze.

Ana took a CD out of its case and popped it into the player. She turned the volume up, like Emmett seemed to like it, and resumed her dual-eyed stare out the window.

"*I see the bad moon arising*," the stereo sang. "*I see trouble on the way.*"

CHAPTER FOUR

Main Street widened toward the center of town. Emmett stopped the truck at a traffic light and cleared his throat. He gestured to the rest of the road in front of them and said, "Welcome to Hadley," as the truck rolled slowly past quaint buildings that reminded Ana of the ghost town facade she once saw in a book about old Hollywood movie studios.

There was Mariner's Antiques on the left with a replica of an old ship occupying most of the cluttered window. To the right was the Hadley Pie Company, shaded by a lemon yellow awning that flapped above whitewashed chairs and tables. There was a tiny sweets shop next door with the words "Sugar Pearls sold here!" and a bookstore called, simply, BOOKS—all caps—that looked as though no one had rung its rusty doorbell in decades.

"It's not what I imagined," Ana said.

"I know it's not much, but it's home."

"I mean that in a good way—it's the opposite of what I

thought it'd be," she continued. "I expected it to be bigger, not like a city or anything, but more populated with people and horses. This—this is . . ."

Again Emmett Garber cleared his throat in a way Ana couldn't decipher.

"We're a small town, full of good people," he said. "Got some horses too."

"It's like out of a children's book or a classic movie or something."

Suddenly, Emmett hit the brakes. A tall, bearded man with long gray hair sauntered in front of the truck, his hand held out in front of him commanding them to stop. His face was deeply lined, and he wore an expression of beatific satisfaction. There was a blue bandanna tied around his forehead and various necklaces dangled over his faded denim overalls, stained thermal shirt, and olive green work jacket, much like the one Ana herself was wearing. The man was dripping with bits of indecipherable totem detritus—turquoise here, leather-tethered rocks there, a ukulele made out of an animal's skull hanging from a random belt loop, and on his left hand, wrapped tightly around his wrist, he wore what looked like a swollen fur glove.

Before Ana had any time to make sense of it, the rest of the glove jumped into view, revealing itself to belong to a very real, very large black bear who stood on its hind legs licking a blue snow cone. The man saluted Emmett, who saluted back, and then he and the bear continued their slow-motion saunter across the street toward the red brick building marked SAL'S SALOON.

"That was Alder Kinman," Emmett said. "If Hadley has a mascot, he's it."

"And the bear?"

"Never seen him before. Must be new to town."

Ana couldn't tell if Emmett was kidding or not. He stared straight ahead as the truck coasted forward. Ana noticed a few people loitering around a cheerful-looking storefront with a giant crescent moon hanging above it. A girl her age, with a swish of short, dark hair, was washing the windows out in front while simultaneously peeking into the window of the record shop next door. Watching her as they drove past, Ana remembered how unremarkable her last day of school had been earlier in the summer. Not that she missed it. Not that anyone was missing her.

The truck continued down Main Street. Emmett turned a corner past a tired corner café. A man with shoulder-length hair, tattooed forearms, and considerable brawn diligently swept the threshold. Emmett decelerated.

"Is that a friend of yours?" Ana asked.

"Nope," Emmett said, taking a menacing glance in the man's direction. "Guess he bought the old place. 'Bout time somebody did, even if they're definitely not from around here. But if he's thinking of turning it into a biker bar, he's in for the fight of his life."

As they rolled out of town, old-fashioned streetlights flickered on. Emmett drove past a few of Hadley's famous Victorian mansions as well as the town's oldest church, which was backed by a hill dotted in gravestones.

"We're almost there," he said.

Ana lifted her backpack onto her lap and peeked inside for a moment before shutting it again. It was funny, she thought, how her whole life fit into this bag.

"Mr. Garber?"

"Emmett is fine."

"Emmett," she said, taking a breath. "I just wanted to say thanks."

"For what?"

"For giving me a ride to your home today. I know I'll probably be going back tomorrow—my mouth gets me in trouble all the time; you can ask Mrs. Saucedo or any of the foster parents or teachers I've had in, I don't know, the past ten years—but this journey, even if it's a truck ride from the airport, has been incredible. It's a moment in time I'll ponder forever."

Emmett remained silent. His jaw ached from clenching.

"What I'm trying to say is I want to do the farmwork. I'll keep to myself because I mostly do anyway, and I know it doesn't look like it, but I'm good with my hands."

The front seat shook as the truck rattled off the road and onto a dirt path past a wooden fence painted with barely legible letters that read LIVE, LOVE, GROW.

"Just because you want to do it doesn't mean you're *fit* to do it. Farming takes focus, hard work, and patience," Emmett said. "There'll be long hours and difficult days. It's intensely physical and requires you to do exactly as I say. I don't allow tardiness, daydreaming, or talking back. Frankly, if this ride is any indication, it doesn't seem like you can handle that."

"I'd like to try if you're willing to give me the chance."

"We're here," Emmett said, ending the conversation.

Along with the glass sconces flickering with electric candlelight on either side of the door and brightness peeking out from under the eaves, there were fairy lights igniting the nearby trees. In the center spotlight of the porch, Abbie Garber waved one hand, then two, beckoning them closer.

"She's got the place lit up like Christmas," Emmett sighed, throwing the pickup into park.

Ana took in the house. Neither grand nor humble, rather pleasantly in between, it was Victorian, like the ones they'd passed on the way.

Emmett leaped out of the truck and walked toward the house, forgetting the passenger who was still inside. Ana watched as the two siblings exchanged words.

Abbie waltzed right past Emmett and over to the pickup truck, her hair bouncing defiantly along her shoulders.

"Hi, there!" She waved again as she approached. "Welcome!"

The passenger remained frozen inside.

"I'm Abbie Garber," she said, opening the truck door. "You must be Ana?"

"Yes, ma'am."

"May I help you with your bag?"

"No, tha—yeah, sure. Thank you."

"I'm so happy you're here," Abbie continued with a gentle smile. "Don't mind him. We're delighted to have you. He's nothing but a bulldog in a baby basket."

Abbie slung Ana's backpack over her shoulder and gestured her to follow her into the house.

"You're a light traveler. I like that."

"I don't have much."

"We've got plenty," Abbie chirped. "And grilled cheese sandwiches and tomato soup in the kitchen. I took a gamble since most people like both, and if you're vegan, you can have the soup with toast."

"I eat everything. Thanks for asking."

"You're very polite," Abbie said, as they made their way through the front door.

Ana took in the warm, cozy living room. Abbie Garber

was all that Mrs. Saucedo described her to be—pleasant and thrilled to have her. A tall and athletic woman with strong arms and shoulders, she was dressed in a simple T-shirt and slim-fitting jeans that belied her forty-seven years. Her face was fine lined and makeup free. There was no embellishment about her, not a trace of polish or intentional color, just unadorned simplicity.

"I'll give you a tour of the house after we eat," Abbie said. "Follow me to the kitchen and we'll see if we can find Emmett along the way."

There was art on every wall, Ana noticed. She passed a portrait of a dignified older woman and a small watercolor of a dormant beehive. She wanted to stop and inspect each one with a careful eye, but she didn't dare, knowing she'd soon be leaving. Remembering the words of her abuela, she reminded herself to always extend a hand, either physical or metaphorical, even toward those who recede.

"Your house . . . It's really nice."

"Thank you," Abbie responded. "It's been in our family for years. Bit of a rickety old thing, but we love it."

They entered the kitchen. Ana had trouble focusing; it had been a long forty-eight hours. "Wow," she whispered.

"Have a seat," Abbie said, filling a glass goblet with water and a slice of lemon. "I'm guessing Emmett made a pit stop to the barn, so I'm just going to arm wrestle him over for dinner. Make yourself comfortable at the table."

Ana had never seen such an elaborate kitchen table before. There were plates decorated in climbing roses on top of cloth placemats and napkins, all neatly arranged with polished silverware and a jug full of mismatched flowers. She forced herself to stay awake and keep it together. Emmett might want to send her back, but Abbie seemed kind—perhaps a little strange and overly cheerful, but welcoming. So far, it was unlike any other foster transfer she'd undergone.

"Stop screwing it up," she whispered to her reflection in the plate.

Outside there were voices, the same hushed conversations she'd heard her whole life. Next, she imagined, there would be downturned eyes entering the kitchen, followed by a "We gave it a lot of thought" or "This isn't working for us." At least this time around she'd get to eat before being sent back, a real meal not birthed from a microwave or rescued from a refrigerator a week after the sell-by date either. If this was to be her first and only night in this place, she decided she'd try to enjoy it.

The screen door creaked open and slammed shut. Emmett ambled into the room, pausing for a moment by the table before heading to the stove. Abbie was right behind him.

"Soup and sandwich, Ana?" she asked. "I'm sure you're famished."

"Sure. I really appreciate it."

Abbie placed a tray of sandwiches on the table and brought bowls of soup ladled from a well-loved copper pot. The soup was thick and hearty, most unlike the thin soup from a can Ana was used to. She watched as Emmett tossed two sandwiches onto a plastic plate he'd fished out of the cupboard. He stuffed a paper towel into his back pocket before turning toward the table.

"Five o'clock sharp," he said to his plate.

No one responded.

"I'm talking to you."

He looked directly at Ana, waiting for her to meet his eyes.

"Five a.m. out in the field," he continued. "That means you'll be standing next to me at that time, not walking out of the house. Wear comfortable layers, the sneakers you have on now, and find a wider brimmed hat."

"Okay," Ana said, having forgotten she was already wearing a cap. She removed it quickly and smoothed down her hair. "Thank you."

"Don't thank me yet. This is a trial period."

Emmett walked past the table and out the screen door, taking his dinner with him. A dog barked in the distance.

"Please eat," Abbie said, sitting down next to her and taking a bite of a sandwich in hand. "These are good, right? The secret is extra crunch and a bit of caramelized onion."

Ana nibbled the sandwich, careful not to inhale it whole. She took a few spoonsful of soup, surprised by how it coated her throat with a savory sweetness, and told herself not to appear too eager or ravenous, despite how delicious it may be. The chimes of an old clock filled the kitchen.

"You must be tired from your trip," Abbie said.

"I'm okay," Ana said, keeping her gaze down at her plate, taking a rest between bites. She was starving, but her stomach was clenched with nerves.

"You can barely keep your eyes open. I can show you upstairs if you'd like."

"The food is great, really."

"You're not hurting my feelings if you'd rather get some sleep. I'm sure it's been quite the whirlwind day. I'll send you up with some oatmeal cookies. Who doesn't want dessert for dinner?"

Ana stood up abruptly, nearly knocking her head on the light fixture hanging above the table. She fumbled for her baseball cap before picking up her plate and reaching for Abbie's.

"Shouldn't I clear all this first?"

"Just leave it here, hon," Abbie said with the same warm smile. "C'mon. I'll show you to your room."

Ana followed as Abbie led the way out of the kitchen, guiding them with a small plate of cookies in her hand. Ana couldn't help but wonder if she was being put to bed early because of something Emmett said about the ride from the airport. It wasn't the first time she'd been sent to a room— never hers, always shared—but either way, she was relieved to have time alone to ruminate on the day.

Abbie stopped at the top of the landing and waited for Ana, who gazed down the long upstairs hall. It was lined on either side, top to bottom, with built-in bookshelves, tiny bursts of color popping from the multitudes of spines.

"You're welcome to take any of these you'd like," Abbie said. "I'd like to think of it as a lending library, but I don't get many visitors up here anymore." She snorted or swallowed, Ana couldn't tell. "I mean, it's pretty much just me in the house most of the time."

She gestured to the open door on the left. Ana followed her into the room, which was like walking into one of those wallpapered home stores she had visited once when living with a family in Pasadena. Though her time with them had been brief, they'd been kind, and the mother, Mrs. Ferguson, had always seemed busy redecorating room after room of their home with new pillows and faux flowers. Unlike the catalog feel of the Fergusons', here it felt to Ana as if she were stepping back in time.

The wallpaper was covered in faded flowers, intertwining bouquets of dusty pink roses tied with fraying blue ribbons. The wooden floors, which creaked a little even when she was standing still, were covered in woven rugs. There was a good-size bed, black iron and simple, with a quilt folded at the edge of the striped bedspread. The bedside table, mint green and chipped in places, was lit by a metal lamp in the shape of a mouse reading a book under a pleated cream-colored shade.

"It's a time capsule of cozy," Ana said, though she thought she said it to herself.

"Indeed." Abbie chuckled as she placed the plate of cookies on the bedside table in front of the old-fashioned alarm clock. "I put your bag in the corner, hope you don't mind," Abbie said, pointing to a blanketed chair near the curtained window. "And you're welcome to hang your clothes in the armoire over there. We're somewhat short on closets around here. But this is your space, so please settle in."

Ana nodded, not knowing what to say.

"The bathroom's small I'm afraid, but it's yours and right across the hall," Abbie continued. "My room's a few doors down at the end, and Emmett sleeps out in the barn. We're here if you need anything, so don't hesitate to wake us. I set the alarm clock to four thirty a.m. That should give you enough time to get ready and come down for breakfast. Please don't be late."

"I won't."

"As I'm sure you experienced today, Emmett is strict and sometimes lacking in tact, but we both want you to do well here."

"I understand."

"Oh, I almost forgot! I called Mrs. Saucedo back in L.A. I was supposed to have you call her, but we agreed tomorrow might be better. She's aware that it's a tryout, but she wants to speak to you after your shift in the afternoon. She told me to tell you to remember what she said. I thought that sounded ominous, but she was rather insistent that I deliver the message."

Ana remained still, both hands at her sides, her thumbs fidgeting in and out of closed fists.

"You sure you're okay?"

"I've never slept in a bed this size."

"It gets cold at night, so make sure to use the blanket," Abbie said before making her way to the door. "And get some sleep. You'll need it."

The door shut quietly. Ana stood there for a moment, listening to Abbie make her way down the hall before all fell silent behind another closed door. She unlaced her sneakers, trusty old black Vans pockmarked with holes, and placed them beside the bed. She folded her jacket and draped it on the back of the tapestry chair, topping it with her base-ball cap. Afraid to leave the room, even to brush her teeth, she removed her jeans and pulled on the crumpled pair of boxer shorts from the bottom of her backpack.

As always, she unpinned the square of fabric attached to the front of it, which had been cut from her abuela's favorite dress, and made her way to the bed. Careful not to crawl under the covers while still wearing unwashed clothes, she peeled back the bedspread, got in over the top sheet, and then pulled the cover over her head, leaving just enough space in which to breathe. The house echoed and moaned. A restless breeze rattled the window. Ana closed her eyes and squeezed the fabric in the palm of her hand, hoping it would continue to keep the shadows away.

CHAPTER FIVE

She expected roosters, but it was too early even for the birds. Awake for hours, Ana checked the clock at 4:18 and decided to get out of bed. Worried she might wake Abbie, she was afraid to shower, so she threw a clean sweatshirt over her T-shirt and jeans.

It was dark outside except for the moonlight bathing the grounds. She parted the gauzy white curtains. There was a large tree just outside the window and beyond it flat land. It was like staring at an alien landscape, everything slightly foreboding and new. She shut the curtain and caught her reflection in the armoire's mirror. Her eyes were still rimmed in dark circles—"raccoon smiles" she used to tell her sort-of siblings—and her hair was its usual mess of curls.

"The bane of my feral existence," she whispered to the mirror while sweeping the last strands back into a low ponytail. The alarm wailed. Ana leaped for it, and her stomach moaned in unison. She opened the door and was greeted by dim light, the scent of something savory beckoning her downstairs. Hung on the bathroom door directly across the hall was a straw hat lassoed with leather. She ran her fingers over a snag in the brim, assuming Abbie had left the hat for her. Remembering Emmett's explicit instructions, she took it and headed for the stairs.

"Sleep all right?" Abbie asked as Ana peeked through the doorway into the kitchen.

"Sort of."

"I'm sure it's strange being in a new place. Come and have a seat. I'm making eggs Benedict, but please help yourself to coffee or juice on the table."

Ana sat in the same chair as the night before and sipped a glass of orange juice. Abbie was right. The first morning was always difficult, she reminded herself, thinking back on all of the first mornings over the years. Though Ana's inclination was to fill the silence, Mrs. Saucedo had warned her over and over again that this was part of a pattern she needed to change. She watched as Abbie tended to a skillet on the stove and wondered if she cooked like this every morning.

"I took the hat on the door," Ana said. "I hope that's okay."

"I left it for you. It's my old gardening hat, a bit worn, but it'll keep you shaded in the sun."

The frying pan sizzled.

"Canadian bacon is Emmett's favorite," Abbie said, scooping the circular pieces of ham out onto a paper towel–lined plate. "He doesn't care for my French toast or anything else 'shellacked in syrup,' so I thought I'd make us all something special this morning."

She composed a plate and set it down in front of Ana. It was heaped with English muffins topped in ham, poached eggs, and a slathering of hollandaise sauce, a small bowl of berries off to the side. It was the opposite of Ana's usual breakfast, which is to say it was something instead of nothing.

"I hope you don't mind if I join you," Abbie continued. "I usually eat after Emmett and the gang start their work, but I thought you might like the company."

"Sure," Ana answered, filling her mouth with another gulp of juice, careful not to show any sign of discomfort.

Abbie sat down next to her and poured a cup of coffee from a ceramic coffeepot. Her fingernails were short, Ana noticed, as if periodically chewed or meticulously clipped, and she thought she glimpsed a small tattoo of a heart in the crease of Abbie's ring finger. There was something about her controlled expression, something about Abbie's arrowed posture, that seemed forced, as if kicking back might come more naturally to her.

"How's everything?"

"Good," Ana said, swallowing a few berries. She didn't know where to begin with what she thought must be eggs covered with lemon sauce.

Abbie sensed Ana's discomfort and worried she'd chosen the wrong first-day breakfast. She was delighted to have company in the house but wondered if she'd gone overboard.

"We have toast and cereal if you're not that hungry . . ."

"I'm okay," Ana said and continued to chew.

"Not a fan of eggs Benedict?"

"Never really had it before, but it kind of looks like a deconstructed Egg McMuffin."

"I've never thought about it that way, but you're right, it does." Abbie smiled. "You don't have to force yourself to eat it if you don't want to."

Ana didn't want to be rude, especially on her first day, so she cut an edge off and gave it a try.

"Holy wow," she said, taking another bite.

"Not really what you've been used to?" Abbie asked, then wished she hadn't asked it.

"Are you kidding?" Ana said. "I usually get a square of sprinkled cardboard from the toaster or yogurt squirted from a tube. Or, you know, nothing at all."

Abbie couldn't tell if Ana was joking or not. She wanted to get her talking more and let her know that Garber Farm was a safe place, and not at all like the situations Mrs. Saucedo had described.

"I heard from your caseworker that it's been a busy few days," Abbie said. "I want you to know that you are welcome here. I'll make you anything you'd like."

It didn't seem real, this room, this food, this woman, Ana thought, and that raised a caution flag. She'd rarely been around adults who were interested in what she might desire, even for breakfast. She'd learned there was no point in asking for anything. She'd read *Oliver Twist* at the library, and laughed grimly about how some things never change. Why this solitary woman in a lonely farmhouse was going above and beyond to please her seemed suspect. All the times she had allowed herself to be taken in before had resulted only in having to give up something much more in return.

"This sauce is ridiculous," Ana said, finishing the last few bites left on the plate. "I seriously thought it was going to be lemon flavored, which would be weird. I hardly ever eat eggs, but my abuela used to cook them in chile sauce for me."

Abbie decided not to mention that the hollandaise was indeed made with lemons. "Who is your abuela?"

"Oh, um, my grandma. She was the best cook on the planet. She was big on breakfast, always telling me, '*Mija,* you have to start the day right.' But it's been a while since, you know, since I've eaten anything like this. It's hotel style, right? Not that I've ever stayed in a hotel. But if I did, this is what I'd imagine."

"I'll take that as a compliment," Abbie said, noticing the clock. "I should send you out there. You'll be working all morning until lunch, and then run deliveries with me this afternoon. I want to make sure we're making this transition easy for you . . ."

"So far, so good," Ana said, taking the last gulp of juice.

Ana picked up her plate.

"You can leave it there, hon."

"I'd like to put it where you need it to go if that's all right."

"You're welcome to set it in the sink," Abbie said. "I appreciate the help."

Ana took the plate over to the sink and looked out the window into the garden outside. "Don't screw it all up," she reminded herself again.

It was brisk and dark outside, the air thick with a tingling mist. Ana did as Abbie told her and followed the gravel path through the fenced garden, light from the house rippling across the bushes and rows of vegetation. There were rows and rows of crops, raised stripes of earth and foliage that stretched as far as she could see. Ana continued walking toward the white domes in the distance, where a few people gathered around a tractor silhouetted against the charcoal sky.

It was quiet. She listened to the sound of her breath as her sneakers sank into the damp earth. She thought she heard a second set of feet mimicking her footsteps. She told herself not to turn around and instead quickened her pace, but the steps multiplied behind her, becoming louder as they broke into a gallop.

"Dolly!" someone yelled in the distance.

Ana whipped around at the exact moment a blur of golden fur leaped toward her, catapulting her to the ground. The dog's rough, wet tongue found her face, hot breath blanketing her ear. She made a move to reach over and introduce herself, but the dog ran around her in circles, barking happily.

"You all right?" Emmett said, out of breath, as he approached her.

"Yeah, I'm fine," Ana said.

"Manny, let's take Dolly over to the barn. You sure you're all right?"

Ana took a moment to glance around at several faces watching her and nodded her head. She stood up and brushed off her jeans.

"I should have warned you about the dog," Emmett said with a disconcerting frown.

"Am I late?"

"You're early. This is Manny Lavaca, manager here at Garber Farm."

"Hello," Manny said, tipping the brim of his hat in her direction while holding the panting retriever by its collar. Manny had a weathered face, an overgrown mustache, and kind eyes that made her feel more at ease. "No need to worry about this one, she won't bite—just excited to see someone new."

"I'm not scared or anything; she just startled me."

"Good ol' Dolly," Emmett said, patting the dog's head. "Always wanting to say hello."

Nosy and eager with wriggling ears and a goofy, wide-mouthed grin, the dog strained against Manny's grip and whined desperately in Ana's direction. Though her inclination was to let Dolly sniff the back of her hand before reaching out and smoothing the fur on the dog's enormous head, Ana remained still. She wanted to tell all of the men standing there that she knew about dogs because she'd had one once. But she stopped herself and stuffed her hands into her pockets instead. None of them cared about her past, she told herself. Emmett hadn't even wanted her there in the first place.

"I'll take her, Boss. Let you get started," Manny said, pulling Dolly in the direction of the barn. Once they were far enough away, he let her go and released something from his pocket high up into the air. Dolly jumped and caught it, her cheerful barking nudging the farm's only rooster awake, the fields igniting with their usual morning song.

"Let's get to work," Emmett said.

The workers continued to stand nearby waiting for direction. They all wore variations of the same uniform: jeans, sweatshirts, caps or cowboy hats, boots or sneakers. Some had a bandanna covering their ears or neck. None of them acknowledged Ana, but a couple glanced her way. Emmett cleared his throat and began his sermon, punching certain words for dramatic effect.

"All right, guys, we're ramping up Community Supported Agriculture and farmers' market *next week*. It's been a great month, but we need to finish up *strong* without any distraction. We'll split up as usual. René and Hector are on field duty again; Joey is with me back at the houses where we finished off yesterday.

"Vic and Rolo," he said, pointing to a slender man who

kept his eyes trained on the ground and a shorter, squatter man standing nearby wearing a Fanta sweatshirt, "you're doing *the usual.* Ana, I want you to join them and grab a bucket from Manny. You'll be picking blackberries to start. I want to remind everyone that Manny's inspecting *throughout the day*, and I'll be on watch, so don't forget to drop off as you go, especially the berries. We had a considerable amount rendered unusable last week, so don't let your buckets get too full before coming in for packaging."

This last bit of information was directed at Ana's group, who were wearing large cans strapped around their waists. They continued their expressionless stare in Emmett's direction.

"*¿Comprende, amigas?*" Emmett said, attempting some Spanish. Ana tried not to giggle. She was sure Emmett hadn't meant to call them "girlfriends."

"*Sí, señor.*" They both nodded with straight faces.

Manny approached the group and mumbled something Ana had difficulty hearing, but all of the workers nodded in unison before quickly dispersing across the fields. It reminded her of the games of touch football she'd been forced to play in gym class. How the teacher had gathered everyone around before barking out a bunch of plays only the boys seemed to understand. She'd listened, but somehow managed to score for the other team.

"We're good to go," Manny said to Emmett. "I'll get her set up."

"Ana, I want you to listen to everything Manny says," Emmett continued. "Do exactly what he tells you to do. I know it's your first day, but it's best if you jump right in. Do you have a hat?"

"Yes, sir. I mean, it's right here." Ana turned around to

show him Abbie's gardening hat, which should have been dangling from the cord around her neck.

"Is there something I'm supposed to be seeing?"

Ana clutched her collar.

"I thought I had it. I mean I put it on before I left the house, but maybe I left it at the table . . ."

"*¡Aquí! ¡Aquí!*" one of the workers shouted as he jogged over clutching the crumpled hat.

"There it is," she said. "I probably dropped it."

"Nah," Manny interjected as he approached, thanking the much older worker he called René. "This is Dolly's work, no? I bet she grabbed it when you were down." He smiled and dusted the hat off before handing it back to her.

El Perro de Peril, Ana wanted to say to him, imagining them all laughing along to the "crazy ol' dog" sentiment before going back to work and patting her on the back.

"Good to go then?" Emmett asked.

"Yeah. Yes, sir, Emmett."

He clenched his jaw and shook his head before walking toward the tall white tunnels floating above a section of the fields. Ana turned to Manny and extended her hand.

"*Mucho gusto, señor,*" she said.

"*Mucho gusto,*" he responded, shaking her hand and smiling. "*¿Habla español?*"

"Not really. I mean, my abuela used to speak it to me, but that was forever ago."

"You from L.A.?" he asked.

"I am."

"I have family down there. Came from San Ysidro myself, but spent some time in L.A. Couldn't take all those cars. The clean air up in these trees is worth all that it takes to get up here, so enjoy it. And don't worry about Emmett, okay? He's serious out here and he's gonna be the boss because that's his job. We work hard and with respect. Not just for each other, but the land," Manny said, patting his jacket over his heart. "Something tells me you can handle it. I recognize the look. So, listen. Everyone gets a break in the morning, but if you need another, you come find me. I'll give you some water to carry along while you work. Drink it, *mija*, okay? Even if you're not thirsty."

Ana couldn't help it. The tears were there, pushing at the edges. *Mija* was what her abuela used to call her.

"You're gonna pick blackberries and fill these cans. If you focus and try not to think about it, time will pass like that." He snapped his fingers and smiled again before offering a homemade contraption of an old belt with two oversize coffee cans attached to it. "*Café*?" he asked in a silly voice, assuming the stance of a daffy waiter. Ana couldn't help but smile, the workers nearby laughing along with him. "Pick the ripe berries carefully but firmly, and fill these—not all the way to the top or the weight will squish the ones at the bottom. Fill 'em a little more than halfway, okay? And then come see me at the station out in the field. We'll sort 'em then pack before sending you back out. Oh, and we pay per container. You'll be getting the same as everybody."

"I'm getting paid?" Ana asked, which seemed like a joke.

"Of course! You sixteen?"

"No, sir, but I will be soon."

"Well, let me know, because we'll save your wages and pay you then. Something to look forward to."

"You're serious?"

"You're working for us, right?"

"Yes . . ."

"Well, then you're getting paid!"

"Is this what I'll be doing every day?"

"*Más o menos*, yes and no. We'll try a few different crops this week and see how it goes, okay? Not to worry," he added with encouragement. "You'll be with Victor and Roberto, but you can call them Vic and Rolo. The bushes are just past the hoops near the woods."

"So I'll be out there with just the two of them?"

"Yep. Emmett will check on you, and I'm just over there," he said, pointing to a large truck and a series of tables in the fields along the road. "There's nothing to worry about, just keep busy. We're all out here together."

Ana Cortez didn't need anyone to explain it to her; she understood the rhythm of repetitive work, knew all about aligning oneself to the synergy of tedium. She was aware of all of the orphan clichés—the Pips, Pollyannas, and Ponyboys whose optimism triumphed over difficult circumstances. She'd read all the books. That's why standing in a thicket of tall bushes, with rolled-up sleeves, she found it easy to get lost in the process of plucking berries the way Manny instructed.

She'd labored in laundry rooms, served time in backyards littered in animal feces. She was good with a sponge, and good with a brush too, be it for scrubbing, cleaning, or detangling—teeth or hair, hers or otherwise. And if the labor ever became rough, in that way where a bandage wouldn't do, every inch of her, inside and out, knew the right way to callus, the secrets to hiding a bruise.

If there was anything Ana had learned in all of the years she'd been put to work, it was—as Manny alluded to—to focus and keep her thoughts to herself. Why this seemed a punishment for adults to dole out to young people continually confused her. Why wouldn't anyone want to luxuriate in his or her own imagination all day?

The first few hours flew as she softened her eyes and zeroed in on the dark berries, carefully pulling them from the branches, layering them delicately one by one into the cans around her waist. But it took everything not to pop one or two into her mouth. She watched as the man called Vic— the slimmer of the two—took care with his pickings in a similar way, how his thumb and forefinger reached up and pulled delicately from underneath the bush. Rolo plucked with rapid abandon, picking and holding a few in his hand before tossing them into his rusted cans. His eyes met hers from time to time, so she returned to her daydreams. Ana couldn't believe how she had escaped the streets of L.A., literally, just the day before, how she'd ended up in Mrs. Saucedo's office, then the airport, and now here, on the edge of a Northern California redwood forest with her fingers periodically squashing blackberries. "Wild," she thought to herself. "Literally."

"*¡Ándale, chiquita!*" Rolo shouted.

"*Cállate,*" Vic responded, his back turned to both of them as he plucked the highest part of the bush.

Ana began to pick faster per Rolo's not so subtle suggestion, but she was glad Vic had told him to shut his mouth. The two men mumbled to each other in Spanish. It had been a while, but Ana understood parts of what they were saying. Some words or phrases were more audible than others, but there were certain ones she'd heard again and again over the years, especially the ones uttered bemusedly by Rolo—"*ay, ay, ay*"—which she wasn't sure was said in jest or if his part of the blackberry bush had thorns. Vic remained quiet, chiming in every now and then, telling them to get back to work, said in English for Ana's benefit.

"*¿Listos?*" Rolo asked, walking over to Vic to see if he was finished.

Vic threw a few more berries into his own modest haul before turning to Ana.

"Done?" he asked from under the brim of an old straw cowboy hat.

"I think so. I mean, they're a little more than half full like Manny said, but that's what I'm supposed to do right?"

"*No sé, bebe,*" Rolo said, his face contorting into something that reminded Ana of a hippopotamus clown, cherubic and inflated with a wide grin full of tiny teeth. "You good, *chiquita.*"

"*Vamos,* let's go," Vic said.

Ana followed a few steps behind them through the fields, the morning's sunshine beginning to warm her shoulders. Her stomach somersaulted at the thought of lunch and, even though she was still desperate to sample a few of the blackberries strapped to her waist, she took a swig from the water bottle instead. Rolo continued to antagonize Vic, taunting him in Spanish, mock inspecting his coffee cans, and taking a tone of voice she imagined was his version of Manny. They reminded her of a cartoon comedy duo, much like the one she used to watch as a child that featured a skinny Chihuahua and a fat cat who got into all kinds of outrageous mischief. She wondered where these men came from, how long they'd been working on the farm, and if they had families of their own. Her mind flitted to even more comedy duos, Bert and Ernie, Tom and Jerry, Cheech and Chong, who had been her parents' favorite, and she decided that Vic and Rolo were worthy of their own show set on a farm and starring a squealing pig and eye-rolling chicken.

Manny waved as they approached the packing station.

"How'd it go?" he asked, though Ana was unsure to whom he was speaking.

"Fine, I think," she said as Rolo hoisted his cans onto the table with a heavy thud.

Manny gave Rolo a look before scolding him in Spanish, his voice light yet stern.

"This is a lesson in what not to do," Manny said. "Nothing but a show-off."

Rolo smirked as Manny and Vic patted his back, picking on him in Spanish. He seemed to blush, she noticed, and then gave a thumbs-up to what he deemed a perfectly unblemished batch of berries, even though he'd picked too many. Another man, older than the rest and dressed in an oddly formal buttoned-up shirt, sorted through Vic's berries. It was the same man who had rescued Abbie's gardening hat. He caught her staring.

"*Hola*," he said. "*Me llamo René.*"

"Ana," she responded. "*Mucho gusto y gracias.*" The gardening hat slid down her forehead as she tipped it toward him. She watched as he put all of the perfect blackberries into multiple plastic containers, packing and closing them with a delicate hand. Manny tossed the empty coffee cans back to Rolo and Vic, who slung them over their shoulders and walked over to the wooden fence to lean up against it, Rolo resting one hand on his rotund belly in triumphant satisfaction.

"Ana, let's take a look," Manny said, beckoning her over.

He and René went through her berries, removing quite a few of them. "Not bad, especially for your first batch."

"Why are you separating so many?"

"Well, we're going to have to toss a few, but this is a good start. Come over here." He motioned for her to join him on the other side of the table. "See how these over here are dark black and yours are more red and purple?"

"Yes."

"Well, we want the black ones, not the others. And these over here have a little bit of fuzz on them? No good."

"Oh. I didn't know."

"It's okay. It's your first time out."

Rolo shouted something Ana was sure was meant for her as Manny, René, and Vic all shushed him. He continued in Spanish, adopting a female voice and batting his eyelashes. Ana wasn't sure, but she thought he mentioned something about her hair, something about the curls, and the back of her neck. Instinctively, she checked to make sure it was covered, not realizing that at some point while she worked, she must have swept her hair up into her hat in the sun's heat. She pulled her ponytail back down again; covering the area she was sure he had seen. He made an ooh sound, and without hesitation, she turned toward him.

"*Cállate*, Roly-Poly!"

There was a silence before Manny, Vic, and the rest of the workers who had since gathered along the fence all erupted into laughter as Emmett approached.

"What's going on here?"

"Ana's reminding Rolo to watch his mouth," Manny chuckled. "And his gut."

"Roly-Poly!" one of the men along the fence shouted, to another round of laughter.

"Good advice," Emmett said. "How'd she do?"

"How'd you do?" Manny asked, deflecting Emmett's attention in Ana's direction.

Ana looked at the ground.

"She did just fine," Manny assured him. "Kept a good pace."

"Well, it wouldn't hurt everyone to kick it up."

The rest of the morning consisted of picking more berries, some sprouts, and a row of carrots. Ana was baffled that the carrots she yanked from the earth were sometimes yellow or purple and misshapen, unlike the perfect orange ones in grocery stores. She stood at the end of a long row and stretched her back, surprised at the exhaustion setting in. A bell rang out over the fields. She followed the rest of the workers to the sorting station, bunches of carrots in hand.

"Lunch break, boys," Emmett said as they approached, "and, um, girl."

Some of the workers headed over to Emmett's pickup truck with Manny, bringing back peaches, water, and sandwiches made by Abbie. Ana knew they had come from her kitchen, judging by the white parchment wrapping tied together with red string. She joined Vic and a few others leaning against the fence and inhaled the roasted vegetable pesto sandwich. Emmett stayed in the driver's seat of his truck to eat alone.

"Boss doesn't eat with us?" she leaned over and whispered to Vic.

"Boss eats with boss."

She watched as Emmett fiddled with the stereo, the faint sounds of Neil echoing across the farmland.

"He's a perfect stranger, like a cross of himself and a fox."

Ana wasn't sure if it was the food, the lulling background music, or if she was hallucinating, but she did a double take as a giant purple caterpillar suddenly made its way up the road.

"*¡Órale!*" the workers hooped and hollered as Emmett honked the truck's horn.

Ana wondered if this is what sunstroke felt like, because behind the caterpillar there was a spider, a metallic dragon, and a winking chicken lumbering along in stride. The creatures rounded the bend near the entrance of Garber Farm, coming closer into view, and Ana realized they were part of a parade of elaborate floats fashioned out of bicycles. There were single bikes and tandems powered by two or three people smiling and waving in hats that matched the theme of their vehicle. Everything from fire ants, snapping turtles, and even a man in a clown costume on a unicycle ambled along the road to cheers from the workers.

"What's this?" Ana asked Vic, who was also staring in awe.

He shrugged in response.

"Kinetic Sculpture Race," Manny said as he took off his hat and waved it toward the road. "Happens every year all along the coast. People spend months building these crazy things. Fun, no?"

The people powering the dragon pulled a lever and the makeshift beast roared to life, shooting a plume of fire out of its mouth that made everyone cheer. It was unlike anything Ana had ever seen before, and she couldn't help but cheer along too. She'd been to the Pasadena Rose Bowl parade once, when she was living with the Fergusons, but had caught only a glimpse of the floats through the legs of the crowd. A lobster with working claws, followed by three guys peddling a shoe the size of a car, passed by. Manny seemed to know a few people and tipped his hat every now and then, earning him hoots and honks.

Ana finished her lunch, as did the others, and they all watched the end of the parade. Her back ached and her eyes were heavy, so she shook herself up as the last bikes approached. They were louder than the others and unadorned. It took a moment before she realized they were motorcycles of various colors and shapes; their only embellishments were the riders themselves, who wore costumes like silver disco suits, cowboy outfits, and more than a couple roughed-up versions of Elvis. They weren't as lively as the homemade sculptures, but they'd dressed up for the event and revved as they passed the farm.

The last two riders rode alongside each other. The larger rider was outfitted in blue and green, and a few flags attached to the back of his bike flapped along in the wind. The smaller rider wore a yellow and black jumpsuit with a pair of wings, which fluttered like a bumblebee as both riders slowed their bikes as they passed. Ana didn't know if the sunstroke was setting in for real, or if it was just her tired delirium, but she let her hand float up and sweep the air in a slow-motion wave.

Abbie couldn't help herself. She waited until she saw everyone head back out into the fields and went up to the guest bedroom. Nothing was out of place, so she opened the backpack that remained tucked into the bottom of the armoire. Abbie was already aware of Ana's limited wardrobe—which she was prepared to launder regularly with nary a word that might blemish her pride—but as she fished around in the old army sack, she pulled out a notebook. Page after page was covered in elaborate pen drawings. One was the backyard of a dilapidated house, its yard barren and swirling with ribbons of dust. Another depicted a schoolyard with dried grass that resembled thick hair entangled with insects and bits of torn paper, remnants of truncated poetry. She flipped the page and stopped at an unfinished portrait of a sad-looking dog with a torn ear. It was rendered in almost photographic detail and backed by a tattered quilt. Underneath, written in letters resembling spray-painted graffiti, was the word CHELO.

"Astonishing" was the word Abbie said aloud, scaring herself, and her reflection in the armoire, in the process. She couldn't help but flip through the entire thing, heart racing, mouth agape, as she uncovered what felt like secret maps to a neglected city most startlingly alive.

She put the notebook back in the bag when she heard the screen door open downstairs. It was only Emmett coming in with a box of beets.

"What's with the expression, Sis?" Emmett said, taking a cookie from the tray on the stove as Abbie entered the kitchen. "Up to no good?"

"I'd say the same of you. Those cookies are for later."

Emmett gave her a wan smile.

"Listen, I'm taking Ana on deliveries this afternoon. I want to introduce her to Rye Moon."

"What's the point?" Emmett said, grabbing another cookie.

"I think it's important she meet girls her age."

"Mm-hm."

"This town is minuscule, Emmett, and people are naturally curious. It's best if we keep from hiding her right from the start."

"Why do you care what other people think? She's our summer intern, and she's staying only a month."

"Honestly." Abbie sighed. "It's her first day. Let's give her a chance, shall we?"

Emmett looked out the window and across the fields. He watched as Ana seemed to struggle with a carrot that wasn't yet ready to be picked.

"If this morning's any indication, I'd keep her for less than a week."

"I'm taking her to meet Rye, and there's nothing you can do about it."

"Okay. But, I'll warn ya. You've never experienced that girl in a moving vehicle."

Ana didn't have time to change. Her faded jeans were covered in dirt and sagging in the knees. She had one of Abbie's stained work shirts unbuttoned over her favorite band tee. The thought of meeting someone her age, especially a girl, twisted her stomach into a nauseated loop.

Ana dropped the box of produce on the front porch as Abbie had asked and made her way past Abbie's lopsided van. GARBER FARM ORGANIC PRODUCE was splashed across the side of it in fading letters. She continued down the pebble pathway to the potting shed on the other side of the house just beyond the garden. The tin-roofed shed was tiny, and covered in flowering vines. The Dutch door's top half was open, framing Abbie as she worked. There was a stained glass window above the entrance, unusual and charming, adorned with a blackbird surrounded by olive leaves.

"So, now that we have a moment, how did the morning go?" Abbie asked.

"It's debatable," Ana said. "According to Manny, I did

just fine. According to Emmett, I need a bachelor's degree in farmer's science, if that exists."

"It'll get easier," she said.

"Should I change clothes?"

"You're fine the way you are."

"I'm filthy."

"We're farmers, it's part of the look," Abbie said, tying bundles of cornflowers with twine. "Let me see your hat."

Ana took off the gardening hat, worried Abbie would notice the stained ring of sweat that had accumulated under the brim.

"Apologies. My hair is an aberration," Ana said.

"Nonsense," Abbie said. "But bonus points for word choice." She snipped a few of the flowers and tucked them under the band around the brim, making them shoot out of the side of the hat like a miniature fireworks display. "My mother used to call this 'pizzazz,'" she said, handing the hat back. "Draws attention to the eyes, and yours are lovely."

Ana put the hat on and swept her hair behind her shoulders. It wasn't really the look she'd normally go for, not that she'd ever been able to cultivate the look she liked, but she felt slightly better.

"Very 'of the land,'" Abbie continued. "Which is to say, just like the rest of us country folk. Trust me, no one in this town is judging."

They made their way to the van and added to the already ample load in the back, which included boxes of jars and bottles, wildflower arrangements, and a few loaves of fresh bread in paper bags stamped GARBER FARM. Ana climbed into the front seat, which was strewn with various odds and ends that included a potato sack, a magazine with the front cover torn off, a to-go coffee mug in one cup holder, a gardening tool sticking out of the other cup holder, and a half-eaten bar of baking chocolate melting on the dashboard next to *Crystal Visions—The Very Best of Stevie Nicks*. She smiled to herself. "The yin and yang of siblinghood," she thought, remembering the scene in Emmett's truck—so much similarity in the differences.

They made their way out of the farm and down the road, passing dainty Victorian houses with manicured yards. If Ana had to pick a favorite, Garber Farm would win, she thought, and not just for the wildness of its surroundings, but also for its restrained authenticity. "The farm is so different from the rest of the houses," she said.

"Well, we've been here a little longer. But yes, we Garbers have always embraced subtlety over ostentation. Believe me, when I was your age, I would have killed to live in one of these houses. One of my childhood friends did."

"I bet the lawns are full of forgotten Easter eggs and polka-dot horses out in back."

"You might find a few." Abbie laughed. "Most of these folks are grandparents, or great-grandparents."

"Did you ever want kids?" She didn't know why she asked it, regretted it from the moment it tumbled from her lips.

"Well, hon, to be honest, it just never happened for me," Abbie said, leaning forward to switch the stereo on. "Some of us are built for a different kind of life, I guess."

Though Abbie had meant to replace the *Crystal Visions* CD still missing from its case—"borrowed" by Josie nearly a year ago—she was glad she'd refused to lend out Stevie's *Wild Heart*, which she preferred.

"My mother was built for a different life," Ana said, continuing to stare out the window as Stevie sang. "But she accidentally had me."

"Sometimes that happens."

"It's funny, all the kids who have kids, the ones who can't take care of themselves being forced to take care of someone else they don't want. Then there are all those people desperate for kids, who are old enough and ready and waiting. I know girls my age—girls younger even—who are pregnant and don't want to be, and I've lived with foster parents who would do anything to have kids of their own. It doesn't make any sense."

"No, it doesn't," Abbie said. "But life isn't fair, and you can't choose who you're born to. It's all beyond our control, I'm afraid. There's power in how we react to our situations, though."

The van continued ambling toward the center of Hadley. They hadn't passed any other cars or signs of life on the road, which Ana thought odd and wonderful. "What would L.A. look like if the same were true?" she wondered.

"*. . . Hopelessly enchanted, wild in the darkest places of your mind.*"

"It's ridiculous how much Stevie truly gets it," Ana said.

"She does, doesn't she?" Abbie responded, forgetting to whom she was talking for a moment. "How did you know this was Stevie?"

"Are you kidding?" Ana asked, her eyebrows rising in mock horror. "*Stand back*, Abbie, please."

They parked the van in front of Moon Pharm General Store, which was hard to miss with its dark facade and bright yellow crescent moon sign hanging above the door. It stood out from all the other storefronts on Main Street, with overflowing flower boxes and dream catchers decorating its front

windows. The door was set back from the sidewalk, the
walkway lined with hand-painted ceramic pots filled with
various plants. The door chimed as they entered, little bells
and clinking pottery pieces strung together on the handle.

Ana breathed in the scent of varnished wood and burning herbs. She realized, for the first time in her brief tour of
downtown Hadley, which was quiet for a late summer afternoon, that she was actually in a bustling place of business.
It wasn't completely unlike some of the corner stores in
Boyle Heights. There were aisles of grocery items, glass re-
frigerators lining a wall, and a sign above the front counter
pointing to the pharmacy and "licensed herbalist" in the
rear of the store.

Abbie waved at the gentleman behind the counter who
was helping a few customers. He was a smaller man with
glasses and a starched shirt tucked into high-waist khakis.
He nodded, giving Ana the once-over with a gentle yet dis-
cerning eye.

"That's Charlie Moon," Abbie said. "We'll say hi in a bit.
I want to introduce you to Della, one my oldest and dearest
friends. I'm sure Rye is around here somewhere. . . . I'm just
so thrilled for you to meet them!"

They rounded a corner of homeopathic remedies and
shelves of homemade soap and oils before being intercepted
by a woman with long dark hair swinging all the way down
to her ample hips. She smiled at them both before embracing Abbie. They held on to each other for longer than
normal, the woman's eyes closed and a smile on her face.

"You must be Ana," the woman said, reaching her arms
out to grab Ana's hands and squeezing them with the same
concentrated warmth she gave the hug. "We're so honored
to have you here. Abbie told us all about your coming to

work on the farm, and we wanted to welcome you in person. I'm Della Moon. My daughter, Rye, is checking inventory and will be out in a moment. Why don't you two follow me?"

"I need to make a quick delivery," Abbie said. "Are you okay for a few minutes? I promise I won't be long."

"Sure," Ana said. She was thrilled at the chance to explore the store. There were so many products she'd never seen before, small vials of tonics, lotions bearing labels with suns and flowers, a black jar with symbols surrounded by tiny bolts of lightning. There were glass containers lining multiple wooden shelves along the back wall, like an old-fashioned candy shop that peddled ginseng and rhubarb root instead of sweets.

"What's all this?" Ana asked.

"My laboratory," Della said with a proud smile, adjusting the multiple strands of beads draped around her neck. "We run the local pharmacy, but I specialize in herbs and natural remedies too. Even tea, if you're into it."

"What's that?" Ana pointed to a jar of slivered twigs.

"Astragalus," Della said, reaching for it, the multiple rings on her fingers clinking against the glass. "Good for preventing illness."

"Do you ever buy your stuff from the farm?"

"As a matter of fact, we do. Abbie grows our gingerroot, and we've found some wonderful varieties of wild mushrooms in the woods behind the farm. Quite potent."

"I'm not allowed back there apparently."

"Oh, but it's breathtaking! I'll see what I can talk Abbie in to," Della said with a knowing smile.

"My abuela would say you look like Dolores del Rio."

"Oh? And who's that?"

"She's a famous Mexican actress with a very distinct

nose, something my abuela and I find to be a treasured mark of distinction."

"Or a wicked curse of nature," a voice said from behind the counter.

"Rye," Della said, adjusting her shawl over her long dress, "there's someone I'd like you to meet."

A petite young woman came out from behind a swinging door. Despite her remark, her nose, as with the rest of the features on her face, was delicate and feminine and was offset by a severe black bob and short bangs, all of which was highlighted in shades of purple. She was striking, with long-lashed eyes that swooped up toward her hairline, cheekbones that matched her mother's, and bright red lips. She looked over Ana from top to bottom, so Ana did the same. There was a lot to take in: Rye's buttoned-up blouse tied at the top with a black satin ribbon, skinny suspenders, and tailored men's trousers rolled up at the bottom to reveal a pair of black-and-white saddle shoes. Ana had rarely seen such deliberate attention paid to personal style. Back in L.A., it was mostly sneakers and jeans. Rye raised her eyebrows but said nothing, so Ana said, "Hey," and left it at that.

"Why don't you girls head to the stockroom?" Della suggested. "I've got customers on the way, and, Rye, you can let Ana help herself to some samples."

Rye rolled her eyes, though her mother didn't notice, and pushed open the door, not bothering to hold it open for Ana. They walked down a long hallway past a locked door. Ana noticed a striped silk handkerchief hanging out of one of Rye's back pockets.

"Is that for random sneezes?" Ana asked.

"What, my hankie? Nah, just for show, but it does come

in handy when you need to clean your sunglasses. Not that we're burning with sunshine up here."

"Tell me about it," Ana said. "It bleeds sunshine where I'm from."

Rye continued walking, so Ana continued to follow as they ducked under hanging pieces of printed fabric into a storage room full of boxes stacked in precise rows.

"FYI, no one in this town likes the Hex," Rye said, pointing at Ana's T-shirt before settling into the only chair in the room. Ana had no choice but to lean up against the wall. "You're the first person I've seen wearing one of those around here."

"Are you serious?" Ana said, hesitating, not knowing if Rye was taking a dig at her favorite band or at Hadley's residents. "I'm not ashamed to say they're my favorite, and they're not afraid to shout what's what. I happen to think that's a miraculous thing."

"You feel very strongly about this."

"I do. So what?"

"So nothing. So, you're a fan then?"

"I think I just made that clear."

"Why are you so touchy?"

"I'm not," Ana said, reminding herself to calm down.

"But you are," Rye said, crossing her legs and leaning back in the chair. "So, what's your deal?"

"My deal?"

"Yeah, what are you doing here?" Rye crossed her arms.

"Why are you asking so many questions? What's *your* deal?"

"My deal is I'm a Chinese Native American named after a type of grass who has a short attention span and a penchant for the absurd. This is where I work, those people outside are my parents, and I can't wait to get the hell out of here. Your turn."

Ana didn't know where to begin.

"Isn't the whole point of this setup to get to know each other?" Rye continued.

"I guess. I don't know. It was Abbie's idea."

"Just like it was my mom's idea."

They were quiet for a moment, the sounds of Della Moon's laughter echoing from the counter down the hallway.

"Have you ever even *seen* the Hex play?" Rye asked.

"I saw them at The Smell a few months ago."

"Where's that? The Smell?" Rye said, scrunching up her face and bobbing one foot up and down.

"Back in L.A."

"Wait. What? You're from Los Angeles?"

"Yeah, so what?"

"Holy lady balls, woman, you need to tell me *everything*!" Rye's entire demeanor shifted as she slid to the front of the chair and gestured for Ana to sit down on one of the boxes. "Okay, full disclosure? They're my favorite band too."

"For real?"

"Yep."

"Weird."

"Supremely."

"I thought you said no one here likes them?" Ana said, sitting down.

"People in this town don't get it. I was trying to see if you were a real deal fan or not because I've been duped once before. Anyway, I wanted to see their show in San Francisco last month, but the 'rents wouldn't let me go. They're the only band that matters in my life, but my mother can't seem to see the importance of experiencing them live and in person, even if she did run off with Abbie once to see Stevie Nicks."

"Don't knock The Stevie; she's a gold—"

"Dust woman, yeah, yeah, yeah. So, tell me about this show. You have no idea how lucky you are. Details."

"It was in this tiny club in downtown L.A., walls covered in crazy paintings, and the place is all ages too," Ana said as Rye's eyes widened. "I kid you not; Rosa Hex effing shredded the place. It was so packed there was sweat dripping off the ceiling. Not that I need to explain this to you since we've established that you're a fan, but it was one of the most monumental moments of my existence. She looked out over everyone—and I'm standing in the back, right—and she points and says, pretty much directly into my eye sockets, 'Stay calm, surrender, and always pretend you're wearing a raincoat of mace.'"

"Holy Shesus."

"I know. It was a religious experience."

"I bow to you," Rye said. She stood up and bent over gracefully. "So, your parents let you go to the show?"

"Not really. I happened to be between houses at the time. . . . I don't have any parents."

"None?"

"Nada."

"You're living my dream!"

"It's not really like that. And your mom seems genuinely nice."

"It's the Wiyot way." Rye sighed. She sat back down and stared down the hallway.

"What's that?"

"My mom's birth tribe. They're native to these parts, the very first people here *ever*, until the settlers massacred them. Not that my dad's people weren't totally driven out during the gold rush too. Hadley's full of the descendants of money-gobbling marauders, FYI, so watch yourself. Why are you living with the Garbers if you're from L.A.?"

"They're my guardians at the moment, I guess, and my bosses. Well, Emmett is. I got sent up here to work on the farm for the rest of the summer."

"But you're from L.A . . ."

"Born and raised, well, semi-raised, I guess. I grew up in East L.A."

"What are you, Chicana? Homegirl type of situation?"

"Wow. Um, I'm Mexican, if that's what you're getting at."

"Unreal. So did you see cholas and everything? Because their style is rad."

"Yeah, it's not really a style so much as . . . I don't know. The whole change from there to here and the farm has been monumental. So far it's interesting, but also kind of a drag. I've been told I may have to work around worms. How people find joy in composting, or whatever you call it, is beyond me."

"Isn't Abbie the best, though?" Rye said. "She's the only person who's ever made it out of this stupid town, even if she had to come back. She's got stories, you know? Like, the real deal."

"Abbie?"

"Oh, yeah," Rye said, pursing her lips and nodding as if she knew way too much. "Ask her sometime. She's into music, was *really* into it at one point, not that anyone ever talks about that. So, have you heard their new cover of 'Heaven Knows I'm Miserable Now'?"

"Not yet. The Hex is my life's soundtrack, yes, but I only ever listen to them at the library, which I haven't been to in a while."

"You're joking."

"I'm not."

"Well, then, you need to come over and get with this business. When do you get a break?"

"Never. It's part of the deal."

"We're going to have to change that."

"Not really an option . . ."

"And we've got to change whatever it is that's dimming the aura of your T-shirt, which is shamefully baggy for what is sure to be something special underneath. And apologies, but those jeans are pushing turn of the millennium, and your hair, though undeniably gorgeous, could use an oil treatment and a slash of blue. Have you never heard of eyeliner? Tweezers? You're like Frida Hayek, only desperately sans film lighting."

"I love Frida *Kahlo* and the *Frida* movie. No dissing."

"I'm not knocking a strong brow and thick head of hair, but this is a fiesta that needs to be tamed."

"You do realize you're insulting my people."

"Your people and my people got the bottom end of the boot, sweetheart. We're in this mess, aka town, together, and I assure you that one of us is way more of a mess than the other."

Before Ana had a moment to decipher which one, the door swung open at the end of the corridor.

"Girls?" Abbie called.

"Back here!" Rye shouted before whispering to Ana, "Seriously? Abbie's *lived*, you know?"

"No, I don't . . ."

"We have to be on our way," Abbie said, peeking into the storage room. "Emmett is expecting us back at the farm, so let's get going."

"Oh, I almost forgot," Rye said. She jumped up and ran across the room to an open box, pulling out a handful of small bottles. "Here," she said, dropping them into Ana's hands.

"What's this?"

"Camellia oil. It's good for the hair. My mom said you're supposed to get some samples, so here's a special welcome gift from one fellow Hexagon to another." Rye put her hand over her nonexistent left breast in silent salute. Ana tried to do the same without dropping the bottles, but she managed only to briefly touch her overflowing hands to the center of her chest.

"Thanks," she mumbled.

"No, thank *you*."

"For what?" Ana wanted to say, not knowing how to respond to Rye's beaming smile.

Abbie rattled her keys. "Rye, please tell your mother thank you from me."

"No prob," Rye said before turning back to Ana and mouthing, "Later."

It was late afternoon when they headed back to the farm. A light fog rolled in from the ocean, dimming the light and blurring the woods and fields surrounding Hadley.

"So, that went well," Abbie said, fiddling with the stereo. "With Rye?"

"It wasn't what I expected," Ana said.

"In what way?"

"It wasn't typically how it usually goes. I'm good with kindergarteners, not so much with anyone else my age. But Rye seems intriguing."

"I've known her all her life, and she has an interesting way about her. Something told me you two would get along."

"She likes the Hex."

"The Hex?"

"The band on my T-shirt? They're this all-girl band from L.A. and are my favorite of favorites."

"Oh, yeah? What do they sound like?"

"Well, there's some yelling involved," Ana said, wondering if she should continue, if Abbie cared about this sort of thing. No one had ever asked before. "It's sort of fused with these beautiful, guttural melodies and lyrics of poetic truth." She figured she'd stop there, but Abbie turned the music off, so she continued. "The lead singer—Rosa Hex—has this incredible voice, but she distorts it and lets the beauty come out only when she wants it to. Each member took 'Hex' as their last name, like the Ramones. But unlike the Ramones, the guitars aren't simple or anything. They have a complex and stubborn sound, fast and howling, and Rosa sings about standing up and facing whatever terrifies you even if it makes you shudder. Sometimes they play topless, but it's about empowerment and not giving a f—well, not caring what other people think, which is important, especially if you've got fear sprinting through your veins."

"They sound fantastic."

"They're sick, no other way to describe them—and so loud even when they're quiet. And they always wear black and white, which dims their outside in order to magnify what they're expressing from the inside, or so I like to think. Their bassist paints these delicate scenes that hang behind them when they play, these murals painted on tarps that are hypnotic and horrifying, kind of like the paintings by this guy Henry Darger but way less uncomfortable."

"You know so much about art and music for someone your age." Abbie flinched, hoping Ana hadn't read anything into the art part.

"It's weird, but sometimes it's all I've had, you know? Like the only thing I can always go back to if I need something to feel familiar . . . a song, a painting, an old movie, picture books or stories that remind me of people, I guess, since I don't have any photos of my own. I've spent so much time in the library—it's the only real home I've ever known. And even though it's open only at certain times, it's always welcoming; no matter who you are or where you come from, it's there for you without judgment."

Abbie hadn't realized how alone Ana had been for most of her life. She hesitated to ask anything more, even though she was curious and delighted that Ana was opening up, but she couldn't help herself.

"Did you go to libraries after school?"

"Yep, pretty much every day, and then all day on Saturdays and Sundays. Sometimes I'd get dropped there with my younger foster siblings. I used to read them stories in the children's section. But on days I was there alone, I'd ingest whatever struck me in the moment, you know? Other times I would explore a little further."

"Other types of books you mean?"

Ana didn't know if she should continue, but Abbie still seemed interested in listening. "I'd take the bus places. Nowhere far or anything, and it's not like anyone ever knew I was gone, but the city's so big and there are places like Little Tokyo where girls dress like intergalactic princesses, whole streets full of weird shops, entire neighborhoods built out of tents. There's this store in Boyle Heights that sells Frida socks and vintage reggae records and they have poetry nights and a radio show and everything. Even though I never had any money, the guy who owns it would always tell me about stuff he thought I should learn about. He gave me a book about Chicano punk rock once too, but it was taken away, of course."

"There's so much more to see and experience in a city like L.A.," Abbie said with a faraway sigh. "I hope you aren't bored here. We don't have that much to offer, I'm afraid."

Ana sat in one of the rocking chairs on the front porch. She listened to the breeze rustle the trees and the sound of Abbie clanging pots in the kitchen. It hadn't been such a terrible first day, she thought. The sun began its slow descent, turning the sky a dusty pink. The front door opened and Emmett walked out holding a beer. He wasn't a man of many words, but he cleared his throat to announce his arrival. Neither one of them knew what to say.

"Where's Dolly?" Ana asked, attempting to break the silence.

"Up in the barn," Emmett said, taking a sip from the can.

"I feel like we didn't get properly acquainted."

"Properly acquainted?" he asked with a snort that wasn't unfriendly. "I'm sure you'll get the chance."

"Does this mean I can stay another night?" she said, figuring she should double-check, just in case. She'd used this tactic before—getting verbal permission before she knew circumstances might change.

"I told you I'd give you a month. I'm a man of my word," Emmett said. He was already counting down the days.

They continued staring out over the land, the sound of barking coming from the barn in the distance.

"I used to have a dog," Ana said.

"Did ya?"

"Her name was Chelo. She wasn't around very long, but she was beautiful—very sweet natured and strong before she got sick."

"Sounds like a good dog."

"She was a champion among pups."

"What breed?" Emmett said, forcing himself to give in to the conversation.

"Pit bull. She had half an ear."

"That's a shame."

"I always thought it made her unique. The last time I saw her, though, she had a whole lot less than that. It was a tragic situation. She was sweet even when she was in pain."

"You were with her then? When she died?"

"No. She was always tied to a fence in the backyard. They took her away one day and then brought her back in terrible shape. I remember I wanted to hold her because she was trembling and crying so much. There was blood." A tremendous amount, she wanted to say, elaborating further on the ghastly mess of a thing that twisted her heart apart every time she thought about it. She remembered how she and Chelo seemed to share their fate quietly, how they would make the most of what they both knew would be very little time together. "I snuck outside, and she stopped whining when I got close. She licked me, and I remember trying to hug her around the neck, but someone took her away again, or me, I can't remember. We were always being taken places we didn't want to go. Anyway, she never came back."

"I'm . . . I'm sorry to hear that."

Abbie popped her head out of the front door and waved an oven-mitted hand before shutting the door again.

"Tell my sis I'll join you a little later," Emmett said. He walked down the steps and headed toward the barn.

Abbie prepared an elaborate dinner to match the morning's breakfast. There was roast chicken, carrot salad, fresh rosemary corn bread, and lavender lemonade. It was the first time in a long time Ana had asked for seconds. After dinner, she checked in with Mrs. Saucedo. It was a brief conversation and not the usual barrage of uncomfortable questions, but she was reminded, yet again, to mind herself. Ana sat in the living room for a moment, taking in the dim light and cozy appeal. She understood why Abbie had come back and never left again.

Before heading upstairs, Ana went into the kitchen to say good night. There was a knock on the back door.

Abbie put her book down and shrugged her shoulders.

"I've got something for Ana," Emmett mumbled from outside.

Going off Abbie's gesture, Ana opened the back door and saw Emmett standing with Dolly. She anticipated the dog's leaping in her direction, but with Emmett's firm hand holding the leash, Dolly remained still, licking her lips eagerly as Ana walked outside.

"What's up, Dolly?" Ana said. She crouched down and rubbed vigorously behind Dolly's ears as the dog flopped over to one side, exposing her belly.

"Be careful," Abbie warned from the screen door. "That dog will charm you into submission."

"Or the other way around," Emmett said. "Dolly, this is Ana . . . Ana, Dolly."

Ana shook one of the dog's upside-down paws. "Pleased to meet you."

Emmett cleared his throat. "There you go. Properly acquainted. Feel free to, uh, to drop by and visit her if you want. See you both in the morning." He and Dolly walked back across the garden toward the barn.

Ana thanked Abbie for dinner and said good night again, this time waiting for Abbie to respond as if she needed permission to leave the kitchen. She crept upstairs to the small bathroom. There was a claw-footed tub, and she had to turn the knobs several times before figuring out the right temperature and what to press, or in this case pull, to get the shower to work. Not knowing the Garbers' policy, she did as she always had and counted to 120 as she washed, being careful not to use up too much of the soap and water. She couldn't believe she didn't have to share the bathroom with anyone else—a first, she thought. "But don't get used to all this," she reminded herself.

She tiptoed back to the bedroom and hung what few pieces of clothing she had in the armoire. She peeled back the covers before slipping into the tall bed. The sheets were cool and soft, the whole bed a feathered cloud with room to stretch out on either side. Abbie had left a small glass of water on the nightstand along with a couple of books to read, but Ana propped the notebook she fished out of her backpack on her knees, clearing her mind, and letting her ballpoint pen move across the page.

Not sure where the sketch ended and the dream began, her eyes became heavy as the paper filled with images. Flying dogs, barking birds, a cat-pig, and a Chihuahua-chicken.

Overripe berries twinkling across the sky like stars; their juice raining down upon a tangled garden. Up in the trees, a figure clutched a swaying branch. Her pen traced the shape over and over again. There was no face, just a shadow hidden behind a curtain of leaves.

CHAPTER SIX

It was a dark Tuesday morning nearly two weeks later when Ana awoke, got dressed, and headed downstairs, realizing when she got to the kitchen that this routine felt alarmingly normal. She treated the morning like any other, even though it was the one day of the year she always tried to forget. Abbie said hello while standing against the counter reading the latest issue of a farming magazine. Ana fixed herself a bowl of cereal and topped it with milk and a handful of blackberries before heading out to the fields.

The first week spent working the land wasn't what she had expected. She was aware of the hard work, at times backbreaking, especially if she was working on rows of strawberries or pulling and stripping bulbs of garlic. Manny explained the importance of cover crops and had given Ana a lesson on sprouts the day before. Even though she thought "alfalfa" was one of the best words ever, she renamed it "awfalfa" because, as she explained to Manny, who would ever want to eat plant hair on a sandwich?

Ana began to look forward to the work, however difficult she still found it. What she enjoyed most was the morning waltz through the rows of mysterious fruits and vegetables, quiet but for the crunch of her weight in the dirt.

Her week of work even resulted in a new appreciation for the coworker she deemed "Roly," who made faces at her when the picking became tiresome. Though they spoke very little, she felt she'd been accepted into the Vic and Rolo duo as a third wheel, mostly ignored but clearly tolerated, the field mouse of the crew.

The workers had changed since her first week. There were the regulars—Rolo, Vic, Joey, and René—but the rest of those reporting to duty had shifted. She wanted to ask a million questions—about where the workers lived and why some never came back—but she kept her mouth shut, even though it pained her.

On days that were difficult, or when she couldn't seem to do anything right, she turned her soft focus further inward, allowing whatever crop she was working on to blossom in her mind's eye, a carnival of twisting roots and branches upon which numerous stories took her to distant universes. She was lost in one such daydream when Emmett approached.

"Cortez," he said. "I'm going to put you on weed duty for the rest of the morning. Vic and Rolo will finish up here."

Both men nodded and continued working. Ana stood there holding her gloved hands in the air.

"Just leave the gloves on the ground along with your cans. The guys will take your haul in and have it sorted for you."

Ana did as she was told. The work shirt tied around her waist and her favorite white Hex T-shirt were covered in dirt and tiny speckles of juice. She followed Emmett back down the path.

"The parsley's a mess," Emmett said. "I'm going to have you weed it."

They passed a row of tiny plants shooting up from the ground. They reminded Ana of miniature palm trees only with much more interesting fronds. She had never thought to ask what they were.

"What are these?"

"Kale," Emmett said, quickening his pace.

"What's that?"

"Kale?" he said, exhaling a little too sharply, as if this were something she should know. "It's a type of brassica."

"A what?"

"Like broccoli or cauliflower."

"Oh," Ana said. "Appetizing."

"You're from Los Angeles and you've never heard of kale?"

"No. I never saw the ocean until the day I flew here, either. Shocking, isn't it?" Ana reminded herself to control her tone. "My abuela always wanted to take me, and I think my parents might have driven me to Long Beach or something when I was super little, but I don't remember. So how do you eat this stuff?"

"Kale?"

"Yeah, brassica. Much better name if you ask me. Like a forgotten orchestra section."

"You steam it or sauté it, I guess. You can also eat it raw. Abbie's always going on about how it's full of nutrients—customers love it. You've *never* heard of kale?"

"I've. Never. Heard. Of. Kale." She enunciated each word for emphasis, and Emmett went silent. Before she gave herself any time to ponder whether or not she was about to be fired for lack of vegetable knowledge, Emmett stopped in front of a long row of thick green bushes.

"You know what parsley is, don't you?" he asked.

"It's the curly green stuff sprinkled on nondescript Italian dishes, only it's kind of inedible."

"Yes, but we grow flat-leaf parsley, which is the opposite of the curly-leaf kind." He seemed impatient, Ana noticed, and didn't elaborate in the way Manny did. "Do you know what a weed is?"

"A type of plant . . . ?" Ana asked, not knowing which definition he was referring to and worried she'd choose the one that would get her arrested.

"Yup. It's basically anything you don't want growing in your fields."

"But it's a plant."

"Yes, it's a plant, one that inhibits the growth of other plants, so we have to get rid of weeds sometimes. They're taking over our parsley."

"Even though they're just growing where they want to grow?"

"Yes," Emmett said.

Ana wondered why anyone would plant parsley in the first place, if it didn't even taste good. She was on the weeds' side, for sure.

"You know what parsley looks like, right?" Emmett continued, somewhere between mystified and frustrated. "It's the opposite of the flat leaves, so pick those and throw them into the middle of the row. The parsley's not ready for picking until tomorrow morning, right before Abbie heads out to the farmers' market, got it?"

"Pick the weeds, toss them into the middle of the row."

"Exactly," Emmett said, nodding his head.

Ana watched him make his way across the fields, and when he was safely out of sight, she kneeled down to take a closer look at the bushes. There were two types of plants growing: some that were longer, flat and narrow, and some that were more in the shape of a four-leaf clover. The longer, narrower ones seemed the flattest, more the opposite of curly, as Emmett suggested. She took a deep breath and wondered if she should double-check with Manny or one of the other workers, but everyone was busily working much farther out in the fields.

So, Ana made an educated guess. She began pulling the clover-looking plants because they were wilder and more abundant, "taking over," as Emmett had said. She accidentally snapped a few off at the center of their stems, not realizing you had to grip from closer to the bottom. Once she got the hang of it, she worked fast and efficiently, getting lost in the pulling and throwing of weeds, finding joy in the tossing of them all over the middle of the row. She imagined the praise she'd get from Manny, who would then tell Emmett— in front of everyone else—and how maybe she'd get a nod of respect. She envisioned Vic and Rolo high-fiving her and René giving her a gentle bow. She became so lost in the work she didn't notice the bell ringing out across the fields. The workers began gathering at the packing truck for lunch. She continued picking, wanting to prove her enthusiasm to Manny, who walked toward her through the rows of kale.

"Ana!" he said cheerfully. "Working hard! Let's take a look—"

He stopped abruptly. Ana watched as horrified alarm swept across his face.

"Did Emmett tell you to do this?"

"Yes, sir," she said, her heart pounding. "He said to pick the weeds and leave the parsley. He said to leave the flat ones intact."

"*Ay-ay-ay,*" he said, exhaling, shaking his head. "Did Emmett tell you which was which?"

"Well, he said your parsley was the opposite of curly parsley, that it was flat, and that the weeds were everywhere. So I left the long flat ones and picked the other ones, which seemed to be the plants that were taking over."

Manny shook his head and cupped his hand over his mouth, keeping his eyes locked on the piles of green resting in the dirt.

"I picked the wrong ones."

"Yes, *mija.*"

Ana didn't know what to say. She wanted to cry but told herself not to. The thought of disappointing Manny, let alone Emmett, again made her want to turn around and sprint into the forest to embrace whatever dark fate was surely waiting for her. They both looked up, not realizing Emmett was standing behind them.

"What is this?" he said.

"It's not her fault," Manny said, remaining calm and giving Ana a look that implored her not to say anything. "She didn't know, okay? She thought she was picking the weeds."

"But I explained everything to you," Emmett said. "How could you not understand?"

Ana looked from one man to the other. "I guess I don't really know what flat-leaf parsley looks like?"

"But I was standing right here," Emmett said, exasperated. "You could have asked me to show you."

"You didn't ask me if I had any questions."

Emmett took off his baseball cap, squeezed it in his hand, and put it back on again. He looked down at the pile of parsley and then over to Manny.

"I, I'm really sorry," Ana said. "I thought I was doing it correctly. And, to be fair, I didn't completely understand your instructions." She looked over at the trees and picked a spot to run to.

"I should have checked on her sooner," Manny said. "It's my fault."

They stood there for a long, quiet moment, the sounds of the workers conversing across the fields in the background. Emmett bent down and picked up a small bunch of parsley. He handed it to Ana.

"Smell that," he said.

Ana put the leaves up to her nose and took a deep breath.

"What does it smell like?" he asked her.

"Um. Kind of fresh? A little bit like pepper."

"Okay, rip off a leaf and give it a chew."

Ana looked up at him and wondered if this was her punishment, but Manny nodded. She tore a small leaf from a flimsy stem and put it in her mouth.

"What does it taste like?" Emmett asked.

"It tastes like what it smells like," she answered, then swallowed. "Sharp and pungent, but not in a bad way."

"The next time we ask you to weed the parsley and you're confused, rip off a leaf, smell it, and taste it."

"Yes, sir." She looked from one to the other. "Am I going to be fired? I completely understand if that's unavoidable. I deserve the punishment even though the instructions weren't explicitly delivered." She looked up at Manny, who shook his head while staring at the ground.

"Manny, let's gather all this up and take it to the boys."

"No problem," Manny said, scooping a portion of the picked parsley into his arms. He gave Ana an encouraging smile on his way to the truck.

"I screwed up big time," Ana said, but Emmett didn't answer.

In truth, his mind was elsewhere, specifically on the thought of Josie, the anniversary of her departure looming. He knew he should have given a better explanation of what to do, going so far as to pick a few weeds himself, but he resisted an apology. He wasn't keeping Ana for much longer anyway, he reminded himself.

"Why don't you grab lunch and head on in with Abbie," he said.

Ana watched as he walked away.

"What's the deal with compost anyway?" Ana asked Abbie on their drive into town.

"I mean, I get that it's good for the soil or whatever, but worms?" Ana continued. "However full of protein Manny says they are, they're disgusting. My abuela sometimes ate grasshoppers, and I won't even get into what she did to cow's tongue, but 'learning from worms' makes no sense to me."

"Emmett's methods don't always make sense, but he's teaching you for a reason."

"The reason is punishment."

They passed a few modest brick homes and small bungalows before slowing to the curb and coming to a stop at the bottom of a sloping green lawn. Abbie turned the ignition off and they both sat there looking out of the passenger-side window.

"Monarch Mansion," Abbie said with a cluck of the tongue. "Pretty nuts, right?"

If there was any home in all of Hadley that was the antithesis of Garber Farm, it was Monarch Mansion. Though elaborate Victorian mansions were common around Hadley, Monarch Mansion was in a class of its own. There was no mistaking the theme. Painted in alternating shades of warm yellow and burnt orange, it was covered from top to bottom in anything and everything related to butterflies. There were stained glass butterfly scenes in the windows and butterfly carvings in the railings of the stairs leading up to the front porch. Rocking chairs, painted in shades of pale pink and electric blue, flanked the entrance, along with butterfly-shaped pots planted, of course, with flowers to attract the real things. The wooden sign, swinging ever so lightly in the breeze, advertised the property, in looping cursive, as An Award-Winning Bed and Breakfast. In slightly larger letters underneath, it read PROPRIETOR: MINERVA F. SHAW.

"I think we passed this on my first day," Ana said, "but I don't remember its being so . . ."

"Ridiculous?"

"I was going to say 'insane,' but in sort of a glorious way."

"Wait until you see inside."

Ana jumped out of the van, smoothed her T-shirt and jeans, and tightened the work shirt around her waist. She pulled her hair out of the ponytail, letting it fall loose around her face. They wound their way up the pebble path, passing an ornate gazebo as they ascended the steps to the front doors of the mansion. Abbie threw open the doors as if she owned the place.

"Minerva!" she called into an empty entrance room awash in floral wallpaper that enveloped a grand staircase leading up to what Ana imagined were the guest rooms. They peeked into a sitting room, also empty, but filled with antiques. A framed photograph of a balding man wearing a loud bow tie sat atop a piano in the corner. Ana followed Abbie through a larger living room crowded with couches, butterfly paintings, and windows with heavy drapes. There was a connecting formal dining room, its enormous wooden table laden with flowers and candles, and just beyond it a smaller breakfast room just outside the kitchen, where, framed in the doorway, a peacock in heels leaned against the counter smoking the longest cigarette Ana had ever seen.

"There you are!" Abbie said. "Ana, this is Minerva Shaw. Minerva, I'd like you to meet Ana Cortez."

"You caught me at a moment of weakness, girls," Minerva said, stubbing the cigarette out in the sink and spritzing the room with the overpowering scent of wilting gardenias.

"Your house, your rules," Abbie said.

"Don't tell the authorities," Minerva responded with a wink.

They had an easy banter, Ana thought.

"Hi," Ana said, extending her hand. "Your home—I mean, inn? It's magnificent."

"Well, aren't you polite, Anna," Minerva said, barely shaking the tips of her fingers.

"It's Ana, one n, like 'fauna'—not Anna like 'banana.'"

"I see."

"It's just the way it's pronounced."

"Noted," Minerva said, scrunching her face into a forced smile. "Abbie, good to see you; expected to see you earlier this morning, but no bother."

"I thought it'd be fine seeing as how it's well past breakfast and check-in isn't for another several hours," Abbie said, setting a box on the kitchen counter, which was spotless save for a half-empty tray of muffins and a lipstick-stained coffee mug, its handle a butterfly in repose. "It's not like guests are wandering about the parlor."

"A phone call is always appreciated, my dear. I could have been taking a reservation or meeting with the housekeeping staff . . ."

"I saw Teresa scrubbing the gazebo outside."

"Not all of us are as by the book with our routines, Abigail."

"Clearly," Abbie said. "So! I brought extra flowers for the weekend—your favorites—and blackberry preserves, peach chutney, tomatoes, plums, a bag of arugula, and I'm throwing in a fresh loaf of zucchini walnut bread."

"Always more than I asked for, but that's why we love you," Minerva said, applying a lacquer of coral lip gloss and popping a peppermint as she glanced at the contents of the box. "So, Anna, you're the one living with the Garbers, yes? Tell me everything. Is Emmett cracking the whip?"

"It's Ana," Abbie said with a smile, reacting to Ana's noticeable wince.

"Let her answer for herself," Minerva continued. "And from where do you hail?"

"Los Angeles."

"How exciting—the land of dreams! When I was your age, I was always being told to head out there myself, sit in a diner on Hollywood Boulevard, that sort of thing. Can't imagine leaving there for Hadley, though," Minerva said, wrinkling her tiny nose. "Are you enrolled in FFA at your school?"

"What's that?"

"It's Future Farmers of America," Abbie answered. "And, no, she's just helping us for the rest of the summer."

"Like an intern?"

"Sort of . . . ," Ana said.

"Oh?"

"I didn't really have a choice."

"She's on a special program," Abbie interjected, "and she's doing a brilliant job. Anyway, we should be going. I have cider in the van for you."

"And what did you say your last name was?" Minerva asked.

"Cortez."

"Oh, like the sea. Is that Spanish?"

"It is, I think, but my grandparents were from Mexico."

"How exotic! I went to Acapulco once, with my first husband—not really my thing—kept getting sick from all that food, or maybe it was the water? Never could be sure, but I'm sure you're used to it."

"Yeah, I guess you can say we're made of heartier stock, able to ingest all of the grease and spice."

Abbie cleared her throat.

"Indeed," Minerva continued. "Not really a beans-and-cheese kind of gal myself, but to each their own! Well, I'm sure this place pales next to the glitz and glamour you folks are used to down in L.A. Tell me, what do you miss most now that you're stuck in Hadley?"

"Mexican Coke."

"What's that?" Minerva said, holding on to the kitchen counter, certain she'd heard incorrectly.

"Mexican Coke. It's hard to find, but it's the best. You should try it sometime. Or at least have it on offer for your guests. It's way better than regular Coke."

Minerva stared, dumbfounded, at the young woman in front of her. Abbie looked from one of them to the other.

"Regular Coke just doesn't compare, taste wise," Ana continued. "I think they use different ingredients—"

"Just what is this, Abigail?" Minerva said, crossing her arms. "Do you condone this type of behavior in your house?"

"I'm not sure I know what you mean—" Abbie said.

"Oh, you're a clever thing, aren't you?" Minerva continued. "Well, I don't want any gangbanger business around here. You may be more progressive over there at Garber Farm, you and Alder Kinman and the rest of the landowning hippies, lippies as I like to call them, but not under this roof. Monarch Mansion is a respectable place. It's an institution!"

"Listen, Minerva, I'm sure—"

"What do you mean by 'gangbanger'?" Ana asked.

"I do *not* want a scene in this house," Minerva said, walking past them, making a wide berth around Ana, and continuing through the dining room and toward the front door. "This Mexican business is not something I even want discussed! I'll see you both on your way."

"Mexican business? What *Mexican* business?" Ana asked as she followed Minerva to the door.

"I think there's been a misunderstanding," Abbie said, following close behind. "I think what Ana means is Coca—"

"'*Misunderstanding*'?" Ana began to raise her voice not bothering to control it. "The only misunderstanding is when she said '*that*' food and '*dirty*' water and was actually being horrifically racist, never mind that she went on to reduce my heritage to 'beans and cheese' in such a way that I have to defend a misguided, ignorant, fast-food assessment of it— well, it's not something I'm just going to stand here and be silent about. I don't know what your problem with me is, lady, but if you're worried about 'gangbangers' all up in your fancy inn, then you might want to take a step back. It's in my blood . . . so to speak."

Silence descended on the foyer.

"Ana's been up since four thirty," Abbie said, stepping in between them, touching Ana's arm, causing her to pull away.

"Does that excuse her defiant tone?" Minerva said. "It's as if she's primed for violence; just look at the way she's standing there glaring at me—those eyebrows say every-thing. I am not at *all* comfortable with this!"

"Are you serious?" Ana asked, still not looking at Abbie. "Do you have any idea what you're even saying? Since I'm probably going to be sent back to L.A. anyway, I should tell you that going to Acapulco *once* is hardly enough time to judge an entire country, not that I've been there myself. But not all Mexican food is spicy nor is the water always the culprit. Not all of us are gangbangers or the product of Taco Bell."

"You've never even been to Mexico?" Minerva asked.

"No, I was born in L.A. But that doesn't mean—"

"But you *do* have family living down there . . ."

"I don't have any family."

"None at all?"

"Correct."

"I see," Minerva said, running her fingernail along her forehead and checking to make sure her hair was still in place. "So, you're an orphan?"

"I prefer 'parentless,' but yes."

"Well, that explains everything."

"It's not exactly like that," Abbie said as she watched Ana's hands ball into fists.

"Is there something wrong with the fact that my parents are dead?" Ana asked defiantly. "It's not like I have any control over that. I know what I am, and I can tell you that it's not something most people want to be."

"Of course there's nothing wrong with it, dear, quite the contrary. I now have a better understanding of your predicament and that helps forgive your little outburst—"

"My '*predicament*'? The only predicament I have is explaining to people what that even means when they have no clue about life outside their own perimeters. You couldn't possibly imagine it or understand."

"I think we adults can imagine that it's not been easy—"

"Do you know what it's like to be locked alone in a dark room for hours, not knowing if anyone's coming back?"

"Well, we've all had certain—"

"Have you ever hidden under your bed because you know the popping sounds down the street are bullets and not fireworks? Do you stay awake at night guarding yourself from real monsters and not the imaginary kind? I doubt you have any idea what kind of *predicament* I live with."

"Well, I'm sure I don't, but knowing what I know of Abigail Garber, the fact that you've been allowed to come out to her farm with all that you have going on is an act of utmost charity, in my opinion, and something you might do well to be thankful for, my dear."

"Minerva," Abbie said. "Ana's fifteen and she's working very hard to take care of herself. Emmett and I are happy to assist her in that journey . . ."

"I'm sixteen, not fifteen."

"Oh," Abbie said with surprise.

"Today's my birthday. Not that it matters to anyone, not that this isn't the way it normally goes every year."

Ana shifted her weight and lunged for the door, causing Minerva to jump out of the way, thinking she was on the verge of an oncoming attack. Ana walked outside pretending she didn't hear the voices trailing behind her on the way down the stairs.

"She'll cool off," Minerva said. "It's perfectly natural for someone like her to get fiery from time to time, especially with all that Mexican Coke . . ."

Ana sat in the front seat of the van taking deep breaths. "That's it," she told herself. "If they don't send you back, today's the day you can actually leave if you want to." She watched as a lone bumblebee buzzed around the shrubs lining the front of Monarch Mansion, wondering what was taking Abbie so long, hoping there was a bus station nearby. She glanced at the neighborhood reflected in the side mirror, all of the houses lined up in white picket fences down the street. "It's not like I belong here anyway."

The door to the mansion opened and closed. Ana stared straight ahead as Abbie made her way to the van, jumped inside, and pulled away without saying anything. They both remained silent on the short ride to Main Street. Abbie parked across the street from the corner restaurant, her last delivery of the day. The restaurant looked empty, most of its windows covered in paper. She turned off the ignition and faced Ana.

"I want to talk about what just happened," she said.

"I don't know what got into me, but I'm fully prepared for the consequences."

"You were provoked, for one," Abbie said with a sigh. "But not in the way you took it." They both watched a young mother push a stroller across the street, tugging a little girl behind her. Abbie took a moment to gather her thoughts before delivering them, doing what she wished her mother had done with her. "I had no idea it was your birthday. If I'd known, I would have planned something to celebrate."

"It's okay. I never told anyone when it was."

"Let me finish, please. Minerva Shaw is a single-minded woman, yes, but she isn't cruel, or intentionally inhospitable. While I completely agree with you that her comments were way *way* off, I know she didn't mean to hurt your feelings. But she deserves an apology for the way you acted in there. Beyond that, she deserves the chance for you to perhaps educate her on your differences. She's spent her whole life in Hadley. Not a lot changes around here."

Ana wanted to tell Abbie that she'd encountered dozens of Minerva Shaws in her lifetime, and that the only way to deal with them was to fight back. She had no intention of apologizing for defending her past, or her heritage—even if she was afraid to admit she rarely gave much thought to it.

"The same trouble follows me wherever I go," Ana said, "especially today. My birthday is cursed with bad luck." She knew if she told Abbie the whole story it would sound like an excuse for her behavior. Besides, Ana didn't want to go into the details of the day her abuela died.

"Do you think this trouble seeks you out or do you court it?" Abbie asked with a sincerity Ana found touching.

"Both probably. I don't know."

"I think it takes a strong person to realize that when

there's a plague of difficulty, it doesn't define them. That's something I learned the hard way. You're lucky to have such a strong connection to your past, Ana, and whether or not you see that as strength is up to you. But I saw it back there. And I can assure you that Minerva feels terrible and never meant to kick up a fuss. She would like to apologize, and I think it would be polite for you to do the same."

"Are you sending me back?"

"Of course not. Do you want to go back?"

There was a knock on the window. They both jumped.

"Sorry to startle you." It was the same man Ana had seen as she and Emmett drove through town on her first day. He scratched his head waiting for a response, both of them taking in the tattoo of a butcher knife carved on his forearm. "Abigail Garber?" he said.

Abbie rolled down the window.

"Yes? Are you Will Carson?"

"I am indeed. Pleasure to meet you," the man said, thrusting a giant hand through the open window. "We're doing some painting today, so whenever you're ready, come on in. I saw you idling out here and wondered if you thought we were closed. Front door's open."

"This is Ana," Abbie said, flustered. "We'll be right there."

"Right. Apologies for interrupting."

Abbie rolled up the window. They watched Will walk back to the entrance of the restaurant.

"I thought he was going to tear our heads off," Ana said.

"Not in that cologne," Abbie replied.

They sat for what seemed like several minutes in silence.

"If you need to send me back, I'll understand."

"Is this normally how it goes?" Abbie asked, turning

back toward her. "Something uncomfortable happens and you get sent somewhere?"

"Pretty much."

"That's not happening here. But I think you should hear Minerva out. I leave that up to you."

Abbie opened the door and headed to the back of the van, so Ana followed. She handed Ana a crate of produce and they made their way to the entrance of the former Main Street Corner Café, its hand-painted sign fading along the side of the brick building. Ana quickly looked up and down the street, hoping to find a bus sign posted somewhere, just in case, but didn't see anything. She could always walk to the highway and hitch from there, she thought.

They made their way inside the restaurant. It looked like a diner, a dark wooden counter lining the back wall, the front area empty, its black-and-white tiled floor in need of tables. Watching over the place, just above the open window to the kitchen, was a stuffed deer wearing a dried Christmas wreath around its neck. There were a few booths lining the wall of windows opposite, most of which were covered in paper, and the back wall was painted in rectangles of varying shades of navy and gray.

"Come on in," Will bellowed from behind the counter, paintbrush in hand. "Make yourselves comfortable—that's a joke—it's a mess in here."

"Where do you want the produce?" Abbie asked.

"On the counter's great."

There was a tailored sensibility to the man, Ana noticed. Everything he wore seemed made to fit, as if he'd paid careful attention to the right combination of colors and textures, even if they were his grungiest clothes. Up close, she noticed his hair was graying in places, but he possessed a youthful, easygoing confidence that made it difficult to calculate his age. Behind the counter, he didn't appear as menacing, though the stereo, resting on the back bar, was playing some sort of heavy metal guitar Ana couldn't make out. Will turned it down.

"I've brought a selection of what's currently in season at the farm," Abbie said, in a way Ana thought more stilted than usual. "It's a sampling of every fruit and vegetable we have right now, plus herbs, preserves, lavender, and some dahlias, which are a sampling from our garden. I can do simple flower arrangements if needed, and we'll have more peaches, cucumbers, brassica, and various peppers in the coming weeks."

"You have any roots?" he asked. "Legumes, tubers, foraged fungi?"

Abbie hesitated. "We have potatoes, sweet potatoes, and will have parsnips this year. I included some heirloom carrots which we sell at the farmers' market, along with sugar snap peas. And celeriac and burdock root are out next month. We don't currently offer anything foraged."

"Interesting," Will said, inspecting the crate of produce. "Honestly, this is better than I'd hoped—not that I didn't have high expectations—it's just that I had no idea what kind of farms I'd be dealing with around here. But I've heard great things about Garber Farm."

"Where did you hear about us?" Abbie asked.

His eyes lingered on Abbie for longer than Abbie found comfortable.

"From a few customers up and down the coast," Will said. "Even some in Berkeley, where I moved here from. Seems you have fans. If it's not too much to ask, would you mind walking me through each piece, please?"

"Um, sure," Abbie said, gesturing to Ana to start unloading the produce. She turned back to Will, careful to keep her voice light and breezy. "So, did you work in restaurants down there?"

"I did. A few in L.A., San Fran—put in some much-needed time with Alice and the gang over in Berkeley—and now I'm here."

"Why here?" Abbie asked, curious.

Will smiled. "I'm attempting to get something of my own going. Didn't want to do the whole big-city thing, you know? It's been done, and everyone's always getting poached or moving around from restaurant to restaurant anyway. Wanted to try something new. I grew up about an hour up north from here—used to come down to the beach as a child. Hadley's always had a kind of renegade magic, I guess."

"Huh," said Abbie, busying herself with the vegetables.

"Ana, is it?" he asked.

"It is. Wait . . . you lived in L.A.?"

"I did. Worked for a French chef down there, crazy guy. Set up a Michelin-starred restaurant in an abandoned pizza parlor. Freaking genius if you ask me."

"I'm from L.A.," Ana said.

"Yeah? Whereabouts?"

"Boyle Heights originally."

"Guisados, yo! The best! Their *bistec* taco with the *salsa roja*? Doesn't get better than that."

"Right? But it's all about the *mole poblano*. Don't even get me started on the *horchata*. King Taco's where it's at for *al pastor*, though. My abuela used to take me there all the time when I was a kid. That's original Boyle Heights, *esé*."

Abbie continued to look from Ana to Will as she held a peach in one hand, zucchini in the other.

"So, you both lived down in L.A.?" Will asked, hesitating and not wanting to seem too obviously curious.

"Yes," Abbie blurted, surprising Ana. Why hadn't Abbie ever mentioned that before? "I did a brief stint."

"I wondered. I'm sorry for staring, but you seem *really* familiar," Will said, leaning across the counter. Abbie kept her distance behind the produce box. "When did you live down there?"

"It was a long time ago, way before your time. So, here's what we have at the moment," Abbie said, gesturing to the counter. "I threw in a few of my preserves, including the ginger, which works with sweet or savory dishes, and some pickled beets and carrots, which are popular around town— served over at Monarch Mansion during their wine and cheese hours. I'm sure you'll be doing in-house baking—are you doing in-house baking? If not, I bake breads every week and included some zuke—I mean zucchini bread—which came out of the oven this morning. We participate in Community Supported Agriculture every Wednesday, and I can easily set up a business account as we do with another restaurant up north . . ." Abbie had gone pink and breathless. "Ana, the bok choy, please," she continued.

"The what?" Ana said, looking over the piles, not knowing which one to pick.

"The bok choy."

Will leaned over and picked it up. "Looks fantastic to me," he said, smiling at Ana, holding it out for her to inspect.

"That's new this season. We also have Japanese eggplants," Abbie said, looking at Ana again, who scanned the piles before picking up a turnip.

"You weren't kidding about your brassica. These are gorgeous turnips," Will said, taking it out of Ana's hand before picking up the eggplant and wiggling it. "Eggplant is equally as exquisite."

Ana stuffed her hands in her back pockets, hoping Abbie hadn't noticed her mistake.

"I'll take whatever's in your box next week as well as anything and everything else you have on hand," Will said. "I'd love to try it all."

"All of it?" Abbie asked. "Like, *all* all?"

"Yep. I like everything I see."

"Great! Let me just run out to the van for the paper-work." She hurried to the door, before turning back around. "Ana?"

"Oh, yeah! Sorry. I'm still trying to wrap my head around the bok soy."

"Choy," Will said. "Though it's delicious grilled in a little miso butter with a drizzle of fermented soy."

Ana followed Abbie outside, trying to keep up as they crossed the street. Abbie threw open the back doors of the van, jumped inside, unscrewed a bottle of water, and drank half of it as she sat down on an empty crate.

"Whoa, dude," Ana said.

"What was that?"

"I think Mr. Carson likes *everything* he sees, if you know what I mean."

"Excuse me?"

"Dude's into you. It's totally obvious."

"What are you talking about?"

"Mr. Carson? Will? He couldn't stop staring at you. 'Gorgeous turnips'? Please." Ana laughed but then stifled it because Abbie had gone completely white, downing the rest of the water bottle and pushing sticky strands of hair from her forehead.

"Sorry, what did you say?"

"Mr. Carson seems super rad. How old do you think he is?"

"Not old enough."

"Huh?"

"Too old for you."

"He's definitely good-looking in a kind of superhero vampire kind of way, but he's not my type and, yes, way too old for me. *You*, on the other hand . . ."

"What time is it?" Abbie asked, looking for the watch she never wore. "We've got to get going. I still need to make one more stop, and I wanted to take you to the bookstore, have you pick something out for your birthday."

Ana had forgotten that part of the day again.

"Listen, I've still got to go over the produce list with Will, I mean Mr. Carson," Abbie continued. "The bookstore is right across the street; you can see it through the windows on the other side of the café. Why don't you head over there, and I'll meet you in a minute. I trust you, but I'll be watching from the window. Is it just me or is it a hundred degrees outside?"

Ana tossed her hat into the van and headed across the street in the mid-August heat. Summer up here was nothing like the summer in L.A. Despite Abbie's protestations, it was a perfect day with a cool breeze and periodic clouds breaking over the town. She took a moment to let the sun warm her face before looking up and down the street, mapping it to memory. There was a lone man smoking a cigarette along the curb and two women in vintage-looking dresses chatting in front of Moon Pharm General Store just a few doors away. Even though she'd rather pop in and see Rye, she did as Abbie said and headed for the bookstore. Though she hadn't noticed it since the day she arrived, there was a sliver of a store next door to the Moons' with a handwritten sign in the window that read BUNGLE RECORDS, USED AND NEW VINYL. She made a mental note to check it out, that is, if she was staying. Ana stood there for a moment trying to decipher the band stickers in the window from across the street when the door swung open. Out walked someone dressed from head to toe in dirty motorcycle gear complete with helmet, a record tucked under his arm. She could only see the rider's eyes, which met hers briefly. She took that as her cue to duck into the bookstore.

A bell above the door rang as she entered. Though the space wasn't intimate, it felt inviting with its creaky floorboards and shelves stuffed with books. The whole place was lit by lamps that cast a golden glow—the kind of place you'd want to linger inside of on a gray day, she imagined. Behind the counter a scrawny young man Ana assumed must be in college, judging by his university T-shirt and cardigan, sat up. He appeared startled to see a customer walking toward him.

"Good afternoon," he said, adjusting his glasses.

"Hello," Ana said.

"May I help you?"

"Just browsing."

"Any particular genre?"

"Art books, I guess, and poetry, please."

He pointed to the shelves nearest to the door. "Poetry is next to fiction over there and art," he said, gesturing to the rear of the store, "is just past psychology in the back, though our selection is limited."

"Thanks," Ana said. "Is this your shop?"

"Kind of. Not really. It's my grandfather's. He's not feeling well today. Who is?"

"I feel you," she said.

"If you're looking for hiking maps, guidebooks, or more information about the area, that kind of thing, I've got it all here at the counter. Might be helpful if you're new to town."

"Actually, I'll take a look at a guidebook with a map, if you have one."

He handed her a travel guide, more like a brochure. She carried it with her to the back of the store, passing a table full of books with handwritten signs advertising recent employee picks. From what Ana could tell, there was only one employee doing all the picking, and that employee enjoyed graphic novels and noir. The art section took up half a bookshelf in the back corner. She scanned it for her favorite, Frida Kahlo, finding a large picture book to flip through. She opened it to an image of the artist lying in a desert, leaves springing from her open chest, and placed the guidebook with the map of the coast inside to study it. Though she wasn't ready to bolt just yet, it was important to figure out exactly where she was in relation to where she could go if need be.

The bell above the door rang. She shut the Kahlo book, hiding the travel guide inside, and turned around expecting to see Abbie. Instead, there was a flash of helmet. She returned to the map until someone began loudly opening and shutting books at the table behind her. She turned around and faced the same biker from across the street. He was still wearing his helmet, and his half-unzipped uniform was streaked with dried mud. She glanced at him as his hand floated up in a slow-motion wave.

He removed the helmet and smiled. His eyes—panther eyes, she decided—were tired and murky green. He looked a little older and taller than she, with a bad case of helmet head. He was slender, so if anything went down, she thought, even right there in the store, she was confident she could semi-take him even without a weapon.

"The Hex. Great band," he said, pointing to her T-shirt. "For a girl band, that is."

"You're kidding, right?"

"I'm not being sexist, I just prefer my punk with a male bravado."

He had one of those smiles that curled up at one side, purposefully sly, she thought to herself, dangerously confident.

"Let me guess," she said. "Henry Rollins?"

"Ha. Typical. Ian MacKaye."

"Not ruling out a Black Flag T-shirt hidden somewhere in your gym locker, but Fugazi's an obvious second if we're talking old-school American punk."

"Minor Threat, actually," he said. "Fugazi's post-hardcore."

"Unlike you, right?" she said.

"Wow. Burn. Let me guess," he continued, moving a little closer. "Frida Kahlo."

"You saw me reading it."

"I didn't. Like you said, it's the obvious choice. Also, I know that shelf doesn't have much beyond Monet and Norman Rockwell. Which Frida are you looking at?"

She shut the book.

"Why are you so curious?" she asked.

"You don't remember me?"

"No. Should I?"

He repeated a slow-motion wave.

"I don't understand what—"

The bell clanged and Abbie walked through the door, stopping for a moment at the counter.

"We had a moment a couple weeks ago," he said.

"Look, dude, I don't know if this is your go-to pickup maneuver or whatever, but I'm not from here, so there's no possible way we've ever met."

"C'mon, Curls," he said. *"Think."* He smiled and did the slow-motion wave again.

"What did you just call me?"

"Ana!" Abbie said, making her way to the back of the store. "What did you find? Oh, Frida! Love her. Hand it over."

Ana remained silent, still eye to eye with the stranger.

"Hello, Ms. Garber," he said, turning toward Abbie.

"Oh. Hello, Cole," she responded, looking from one to the other.

"How's everything over at the farm?"

"Fine," Abbie said, her shoulders suddenly stiff with tension.

"And how's Mr. Garber these days?"

"He's fine," said Abbie, in a tone that did not invite further discussion. "Please give my best to your mother. Shall we, Ana?"

Abbie headed to the front counter, so Ana followed, glancing once over her shoulder.

"Seriously, you don't have to do this," Ana whispered.

"I want to. It's your birthday, hon."

Between this and the stranger—Cole—still somewhere in the back of the shop, Ana was at a loss for words. The way he'd said "Curls" echoed in her head.

"Happy Birthday," the bookstore clerk said. "How old are you?"

"Sixteen."

"Sweet. All I got on my sixteenth birthday was a cow

and a black eye. I'll go ahead and throw in a bookmark for free. It's not like anyone ever buys one."

"How kind of you," Abbie said. "Tell Grandpa Henry I hope he feels better soon."

"He has a headache every Friday, you know. He's probably over at Sal's downing a pint. . . . You ready?"

"Just this," Cole said, suddenly standing behind them, placing a book on the counter.

"*The Beats: A Graphic History*!" The bookstore clerk beamed. "I've been waiting for someone to buy this! You won't be disappointed, I promise."

There wasn't much room to move between the counter and the front door, but Abbie turned and made her way toward the exit. Ana stood wedged in between the counter and Cole.

"Hey, man," the store clerk continued. "I'll call you when *The Subterraneans* comes in. Still don't know why you don't just order it yourself, but thanks for actually giving me work to do."

"I like to support local business," Cole said, turning to look directly at Ana. Did girls really fall for that sort of thing?

"Kerouac," she said, looking right back. "As obvious as it gets."

She squeezed past him to the door, willing herself not to turn around at either his "Hey" or "Wait."

Abbie held the door open and glanced inside the bookstore before shutting the door with purpose and giving Ana a look.

"How did the meeting go?" Ana asked, not making eye contact.

"Great. We're in business. How was your conversation with Cole Brannan?"

"Who?"

"Cole. The boy in the motocross getup."

"Oh. We didn't converse. At all."

"Seems like I interrupted something."

"He was asking about the book."

"Was he," Abbie said, peering through the window. "Well, he's not someone you should be interested in conversing with."

"I have like no interest."

"Good. Let's head home."

"Home," Ana thought. She liked the sound of it. Though most of her guardians had used the word from time to time, none of them knew what it meant for a foster kid to hear it. Ana had learned not to get her hopes up long ago, as "home" was always a temporary state or place, and usually not particularly appealing. She forced herself to dismiss the comment as they crossed Main Street and, instead, she wondered what it was about Cole Brannan that Abbie didn't like. His lopsided smile was fixed in her mind's eye. Not that she hadn't been infuriated by boys her age before—or teased, for that matter—but—

"Curls," she thought to herself again . . . at least that word wasn't as revolting as "gangbanger."

"What is *wrong* with people?" Ana said.

"Where do you want me to start?" Abbie answered.

When they got back to the farm, Abbie suggested Ana head up to her room to freshen up for dinner, which was never something she'd suggested before.

"Your room," Ana repeated to herself, hearing Abbie's voice, trying not to let it mean anything as she ascended the stairs and tossed the paper bag on the bed. She pulled out the Frida book as well as a blank sketchbook and a box of colored pencils. Had Abbie meant those for her? She slipped on Abbie's work shirt and pulled her hair back, braiding the curls away for dinner. "Just one look," she said to herself as she flipped through the Frida book, taking in the images, pausing at the one with the flowers in her hair and thorns around her neck, until the book fell open to the middle where the guidebook sat unfurled to the map of Hadley.

"Oh no," she whispered as her stomach sank and chills crawled up the back of her neck. She threw open the armoire and stuffed the book behind her backpack. "Adding thief to my list of wrongs," she said to herself.

"Ana!" Abbie called.

She grabbed the notebook and pencils and made her way downstairs, creeping into the kitchen, her mind tumbling over itself trying to come up with what she should say.

"I did something—" Ana blurted as she entered the kitchen.

"Ah, you found your gifts!" Abbie said. "I always see you doodling around the house and thought you might want some fresh paper and pencils."

"I can't accept this."

"Nonsense. Set it there and come outside."

Ana followed, trying to speak, but Abbie shushed her as they walked outside to the picnic table in the garden. There were sunflowers in a watering can in the center of the table next to a pie with the number 16 written in haphazard yellow icing. The fairy lights in the trees were on, throwing a halo of light over the table. Emmett and Manny stood by the table, holding their hats in their hands.

"What's all this?" Ana said.

Emmett cleared his throat. "Happy birthday."

"We didn't have a ton of time," Abbie said, "but I called Emmett and ran into the pie shop while you were in the bookstore. I hope you like chocolate cream."

Ana didn't know what to say. There was a part of her that wanted to hug Abbie—something she told herself she should *never* do—and another part that wanted to run through the fields, back into town to the exact location of the bus station, wherever it might be—suddenly thinking that maybe the stolen map was good for something—even though she'd be going back to nothing.

"I don't deserve—"

"I got the last one," Abbie said, shushing her again. "Lemon is the best, but it was sold out. Come and sit and have a slice. I don't want to embarrass you with a big deal or anything, but we must celebrate your sweet sixteen."

"I love chocolate," Ana said, taking a breath.

They all sat down, Emmett and Manny next to each other, and Ana opposite them. Abbie handed out plates. Manny winked as Emmett reached into his vest pocket and pulled out an envelope.

"Your pay from the last couple of weeks," Emmett said, sliding the envelope across the wooden table. "I suggest you put it away and use it wisely."

"Good work," Manny said, nodding at her. "You earned it."

She put the envelope in her back jeans pocket and went quiet again, not knowing how to relay her gratitude for the only birthday party she'd had since she celebrated her sixth with her abuela. She could hardly believe that ten years had passed since everything changed. It had been sunny that day, and they'd had *pan dulce* for breakfast, she remembered, along with a mug of hot chocolate with cinnamon and vanilla. "Too sweet for every day," her abuela had said, "but just right on your special day." Ana was promised a piñata, so they'd headed out to pick one up a few streets away. She yammered on about which one she was going to get—"The rainbow donkey or the white kitten with the pink bow?" she'd asked. But they never made it past the shots at the end of the block.

"*Feliz cumpleaños, mija,*" Manny said, forcing her to look up. There was a single lit candle in the middle of the pie.

"Make a wish," Abbie said.

"Wow. This is . . . too much," Ana said, biting her lower lip, not looking at anyone. "But thanks. It means more than you could ever possibly know." She blew out the candle, and they all clapped.

"Dessert for dinner!" Abbie sang as she handed out slices.

Manny took a bite and chewed, oblivious to the meringue mustache on his upper lip. "What's the matter?" he said, looking around the table.

Ana couldn't help but laugh; Abbie did too, though Emmett did the usual and shook his head. Ana wondered if he ever laughed, or even smiled enough to show his teeth, if he had any, the very thought of which made Ana laugh again. Conversation floated around the table, mostly about the day's work, to which Ana listened. She felt strangely comforted by the easygoing timbre of the voices around her. The sounds were soothing enough to keep the waking visions away, at least for the rest of the evening and all the way to bed that night, where her lingering smile, like a gentle bell, lulled her to sleep in placid waves.

CHAPTER SEVEN

She'd been dreaming about worms, small white ones burrowing into the space behind her earlobe, whispering messages into her ear. It wasn't the kind of nightmare she wanted to wake up from, more mysterious in the way that she wanted to hear what the worms had to say. There was a flash of light, and then a loud bang, so she pulled the covers over her head.

"Are you awake?"

It took a moment for Ana to realize her room was flooded with sunlight and someone was at the door.

"What day is it?" she said, speaking to the voice she thought she'd heard in her sleep.

"It's Saturday morning, almost six fifteen," Abbie said through the door. "Why aren't you in the fields?"

Ana sprang out of bed, pulled on jeans and a work shirt, and grabbed her sneakers before throwing the door open.

"Is everything okay?" Abbie asked, standing in the doorway, eyes wide.

"I don't know what happened," Ana answered, deflecting Abbie's concern and heading straight for the stairs. "I didn't set the alarm because I never need it."

She ran down the stairs. Abbie followed close behind.

"Slow down . . . are you sure you're feeling well this morning?"

"I'm fine, I just overslept. Emmett's going to kill me."

"I've been out in the shed since early morning," Abbie said. "But I thought you beat me out there, otherwise I would have checked on you. I'm worried. This isn't like you."

"I had a nightmare," Ana said, not wanting to tell Abbie the real reason was that she'd been up most of the night sketching.

"Emmett will be furious." Abbie sighed. "It's entirely your responsibility to follow the farm rules, and that begins with being on time. He was very strict about my not intervening in that regard."

"He's going to kill me."

"Probably. But if it makes you feel better, I had trouble sleeping last night too. Must be something in the air . . . but that won't be a good-enough excuse. You need to run out there and apologize, then offer to work late. Say you'll do whatever it takes. He'll be angry, but if you keep quiet and do as he says, it'll be fine."

Ana ran out the back door and sprinted toward the fields. Dolly shot out from behind the barn, barking and loping alongside her as if they were in a race. Ana passed Vic and Rolo, already busy with work. They both bowed their heads in unison, signaling the extent of her transgression. René and Joey were at the truck, but there weren't any other workers in the fields, which had been more typical lately. She couldn't see Emmett or Manny anywhere, so they had to be in the hoop houses—exactly where she was supposed to be. She'd only very recently earned the opportunity to be working in there with them. She continued running toward the white-tunneled houses, stopping in front of the one with the shadows of two figures inside.

"Grovel," she told herself, hoping her heart wouldn't leap out of her mouth. "And then shut it."

She peeled back the plastic flap. Manny glanced up, then back down again, disappointment mixed with something she couldn't quite detect. She walked toward Emmett, whose back was turned, his hands buried in the wire tomato cages.

"I'm late and I'm sorry," she said, out of breath, making a point to be direct yet remorseful. Emmett continued working as if she weren't there. "I don't have an excuse because I know you won't accept one. I usually set the alarm, even though I don't need it, but I forgot to last night for some reason. I slept deeply, unusually deep, and thus I overslept. I'm willing to work late every day this week—the rest of the summer— weeds and compost duty too. I've already spoken to Abbie, who was not happy about my tardiness, either. It's entirely my fault, and I'm willing to do whatever it takes to fix it because I know it's wrong. Did I say I'm sorry? I'm truly sorry."

"Is that all?" Emmett said, the small hole in the back of his blue work vest ripping farther apart as he made a point of continuing to do Ana's work for her.

"I can work every Sunday too. No more afternoons off."

"You're an hour and a half late, and I don't condone tardiness. The one rule you had to follow, without exception, was arriving to the morning meeting five minutes early every day. That rule is for everyone."

"You have to believe that I had trouble sleeping last night and—"

"I have trouble sleeping, but I'm never late; neither is Manny or any of the workers out there, a few of whom don't have a comfortable bed like you do to sleep in every night."

"But what does this mean?"

"It means compost and weeds, no arguments," Emmett said, pulling his hands away from the tomato cages and wiping his brow. The month was almost over, he reminded himself. If anything solidified his decision to let Ana go, it was this.

Emmett stood up and brushed off his jeans. He looked at her and then looked away. Ana knew there was no changing his mind. Manny gave her the look that meant she should say nothing more. He had an uncanny way of shifting his eyes ever so slightly, enough that the reprimand fell harder on her than words.

Ana nodded, turned around, and pushed the flap of the house open to walk back out into the fields. She scarcely felt her feet moving forward, but let them carry her back to the composting station. She kept her eyes focused ahead, ignoring the looks from her fellow workers in the periphery, ignoring the barks of an enthusiastic Dolly, who darted to and fro behind her knees and paid no mind to the odd chicken wandering by itself through the cauliflower. "This is it," she told herself. "You're done."

Ana thought about the evening before. She'd been hanging out with Rye Moon on the front porch of the farmhouse drinking lemonade and talking about their favorite band for an hour. It was what Rye called a proper hang session. Della Moon dropped by ostensibly to bring Abbie some new tea she made, but Rye divulged to Ana that she'd been begging her mom to bring her over ever since the day they'd met on Main Street, not that Ana had had much time off since then.

"You're the only person I've met who cares about this stuff," Ana said, hoping she hadn't said too much. Any time she'd opened up to someone before, they eventually fled in the other direction. "The Hex is something I've always kept to myself. That and pretty much every other band I like or book I've read."

"Ditto, woman," Rye said, twirling a strand of purple between her fingers. "No one in my stupid school gets the impact of a monochromatic ensemble onstage, or the power of the goddess who is Rosa Hex. We were meant to find each other."

"Fated."

"Belated."

"And maybe possibly related."

They both laughed and pushed on the rocking chairs, rocking in opposite tandem as they watched the golden moon peek over the treetops. "Seriously, you're the most interesting person in this town by far," Rye said, pushing the chair back with the heels of her oxford shoes. "You've seen more than most people in this pinprick of a place."

"I've only ever lived on the east side of Los Angeles. It's not like I've traveled the world or anything."

"That's more than anyone else I know, except for Abbie, of course." Rye went quiet and stopped rocking. "So, now's probably the best time to tell you that I'm the big L."

"Huh?"

"Lez. Lesbiana or whatever your people call it."

"Okay."

Rye waited for another response, but Ana continued rocking. "That doesn't bother you or anything?" Rye asked.

"No, why would it?"

"Because it's something everyone in this town seems to not understand. Not that anyone would in Hadley, population Homo sapiens zero. My parents are fine with it thus far, but they don't ever ask me any questions. And it's not like I've had a girlfriend before, not that I'd ever be able to have one around here. I'm not professing anything major to you FYI—"

"I didn't think you were."

"Good. It's just . . . I don't need to explain myself to people, you know? Still, I'm not exactly popular in the amigo department since word was blasted all over school last year."

"Well, you're popular with me," Ana said. "But you and I should never go anywhere near Monarch Mansion. Deal?" Ana put her hand over her left breast.

"Deal," Rye said, doing the same. "So, tell me about the Lolita girls hanging out in Little Tokyo again. I need details on their ruffled dresses, if any of them carried parasols, and if you were ever compelled to squeeze one of them like an overstuffed human doll baby."

Though they'd spoken for only about an hour, Ana knew she'd quite possibly found a friend. It was the first time she'd ever had a visitor at the house she was living in, someone who came over to see her for good reasons rather than bad. She couldn't help it if she'd been amped up enough not to be able to sleep the night before. But Emmett would never understand. The very thought made her churn the compost harder.

Abbie tried to pay attention to the road, but she was distracted by her own noisy thoughts replaying her latest meeting with Will Carson. She had walked into the café that morning to drop off a selection of fruit he'd requested, along with a new batch of smoked tomato jam. The back wall had been painted charcoal gray since the first visit, and there were new black leather booths installed along one of the walls with windows. Though Will was nowhere in sight, his music of choice, late eighties heavy metal, blared from an unseen stereo. Abbie knew the song all too well. She'd sworn off ever listening to it following her lost decade. But hearing it had so surprised her, so uprooted the suppressed memories, that she had left the box of produce on the counter without a word. She sat in the van for a moment cursing herself, seconds away from going back in, when Will appeared in the window across the street with a furrowed look of confusion on his face. He held his hands up as if to say, "What gives?" and then waved at her to come back in. And with that, Abbie sped away, the image of his dark features, perplexed and shaded in morning stubble, playing on a constant loop ever since.

Forcing herself back into the present, she focused on the road. Ana sat beside her staring out the window. Ana's tardiness that morning was ammunition for Emmett. Abbie knew she'd eventually have to fight him on whether Ana should stay. She drove up over the forested hills behind Garber Farm, nearly forgetting where to turn. Abbie jerked the van onto an unmarked road, slowing the vehicle as it bounced up and down erratically along the slippery rock path.

"Where are we going?" Ana asked.

"The Honey Pot," Abbie said. "We're dropping off and picking up."

Not many people knew the whereabouts of Alder Kinman's honey farm, and those who did kept it secret. Alder was a man dusted in mystery—by his own choosing, of course—and his business, though modest, resulted in the kind of profits that garnered many a head scratch. He never explained beyond "My bees are hearty." His family owned a portion of the land adjacent to Garber Farm, and the two families had been neighbors for generations. Abbie and Emmett grew up running to and fro in the shared woods, and Alder was often a willing playmate. Children loved him, however odd the adults in Hadley found him to be. Both families had suffered misfortunes over the years, so they'd agreed together to sell a portion of their adjoining land. It had pained Abbie's father, she remembered, and quite possibly catalyzed his death. Alder, a faithful friend to the Garbers, was the only real family Abbie and Emmett had left.

The road twisted and turned as they drove farther down into the trees, which were covered in dust and were an eerie shade of grayish green. They finally made it to a wide clearing. At the bottom, surrounded by the tallest of redwoods, an ominous cabin sat lopsided in the middle.

"Don't let the creep factor scare you," Abbie said. "He built this place for that very purpose."

They got out of the van, and Abbie watched as Ana took in the wall of antlers lining the front porch. Abbie waved to Alder, who rocked back and forth in an imposing high-back chair as he puffed on a pipe.

"What's doin'?" he called to them as they approached.

"We have your pickles and veggies, came for some honey," Abbie said. Ana trailed behind her. "Thought you might give us a peek at the hives before we're on our way."

"Who's that?" he said, scrutinizing Ana, who was hiding behind Abbie.

"Ana, this is Alder Kinman," Abbie said.

"We've met," Ana said. "I mean, I saw him on Main Street on my first day."

Alder rose from the chair. His whole body rattled from the various necklaces, dangling arrowheads, and beaded chains hanging off his overalls.

"Where ya from, Squirrely?"

"Los Angeles," Ana said, assuming he was speaking to her.

"Thought so," he said with a huff. "Why don't you leave the box on the side steps, and I'll meet ya 'round back."

He opened and shut a noisy screen door and headed inside.

"What's it like inside that place?" Ana asked.

"More antlers, heavy wood, books, tobacco, and some unusual paintings, if I can remember correctly. He hasn't let me inside in about thirty years."

They walked around the side of the dark house with a box of produce and pickles and set it on the steps leading up to a chipped door with a hand-painted sign that said KEEP OUT. Ana thought it strange that the sounds of birds were much louder than what she heard regularly at the farm, even though the atmosphere was much gloomier. It was like the place existed on its own, separate from the world, a planet in and of itself tucked back into the forest. There were more than a few signs marking the area as private property. Abbie and Ana came to a tall wooden gate and pushed it open, walking out into a much larger field, which was clear and open to the sky, covered in multicolored flowers and several towers of white boxes.

"Breathtaking, isn't it?" Abbie said.

"I feel like the Ewoks are going to emerge from the trees at any moment," Ana whispered. "What are all these boxes?"

"Those are the beehives."

"Get in costume, m' ladies!" Alder called out as he lumbered across the field wearing a netted helmet. He handed one to each of them, along with a couple of pairs of gloves, taking a moment to look deep into their faces. "You afraid?" he asked.

"No, sir," Ana answered.

"I can see it all over ya. Ever been around honeybees before?"

"I don't think so."

"Not surprised. Cities need more bees. Don't we all. But, listen; they're not here to harm, just here to do their job for the queen and the flowers. Even so, we don't want to get in their way. They're miracle creatures, like the butterfly and the ladybug. Miracles often come in small packages."

He led them out to one of the hives, along the way scratching his beard through the netting and humming a tune of his own making.

"What happened to all those deer?" Ana asked.

"What do you mean?"

"All the antlers. Do you hunt them?"

"Never killed a deer in my life," he said. "That's not true. Killed one once, but that was out of mercy—poor thing been hit by a truck off the highway. Believe you me, I still think about it."

"Then why do you have so many antlers hanging on the front of your house?"

"Bringing 'em back to the land, so to speak. I rescued most of those from garage sales or other folks who didn't want them in the house anymore. Few I rescued without anyone even noticing."

Alder approached one of the stacked white boxes, which

was faded and splintering with age, and began pumping small puffs of smoke from a silver can around it.

"Put the nets and gloves on, you two."

"What are you doing?" Ana asked.

"Giving 'em a little smoke. Calms the nerves, makes everyone a little less aggressive. Come take a look, but stay on that side of the box."

Ana and Abbie wandered over in their nets and gloves. Alder lifted one of the boxes to reveal rectangular pieces of wood inside with a few bees crawling in and out of them and several flying out and into the air before making their way to the wildflower field. Ana remained motionless.

"Don't worry. I guarantee you they don't want to waste their lives stinging you."

"What do you mean?" Ana asked, terrified to move.

"They die once they sting ya," Alder said, which made Ana even more rigid. "Get a little closer; I want to show you the queen."

Ana shook her head no and refused to budge. "I'm fine over here."

"I promise nothing will happen to you," Abbie said. "It's something special to see."

"If they die when they sting you, then they should definitely stay away from me. *Far* away."

Alder and Abbie exchanged a look that Ana couldn't see beneath all the netting.

"Your choice," Alder said, dipping into the box delicately and pulling out a rectangular frame covered in bees. "Might've taken you for a squirrel, but never a chicken."

Abbie had no fear, as she spent her days with bees in the garden, so she took a frame to inspect.

"Extraordinary," she said.

They continued to ignore Ana, who stood there looking at the ground, then the trees, until she worked herself up and headed over.

"If I get stung, I get to take a pair of antlers," she said.

"Fair enough," Alder replied.

He tilted the frame for her to see.

"Check out this gang of wise guys right here," Alder said. "Been around longer than the rest of us. They have much to teach about a working society. Can't say that about most of the rest of us, but these bees know exactly what they're doing right down to communication and community spirit. They even dance better than we do."

"You said they're like gangs," Ana said.

"And they are! They gather socially to protect and defend what they hold most dear."

"Do they kill each other, though?"

Abbie looked at Alder again, but he didn't look back.

"Well, you've got your drones and your worker bees, which work together for the protection of the queen bee and her eggs. Sometimes, when the drones are no longer needed and pose a threat to the hive, the worker bees will kill them. It sounds brutal, but it's all to serve the betterment of the hive."

"Sounds exactly like a gang," Ana said.

"Yes, and what's fascinating is that in the land of the bees, it's the sisters taking the brothers out. Come over here and check out the honeycomb. Fascinating hexagons!"

Without hesitation, Ana came around to the other side of the hive, so Abbie moved out of the way.

"What do you mean, 'hexagons'?"

"See here, that's the shape," Alder said, delicately running a gloved finger over the wax-covered combs crawling with bees. "Eventually, we'll take these frames out and extract the honey from 'em. And if you've tasted my honey, you know it's the best in the area."

"And some of the best surrounding crops too," Abbie said.

"What else do you grow?" Ana asked.

"Oh, just wildflowers and such and so on," Alder said, coughing into his netting. "Shall I send you on your way with some fresh honey?"

Rocks and pebbles ricocheted around the van's wheels. Abbie maneuvered the van back up to the road, trying and failing to pick up speed. Ana stared out the window, a pair of antlers in her lap. The sky had gone dark with incoming clouds.

"It's weird isn't it," Ana said.

"It is," Abbie agreed, though she didn't know to what Ana was referring.

"How if you listen, sometimes the signs present themselves to you, like those moments when someone else randomly says what you're thinking. Or when you've been thinking about someone and you see them, or you've had a dream about something that doesn't pertain to anything in particular, but then you see that thing or that image in real life? I think those are signs pointing you in the right direction, or at least toward the way you're supposed to go."

"I think I know what you mean," Abbie said, knowing full well what Ana meant.

"My abuela was into signs. On this one particular morning, a pretty good one, my birthday actually, she said she hoped we didn't see any devil piñatas. But then we did. A whole group of diablos."

"Coincidence, I guess."

"Or something more. You know when we were leaving and Alder said he thought bees were really angels on earth?"

"Yes . . ."

"Maybe they have stingers for that very purpose. To give life, take it, and also to maybe keep the rest of us from realizing how good they can be. And maybe when we see one, away from any others, nowhere near a hive, maybe it's there to remind us that goodness in disguise is always buzzing around in the periphery."

CHAPTER EIGHT

The rain was falling in a light mist over the fields and Ana felt as if she were walking through television static. It hardly ever rained in L.A., so she relished the moment. She crossed through the crops and made her way to Manny, who was helping Vic haul beets to the sorting station.

"I finished the squash," Ana said, approaching them.

Manny nodded at Vic to go on without him.

"Good," Manny said. He was quieter than usual.

"What's next? Do you need me to help you?"

"*Mija*, we need help with everything today," he said. "We've been short on workers, as you know, and the new guys didn't show this morning."

"How come?"

Manny sighed. He seemed older somehow, Ana thought, and preoccupied. "Old farm up in Keyserville got bought by the big guns," he said. "They're hiring anyone they can and offering a higher wage. Some even get shared living in the empty stables, and many of them don't have permanent homes. Guys go where the better work is, you know? But it's something we're dealing with more and more. Emmett's not in the best mood."

"What can I do?"

"Pull the garlic before the downpour, strip it for market."

Manny looked up at the sky. The dark clouds were ominous and rumbling every now and then. He looked out over the fields where Vic, Rolo, and René were gathered at the tented station near the truck. "Go ahead and start on the far row since those are ready to pull. I'll find Emmett and see where we're at today. If the rain gets worse, come on in."

The wind kicked up, whipping Ana's hair around her face as she headed straight for the rows with sprays of green. She reached down and gave the first bulb of garlic a pull, checking that its resistance wasn't too firm before yanking it from the earth. There was a tiny victory in pulling each one, she thought. She began tossing them one by one into a pile behind her as she'd been taught, dirt flying all over her sneakers. She made sure to go for the ones that were slightly loose, wiggling each one, holding off on any that were too difficult to pull, having nearly fallen down trying to pull with two hands more than once. When she had a sizable pile, she began stripping the outer layers, piling the unwanted bits at the end of the row. She looked up from time to time, but she didn't see Manny or Emmett, so she gathered the bulbs in her arms to take over to the others.

René wasn't expecting Ana. His focus was on Vic and Rolo, who were up against the fence in a heated conversation with Joey. He nodded at her when she dumped the garlic on the table and began sorting it while also turning around from time to time to listen to what was being said.

They all looked over at her standing there but said nothing. Ana's Spanish wasn't perfect, but she heard Rolo tell Joey that "she" didn't understand enough to know what they were talking about and to continue. She played dumb and smiled at René, who continued working despite the fact that they were all discussing whether or not they should leave the farm. She couldn't make out all of the details, but from what she understood, Joey's cousin had taken a job at the farm in Keyserville, and he wanted more workers to join— there was something about his getting more money too if he brought in more people. Rolo and Vic said yes, though Vic seemed to be wavering, and René remained mum. They were talking about how to break the news to Manny before lunch.

A crack of thunder rolled across the fields, but the rain remained light and steady. Ana wondered what she should do or say, although one part of her wanted to ask the guys if they thought the farm at Keyserville might give her work too. She had only one week left on the farm and neither Abbie nor Emmett had mentioned whether or not she'd be staying. She didn't want to leave—the very thought of it made her chest ache—but she might not have a choice. "Fix your mistakes and move forward," she thought, echoing Abbie, "whatever the consequences."

The conversation tapered off as Manny emerged from the hoop house and made his way over with a look of concern, bypassing Ana at the station and heading straight for the others, who were still in midconversation. To her surprise, he seemed to have already been made aware of the situation, though he hadn't taken the men seriously. He pleaded for them to reconsider, but Joey and Rolo said they were leaving, especially because they'd not received their

Friday paychecks. Ana had never seen Manny so distraught. He took off his hat and apologized on Emmett's behalf, or so Ana assumed, as Emmett's name came up every now and then. She had forgotten about getting her pay for the week, which was in fact a day late. It wasn't like Emmett to forget. It was just as out of the ordinary as Emmett's current absence.

"I'll be right with you," Manny said to Ana, noticing her listening, but like the rest of them, he had no idea that she'd understood nearly every word that was said. And from what she could tell, the workers said they had no choice. They didn't want to leave; they needed more than the Garbers were able to give.

"¿Y tu, René?" Manny turned and asked. René put his head down and shook it in the affirmative. Ana realized that all of them, with the exception of Manny, right then and there had decided to go.

Another hush came over the fields—just as much for the lightning in the distance as for Emmett walking up over the hill from the barn. There was nowhere to hide, but Ana stepped to the side of the table nearest to René. She saw Emmett notice her, his brow inverting and his pace—like her pulse—suddenly quickening.

"Who stripped the garlic?" he asked.

"I did," Ana said.

Emmett looked furious.

"Manny, did you know she did this?" he asked.

"I told her to do it, Boss," Manny said. "They need them for market tomorrow."

"Did anyone think to ask me what I thought? I wanted this garlic kept as is and hung to dry. We need to age most of these, not strip and sell them. Is no one paying attention around here today?"

Ana had seen Emmett frustrated and irritated, but she had never seen him bordering on out of control. He took a breath and closed his eyes.

A bell sounded on the breeze, signaling that lunch was ready. There was another clap of thunder.

"Who's going to pick up lunch?" Emmett said, finally calm, but no one responded. "Whose turn is it?"

"I'll head down there," Manny said, "but I need a quick word."

"Now's not the time," Emmett said. "Vic, Rolo, head on down to the house and grab lunch. We'll have to eat under the tent and figure out what to do if it rains this afternoon."

Vic and Rolo didn't move other than to look over at Manny, who looked back at them and then to Joey and René, but no one said or did anything.

"I don't know what's going on here, if it's the rain or what," Emmett continued. "But we need to shift our focus, everyone. I'll grab the lunch." Emmett walked away toward the farmhouse while the others remained quiet until he was out of hearing range.

"Why are you all leaving?" Ana said, not being able to hold it in any longer. "I mean, I get why, and I know we need to get paid, but maybe there's a reason the paychecks are late. Maybe we should give Emmett the benefit of the doubt. I know it sounds better over at this other farm in Keyserville or whatever, but you can't leave the farm. In case you guys have forgotten, I'm probably being sent away too. Abbie and Emmett depend on you, and not just for work, you're like—I don't know—you're more than that to them."

"This is about business," Joey said. Rolo shook his head in solidarity.

They continued talking. Manny walked over to her and put his hat on the sorting table.

"Did you understand everything they said, *mija*?"

"Most of it."

"I don't want this to alarm you. You've done good work out here, and you made a real effort today, okay?"

"But this is partially my fault. I just screwed everything up again with the garlic . . ."

"This has nothing to do with you."

"They can't just leave without saying something. You need to tell Emmett."

"I don't know what to do." Manny sighed, and she could tell by his expression that he didn't.

"Well, I'm going to fix it then."

"Wait—" Manny said.

But Ana was already sprinting toward the farmhouse as the rain began to fall in sheets, thunder forcing her feet to run faster. She got to the back door of the farmhouse and pushed the door open, heading straight for the kitchen without wiping her feet. Abbie and Emmett were in a tense conversation at the counter and went silent when Ana, muddy and dripping, trampled in.

"What on earth—" Abbie said.

"You've got to listen to me—" Ana said, out of breath.

"And you need to march right back outside," Emmett said, walking toward her.

"Please, just listen to me for a minute. They're leaving."

"Who is?" Abbie asked.

"All of them—Rolo, Vic, Joey, and René. They're all going to the farm in Keyserville."

"What's going on?" Emmett said, his voice rising in alarm.

"I heard them talking, in Spanish, about wanting to go today, that they couldn't afford to do this anymore. Joey said it was a business decision."

Emmett rushed over to the window above the sink and looked out. "Did Manny send you?"

"No, but he said it was about the paychecks and that they had to go where the work was better."

"And you heard them say this?" Abbie asked.

"Yes, but I don't think they really want to leave, deep down. I mean, that's what I believe. But they said they're going, soon, and I want to help."

Emmett remained quiet as he continued to stare out the window.

"I don't want my paycheck," Ana said. Emmett turned to look at her. "If it will help everyone else get paid, so they can stay, then I don't want mine."

"Ana—" Abbie said.

"I know I screwed up this morning, and pretty much every morning I've been here, but please let me fix it. I just—I don't want to leave. What if I stay and work and you pay me in room and board? It'll be like having an extra worker but with one less paycheck."

No one said anything, but Abbie looked at Emmett and held his gaze.

"I was planning on paying everyone today, just didn't know how to break it that the checks would be less this week," he said quietly.

"But without my paycheck it'll be fine, right?"

Emmett nodded his head, looking at the floor. "I think it'll help, yes."

"Wait here," Ana said. She ran upstairs to her room and

pulled out the envelope of cash from her backpack. She ran back downstairs and handed Emmett the envelope.

"Here's all of my pay from the past few weeks," she said. "I don't want it. They said they wanted to go before lunch, so you better hurry."

Without a word, Emmett headed out of the house and across the garden to the barn. Abbie looked out the window and then turned back to Ana.

"Well, that was above and beyond," she said with a smile and a shake of her head. "Not that we knew we were about to lose it, but I think you just saved the whole goddamned farm—I hope—excuse the language."

Ana liked the way Abbie was looking at her, almost as if she were proud.

"Well, what are you standing there for?" Abbie said. "Go get everyone and tell them we're eating lunch inside. Take some umbrellas."

Ana put her hat on, grabbed a few umbrellas, and ran out of the kitchen, through the garden, and across the fields. Dolly escaped the barn again, out the half-open front door, and raced alongside her. Ana shouted out to Manny and the workers, all huddled under the tent, and hoped they'd hear her over the thunder.

"What are you doing?" Manny said as she ducked under the tent, covered in mud.

"It's lunchtime," she said, full of excitement, her heart racing.

"*Mija*, I don't know if everyone's coming down to—"

"And pay time."

The workers exchanged looks. Vic, in particular, had an expression that said "I told you so," while Rolo and Joey remained still as if they wanted to go.

"Give the guy a break," Ana said, handing out umbrellas. "He's a day late, but he's got our pay. Have some lunch, get your money, and then you can decide to go." She popped open an umbrella and held her arm out for René, who took it and walked alongside her and Dolly back down the hill as the others mumbled and followed. Abbie was waiting for them at the back door, though most of them hesitated, not wanting to track in so much wet dirt.

"Everyone inside," Abbie said. "C'mon. Everyone but Dolly."

One by one they walked into the house for the first time. She insisted Vic, Rolo, Joey, and René take seats around the country table, which was set for four. Manny and Ana sat on the bar stools near the counter, and Abbie handed out plates—on the same china she had used on Ana's first day— with almond butter and raspberry jam sandwiches, thick-cut potato chips, and fruit salad with rose water and mint. Ana jumped up to fill glasses of lemonade and was passing them around when the back door opened and shut.

Emmett walked into the room. It took a moment for him to register that the kitchen was suddenly fuller than it had been in years.

"We're eating inside today," Abbie said to him. "Come and have a seat at the counter."

"I'd like to apologize," Emmett said, not looking at anyone. "I'm a day late with pay, which is unforgivable." He reached into his coat pocket and pulled out several envelopes, which he handed out, personally, to Joey, Vic, Rolo, René, and Manny. "I hope you'll accept this with my apologies. I know it's been rough lately—well, I've been rough— but I promise this won't ever happen again. The farm exists only because of all of you. I don't know what Abbie and I would do if . . ." His voice trailed off and he cleared his throat.

"I also want to thank everyone for the hard work," Abbie said, raising her lemonade glass. "Emmett and I are both grateful to have you in the Garber family. Let's eat!"

The workers remained silent, staring at Manny, but on Abbie's cue they began to eat. Manny looked at Ana and then back at Emmett with concern.

"Are those all the paychecks—" Manny said to Emmett.

"A word outside, please," Emmett said.

Manny stood up and followed Emmett out. They huddled under the eave of the back porch as the rain continued to fall.

"Ana deserves a paycheck just like all the rest," Manny said. "The garlic was my fault—"

"I know," Emmett said. "She forfeited her paycheck, all of them, so I could pay everyone else—told me she didn't want any more pay if it meant the rest could stay."

Manny was silent.

"I know we're in a tough spot, what with Keyserville and the shady way those guys do business, poaching everyone and promising what they can't deliver. I don't ever want this place to be like that. I don't know how to apologize enough for being late on these paychecks, let alone not being able to pay them. But I don't want you to leave. I don't want anyone to leave. Don't know what I can do to convince you to stay."

"I'm not going anywhere," Manny said. "The others, I'm not so sure about. But let me see what I can do."

They went back inside, scuffing their feet on the doormat, listening to a rousing commotion as they walked back into the kitchen. Rolo was doubled over with laughter, pounding the table with his hand while the others laughed along, but René, his head down, appeared to be crying quietly into the collar of his shirt.

"Oh, it's absolutely perfect, Ana," Abbie said.

Ana swiveled around on the bar stool to show them a jar of jam with a rectangular piece of sketchbook paper cut up and taped to the front. "You see, René?" she said. "You're perfect."

"Look what Ana made," Abbie said to Manny and Emmett.

Ana passed the jar to the workers at the table, who continued to snicker, before passing it to Manny.

"René's Red Raspberry Jam," Manny said, taking in the lettering, spare and elegant, and the uncanny pencil portrait of René in the middle, framed by raspberries and leaves. "Did you draw this?"

"Yep," she said, smiling and proud.

"Incredible! It's him, right down to the hat and dimple. *Muy bueno*," he said to René. He handed the jar to Emmett, who looked at it for a while, shaking his head, but not in a bad way.

"I have more, one of everybody," she said, grabbing her sketchbook from the counter and opening it up. "I even have one of you," she said, turning the book around to show everyone a colored-pencil rendering of Manny, complete with mustache and red bandanna around his neck. "I was thinking you'd be good for a jar too, though I don't know what Abbie pickles that starts with an M."

"Magic?" Manny said with a wink.

"I was thinking mustard greens, which could work, I guess, if we ever put labels on the CSA bunches. Oh, and

there's this one." Ana flipped the page to an elaborate cartoon farm scene featuring a Chihuahua with chicken legs
and a creature that appeared to be a cross between a cat and
a pig. The "animals" had their arms around one another
like long-lost pals and were standing in front of a blackberry
bush made to look like a hungry monster.

"Who's that?" Rolo asked.

"You and Vic, of course." Rolo remained straight-faced,
while everyone else burst into another round of laughter,
heartier this time. Even René and Emmett cracked smiles.

The gang left after lunch. Emmett gave everyone the rest
of the day off because of the rain. Manny and René said
they'd both be in the next morning to help with the farmers'
market haul. The rest, Ana hoped, would be showing up
with her early on Monday. She kept her fingers crossed in
her coat pocket as they left, each one thanking Abbie as
they did, and then nodding to Emmett before shaking Ana's
hand. René gave her a courtly bow and kissed her hand.

It continued to rain steadily throughout the afternoon.
Ana headed upstairs and took Abbie's advice about having
a bath, though she couldn't remember ever having had one
before. She did as Abbie said and poured the bottle of blue
liquid into the tub, watching as the bubbles rose until they
nearly spilled over the edge. She got into the warm water,
blissful at first, tedious after a while, and stared at the white
wooden ceiling. "How long am I supposed to stay here?" she
wondered.

Emmett finished feeding Dolly out in the barn. He went
back to his bedroom and began picking up the glass from

the photograph he'd thrown earlier, the one of him and Josie on their wedding day. He shook the photo from the broken frame and shoved it in the back of a desk drawer before he swept up the pieces. It had been exactly one year since Josie had gone out with friends, or so she'd said; needing a "girls' night" was the way she put it. Emmett didn't normally wait up, but he had awakened in the middle of the night, unable to sleep, so he had stayed up until dawn. When she hadn't returned by the time he needed to head out to the fields, he walked outside to find a letter taped to the front door. He opened it, read it through once, and then burned it in the sink.

Emmett hadn't anticipated the anger that would return on the anniversary of that day. He hadn't expected it to affect his work. He tied up the trash bag and took it outside, shielding himself from the rain with an umbrella. He walked over to the farmhouse and let himself in through the back door. Abbie was busy making a supper of spicy chicken, black beans, and grilled corn, with a crème caramel from a recipe she found in their mother's *Joy of Cooking* cookbook. She smiled at him as he entered.

"Thought I'd eat here tonight, if that's okay," Emmett said.

"Absolutely. I already set the table. Would you mind running up and asking Ana to come down?"

"I'd like to discuss something first."

"About Ana?"

"Yes," he said, removing his baseball cap and smoothing down his hair. "I've been thinking lately, too much probably, but having her here has been—"

"A burden for you? Too much to handle?"

"No, actually." He didn't know if it was the poignancy of the day or what had transpired earlier, but Abbie's exasperated look, even more than her words, bruised him. "I was going to say—before you jump to conclusions—that it's been more helpful than I thought it would be. We need it, frankly, and what with the whole payment thing—"

"Pretty selfless, if you ask me, and quite wonderful. All those labels, all that time she took working on them . . ."

"I've been thinking about how you and I grew up, how we juggled our schedules," Emmett continued. "We used to help each other when Mom was sick."

Abbie put down the dish towel she was holding.

"I remember," she said. "It was hard . . . it's been hard."

"It was harder when you left."

Abbie took a breath. Though she and Emmett had never discussed it, she always imagined that he and their father had been better off.

"I was young," she said. "I couldn't handle being here without her."

"I understand the feeling."

Emmett continued, wringing the baseball hat in his hands. "Today's the day, you know."

"What day?"

"The day Josie left."

Abbie nodded her head. "I miss her too."

"But what I'm trying to say is, I think we need the help around here."

Abbie smiled. "I know."

"It's more that it's good for the farm, good for the business . . ."

"Emmett Garber you can't bring yourself to say it."

"Say what?"

"That your sister was right."

Emmett went up the stairs looking at the photographs and paintings the way he used to when his mother would tell him to go up to bed. He wondered how long it had been since he'd been upstairs, now that it was Abbie's domain. Something about the creak of his footfalls brought back a flood of memories, from the giggling to the yelling to the week of their mother's death. The hallway had gone quiet when Abbie ran away soon thereafter. He knocked on Ana's door—Abbie's old bedroom—and he turned the knob when she said he could come in.

She was startled at the sight of him, poised as she was, sketching on the bed, her wet hair hanging down her shoulders, wearing his old Tom Petty and the Heartbreakers concert T-shirt.

"Abbie said I could wear it, I swear," she said, eyes wide. "All my clothes are in the wash."

"You can have it," Emmett said. "Don't think I could fit into it if I tried."

They looked at each other, neither one of them saying anything.

"Is it dinnertime?" Ana asked.

"It is."

Ana slid off the bed and tied her hair back as Emmett made his way into the hall. He stopped and turned back around. "I need to say thanks," he said. "For today. I'm sorry I went off on you like that. I know how hard you've been working, and I think I forget that this farming stuff doesn't come easy all the time."

"You said I was supposed to be fit for it, so I'm trying my hardest to be. It's just new, I guess. I told you I had good hands, but I didn't expect them to make such a mess in the dirt, you know? I mean, I still don't understand what kohlsabi is or why anyone would ever want to eat something called that, or why you people worship worms the way you do."

"Kohlrabi?"

"Exactly. But I'm serious about it and want to get better . . . if you'll let me."

"Supper's ready. Abbie made some spicy chicken thing."

They headed down the stairs. Ana thought Emmett looked different and realized this was the first time she'd ever seen him for any length of time without his baseball cap. She took her seat at the table, and Emmett sat beside her. Abbie served plates full of food with glasses of iced hibiscus tea as the rain pelted the windows.

"I've always wished for rain," Ana said.

"Why?" Abbie asked. "What I wouldn't give for all of your sunny L.A. days."

"I always think it's more atmospheric in L.A. when it's gloomy, like all of the gray kind of folds into this two-dimensional wonderland. It makes the trees and flowers pop up against it. Whereas here, where there's so much color, so much green, the bright days are the best because the sun has more to play with. I guess it's about contrasts, always wanting the opposite of what you're used to. Holy geez—" Ana said. "This is outrageously delicious."

"I did my best, used some oranges for the marinade."

"It's *so* good. You used bacon in the beans, right?"

"I did. Is that how your—how you like to have them?"

"I'll take them any which way, really. My abuela did

frijoles de la olla with pinto beans, which is kind of similar. The secret is epazote."

"I've never heard of that before."

"It's an herb," Ana said. "See, I know some stuff, Emmett."

They ate together for the first time since Ana had arrived at the farm nearly a month before. The time had gone by quicker than she realized. Her phone call with Mrs. Saucedo was scheduled for that night. She reminded herself to find out about where she'd be going when she got back to L.A. the following Saturday, not that she wanted to think about it just yet. Abbie asked about her sketches and what gave her the idea to make the labels. Emmett asked about when she started drawing and if she wanted to be an artist. In turn, she asked them if they'd ever been to a famous art museum— Abbie, yes; Emmett, no—and why no one had ever made signs to mark all the crops.

They did the dishes together, with Abbie washing, Ana drying, and Emmett putting everything away. And when it came time for Ana to make the phone call in the parlor, they asked her to sit back down at the table.

"Emmett and I have been talking," Abbie said.

"Good. I mean, not that you weren't. You know what I mean," Ana said.

"We'd like to keep you on through the fall, if you're interested. You'd go to Hadley High, but you'd also continue to work here."

"It's still an internship, so you'll have a morning farm shift before school most days," Emmett interjected. "And a full shift Saturday, plus farmers' market prep on Sunday mornings. It'll be tough, but it's the schedule Abbie and I had when we were in high school."

Ana looked from one to the other. "You're serious?" she said.

"It's entirely up to you to decide," Abbie said. "But we'd love to have you, if you'd like to stay for the semester. We want to help you with your emancipation."

Ana was quiet. She looked from one to the other and nodded her head. "Yes," she said quietly, holding back her exuberance, worried it was enough to topple them over. "Yes, please," she said again. "Do I tell Mrs. Saucedo tonight?"

"If you'd like to," Abbie said. "There's no pressure, either way. I will speak with her this week."

Emmett stood up from the table, as if it were his cue to leave. "Tasty dinner, Sis," he said. He walked over to Ana and put out his hand as if to shake on the deal.

"Abbie really likes having you here," he said. Though Ana heard the name Abbie, she knew he meant himself too. She said nothing and shook his hand.

"I almost forgot," he said, pulling out an envelope from his coat pocket. "This is for you." He handed Ana a white envelope. There was an M written on the front in Emmett's handwriting, followed by "for magic" written by a different hand. "It's from Manny," he said. "He says to use it wisely. I'll see you both in the morning."

They all said good night as Emmett left out the back door.

"What a day," Abbie said, exhaling as she rose from the table. "I think I'm going to luxuriate in recipes for the rest of this rainy night. Need anything before I head up?"

"No, thanks," Ana said, remaining seated, still not believing she was staying, wondering what was inside the envelope, but guessing what was. "I'll go make the call."

Abbie pulled out a couple of cookbooks to peruse and

tucked them under her arm. She looked over at Ana, who was still at the table facing the other way, and she fought the impulse to embrace her, like her own mother would have done. "See you in the morn," she said, and Ana nodded.

"Abbie?"

"Yes, hon?"

"Good night."

"'Night."

"Today was a sunny day."

CHAPTER NINE

"Curls," Ana said. "So many curls, it's like they're multiplying."

They'd been sitting around Rye's bedroom all Sunday afternoon listening to the Hex. Rye sat cross-legged on her bed, hunched over her laptop, while Ana was on the floor opposite the standing mirror, avoiding her reflection while sketching and enjoying the free time. It was her first visit to the Moons' house, the first time she'd ever left the farm on an afternoon off, and Rye's room was a jolt of inspiration. Rye didn't mind that Ana wanted to sketch her space. Ana was taken with the entire room, the walls totally plastered with posters, magazine cuttings, photos, and assorted objects. She mentioned more than once to Rye that she was thankful for the change of scenery.

It was Labor Day weekend, and the summer was officially over. Ana still couldn't believe she'd ended up working as a farmhand. She knew all about cover crops and irrigation, the intricacies of tomato training, and why cow manure was more balanced than chicken. She'd become so familiar with the farm's chickens, in fact, that she and Abbie had finally solidified their names. There was Edna, Josephine, Mama Cass, Li'l Stevie, and Frida K, plus a few others. The lone rooster had always been known as Earl, but Ana had taken to calling him Diego because he seemed to favor Frida the most but still spent time with Edna and Josephine.

Though the farmwork was difficult at times, Ana found comfort in her gang of fellow workers, who had all stayed at the farm, except for Joey. Ana wasn't surprised he'd left. And though Emmett and Abbie faced competition from the expansion of the Keyserville farm, Garber Farm continued to fulfill its commitments, and its family legacy.

Not that there weren't arguments from time to time. Part of what kept the farm afloat was its most recent client, Will Carson, who ordered produce week after week, even though his restaurant had yet to open.

"If it ever does open," Emmett said to Abbie one night during a particularly argumentative conversation Ana wasn't guilty about listening in on. "He thinks the people of Hadley want fancy food? I'll tell you what, we need a diner with hearty breakfasts, sandwiches, and early-bird spe- cials, not some farm-to-table crap he keeps filling your ears with . . ."

"He has ambitions," Abbie protested. "And he loves our produce and pickles. I'm willing to believe in the guy. Have you heard about the restaurants he's worked with? Two in San Francisco, a few in L.A., and that famous one in Berkeley, the one with the garden."

"I don't care where he's worked, what's up his garden, or

if he grew up fifteen miles from here—no one in these parts wants damned nasturtium foam with their pancakes!"

It was the first time Ana felt any normalcy in her life and the first time she had real responsibilities. Though she sometimes missed the freedom to jump on the bus and explore East Los Angeles, to while away hours in the library or explore the hidden pockets of downtown, she had to admit that having people who actually cared about her whereabouts wasn't that terrible.

She'd even taken to spending creative time with Abbie some nights after dinner, the results of which were new sign markers for the fields. They'd spent the past week of evenings painting scraps of wood with smiling kale, waltzing turnips, and fennel with Mohawk-shaped fronds. Abbie added fanciful text listing the genus and common names of each crop, and Ana added the Spanish translations underneath. Life had become a busy routine, so much so that Ana hadn't once thought about school, which was a few days away. The prospect seemed less daunting in Los Angeles, where it was much easier to remain invisible as the new kid in the vastness of the system, but here in Hadley, population everyone knows everyone, Ana knew circumstances would be different.

"What are you wearing?" Ana asked. "On the first day."

"Trying to figure it out right now," replied Rye. "I've saved a ton of street-style images and am leaning toward something Scandinavian in feel. I want to change it up this year."

"But what do you normally wear?"

"It depends on what theme interests me that season. Right

now, it's all about neutral colors and layers and my ongoing love affair with men's tailoring—and maybe some sort of patch situation, like an old tuxedo jacket covered in slogans. Accessories wise, I'm thinking about embracing the cravat."

"Where do you go shopping for that around here?"

Rye rolled her eyes. "There's only one store that counts, Ellery Pearl, which is this vintage shop on Main Street. They source stuff for me all the time, like shrunken blazers and weird old brooches. I think I'm the only person in this town who actually appreciates what they do. They cut hair in the back room too. What's your theme going to be?"

"Farmer's closet," Ana said, thinking about her two pairs of jeans, few T-shirts, army jacket, and her sneakers, which were thrashed but in working order. The rest of her daily uniform came in the form of hand-me-downs from Abbie's or Emmett's closets. "I'm thinking of accessorizing with a pitchfork."

"Hilarious, also not such a bad idea. Where did you go shopping in L.A.?"

"Goodwill, exclusively."

"Used is the best, right?"

"It's like wearing stories. Speaking of which, what's the story of this room—it's insane. Who are all these people on the walls?"

"My inspirations, muses. They're a constant reminder I need to get the hell out of here one day too. New York, London, who knows?"

Ana looked at the photos surrounding her—women wearing men's tuxedos, elaborate dresses made entirely of purple flowers, and black feathers rendered around a mannequin's body in impossible shapes. Above Rye's desk there was an image of a model wearing an oversize skirt as a dress belted across the chest, the front of it splattered with spray paint. Pinned up around the room there were also several photos of a woman with a severe black bob haircut, sad eyes, and ruby red lips.

"Who's that?" Ana asked, pointing to a photo of the woman wearing a white dress with a giant silver lobster clinging to her neck.

"Isabella Blow. She was this fearless British fashion icon who wore the most outrageous ensembles. And hats! That woman could wear a hat like no one else, except maybe you. You've got the face shape for it."

"Where does she live?"

"With her best friend Alexander McQueen in a tartan castle in the sky. She's dead. So is he. That's them up there." Rye nodded toward a printout of a man wearing a princess gown being chased by a woman in a towering hat, the castle behind them burning. "He was the most incredible fashion designer who ever was, until he wasn't. It's a tragedy."

Ana thought about the word "tragedy" and how it had a different meaning for different people. "My hair is a tragedy," she said. "Look at it. I can't walk into school with it all crazy like this."

"Hasn't it always been crazy like that?"

"Yes. It's my legacy and part of my curse, but I'm sick of wearing it tied back all the time."

"Why don't you pull it up off of your shoulders in a top-knot or something? Let me try putting it in a bun—"

"No," Ana said, suddenly standing up. "It's fine. I'll figure something out. Where's the bathroom?"

Ana made her way through the living room of the Moons' house. As much as she loved the way Abbie decorated

Garber Farm, the Moons' house had an eclectic charm all its own. In addition to the long driveway that wound its way through brush thicket and thin trees, the house sat in the clearing of a redwood grove, a pond fronting the property. Their house was smaller than the farmhouse at Garber Farm, boxy, but two stories with a double-slanted roof. The living room was dimly lit, with low couches and mismatched chairs. Wooden sculptures and woven baskets occupied every surface, and patterned rugs covered the floors. The walls were a brushed gold with various pieces of art hanging from the dark wood trim. Above the fireplace hung a massive oil painting in shades of slashed green featuring an owl with the arms of a man.

"Holy—" Ana said, crossing the room to get a better look.

"Captivating, isn't it?" Della said, walking into the room. "It's a Rick Bartow, an artist very dear to us."

"Is he from here?"

"Not exactly, but he's one of my people."

"Like . . . family?"

"He's Wiyot, as am I. Our people have been on this land for many years," Della said, her slender hand resting on ropes of beads around her neck. "He painted this one as well." She pointed to a painting in the far corner above glass-fronted bookshelves; it depicted a small multicolored bird floating in a sea of pale pink.

"What's it called?"

"*Kestrel on Pink Field.*"

"It's soul crushing how the bird is just sitting there all alone in that empty space."

"It's a very strong piece, emotional. At least, it's always struck me as such. Glad to see it has struck you too," Della said. "You're an artist yourself, correct? Abbie was telling me about your drawings and the labels you made for her preserves. She said you have quite the talent."

"It's the only thing I've ever been good at, the only work I never tire of. I've been drawing since I can remember. When I was a kid, I was sort of forced to draw things I didn't want to, because I'd somehow forgotten what to say. But I realized my voice could sometimes be louder when I didn't have to deal with all the words."

In hindsight, in that moment, Ana wished she'd kept some of the drawings she'd made for Mrs. Saucedo the second time she'd been brought in to child services. It wasn't that she wanted to relive the nightmare of that day; it was more that she wanted to look back into the eyes of the monsters, the ones she'd had the power to draw and put away. She wanted to remember her abuela's face the last time she saw it, and the floral pattern of her abuela's favorite dress, even though she still held a square of fabric from it every night before she went to sleep.

"Well, you'll have to take Susan Darnell's class at school this year," Della said. "She's been making and teaching art in these parts for decades—knows all the area galleries and is a wonderful teacher. Rye took her class last year and is signing up again this year."

Charlie Moon entered with a tray of cookies and sliced nectarines. He was wearing the same uniform he always wore at the general store, a plain button-up shirt tucked into khakis. He was the opposite of Della Moon, Ana thought, who favored a flowing bohemian look, with rich colors and piles of jewelry on her hands, arms, and chest. He set the tray down on the coffee table next to a sculpture of a curious iguana and nodded at them before slipping out of the room again.

"Some snacks for you two," Della said. "I'm so glad you could come over today. You have no idea how happy it makes us to know Rye has found a friend—well, a friend in you."

Ana carried the tray back upstairs to Rye's room, stopping midway to look at a photo of the Moons and a very young Rye, her hair long and flowing, her face open and lit up by an enormous smile. Ana pushed the door open to a wild-eyed Rye, who was wearing nearly the same expression. She nearly toppled over Ana and the tray.

"I have a solution," Rye said, her arms resting on Ana's shoulders, face growing serious. "Three words: 'Brazilian hair treatment.' It's a treatment made specifically for people with curly hair who want to straighten it. My dad bought some for the store, but my mom vetoed it, and I think the boxes are still out in the garage."

"Brazilian hair what?"

"It's all the rage. I just read about it online and the Web site says it can straighten your hair for months, so it's not like it'll be permanent or anything."

"How do we do it?"

"Quick, eat those cookies," Rye said. "I'll take the plate down and then sneak into the garage and get it. My mom was furious at my dad for buying it, but at least it'll work for one customer."

"I don't want to steal—"

"Please. It's already been purchased."

Ana returned to her sketching while she waited for Rye. She nestled herself into an empty corner with a few pillows and took in the room again. Even though she had her own room back at the Garbers', she'd never really known what it was like to make a room her own. Aside from the various shared ones in foster homes, she'd slept in the same bedroom

as her abuela, and when her parents were alive, it was anywhere from a motel to a refrigerator box with a sleeping bag
so as to separate her from her parents' nightly "discussions."
The group houses were a whole different situation she
wanted to forget, specifically the shared rooms and showers.
Ana wondered if Rye even knew how lucky she was.

The door opened and Rye motioned for Ana to follow her.
They tiptoed into her parents' bathroom, which was earthy
in feel with sandy brown walls and cream-colored tile.

"Your parents seem to love baskets," Ana said.

"Are you kidding? We have baskets in this house that are
used for holding other baskets."

"Why are we doing this in here?"

"My parents are downstairs working in the kitchen,
which is precisely why we have to do it up here. Do you
want to tame these curls or not?"

"More than anything."

"Good, then have a seat. I'm supposed to douse you in
serum."

Ana sat in the small chair near a vanity while Rye threw
a towel around her shoulders. Rye put on some gloves and
began squirting a bottle of liquid over the top of Ana's head.

"This is disgusting. It feels like slime."

"Smells like it too."

Ana picked up the box of serum while Rye combed the
liquid through her hair.

"It says formaldehyde is one of the ingredients," Ana
said.

"So?"

"Not that I'm stellar in science, but I don't want to be
embalmed just yet."

"It says you're supposed to wait fifteen minutes, which

is hardly enough time to pickle you from the follicles inward," Rye said, removing the plastic gloves. "Let's just take a deep breath and relax, try to forget the stench, and let our minds wander from the essence of rotten eggs lounging in a Jacuzzi of forgotten milk."

"I was going to ask you, since we have to sit here . . ."

"Yeah?"

"Do you know a guy named Cole Brannan?"

"Why do you ask?" Rye said quickly, her entire body stiffening in a way that answered Ana's question.

"He kind of cornered me in the bookstore a while ago and said we'd met before, but I know for a fact we never did."

"And you've been wondering about him all this time?" Rye said with a strange smile Ana hadn't seen her make before.

"Not really, I mean, it just popped into my head when we started talking about school. Does he go to Hadley High?"

"Yep," Rye said, clearly annoyed. "He went away at the beginning of the summer. But I guess he's back, sadly, now that you've confirmed it." Rye chewed the inside of her bottom lip in a way that Ana couldn't tell was habitual or out of anger. "What did he say?"

"Just that we'd met, and then he did this weird wave. He was cocky and dirty and wearing motorcycle clothes."

"Of course he was. He races."

"So, you do know him?"

"I used to, or thought I did. He's the only person in the world I wish I never met. *What* is that smell?"

"How much time has passed?"

"Barely five minutes. Ew. It smells *awful*."

"I think we should rinse it off," Ana said, looking in the mirror at her dark matted hair sticking together in clumps at the ends.

"But the time isn't up yet. Maybe this is how it's supposed to smell before it does what it's supposed to do."

"I think we should rinse it off. *Now*."

Ana rushed over to the bathtub, kneeling down and bending over while throwing her hair under the faucet. "Rinse!" she shouted.

Rye turned the water on and pushed Ana's hair underneath it. "Ouch!"

"What?"

"It stings. It's making my hands tingle!"

"Get it off, get it off, get it off!"

Rye grabbed some shampoo and squirted it all over Ana's hair, lathering it up under the faucet and rinsing it repeatedly under the water.

"You have so much hair."

"I know."

"It's taking up the entire bathtub, oh—"

"Oh, what? *What?*"

Rye went silent.

"Let me get a towel . . ."

Rye turned off the water while Ana waited behind her curtain of hair.

"Here," Rye said, handing her the towel.

Ana threw her head back, surprised at the lightness of it, and began to towel her hair dry. It took her a moment before she realized a good portion of her hair was still in the bathtub. She jumped back and turned to look in the mirror, stunned silent and horrified at the sight of herself.

"I'm sorry," Rye said, her hands covering her mouth. "I don't know what to do, I'm so sorry."

Ana continued staring at her reflection, which stared back, even though it didn't look like her usual self at all, what with half her hair missing, most of the ends burned off entirely on one side as well as pieces missing in the front.

"No," she said. "Oh, no, no, no."

"You did say you wanted a change . . ."

Ana turned around abruptly and headed for the door.

"Wait! Let me comb it through," Rye said, following her and reaching for her arm. "We can try to salvage what's left, or I can cut it—"

"Stay *away* from my hair," Ana said with more anger than she'd meant.

Abbie was reading in the kitchen when she heard the front door open and shut. She put on her slippers and padded into the parlor, which she was surprised to find had gone dark.

"Who's here?" she asked, wishing she'd brought a knife from the kitchen with her.

"It's just me," Ana said. "I'm in the chair, but please don't turn on the—"

Abbie switched on the lights and gasped. "What happened?" she said.

"I was stupid," Ana said, putting her head in her hands.

"Is this why you're home so early? I thought you were having dinner at the Moons'."

"I asked Della to bring me back. And, yes, my losing half of my hair also has something to do with it."

Abbie sat down on the couch and shook her head. "Tell me what happened."

"I was sick of my curls, so Rye and I decided to try this Brazilian hair treatment and, well, this is what happened."

"Did Rye put you up to it?" Abbie asked, concerned.

"No. We both did it. Rye burned her hands too."

"Oh, hon," Abbie said, noticing tears rolling down Ana's cheeks. "It's not that bad. We can fix it tomorrow."

"I screwed up, and I think Rye is upset because I yelled at her . . ."

"I'm sure she'll understand."

"I'm crying because I'm frustrated."

"I get it, but I'm telling you, we're going to fix this tomorrow," Abbie said.

"But isn't everything closed for Labor Day?"

"Hon, Hadley may go quiet on Sundays, but it's always open the day before school starts," Abbie said.

The tears continued to roll down Ana's face. "What's the matter?"

"It's just—my abuela loved my long hair, so I've never changed it. I've always kept it this length. I told Rye I wanted a change, but I didn't want this."

"Sometimes things happen beyond our control, but maybe you'll like it even better tomorrow after a new haircut."

"If you say so."

Ana was quiet on the ride to Ellery Pearl. In addition to being Hadley's lone hair salon and vintage store, the Pearl also sold needlepoint pillows and small oil paintings crafted by proprietors Ellery Jonas and Pearl Parnell, both longtime fixtures in Hadley. Ana was wearing the gardening hat down low over her face, what was left of her thick hair hanging above one shoulder and below the other. And even though it was a warm day, she'd insisted on wearing her army jacket over her T-shirt and jeans. Abbie didn't ask any questions.

Ana kept her head down when they entered the store, taking in its striped walls, smoky glass countertops, and windows covered in delicate lace. Abbie must have called ahead of time because they crossed right through the boutique in front before going through a door into a small back room that was made to look like an old-fashioned barbershop.

"Is this our girl?" a woman with the voice of a little girl said, entering behind them. "Have a seat."

Abbie gestured for Ana to sit in the lone leather chair in the middle of the room, a wall of mirrors in front of it.

"I'm Ellery Jonas," the woman said, reaching her hand into Ana's view underneath the hat. "You must be Ana."

"I am. Hi."

"Let's take a look at what's going on under this hat." Ellery removed it, making Ana squint under the bright lights.

"I'm a disaster," Ana said. She couldn't even glance at herself in the mirror, so she took in Abbie's look of concern as well as the petite face of Ellery Jonas, who was decades older than her voice. Always one to dress herself in the style of a lost era, she was the type of woman who kept her hair pinned into meticulous curls around her face. She wore a round little hat perched on the side of her head, like a lopsided cupcake, Ana thought. A giant brooch in the shape of a cicada was pinned to the front of her 1940s suit dress, which was prim yet a vibrant shade of clementine.

"You have lustrous curls, despite the ends, which are in an unfortunate state," Ellery said. "But I'm going to fix that. There's a lot of damage, so I'm going to have to cut above your shoulders, maybe to your chin, if that's okay with you."

Ana's heart sank. "Do I have a choice?"

"Not if you want your hair to look better and be in a healthier condition."

She took Ana over to another chair at a sink and washed

her hair—taking forever, Ana thought—giving her a scented scalp massage, which Ana wondered if she'd have to pay for. When she sat back down in the barber chair, Ellery turned it away from the mirrors so Ana was facing Abbie, who looked up from the magazine she was reading and smiled. "It'll be fine," she said.

"Heard you're from L.A.," Ellery said, combing what was left of Ana's hair. "Welcome to our quaint little town."

"Thanks," Ana said, knowing she was being impolite with her lack of conversation. "My friend—this girl I know—Rye says your shop is the best in town."

"She's sweet, isn't she? Fantastic taste. She's one of my best customers. I'm still on the hunt for a 1980s beige jumpsuit for her—very particular about what she wants. Oh, I love your tattoo!"

Ana froze. Abbie looked up from her magazine.

"Is it a symbol for something?" Ellery asked.

Ana remained silent.

"It's such a simple design—very unusual on the back of your neck. What does it mean?"

Ana felt dizzy and out of breath, like she was chained to the chair, the scissors snipping away behind her ear. Abbie knew something was wrong.

"Ana?"

"They're symbols. Not something I wanted, but something I have to live with," she managed to say.

"Oh," Ellery said quietly, continuing to cut. "Even I have one of those. Got it back in the sixties—too many drinks, too much love for a man who never seemed to remember my name, though I will have his forever. And let me tell you, no one, *no one* wants Willie Burns tattooed on their—where it shouldn't be."

"I have one too," Abbie said.

"You do?" Ana said, stunned.

"I regret them both."

"You have more than one?"

"Like Ellery, I got one back in the day that I'm not proud of, but thankfully it's in a place I'll never have to show anyone—don't ask. The other one is this—" She stood up and showed Ana a tiny black heart tattooed on the inside of her ring finger. "That one I regret the most."

"We live with the scars though, don't we?" Ellery said, running her fingers down the back of Ana's head in a way that made Ana want to go to sleep. "But they show we lived in the moment and have survived past it."

"I always imagine the people covered in tattoos have stories they want to tell," Ana said. "But maybe the tattoos tell them better, you know? Maybe that's why they got the tattoos in the first place."

"That's an interesting philosophy," Ellery said. "My Willie Burns story is five seconds long, and I can assure you the tattoo is mute."

Ana thought it curious that Abbie had gone back to reading the magazine, making an active choice not to take part in any more of the conversation.

"Okay, doll, I'm not going to dry it because your curls don't need it, but are you ready for the big reveal?"

Ana nodded her head as the barber chair swiveled around.

"Voilà! Very rock and roll," Ellery said.

Ana didn't recognize herself. Her hair was cut to her jawline, and her formerly long, wild curls were softer at a shorter length, with bangs that framed her face.

"Makes your eyes pop," Ellery said.

"So pretty," Abbie chimed in.

"Pretty's overrated," Ana said, still staring at herself. "But I like it."

"Splendid," Ellery said. "Shall we pick out some school clothes?"

Ellery, along with her partner, Pearl, who was tall and lanky, wearing a linen jacket and crisp white man's shirt over white jeans and a pair of worn moccasins, at first steered Ana toward the dress section, which was rife with 1960s shifts and pastel pinafores. Deeming them too frothy for her taste and meager farm paycheck, Ana chose a new-old pair of jeans, this time form-fitting and cut higher like Abbie wore hers, as well as a simple navy blue sweater embroidered with diving sparrows. She threw in a paint-splattered shirt that reminded her of Jackson Pollock, a striped long-sleeved T-shirt, and a well-worn black leather jacket that was exactly what she had always wanted.

Ellery insisted Ana try on a few dresses with her new haircut, particularly one from the 1940s that was covered in dark roses, its shoulders slightly puffed, bodice fitted, and skirt flowing to just below her knees. They'd gasped when Ana walked out of the dressing room, Abbie especially, and had demanded she add it to her purchases at a discount. Much to their chagrin, Ana added a pair of black leather ankle boots instead.

"Very Patti Smith," Pearl said.

Ana paid for her purchases with a little left over, so she asked Abbie if she could run across the street to the record shop while Abbie did her own shopping. Just as she was about to walk out the door, it swung open and in walked Rye Moon.

"Hey," Ana said.

"Holy Shesus, your hair! It looks incredible! Can't tell you how sorry I am that I ruined it."

"I kind of like it this way, so thanks for forcing me to change it up," Ana said. "Want to come with me to the record shop?"

"Would love to, but I have a hair appointment. Figured if you had to cut yours, I should cut mine too. It can be part of my new theme anyway."

"Can't wait to see it."

"Oh, hey, if you're going across the street," Rye said, leaning in and whispering, "don't forget to check out the heavy metal section."

"Why?"

"Trust me."

Ana crossed Main Street, avoiding stares from a group of girls sitting in front of the pie shop. She pushed open the door to Bungle Records but wished she hadn't. Standing in the middle of the store looking more normal than the last time she saw him was Cole Brannan, perusing the new-releases section. He was cleaner this time, in a gray T-shirt and dark jeans, his hair shorter and brushed to the side.

"Hi," he said from across the small shop.

"Hi," Ana said, remaining still. "Bye." She turned to walk out, but he yelled at her to wait as the long-haired man behind the counter glared at them through round glasses.

"Your hair is different?"

"Perceptive. I cut it."

"It suits you."

"Almost as much as my *curls*?"

"Look, I didn't mean to freak you out in the bookstore," he said. "I thought you would have put it all together."

"Put what together?"

"Where we first saw each other," he said. "It was about a month ago on the road in front of Garber Farm. You were standing by a truck out in the fields with a bunch of men. You were wearing your Hex T-shirt, and I was riding by on a motorcycle with my little sister. It was the Kinetic Sculpture parade. You waved at us."

"What?"

"You waved, in slow motion, as my sister and I rode by . . ."

"That was you?"

"Yeah," Cole said, looking down and not directly at her as he had in the bookstore.

"How would I have known it was you if you had a helmet on?"

"Good point. Anyway, you're the only person who waved at us. My sister wanted us to turn around and talk to you. I probably should have."

"Why?"

"Because we wouldn't be having this conversation right now."

"What makes you think I would have wanted a conversation then?"

He smiled the same lopsided smile.

"I think you better go," he said. "Abbie's out there looking for you. Wouldn't want you to get in trouble being seen with me."

"Why would I—"

"Guess I'll see you in school."

"I guess," Ana said.

"Looking forward to it."

CHAPTER TEN

They were supposed to ring a bell. Instead, there was a waving of hands and frantic yelling from the other side of the fields. Ana knew immediately that she was late—again. Manny assured her the morning of the first day of school would be light on the dirty work and just the usual early morning chores. But they hadn't foreseen a rain shower the night before, so she'd been sent to the green bean trellises to hurriedly pick the remaining beans, her shoes becoming soaked in the process.

She and Manny were working on the overgrown plants together, both with small buckets strapped to their waists. He taught her how to hold each stem lightly under the leaves, so as not to break them, and pull each bean one by one.

"Why can't I just pull six beans from the same branch if they all need to be picked?"

"Rushing can damage them, so take your time, little by little," Manny said.

Ana couldn't think about beans at a time like this. She needed to get ready, double-check her backpack, and help Abbie pack a lunch. Also, there was breakfast, not that she was hungry.

"Worried about your first day?" Manny asked, clueing in to her mood.

"Can you tell? Just nerves, I guess."

"It's always tough on the first day. Remember your first day here? From blackberry killer to—"

"Bean slayer?"

"I was going to say expert weeder and worm handler in training, but you've come so far, *mija*. It'll be the same with school."

"Taste it first, right?"

"*Exactamente*. And don't forget to speak up, not that you have trouble doing that here."

The very moment Ana stopped thinking about school was the moment she shouldn't have. She heard Abbie's voice in the distance as well as the sound of a whistle. She had no choice but to drop everything and run.

"We have to leave," Abbie said when Ana arrived on the front porch, hat askew and panting. "I thought they'd have sent you in by now."

"I have to change—"

"No time. I packed you a lunch, and we can eat breakfast on the way."

"But I can't go like this . . ."

"I've got your new boots, which you left downstairs. Throw those on in the van and roll up your jeans. It'll help cover the splatters of mud."

"Honestly, I *can't* go looking like this. I haven't even showered."

"No choice. We're going."

"I look like a farmhand," Ana said, catching her reflection in the passenger window.

"You are a farmhand, hon. Keep the hat. It's a look."

Ana climbed into the front seat while Abbie continued to load the back of the van. Ana changed her shoes and pulled the brown work shirt tied around her waist over the same faded T-shirt and jeans she'd been wearing for months. It was enough to pass for a normal high school outfit, on a sloppy day, she thought. She remembered how her abuela had worn the same handmade dresses for years, and how she'd changed up her look with different purses or a delicate string of faux pearls. It had never bothered her that she didn't have the money to buy something new. She had always looked dignified simply by the way she carried herself.

Ana rolled up her sleeves and put on some lavender lotion she found in the glove compartment of the van. She nibbled Abbie's oatmeal-flax banana bread and sipped from a thermos of carrot apple juice. Her old backpack was at her feet and full of books and new supplies.

"How are you feeling?" Abbie asked.

"Nervous, I guess. Like I could spew my spleen at any moment."

"You'll be fine," Abbie said. "I put together quite the brown bag lunch. You've got a roasted veggie sandwich on that rosemary bread I made last night, some kale chips—don't knock 'em, they're a tryout recipe—a pear, a granola bar if you need another snack, and a thermos of frozen lemonade."

"Wow."

"There's enough to share."

They drove toward town, sunshine machine-gunning

through the pines. Ana closed her eyes and let the light ric-ochet off her forehead.

"Gorgeous day," Abbie said.

"I've lived in perfect weather all my life—doesn't fool me for a second," Ana replied.

They turned down Common Street, and Ana's stomach lurched. When they stopped at the intersection at Main, she knew the school was just another few blocks down the road. Abbie idled at the stop sign, glancing over at Will Carson's café.

"The paper's off the windows!" she shouted, startling them both.

They both squinted and stared. The lights were off, but there were new light fixtures and bar stools along the long counter. A piece of brown paper taped to the window read CAFÉ OPEN SOON in bold block letters.

They both jumped at a loud honk behind them. Abbie accelerated through the intersection, looking particularly shaken, joining the line of cars making its way to Hadley High.

"How's Will?" Ana asked.

"What do you mean?"

"When was the last time you were over there?"

"Last week, same as always, for a delivery."

"He seems to buy a ton for a restaurant that isn't open yet."

"He's testing recipes with a few people he hired. He men-tioned something about a sous-chef coming up from Berke-ley. He wants to try my cider, but it's more for friends and not something I think I should sell."

"Why not?" Ana said, catching her breath as the cars in front of them rolled forward and the fence around the school came into view.

"He's so serious about everything I make, it's a bit off-putting."

"Maybe because he's serious about you."

"What?"

"About your abilities. I mean, let's get real; you're an amazing cook. The new spicy carrot pickles you're making? They're insane, like beyond restaurant amazing. Speaking of which, should they be Vic & Rolo's Spicy Carrots? I've been trying to come up with a label."

The van jerked to a stop.

"First-day traffic jam," Abbie said.

"I can get out and walk if that's easier."

"We need to park. The main lot is in front, so we'll pull over there. I promise not to cramp your style or give you too much of a pep talk."

Ana pulled her hat down low, peering from underneath it the way Emmett did when he didn't want to be disturbed. Students began jumping out of cars and waving good-bye to their rides. Ana wasn't the only one with an oversize backpack. Some carried their books along with just a purse or tote. There was a lot of enthusiasm, kids shouting or embracing as if they hadn't seen one another in years.

As they got closer to the school, Ana took in the green grass edging the track and football field, which was larger than she had imagined, and pristine. Beyond it stood the school, a low brick behemoth with small windows and a hanging banner that read WELCOME BACK, STUDENTS! There was a steady stream of them making their way through the double doors. More than a few girls were wearing first-day dresses. Ana was surprised not to see metal detectors at the entrance as she had at her two previous schools.

"Here we are," Abbie said, pulling into the crowded lot.

"Rye said she'd meet me here."

"I know Charlie's dropping her off on his way to the store. Did you specify a place?"

"No, I guess we didn't."

"You'll find each other inside."

Ana watched as one mother ran around to the other side of a parked car to hug a kid who looked barely old enough for high school. He had a burlap sack presumably containing his books slung over one shoulder, and was wearing an ill-fitting blazer, jeans, and a pair of cowboy boots.

"Nora! Brady! Hello, you two!" Abbie chirped out the window. Both the mother and son waved as Abbie parked alongside their beat-up pickup truck. "That's Nora and Brady Lawson. He's a smarty pants, that one, and I bet his mother wouldn't mind if you walked him in on his first day."

There was nothing Ana could say, and in truth, she was glad not to have to walk in alone. She gave the thumbs-up and hoisted her backpack out of the front seat. Abbie said her hellos before thrusting open the back doors of the van, revealing heaps of flowers ready for the morning delivery rounds.

"I saved this little bunch for you," she said, handing Ana a delicate bouquet, which Ana tucked into the brim of her hat in keeping with her summer habit.

"Still look like a farmhand?" she asked.

"Not even remotely." Abbie winked.

Ana squashed the lunch bag into her backpack and took a deep breath. Everywhere around them students were rushing toward the school. No one seemed to be hanging out in the parking lot or smoking alongside the fence. She debated whether to articulate the tickle in her stomach, as thrilling as it was foreboding.

"We're going to shake on this," Ana said, turning to Abbie.

"Okay . . ."

"I may be at the loser table by lunch," Ana said, "but I just wanted to say thanks for letting me stay. You're one of the reasons why I hoped I could."

Before Abbie had a moment to register the unfamiliar snag in the back of her throat, a bell buzzed loud and low over the parking lot.

"That dreaded sound," Abbie said. "Takes me back. You should probably get on in there. Nora! Ana will walk with Brady."

"How old is he, by the way?" Ana whispered.

"Younger than he's supposed to be and from one of the oldest farming families around. Spends most of his time indoors reading or puffing on an inhaler," Abbie whispered back.

"Gotcha."

As Abbie and Ana approached, the woman hugged the kid again, wiping away tears and genuinely inflicting a sense of terror into her otherwise determined-looking child.

"Hey, I'm Ana," she said, extending a hand toward Brady. "I'm new too. We should do this thing together, right?"

"Are you a senior?"

"Not quite. Junior."

"I can work with that. I'm Brady and I'm a freshman, even though I should probably be a sophomore. Cool backpack."

"Ditto," Ana said. "You know, I started school a little early too. It's always good to have a pal on your first day, right? I say that more on my behalf because you'll be ruling this place in no time."

Brady saluted his mother, who already had one of Abbie's

protective arms wrapped around her shaking shoulders. Ana followed his lead and saluted Abbie, who winked back.

"Get going before you're late," Abbie said. "I'm serious."

"Wanna race?" Ana asked.

"He can't run! He *cannot* run!" Nora shouted, her eyes bulging with hysteria.

"We'll walk, Mom," Brady said. "And if we're late, I'll just take Ana to the nurse and get us both free passes."

He turned away from the car and began walking, so Ana followed with a quick reassuring wave to the women they were leaving behind.

"She's the most embarrassing woman on the planet," Brady said, moving the sack from one shoulder to the other. "Your mom's way cooler."

"She's not my mom."

"Oh, yeah, duh. They only have a dog and chickens at Garber Farm. So, how are you—"

"Abbie's kind of my guardian, I guess."

"You're lucky."

"Trust me," Ana said, taking his sack from him and slinging it over her shoulder. "You're luckier than you think."

"Where's your homeroom?" Brady asked.

"I missed orientation, so I'm supposed to go to the office first. What about you?"

"Same. But I need my stuff back before we go in—don't want to look like I can't handle this."

Ana handed Brady his sack as they approached the front doors.

"Ready?" she asked.

"Are you kidding? I was born for this."

Ana couldn't help but laugh as Brady strutted into the lobby of the school, which was teeming with roaring voices and slamming lockers in the rush to class. They followed the main hallway sign pointing to the office, aware of all the curious eyeballs suddenly turned toward them. Rye Moon was nowhere in sight. As they walked, Ana realized she still had her hat on. She imagined they made an interesting duo, kind of like the pair in *Midnight Cowboy*, one of the movies she'd watched on the recommendation of her friend at the library. "You're probably not supposed to watch this, but it's necessary if you ever need to find your Miami," he'd said, quoting the film.

They walked through the door of the office and up to a dark countertop guarded by a plant with a ribbon around it and a metal lamp that looked like it had been sitting there since Abbie and Emmett's era. A woman in glasses with delicate chains hanging alongside her rouged cheeks, her hair piled into a time-machine beehive, gave them both a glance before answering a phone that didn't appear to be ringing.

"One sec," she said. "They're here, George."

She put the phone down and gave them a once-over.

"There are no hats allowed in Hadley High," she said. "You can store it in your locker until after school."

Ana took her hat off, shaking out her new haircut, checking to make sure the collar of her work shirt was covering the back of her neck. A wooden door opened and a man in a brown suit, wide-striped tie, and thick mustache walked out.

"Welcome to Hadley High." He beamed. "You must be Brady and Anna."

"It's Ana," Brady said, "Ana like you're turning *on* a light. You must be Principal Tucker. Pleasure to meet ya. Heard a lot about you from my pop."

"I heard a lot about *you* from your pop. Did you both get your locker assignments and schedule?"

"Not even a tour," Brady said.

"Well, Helen will see to that," the man said, clearing his throat. "That's Mrs. Molloy to you both."

The woman slid two pieces of paper over the counter without looking up. She flipped a switch and another bell sounded.

"Those are your schedules, along with locker assignments, combinations, and a map of the school on the back. Brady, I'll walk you to your locker and homeroom to get you situated, and I'll let you navigate on your own, Ana. You two have any questions or problems, come right on in here and see us. Pep rally's on Friday, so I hope to see you both wearing yellow and blue, the official colors of the Hadley Lions.

"Roar," Mrs. Molloy deadpanned.

Ana scanned the map, which didn't appear too daunting. She checked her schedule. "Excuse me," she said, "I'm supposed to have art class, but it says I have independent study."

"Art is full," Mrs. Molloy said, shuffling papers behind the counter.

"I was assured by Abbie Garber that I had a place."

"Brady, would you mind waiting out in the hall, please?" Mr. Tucker said.

They waited for Brady to shut the door behind him. Ana fixated on his diminutive figure outside the window in the hall just as she'd always chosen a point of focus when she knew something was about to be discussed to her detriment.

"We know your situation, Ms. Cortez," Mr. Tucker began, "I mean regarding your farmwork before and after school. I had a chat with both Mr. and Ms. Garber, and Mr. Garber and I wondered if you might need an independent hour to get your homework finished with all that you have going on. We always have such an interest in Mrs. Darnell's class, so I'm sorry to say it's already full for the semester."

"But I *need* to take art. Ms. Garber understands this more than Mr. Garber ever will."

"It's an elective, Ms. Cortez. You're welcome to use your free hour however you see fit in the library, which includes doing your own art research or finishing homework. I believe it is more than fair."

"I believe it's incredibly disappointing and never about having a choice because it's always about you people making the ultimate decision. I'm fully aware that life *isn't* fair."

"I beg your pardon?"

"Independent study is fine," she said. "I accept my fate."

Ana headed for the door; Brady saluted her through the window. She heard Mrs. Molloy whistle faintly behind her.

"Enjoy your first day," Mr. Tucker said as she left.

She gave Brady's shoulder a squeeze before making her way down the dim hallway, her new-old boots clicking along the glossy floor toward the bank of lockers. When she found her locker, she was surprised it was clean and not covered in scratched musings penned by whoever had occupied it before her. Opening it, however, revealed the familiar. Almost every surface was covered in permanent markings proclaiming it the former lair of the football team's most ardent fan with GO LIONS! or LIONS #1! screaming from every surface. She adjusted her books and wedged her hat in above them, pulling a few flowers out from the brim and poking them through a buttonhole on her shirt. "Same here and same everywhere," she whispered into the metal.

As Mrs. Molloy's voice echoed the morning announcements throughout the empty hallways, Ana followed the map to her homeroom class, which was also the same as her first-period class. Ms. Gregg, her new English teacher, waved to her from the slivered window on the door. She took a deep breath, knowing this was always the hardest part. "The audience will soon tire of the same show," she told herself. She opened the door as Mrs. Molloy announced Friday's pep rally over the loudspeaker, which momentarily diverted the classroom's attention into a rousing round of cheers. Ms. Gregg smiled and pointed to an empty seat in the second row, which also happened to be the seat directly next to Rye Moon, whom Ana barely recognized due to her very new, very short hair.

"*Hola*," Rye whispered in the chaos of everyone catching up with one another around them.

"Whoa, dude," Ana said, noticing a few heads turning in her direction.

"It's *The Little Prince* meets breathless French ingenue. You like?"

"I love! It's perfect. You're wearing lipstick."

"I know. And check out my jumpsuit," she said, sitting back in her chair to reveal what looked like an olive green flight suit tailored to her petite frame.

"You look so different."

"Told you, it's all about the mood of the season."

Another bell rang and a portion of the class exited, leaving a few seats empty. Ana took out her notebook as more and more eyes invaded her periphery. She noticed a few of them were watching and whispering in Rye's direction too. Ana turned toward her, but Rye was bent over going through her bag, making a point not to notice them.

"Take a seat, students," Ms. Gregg said.

Ana listened as those around her chatted about their summer vacations, realizing that she'd never had one, ever.

There were also audible whispers about another student, someone who'd gone away for most of the summer, as if this was something people in Hadley just didn't do. It was mostly other girls doing the whispering, with a few guys chiming in.

"I would kill my parents if they made me go away and then grounded me when I got back," said the long-limbed, long-haired girl who was sitting directly in front of Ana and talking to a group of girls. She sat with one pale leg wrapped around the other under a short blue dress the exact shade of her eyes, her wide, post-orthodontic smile perfectly frosted in pale pink gloss. Every bee seemed to buzz around the girl, every bee except for Rye Moon. Rye rolled her eyes at Ana, who smiled. Ms. Gregg continued to write on the chalkboard, oblivious to the chatter behind her.

The buzzing reached a fever pitch as Cole walked in, plenty of people in the busy hallway pausing to watch him cross the threshold. Ana suddenly knew whom everyone was tittering on about. Half the room seemed to treat him as a welcomed friend, the other half froze, pretending not to look anywhere near his direction. It was strange, Ana thought.

Cole slid into a seat nearby to the delight of the girl who curled her entire blue ribbon body in his direction. He said hello as if they knew each other, and then glanced over at Rye, whose body pretzeled back down to her book bag. Ana wished she had her old hair back because it was easier to peek out from behind it without being seen.

"Ana," he said, silencing the room yet again. "Hey."

She glanced up, careful to meet him eye to eye.

"Oh, hey," she said.

"We meet again."

"Indeed."

Both the girl in front of her and Rye shifted their attention in Ana's direction. Another bell rang.

"All right, everyone," Ms. Gregg said. "Hope you had a great summer. Let's jump right in. We're reading two novels this semester in addition to some plays, and we'll be doing essays and in-class debates. I'll know when you haven't done the reading, so do the work and prepare to be called on. Some of you may have already read what I've assigned, but I think it will only add to the spirit of our debates. First up is a book called *The Chocolate War*. Has anyone read this?"

The room remained silent.

"I see one hand in the back of the room. What's your name?"

"Dillon."

"What did you think of the book?"

"Is that the one with the kid who goes to the chocolate factory?"

The room erupted in laughter. A couple of *idiot*s and *derp*s thrown in and the sound of a loud high five.

"No, it is not, but *Charlie and the Chocolate Factory* is a wonderful story. Next up will be Jack Kerouac's classic *On the Road*. Has anyone read it or any other Kerouac?"

Ana and Cole both put up their hands.

"Two of you, great!" Ms. Gregg said. "Cole, why don't you tell me what you like or dislike about Kerouac."

"Well, I like his sentence structure and rambling way of thinking. But mostly, I like that he lived for travel and adventure, that he was all about climbing forbidden mountains, so to speak, and living life to the fullest on his own terms."

"Well said. What about you—it's Anna, isn't it?"

"Close. It's Ana," she said to whispers in the back of the room. She took a breath. Manny popped into her head, reminding her to speak clearly. "Kerouac is one of those guys you either love or hate, I guess. I'd say that my dislike comes mainly from an inability to understand his chaotic logic. A lot of people find him to be sort of a jerky inebriated degenerate, which he apparently was at times. I don't love all of his work, but what I like about him is his ability to champion the riot in people. Because we all have it inside of us, right? Some of us are just less afraid of letting it out. And Kerouac held those with fight in them, those who refused to be ignored, as the ones who were most interesting on the blank page of life. I think that's rad."

"What an interesting way of looking at it," said Ms. Gregg, nodding her head. She went around the room asking each person about their favorite novel. Ana was fascinated to hear revealing bits of background about each of her new classmates. There were more than a few mentions of *Catcher in the Rye*, and one of the guys in the back got a laugh when he said *The Boxcar Children*. Ana chose *Kafka on the Shore*, much to Ms. Gregg's delight, and to Cole's, who made a point of nodding at her when she said it. She noticed that Rye was uncharacteristically quiet through most of the class, her head down until it was time to choose a favorite book. She chose *Breakfast at Tiffany's* before changing it to *In Cold Blood*. When the bell rang, Rye jumped up and catapulted herself out the door, stopping to turn around the moment she realized she hadn't waited for Ana.

"See you at lunch?" she said, looking like she was in a hurry to go.

"Of course," Ana said, making her way to the door. "Where shall we—" But Rye was already headed down the hall.

Abbie checked her reflection in the driver's mirror. She pinched her cheeks to wake them up and put on the lipstick she found in the glove compartment.

"What am I doing?" she asked herself as she fluffed out her hair.

She carried a box of produce and a bundle of flowers across the street to Will's café.

"Great to see you again," Will said as he opened the door. "You ran out before we had a chance to talk last time."

"Migraine," Abbie lied. She followed him inside and set the box on the back counter. There were bistro tables and chairs filling the room and an oil painting of a sea captain on the far wall. "The place looks incredible," she said.

"So do you," he responded.

Abbie blushed and ignored the comment.

"I've got all kinds of goodness for you today. You wanted tubers, right? I brought sweet potatoes and sunchokes, both of which are practically popping out of the ground on the farm."

Will smiled and inspected the produce. "Beautiful," he said. "Still no fungi?"

"Not really our specialty, but I can connect you with Alder Kinman, who grows chanterelles on his property."

"I'll take you up on that. What else are you going to thrust upon me?" he asked.

"Plenty," she said, throwing him a smile, which he returned. "I think you'll find our salsify and purslane are unparalleled. And we're harvesting Asian pears and quinces. I brought both for you to try."

Will picked up a quince and sniffed it. "I can make a *membrillo* with this," he said. "You into Spanish cooking?"

"Not as much as I probably should be, but I've been making Mexican dishes at home. Ana seems to enjoy it. She also enjoys critiquing my recipes."

"I don't doubt it." He laughed. "From what I've heard, you're pretty fantastic in the kitchen. Not that I didn't guess that already."

"I brought a variety of dahlias this time too," Abbie said, changing the subject. "Thought the color palette would go with the dark grays of the restaurant."

Will crossed his arms and nodded his head. "No tomatoes? Eggplants?"

"Not at the moment, I'm afraid."

"No other types of nightshade?" he asked, looking straight at Abbie, whose body stiffened.

"No, um, can't say we have any other types of . . . of that."

He continued staring at her as she fumbled for her keys.

"I should probably get going," she said.

"C'mon . . . ," he said, leaning forward from behind the counter. "I can't just stand here without acknowledging that you are who I think you are."

"What are you talking about?"

"I'm talking about the year 1988 and the release of Nightshade's seminal album *Midnight Angel*. Correct me if I'm wrong, but you're the angel."

Abbie knew there was no way to lie or hide her way out of this. It wasn't as if anyone stopped her on the street. She was certain no one in Hadley was even aware of her brief fame, however short lived. Heavy metal wasn't something on anyone's radar anymore.

"Yes, that was me," she said, deciding to own up to it. "It's not something I'm proud of or acknowledge at this time in my life, though."

"Why not? You're one of the most iconic album cover babes in the history of heavy metal! I had you on my wall!"

"Wow. I feel naked all of a sudden."

"That's what I loved about that cover. You weren't. Nightshade got so much heat for that, remember? Just you in that white dress floating against a black background . . . it's the only album my mother let me hang on the wall. Man! If I could go back and tell my younger self that I'd one day be standing—"

"How old were you when the album came out?"

"Technically, I was eleven," Will said, which made Abbie cough. "It was my older brother's, but it was my favorite. I was obsessed with it all through my teenage years onward."

Will continued staring and shaking his head. "This is so surreal."

"You're telling me," Abbie said. "It was a darker period in my life, one I don't care to remember."

"Sorry if I kicked up—"

"No, it's fine," Abbie said, waving her hand. "I was young and on my own in L.A., running from boredom like every other groupie. I happened to be in the right nightclub at the right time, I guess, and I was up for any kind of adventure, so . . . I used to call them my 'yes' years, not that they didn't devolve into a gigantic no."

They were both quiet for a moment.

"So, we'll have parsnips and persimmons soon," she

said. "I should have batches of cider next time too. Same time, next week?"

"Absolutely. Yes."

Ana followed the crowd of people heading out the back doors for lunch. She had no idea where Rye's locker was, so she looked for her outside. There were crowded picnic tables strewn along the back of the building as well as people tucked into the bleachers above the football field. Most of the tables were occupied or seemed reserved for previously established groups. Quite a few kids were wearing Lions jackets and T-shirts, Ana noticed. She'd thought that school pride was a thing Hollywood had invented. At the far end of the row, near several trash cans, Rye Moon sat in the middle of an empty table. She waved Ana over.

"Roar," said a voice.

"How goes it, Big B?" Ana said to Brady, who was carrying a brown paper lunch bag significantly smaller and emptier than her own. "Shall we have lunch together on our first day?"

"Been waiting all morning."

"How did it go?" Ana asked, walking them slowly toward the far table.

"Pretty awesome. My math teacher made a big deal about me, but everyone was nice about it. Science is going to be a snap, but English was weird. The school is bigger than I thought. Did you get lost?"

"No, but I got stared at a lot."

"Me too. It's 'cause we've got it going on."

They approached the table. Rye was eating an apple and flipping through a fashion magazine.

"Mind if we join?" Ana asked.

"Please. I've been waiting for you forevs," Rye said. "Who's your friend with the boots?"

"I'm Brady. The boots used to be my dad's, and they've been to a rodeo. Once."

"How old are you?" she asked.

"Old enough for sophomore-level algebra even though they're keeping me in freshman. Almost old enough for you."

"I see."

"You're the most beautiful woman I've ever seen," he said, causing Rye's maroon lips to smirk upward. "I would say the same about Ana, but we have an understanding."

"Do you?"

"We're friends, kind of like life support for the first day and everything."

"Why aren't you sitting with the rest of the freshies in the cafeteria?"

"Because he's fine out here," Ana interjected with a wink.

"Of course, I just thought he might like to be around the rest of the kids in his class. They have their own weirdo table too."

"Wait, is this the official weirdo table?" Ana asked, making a joke and not realizing Rye was serious.

"Sorry to break it to you, but we're not part of the bouncy ponytail, milk and shortbread cookies crowd."

Brady gleefully sat next to Rye. Ana squeezed in across the table. She could tell something was bothering Rye and that she didn't want to talk about it.

"What's for lunch?" Rye asked.

Ana pulled out the parchment-wrapped sandwich. It was a two-handed situation, as usual, and noticing Brady's

measly lunch of peanut butter and jelly with carrot sticks
and a juice box, Ana handed him half her sandwich.

"Like I said, Abbie's zee best of zee best. What'd you
get?" Rye asked.

"Mozzarella and roasted vegetable."

"I got a dull hummus sandwich, an apple, and some spelt
cookies. Moms love to make lunches for the first day, huh?
I mean—sorry."

"No biggie," Ana said, pretending, just for a moment,
that it was true. She continued to chew, sliding the bag of
kale chips in Brady's and Rye's direction.

"I don't eat anything green," he said.

Rye pulled them in front of her. "Do you mind?" she
asked, dipping into the bag.

"Go for it," Ana said.

She popped a chip into her mouth before pushing the bag
away and abruptly looking down at the table.

"Hey, *Ryan* . . . I mean Rye," a guy in a Lions T-shirt
called as he walked to the trash cans with a group of friends.
"Like the haircut. That your new girlfriend?"

Rye didn't say anything.

"And who's this little dude?" the guy continued, to which
his friends laughed. "Your plaything?"

"We haven't played yet, no," Brady said.

"Be careful, little bro," the guy said, leaning in to whis-
per. "I bet these two like it rough."

"What's your problem?" Ana said.

"What's *your* problem," he answered to another round of
laughter. "You're the new girl from Hell-A, right?"

Ana hoped her look alone would silence the topic, but
she could feel Rye's anger and Brady's confusion, and no
one else was saying anything.

"Yeah, so what?"

"So, welcome to Hadley, bitch. Or is that 'Butch'?"

The group walked away, but not without making rude gestures. Brady looked terrified, and Rye's gaze was locked on the table.

"Unbelievable," Ana said.

"See what I mean about needing to get the hell out of here?" Rye mumbled. "It's the milkiest, most backward place in the universe. I say that literally and metaphorically with deliberate shade thrown at the amount of dairies in this town."

"My dad has a dairy farm," Brady said.

"Your dad is excluded," Ana said.

"This town practically killed off both my parents' ancestors. Why they stay here remains a mystery, especially when San Francisco seems like a much better option—I admit that selfishly—but it isn't like it hasn't changed in one hundred fifty years. None of us has ever been welcome and we were born here."

"I don't know what to say," Ana said.

"You wouldn't understand. You grew up in a sprawling metropolis full of diversity and Disneyland, and it isn't like you advertise your serape on your sleeve. Honestly, with your smattering of freckles and doe eyes, it's no wonder you're already palsy with Cole Brannan. You fit in better than anyone at this table."

"What about me?" Brady said. "I'm awesome!"

"Honestly," Ana began, taking a second to think before speaking. "Those guys will be jerks regardless of their background or yours. Ignorance can be mean. I've dodged bullets like that all my life, and it never gets easier. I've dodged real ones too."

The table behind them turned toward her. Ana hadn't realized their conversation had other listeners.

"They're just words," Ana continued. "Those idiots have no idea that the weirdo table is the most interesting one, and that's their loss. Personally, I'm glad to even have a table."

The bell rang.

"Gotta run to gym," Brady said, easing out of the table quickly. "Thanks for lunch! See you after school!" He crumpled his lunch bag and scampered toward the doors, along with everyone else sitting nearby.

"What they said . . . ," Rye said before stopping herself.

"Who cares? Let it roll off your amazing new hair, but don't come anywhere near mine."

"We should get to class," Rye said. "We can go together."

"To independent study?"

"My mom said you were supposed to be in my art class. . . ."

"They switched me out of it."

"Typical."

"*Bastardos.*"

"*Bastardos.*"

CHAPTER ELEVEN

Abbie Garber hung up the telephone and leaned against the kitchen counter.

"Hell on a hot plate!" she shouted to the various jars and bowls taking over the counter space. "*Two hours? Who does she think she is?*"

She went to the stove with her tongs and lifted the jars of peach preserves out of their boiling bath, then set them on a towel to cool. She'd dealt with last-minute orders before, but never one in such a short amount of time. Still, surprised as she was to get the call, new clients were a necessity, even if the client was Nadine Brannan. Abbie wondered if there was a motive behind it. The Brannans had never been friendly, even though they owned part of the forest behind Garber Farm, but their recent history—more specifically, the unfortunate ties binding Nadine and Emmett— gave Abbie pause. She'd said yes to the order partially

because she couldn't say no, but also because she was curious as to why she'd been asked in the first place.

"Right," she said to the cupboards. "Zucchini bread, Earl
Grey peach preserves, which I already have, and a pickle
sampler. Easy enough."

She rushed around the kitchen simultaneously cleaning
up and gathering her baking ingredients. And though it had
been a while, she switched on the stereo and cranked the
sound to energize her less-than-pleased mood.

Abbie smiled at the song, however bittersweet the sound.
She hadn't realized how long it had been since she'd listened
to music in the house, but hearing Josie's mix CD brought
her back to the last time she ever saw her best friend. They'd
been up late drinking red wine and baking, laughing about
Emmett—who was in the barn watching a baseball game—
and talking about their best kisses. Embarrassed at the
memory, Abbie recounted a clandestine moment drunk at a
hotel on the Sunset Strip. Josie was particularly wrapped up
in her own story, which remained vague in location but
rapturous in the description of "a week-long kiss." Abbie
gagged at what she could only imagine was Emmett in his
much younger years.

Abbie turned the music up, cracked a few eggs into the
mixing bowl, and began whisking away. She wondered how
long it had been since she'd had a kiss like that. She hadn't
been on a proper date in years. "Probably not since 'Barracuda' was on the radio. Jesus," she thought to herself. And
though she'd already blocked this particular daydream more
than a few times before, her mind wandered all the way
down the road and through the open doors of Will Carson's
café. She wished Josie were sitting in the kitchen with her

so they could dish about the new chef in town, dissecting his looks and gasping at his age, while swooning at the prospect of his availability. And because she knew her friend hadn't meant to destroy their friendship the way she did, Abbie indulged her imagination for a moment, pretending Josie was at the table listening anyway.

"You gonna burn, burn, burn, burn it to the wick, aren't you, Barracuda?"

She sang along while sifting her dry ingredients into the egg mixture, dancing around while beating it all together, enjoying the release. When she turned around to grab the grated zucchini, she screamed—there was someone sitting at the table. Minerva Shaw smiled and put up her hands as if to say, "Please continue." Abbie dropped the zucchini and turned off the mixer.

"Didn't mean to interrupt," Minerva said over the music. "Thought I'd wait to make my presence known until after you finish doing whatever it is that you're doing."

"Did you let yourself in?" Abbie said, switching off the stereo.

"Of course I did—rang several times, but there's no way you're going to hear me over that noise, my dear. I could hear it plain as day from the front porch. But I apologize for interrupting this moment. Lord knows we've all turned to Heart at some point or another during our middle-age crises. More of a Linda Ronstadt fan myself."

"What do you need, Minerva?" Abbie said. She wiped flour across her brow. "I'm right in the middle of a last-minute order."

"Working overtime for that strapping new chef in town? Don't blame you. Word's out, you know."

"What do you mean?"

"Well, there's no hiding it. You're over there every week and, I mean, look at the guy. Best to do what you can until the can is gone."

"He's a client," Abbie said, grabbing her loaf pans and making a point to set them down hard on the counter.

"He's calling the place The Bracken; the sign went up today. It's sure to raise many an eyebrow in these parts, let me tell you . . ."

"Are you here for cider or preserves?"

"Both. And there's another matter . . ." Minerva looked down. "That girl you have living with you. The Mexican girl."

"Yes. Ana."

"I think I might have misunderstood when she was over at the mansion that one time. Apparently, there is such a thing as Mexican Coke."

"There is indeed. I can't speak for her myself, but she was very sorry for the way she spoke to you."

"Well, I share the same sentiment and am here to make it known. You do realize I've hardly seen you since then? I fear the little misunderstanding has somehow soured our friendship, Abigail."

Abbie sighed. She didn't have time for this, but she thought it amusing that Minerva considered them friends, especially because Minerva spent her side of the relationship meddling and passing judgment. But Abbie knew, even after all of their squabbles, their years-long acquaintance was more than that. Minerva had been kind to both her and Emmett after their father died. And she'd known their mother too. "Besides," she thought, "who else do I have left?"

"So this girl, Anna—"

"*Ana*," Abbie said. "Oh my goodness, Ana! What time is it?"

"Just fixing to turn three o'clock."

"You're kidding."

"I'm not."

"Barracuda!"

Ana waited in front of the school, watching the steady stream of students filter around her in the race toward home. She remembered all the bus rides, long walks, or long waits of her past.

Ana looked for Rye on the way out of the building but realized she still didn't know where Rye's locker was. She watched the door periodically and scanned the parking lot, waiting for her to emerge. The time continued to pass—still no Rye and no Abbie, who was supposed to pick her up—so Ana concentrated on the mundane details surrounding her, hoping for tiny miracles shown only to those willing to see them. A hand in a jacket pocket pulling out a lollipop, a snapped broom discarded next to a trash can, a boy nuzzling the neck of a girl in a Jeep with a license plate spelling out DAIRYQN.

She put her hat back on and leaned against the low wall next to the flagpole, wishing Brady's mother hadn't picked him up already. She felt the same stares and kept her head dipped into her notebook, double-checking the homework she'd already finished. It was the first time she truly looked forward to her farm chores and to the ride back to the farm. It was the first time she didn't worry about looking over her shoulder.

"Nice hat."

"Of course it's Cole. Of course he's with his friends. Of

course I'm gnawing on a granola bar at this very moment," Ana thought.

"Need a ride?" he asked.

"No, thanks."

"Just hanging out by the flagpole?"

"Looks like it, doesn't it?"

"I like your backpack. Did you draw all that yourself?"

"Uh, yes, who else would have?"

"I don't know, I don't know you that well. Yet."

"No, you don't."

He continued to stand there, looking at her.

"My buddy Jim's got his pickup . . . we can drop you anywhere you need to go," Cole said as three guys in Lions jackets came into view, the very same ones she'd encountered at lunch. "There's room in the back. I'll sit with you."

"No offense, but that sounds like a death sentence— literally and metaphorically. Your friends are the worst."

"Have you even met them?" he said, taken aback.

"It's one thing to jab at the new girl, which is unoriginal at best, but making fun of—"

"I don't know what happened, but—"

"Ask them," she said, looking over at all three of the guys who were making a point of ignoring that she was even there. "Rye didn't deserve it. No one ever does."

"They said something about Rye?" Cole asked, concerned.

"You can discuss it during your joyride. I need to get back to my homework, thanks."

There was a honk. Manny pulled up to the curb in Emmett's truck, Vic and Rolo waving in the back.

"That your dad?" said the guy Ana assumed was Jim. "Or do you pay them by the hour?"

Ana shut her notebook and slung her bag onto her

shoulder. "The *worst*," she said to Cole before heading to the truck. She jumped into the front seat as Manny maneuvered around the parking lot traffic and Cole walked away with a shake of the head. His backpack was just as worn and scribbled on as her own, she noticed. He seemed to know everyone he passed, exchanging nods and high fives with a select few. Though he didn't engage with his friends, he followed them through the parking lot to an oversize pickup truck with obnoxiously tall wheels. The girl in the blue dress emerged from a car parked nearby. She encircled her long arms around his neck. They exchanged a few words before Cole climbed into the passenger seat of the truck.

"Everything okay?" Manny asked.

"Everything's fine."

"Those boys bothering you?"

"Nothing I can't handle. Where's Abbie?" she asked.

"Ran into some trouble prepping a last-minute delivery, so she sent me. Sorry I'm late. The tractor broke earlier, so Emmett said we're done for the day. I'm dropping off the guys on the way back to the farm."

"I'm not working this afternoon?"

"You're off. Not bad for the first day, no? How did it go?"

"To echo your words, 'Not bad.' Not great, either. I didn't get into the art class I wanted to take."

"Why not?"

"Because Em—. It was full."

"I'm sorry to hear it. I know how much you were looking forward to it, *mija*."

"I have independent study, which means I get to study in the library." She sighed. "The universe keeps throwing me into libraries, Manny. Not much has changed there."

"It's funny. I remember visiting my brother down in Chula

Vista. My nephew always wanted to go to the library instead of the beach, said it was more fun. Always had his face in a book; real curious, loved to learn. Reminds me of you."

"I've still never been to the beach."

"We've got one, you know. Ask Abbie to take you. It's just down the road, borders the end of the forest."

The ride back to Garber Farm was a pleasant one, Ana thought. It was a cool, crisp afternoon and what she imagined autumn should feel like. Before Manny dropped them off, Vic and Rolo opened the window behind Ana's seat to ask her about her first day. They, in turn, told her about the tractor problem and Emmett's subsequent meltdown.

"Reminds me," Manny said as they got nearer to the farm, "Emmett wants you to take Dolly for a walk before he gets back."

"Where did he go?"

"Up to Keyserville to pick up some parts for the tractor; said he'd be back around dinnertime. I don't know if Abbie's still there with Minerva, but I know she's leaving to make the delivery."

"Minerva Shaw is there?" Ana said, wishing she'd never climbed into the truck.

"She is. I'm late getting home, so I'm going to drop you at the gate if that's okay."

"I always forget you have a family. I don't mean it like that. . . . I just hope I didn't make you late."

"Never. Uncle Manny's here to help whenever you need him."

Ana took her time walking down the field road to the farmhouse. If there was one person she didn't want to see, it was

Minerva Shaw. She stopped to pick the remaining in-season blueberries as a quick snack, hoping no one was watching her from the window. When she got to the barn, she jingled the keys at Emmett's door, making Dolly bark before she let her out to run in circles in the dirt. She grabbed a leash from inside and peeked into Emmett's darkened living room. It was spare and cleaner than she imagined, with a small couch and leather chair next to a stone fireplace, a television in the corner. She tiptoed out as if it were occupied.

"C'mon, Dolls," Ana said, putting the dog's leash on and walking her through the garden to the back door of the farmhouse. She bent down to rub Dolly's head as she looked past the gardening shed to the entrance of the forest in the distance. "Stay," she said to Dolly. She went inside to unload her backpack, expecting to see Abbie and Minerva Shaw, but neither one of them was there. In their place was a bottle of Mexican Coke sitting on the counter with a note attached that read "With apologies—Minerva F. Shaw."

"No way," Ana said. She picked up the bottle not believing it was real. Though a part of her didn't want to accept it on principle, she believed the apology was sincere.

She ran upstairs, pulled the map out of the Frida book, and switched her boots to sneakers before running back down again. She unloaded half of her backpack in the kitchen, keeping her sketchbook and tossing some dog treats into it. The Coke sat there still demanding her attention, so she tossed it into her bag as well and headed outside.

"Adventure time, El Perro de Peril."

Ana had studied the map of Hadley enough to know the woods behind Garber Farm were protected lands shared with Alder Kinman and one other property much farther away over the hills. She also knew, per the map and Manny, that the forest edged out along the ocean. Dolly kept to her side as Ana made her way past the shed and closer to the entrance where there was a visible path, worn yet slightly overgrown. She stepped over some branches, Dolly sniffing behind her, and followed it in.

Birds chattered in the branches above as Ana crunched her feet down the winding path. The late afternoon light dimmed, and the sound of flowing water in the distance echoed off the tree trunks. Walls of green surrounded her on all sides as if the forest were swallowing her, she thought. She took deep breaths, stopping every now and then to crane her neck up to the towering redwoods, barely able to see their tops, let alone the sky. The forest was dark and alive, slices of white sunlight crisscrossing along the path. "There's nothing more beautiful than this," Ana thought, imagining unseen fairies floating in the dust that hung in the patches of light.

Dolly sniffed everything around them, so Ana stopped to let her explore the base of a tree that was covered in clinging moss. She bent down to take a closer look at what she thought were tiny white flowers sprouting along the visible roots but realized they were mushrooms. She pulled Dolly away as they continued along the trail. "Why Abbie and Emmett don't spend more time back here is both a mystery and a travesty," Ana said to Dolly. They came to a fallen tree in the pathway. Dolly scrambled right up, but Ana took a few tries before digging her sneakers in and hoisting herself up and over. On the other side, they found themselves at the edge of a gurgling creek. "A good place to stop," Ana said, leaning up against the fallen tree, listening to the flowing water mingle with other unknown sounds hidden deeper in the neighboring thicket.

Dolly sniffed the ground and looked up at Ana, her enormous tongue rolling out of her mouth. "Here you go, girl," Ana said, giving Dolly a treat from her pack. She walked them over to a large rock on one side of the creek and sat down in the middle of it while Dolly rested at her feet. She pulled out her sketchbook and pencil and began to shade the water onto the page, trying to mimic the way the water rolled over the rocks into a deeper pool where dragonflies danced on the surface.

Ana had never experienced this kind of solitude. "You can hear the silence," she thought as she drew in Dolly's silhouette, the dog's ears held up by minuscule fairies. She took out the bottle of Coke but realized she didn't have a bottle opener. She took deep gulps of air instead, letting the air out slowly through her nose, still not fully believing where she was. She likened it to the densest parts of downtown L.A., the trees standing in for buildings, the creek its traffic, the sun blighted by the congested atmosphere. She could almost hear the rush of vehicles, the snarl of an angry driver, until she realized that was exactly what she was hearing.

There was a blur of blue and green camouflaged by the forest foliage until the dirt bike, tipped in silver and red, leaped out of the path on the other side of the creek. It zigzagged up and down making its way to the water, filling the silence with a tremendous motorized roar. Ana remained still, grabbing Dolly's leash and standing up. The bike jumped from the path and into the water, skidding to a halt and spraying water as it passed them, before falling over along the embankment.

"Are you okay?" Ana yelled from across the water.

The rider pushed the bike up and then himself, ripping off his helmet. He sat in the dirt running his gloved hands

over his head before staring up at her. She stared back. Dolly
barked and barked.

"Are you hurt?" she asked again.

"Don't think so. What are you doing here?" Cole answered.

"Was about to ask you the same."

"I'm riding. This is our land."

"I'm sketching. This is *our* land."

"Whose?"

"Abbie and Emmett's—Dolly's," she said, rubbing the
dog's head to get her to stop barking. "Guess you took that
joyride seriously."

"I'm not joyriding, I'm testing my bike and prepping for
a race." He stood up and Dolly started barking again. He
checked his bike and propped it up before turning toward
her, arms crossed.

"What?" she said.

"Can I come over there for a minute?"

"Stay on your side of the creek, please," she said, letting
Dolly stand in front of her. "That is your side, isn't it?"

"Yep. That side's yours," he said with a smirk. "I want to
apologize."

"For what?"

"For my lame friends. I've known them most of my life,
and they've always been that way. I guess I'm just used to it."

"Doesn't excuse their behavior."

"No, it doesn't. If it makes you feel any better, I told
them off."

"My hero," Ana said, shushing Dolly again.

"Why do you dislike me so much?" Cole said. "You don't
even know me."

"Why do you keep trying to get to know me?"

He shook his head, took off his gloves, and splashed

across the creek. Dolly pulled at the leash, barking louder than ever, and when Cole got close, he knelt down and let her sniff the front of his hand. "Hey, girl," he said. Dolly licked his hand, so he rubbed the top of her head and behind her ears, and then continued crossing the creek.

"You're trespassing," Ana said.

"I'll suffer the consequences."

Cole leaned up on the edge of the rock, continuing to rub Dolly, who wanted nothing else to do with Ana. "I'm really sorry if you weren't welcome at school today. It's a small town."

"So I keep hearing."

"I've been away most of the summer and it's like I came back from another dimension. People at our school can be rather limited in their thinking, but that's mainly because they live in a bubble. I'm just putting in my time before I can get out again."

"You sound like Rye."

He smiled what seemed to Ana a sad smile.

"That your Coke?"

"I couldn't open it."

He glanced down at the ground and picked up a flat rock. "May I?" Cole said, to which she nodded her head. He wedged the rock under the bottle cap and popped the cap open before handing the bottle back over. "So, what about you? I heard you're from L.A., and I know you live with the Garbers . . ."

"Hold on," she said, taking a sip of the Coke before chugging half of it. "I thought you were gone forever," she said to the bottle. "Want some?"

"No, thanks. So, what, are you a Garber relative or something?"

"Not exactly," Ana said, finishing the bottle and putting it back in her bag, realizing then she was now full of bubbles. "I'm an intern, I guess, working on the farm, going to school, that kind of thing."

"Your family's still in L.A.?"

"I don't have any family," Ana said, having said it so many times before.

"So the Garbers are—"

"My foster guardians at the moment."

"Oh," he said with a quizzical look.

"What?"

"Nothing, it's just you don't come across like a—"

"Like an orphan? It's okay, we do exist in this post–*Oliver Twist* world."

They both stared at the creek.

"So, the Hex," Cole said, changing the subject, though for his benefit or hers she couldn't be sure. "They're way better than I gave them credit for."

"Of course they are, Bad Brains."

"How did you know I was into Bad Brains?"

Ana rolled her eyes. "Please."

"No one around here is into what I'm into," Cole said, crossing his mud-covered arms. "Well, hardly anyone. For a while I did what was easiest and just went along with the flow, being one person at school, another person after school. I've been riding bikes all my life, with my dad mostly, so I've grown up going out of town for races almost every weekend, living a double life. I've never been as close to people at school as they are with one another."

"Looked like you fit in just fine."

"That's because I know everyone."

He wanted to tell her that it was more that everyone

knew him, or thought they did. "It's always easy coming back to the places where people know your name, until you realize it isn't," he continued. "People make judgments, even if they're wrong, and it sucks when those opinions stick. It's like you can't escape your own situation sometimes, you know? Even if you're trying to move on from it."

Ana's stomach sank thinking about having to go back to L.A. at the end of the semester. She wondered which group home she'd be sent to for the holidays, which fake tree they'd force her to sit around. "I know what you mean. Sometimes it's about duality," she said. "I'm living two lives too, especially here. Where'd you go away to?"

"Back down near San Francisco, where we're from originally."

"You mean you weren't born in Hadley like everyone else?" she said with a look of horror.

"Nope." He smiled. "You and me are the city folk around here. Anyway, I was grounded for the entire summer. I spent the first part of it in Yosemite. It wasn't really my choice. My parents sent me away on one of those forced camping retreats."

"Why?"

Cole hesitated. She didn't need to know all the details, he thought, not that she'd care. "I kind of maybe started a bonfire on our front lawn that may or may not have spread. Luckily it didn't do any damage, unless you call obliterating my relationship with my parents damage. Not that they aren't capable of doing the same."

"Is that why you keep trying to talk to me? You've got no one left."

He laughed at her sad eyes and look of despair.

"That and because I think we're into the same music."

"You mean you're not mesmerized by my *curls*?"

He turned and looked right at her like he did in the bookstore. She looked back.

"I'm way more into the attitude, but yeah the curls work too. Are you going to keep giving me a hard time about that?"

"No. Maybe. Who knows? I better go," Ana said, putting her sketchbook into her backpack and calling to Dolly, who was sprawled at Cole's feet.

"Guess you're set on going 'in the opposite direction in this too-big world,'" he said.

"No, I just have to get back," she said.

"It's a Kerouac quote, lame, I know."

"What is it about guys and Kerouac?"

"*On the Road* is a great book, you said so yourself in class."

"I stand by what I said, but let's not get into some deep conversation about it because it's the only book I've finished of his other than *Tristessa*, which is a whole other conversation. His lead characters are self-centered and always himself. And don't even get me started on his possible homophobia and 'little Mexican girl' fetish. But I get that you're into it. It's written all over you."

"Wow, you have me so figured out," Cole said with a smirk that Ana felt wasn't entirely out of line. "*Tristessa* has its moments, sure, but it's poetic and sad. I think that's the point. He loves her but can't tell her, wants to help but knows it's doomed . . ."

"But what's he in love with?" Ana asked, reminding herself to take a breath. "Tristessa's a beautiful junkie who nods off all the time and won't give him what he wants."

"He's just as messed up as she is, in a different way. The

tragedy is neither one of them knowing how to hold on to the other. It's like he says, 'The beauty of things must be that they end.'"

Ana didn't know what to say. She remembered reading *Tristessa* after finding an old copy of it at the library and being intrigued by the description. She'd read it in one sitting, resisting the urge to throw it across the room at the end.

"I really have to go," she said.

"Do you?"

She was so surprised she paused. It wasn't that she didn't want to continue the conversation, as enthralling as it was talking to a guy her age about something she found interesting. The only other person Ana had discussed her feelings about *Tristessa* with was Ronnie back at the library, who had lived the tale himself. But she paused for another reason too; ashamed as she was to admit it, she liked the way Cole was looking at her.

"I'm not supposed to be back here," she said.

"Neither am I."

"Gasp! Rebels."

"Can I walk you back?" he said, making a move to follow her.

"I think I should go on my own, but thanks for the offer . . . and for the conversation."

"What about my bottle-opening expertise?"

"On point, Brannan. Just stay away from lighters."

It was a quicker walk back to the farm than she'd imagined. To her surprise, neither Abbie nor Emmett was pacing up and down the back porch waiting for her to emerge from where she wasn't supposed to be. She let Dolly off her leash and watched the bouncing yellow dog bark all the way back to the barn, its door opening to let her in and then promptly shutting behind her again. Ana walked through the garden, still lush and flowering in the cooler evening temperatures, and hopped up the back steps into the kitchen where Abbie was busy reheating a stew.

"Did you enjoy your walk?" Abbie asked, not looking up. "Emmett said you took Dolly."

"I did, into the woods. I hope that's okay."

"I'd prefer it if you let me know next time so I can show you which land is off limits," Abbie said, focusing on the stove top.

"Got it. How did it go? With the delivery."

"Made it just on time. She's a difficult client but one I can't say no to at the moment."

"Who was it?"

Abbie sighed and wiped her forehead with the back of her hand. "Nadine Brannan."

"Any relation . . ."

"She's Cole's mother, yes, and not someone used to hearing the word 'no.' Her husband owns most of the dairies around here, some of the smaller farms too—they own half this town, including the land. I don't want to get into it now, but please do your best not to bring her name up around Emmett. I'm handling her orders on my own."

"Okay," Ana said, detecting a mood, understanding why Cole might need the escape. "Can I talk to you for a moment, while you're cooking?" she asked.

"Of course."

"It's about my art class."

Abbie sighed and put down the spoon. "I completely forgot to ask how your first day went. I'm all over the place tonight. Tell me everything." She put a lid on the stew pot and leaned against the counter.

"It was fine except—"

"Was Mrs. Molloy still in the front office?"

"She was."

"Ah, the Iron Lady! She was there when Emmett and I were in school. What about English? Who's your teacher?"

"Ms. Gregg. Do you know her?"

"Don't think so."

"She seemed kind of youngish."

"Then I definitely don't know her."

"Sorry. I didn't mean it like that."

"Didn't take it like that. My English teacher is probably dead. If my prayers have been answered."

Ana laughed, a release of tension built up from the day.

"She was the worst," Abbie continued. "Everyone called her the Succubus. She used to drink from a Shakespeare goblet we all knew was filled with vodka. She sometimes fell asleep on the desk."

"Drama."

"I know. Put me on the spot once too, made me recite something from *Hamlet* like I didn't understand it."

"What did you do?"

"I performed the 'To be or not to be' speech in its entirety."

"No way!"

"It's the only thing I've ever memorized. I'm a sucker for tortured souls with daddy issues."

"Who isn't?" Ana said. "So, the rest of my classes were normal, except for art, which I wanted to talk to you about . . ."

"What about it?"

"Why did you and Emmett cancel it without telling me?"

"What are you talking about?" Abbie said, untying her apron and taking out some bowls.

"I got my schedule this morning," Ana continued, "and it said I had independent study, not art. I asked Principal Tucker and he said he talked to you and Emmett and that someone had suggested I needed a study hour more than art class."

Abbie set the bowls on the table with a clunk, her head dropping back as if she were about to scream through the ceiling.

"I'm going to school with you in the morning," Abbie said, as she began ladling the stew into bowls.

"You are?"

"You will be in that art class. Tucker owes me one. And now so does Emmett."

"I didn't mean—"

"'To take arms against a sea of troubles, and by opposing end them'!" Abbie said, flinging stew at the pale pink rhododendron print on the wall. "Men. To hell with all of 'em."

CHAPTER TWELVE

The meeting lasted minutes. Ana waited on one of the plastic chairs just outside the office, jiggling one leg over the other as she watched Mrs. Molloy perform her shuffling papers routine behind the front desk. The door opened and Abbie walked out, followed by Principal Tucker. They shook hands before Mr. Tucker made an awkward hand gesture that was somewhere between "I love you" and "rock and roll" as Abbie headed straight for the door. Mr. Tucker beamed as he scanned her from her tousled hair all the way down to the only skirt Ana had ever seen Abbie wear.

"Done deal," Abbie said once they were out of the office.

"I'm in?"

"You're in."

"How did you do it?"

"Let's just say Tucker and I go way back. I know what I'm doing," she said to Ana with a wink. "He said you have to keep your grades up with your work schedule and that he couldn't wait to see your artistic genius. I talked you up a bit, all of it true."

"It's a miracle. Thank you," Ana said, wanting to hug Abbie but deciding against it. "I should get to class. You heading back to the farm?"

"No," Abbie said, unconsciously smoothing down her skirt. "The Bracken—Will's café. He's testing a couple of brunch recipes and invited me to a tasting. It's important to keep a good relationship with business clients."

"Is that skirt appropriate for a business meeting, though?"

"Shush," Abbie said. "I'll see you after school."

They said good-bye and Ana headed down the hall, unzipping her leather jacket on her way to class. She'd never had someone stick up for her at school before, let alone talk up her strengths. "Don't screw it up," said a particular voice inside her, one she'd hoped had gone away.

She was only ten minutes late, but when she opened the door, everyone's head turned toward her in silence. Mrs. Gregg pointed for her to sit, so she did, wondering why she was commanding so much attention. Ana set her backpack under her chair as the focus shifted back to textbooks. She glanced over at Rye, who was glancing back at her.

"Where were you?" Rye mouthed.

"Where were *you*? Yesterday?" Ana mouthed back.

Rye shrugged her shoulders and went back to reading. She didn't want to explain how she'd gone straight to the library after school to avoid Cole's group of friends, nor did she want to relive the recent round of harassment. Ana took out her textbook and peeked over at Cole. He was concentrating, but without turning around, he put his left hand up and did a very discreet slow-motion wave across his book. She smiled to herself, catching Rye's eye in the process, and then hunted for the page she was supposed to be reading.

When the bell rang, there was a rush to the door. Ms. Gregg shouted out the homework while students made a wide berth around Ana's desk on the way out.

"What happened to you yesterday after school?" Ana asked.

"I had a yearbook meeting. Kind of forgot I signed up last year," Rye said, lying and noticing Cole standing behind Ana.

"Hey," he said to Rye, who didn't answer.

"I'll see you at lunch," Rye said and darted out the door.

"What's this giant storm cloud between you two?" Ana asked.

"You should probably ask Rye. Where are you heading?"

"Biology. You?"

"Opposite direction—gym."

They walked out of class together, where Ana was immediately bombarded by staring eyeballs, people making a point of getting out of her way as she walked down the hall.

"What, is it the jacket or something?" she said.

"You're the new kid, most exciting attraction in town."

"Why does it feel like every day is going to be the first day all over again?"

Ana watched the clock throughout algebra, waiting for the bell. She knew she was behind in biology and in math too, but she let her mind wander back to the moment in the woods. Why hadn't Abbie and Emmett told her they shared land with the Brannans? There was obviously something going on, not to mention Rye's hatred of Cole. If this town was as small as everyone kept saying, there had to be an easier way to find answers.

When lunch rolled around, Ana made her way outside. More and more heads were turning her way, more fearful than curious. As she walked toward the same table she'd sat at the day before, other tables fell silent.

"What up?" Brady said, putting up his hand for a high five as she sat down.

"That's the question, B. People are crazy staring at me today, like I ate too much garlic or have the plague."

"Yeah, that's probably my fault," Rye admitted, dipping a carrot stick into a container of hummus. "I might have told a harmless white lie in history yesterday."

"What do you mean?" Ana said.

"Two of those idiots from lunch were in my class saying stuff again, making it . . . difficult. They were bringing up your name too and talking about how after school you called them, quote-unquote, 'the worst,' so I might have said you had it out for them."

"Like how?"

"Specifically? I told them you were in a gang back in Los Angeles."

"You *what*?"

"It's not like they've ever been there and you are from East L.A., which is all *mi vida loca* and whatnot—I did some research last night. It made them back off, though, and it's clearly had some resonance throughout the school. The leather jacket helps. Nice touch."

"So, what, do you think gangs are all *Grease* or *West Side Story* or something? Because they're not. It's not something to joke around about." Ana immediately stood up from the table, nausea sweeping across her in waves.

"Why are you getting so upset? It worked, didn't it?"

Ana grabbed her backpack and walked away, leaving her lunch on the table.

It wasn't as if she hadn't spent a lunch period in the girls' bathroom before. She thought it was funny how it seemed the longest or the shortest period of the day, depending on whether you had other people to spend it with. Though there were still several minutes left before the bell, she headed to art class early, just in case there were issues with the recent schedule switch. She was still shaky after what Rye said, but walking down the empty hallways helped. She hoped she hadn't walked away from their friendship entirely.

Mrs. Darnell was sitting at her desk in the art room sipping a cup of black coffee, her long gray hair hanging limply down the back of a smock splattered with paint. She was inspecting someone's watercolor painting, her face puckered like a dried lemon. Ana knocked on the open door.

"Excuse me, Mrs. Darnell?"

"What is it," the woman said, flat and measured, not looking up from the painting.

"I'm Ana Cortez, the new student," she said hesitantly. Mrs. Darnell turned toward her, resuming her concentrated inspection, her eyes creased as if staring into the sun. "Principal Tucker said to tell you I was joining your class today. I have the curriculum from yesterday, and I brought my own sketchbook and colored pencils."

"How proactive of you," she said.

"May I come in?"

Mrs. Darnell waved her hand, but Ana couldn't tell if

that meant yes or no, so she entered anyway. "Are we doing watercolor?" Ana asked.

"There are many ways in which to devise artwork in this class, Ms. Cortez." She stood up and placed the watercolor back on her desk. "My only rules are to free yourself into the work and choose whatever medium you feel would bring your vision to life. I don't believe in being held back by convention, but as I was telling the class yesterday, fundamental basics—as in the proper tools or technique—are paramount in carrying you through the craft of creation. That is what I'll be emphasizing in here."

"That sounds like something I can do. I already do a bit of drawing—"

"It's not a suggestion, it's a requirement for any work in my class," she said, floating around the room straightening the worktables and chairs. "I think you'll find it a challenge despite your enthusiasm. There will be no light assessments, no lackadaisical renderings allowed in here. Many students think this class is a break, but I assure you it is not."

"I'm really looking forward—"

"I do not accept anything less than the unleashing of the inner self."

Ana jumped as the bell rang, though her nerves were already jostled. She stood in front of Mrs. Darnell's makeshift desk, a heavy piece of wood hammered into two sawhorses, the chipped surface covered in paint splashes, art books, and glasses holding brushes and pencils. Students scurried in and found their seats, the silence in the room in marked contrast to the noise of the busy hallway outside. Mrs. Darnell made her way to the back corner of the room and adjusted something heavy on a pedestal next to the only table with two available seats. Ana crossed the room, took a seat, and fished through her backpack. When she turned around, Rye was standing next to her.

"What the *eff* happened at lunch?" Rye said. "Brady practically had an asthma attack."

"Yeah? Well, I had a life attack, or should I say life *attacked*."

The sounds of classical music wafted across the room from speakers sitting on a corner shelf. One by one, each of the heads at the front of the class began turning around, focusing on the area just behind Ana's head. Rye sat down next to her.

"Class, if I can ask you all to turn around, please."

Ana twisted in her seat and was met with a wide ceramic bowl of fruit sitting atop a wooden pedestal at eye height. An apple, banana, pineapple, and pear stared back at her, begging to be rescued from their rigid tableau.

"We did a free draw and paint session to warm us up yesterday, but this week is all about my getting an idea of each of your strengths and abilities as performed through a series of exercises," Mrs. Darnell said, pacing behind the bowl of fruit, her hands clasped behind her back. "Today, we're going to focus on still life, but not in the usual way. I want you to take a long look at this fruit bowl, commit it to memory, then turn back around and re-create it from whatever was impressed upon your psyche. Take a moment to look, reflect, then choose your instrument and begin. I want to remind you that you have forty minutes to complete this task. You may communicate with one another only to divvy up the room's supplies, but once you return to your desk, you must work in silence."

Little by little, the room grew louder as students got up and moved around to find their weapons of choice. There were shelves of pastels and charcoal, countertops stacked with various types of drawing and painting paper, and drawers labeled with everything from paint and brushes to modeling clay and materials for collage. Ana reached down into her backpack and pulled out her sketchbook and pencils, placing them on the table to a deep exhalation from Rye.

"Let's make a trip around the room," Rye whispered. "Please?"

Not wanting to attract too much attention and noticing she was the only one who had materials on her desk, Ana pushed her chair out and followed.

"What's your deal?" Rye asked, leaning over a set of drawers.

"What do you mean?"

"I'm sorry if I lied about you. No one cares."

"Yes, they do, and you know that. You're the one having to lie your way around bullies rather than ignoring them. I've been there too, I know it hurts, but instead of lying to make yourself sound better, why don't you pull a Rosa Hex and use one of her best song lyrics: 'Did I stutter? No, I told you to shut it,' and then walk away. It's worked for me before."

"Maybe you have more of a backbone than I do. Maybe you're stronger and better at handling this than I am. You have no idea what kind of hell they put me through last year."

"And you have no idea what kind of hell I've been through the last *ten* years."

"Is it a competition?" Rye asked, throwing a drawer open.

"Girls, find your materials!" Mrs. Darnell bellowed from the other side of the room.

"There's never any fabric or needles in these drawers," Rye said.

"Find something else then. Expand yourself," Mrs. Darnell said, helping a student tear up a newspaper for what seemed like no reason.

"Look," Ana whispered, "I'm not comparing either one of our situations, but you shouldn't have said what you said. Why do they keep bothering you so much anyway?"

"Why don't you ask Cole for an explanation?"

"I don't know what happened between you two—"

"No talking, please," Mrs. Darnell said from her desk.

Rye grabbed some paper and a pack of markers before crossing back to the table. Ana followed, both of them sitting down and ignoring each other. Ana took a breath and tried to block out the afternoon and envision the bowl of fruit instead. She saw it clearly in her mind's eye, every divot in the pineapple, the sensuous slope of the pear, the unevenness of the bowl as it reached up on either side and held the fruits all together in a warm embrace. She pulled out a regular pencil and began sketching. It was always easy for her to access the images, harder to enter that trancelike state where everything falls away and there's nothing but the mind and heart pushing thought into being on the blank page. Perhaps it was the classical music or desire to please, or maybe it was because her table partner had unnerved her so much, but Ana found it easy to sketch the faint trace of a once-known face onto the paper.

"Utensils down," Mrs. Darnell said, as if only minutes had passed. "Please stop what you're doing while I walk around and observe. You may chat quietly among yourselves."

"Holy Shesus," Rye said, momentarily forgetting they weren't speaking and leaning over Ana's detailed portrait of a woman carrying a bowl of fruit on her head. Though the woman's face was intentionally blurred, her expression was sad and downcast, the fruit and bowl rendered in meticulous detail, almost exactly as they were arranged in the real still life. "Those are some skills," Rye said.

Ana turned toward Rye's work. It was an unusually colorful drawing, almost childlike in its simplicity, of a faceless figure in a mini dress that was shaped like multiple upside-down bowls. Each tiered bowl of the dress was covered in a print pattern mimicking the fruit in the bowl, all rendered in their most basic forms.

"I'm better with my laptop, or with a needle and thread," Rye said.

"It's fun. I could see you wearing that," Ana said.

"Let's see the work, girls," Mrs. Darnell said, picking up Rye's drawing. "Very interesting. You broke free from your desire to use sewing accoutrements for the second day in a row, Ms. Moon, congratulations. I'm excited to see you try some different mediums this year. While I like the concept and use of color in this piece, I'd like to see you ruminate for longer and free yourself from what's most comfortable to you." She handed the drawing back before picking up Ana's, staring at it intensely.

"Can you explain to me what this depicts, Ms. Cortez?"

"It's the fruit bowl but imagined as if it were balanced on the head of a woman carrying it home to her family after a particularly long, hot day. I wanted to pair the realism with a bit of fantasy while also—"

"What in your gut made you want to draw this?"

"Well, it's what popped into my head. It reminded me of someone I used—"

"Why is the woman's face blurred?"

"I ran out of time, I guess," Ana lied. Even if she had had more time, she knew the real face was no longer as clear.

"Aren't the details incredible?" Rye chimed in.

"I will kindly ask that you refrain from comment," Mrs. Darnell said, scrutinizing the drawing before handing it back. "The technicality is good, but there's restraint here. Why is that? What is it about this woman that makes you want to blur her face? That's the meat for the bones."

She shuffled to the next table, leaving Rye and Ana silent.

"Your work is beautiful," Rye said.

"Thanks," Ana said, tucking her sketchbook back into her backpack. "Her critiques are a bit—"

"Cryptic? Get used to it."

They both sat there waiting for the bell.

"What are you doing after school?" Rye asked.

"Meeting Abbie at the café on Main Street. You?"

"Heading to my dad's store, also conveniently located on Main. Here's an idea—want to walk together?"

"Do you really want to walk with me or am I just your muscle now? I can break the nunchakus out of my locker if necessary. Or are we going old school with switchblades and our bare fists?"

"Ha-ha, very funny . . . Sure you're not meeting Cole after school?" Rye said.

"No," Ana answered, though she wondered if he'd be waiting out by the flagpole again.

"Word travels fast around these hallowed halls, and the word is you two have something *caliente* brewing."

"Would you stop? I barely know him."

"But you want to, right?" Rye pressed. "Don't worry, every girl wants to know him better. Kelsey Weaver from our English class wants to know him in the biblical sense. Trouble is, no one has a clue what they're getting into. He's not who they think he is."

"And who is he to you?"

"He's someone to avoid at all costs. Like herpes of the soul. Trust me."

The bell rang, igniting a tidal wave of departures.

"I'm sorry for what I said, even though I unintentionally raised your social profile and mine from loser table to badass table," Rye said.

"You'll need a leather jacket if you want to sit with us."

CHAPTER THIRTEEN

Abbie was surprised the first time Nadine Brannan placed an order with Garber Farm, doubly surprised when she placed a second a couple of weeks later. Nadine had only recently begun hosting parties and charity events, primarily for guests from the Bay Area or the university village up north. Hadley chatter had it that her husband, Nathaniel Brannan, was spending much of his time in Keyserville, after the purchase of two local farms. But Abbie knew otherwise.

Though their properties were close in proximity, just over the hill from each other with acres of shared land in between, there had never been the closeness neighbors in small towns often share. When Emmett Garber Sr. was still alive and struggling to keep the farm afloat, he and Alder Kinman had no choice but to sell their portion of the land to the young Brannan family from Marin County. It was a price they couldn't refuse. They divided the surrounding forest in three, each remaining respectful of the borders of that land. The Brannans agreed to build on a fraction of it, keeping the rest wild and undeveloped—unlike other plots they'd purchased and expanded into corporate farms.

Abbie thought of Nadine from time to time over the years, not that they'd ever formally met, not that she'd ever be invited to any of Nadine's soirées. But like other towns-folk, she was curious about the inside of the Brannans' enormous house. The only person she knew from the area who had even been invited was Minerva Shaw.

"Opulent," Minerva told her over tea at Monarch Mansion one afternoon. "Sprawling but tasteful—an ode to the American dream. The food was divine, the conversation quite over my head; but it was an invitation I simply couldn't refuse. I'm sure you'd find it just as enchanting if there wasn't that spot of bother."

Abbie knew all about the details of Nadine's "bother." None of the locals gossiped—in front of her at least—beyond the fact that Nathaniel Brannan had possibly run away with another woman. Whether they knew the whole truth or not was none of Abbie's concern; it was inevitable anyway. Nathaniel had left his wife for Josie. Abbie wondered if Nadine's interest in deliveries from the farm had something to do with exacting revenge on her spouse. But she decided not to question it. For the sake of her own brother's bit of bother, she was more than happy to deliver.

"Need some help?" Ana asked, removing her shoes as she entered the kitchen, then heading over to the sink to wash away the Saturday farmwork.

"Does it look that bad in here?"

"It's impressive, which is a nicer way of saying yes."

"Last-minute order again for that chef over at the Bran-nans. Nothing to do but fill it fast and deliver it quick."

"Don't you need to change?" Ana asked.

"Why?"

"Your dinner at The Bracken . . . you're having dinner with Will tonight, right?"

"Oh, that!" Abbie exclaimed, her heart suddenly racing. "I forgot about it for a moment."

"You should fance it up."

"Fance it?"

"Get fancy, gussy up, 'tip it out,' as Rye always says. Which translates to doing your hair and wearing pointier shoes. I think. Not to blow his cover or anything, but it's pretty much a date."

"It's just a quick dinner. He said it's a thank-you."

"It's a meeting," said Emmett, flinging the back door shut as Dolly whimpered out on the porch. "He likes what we've got so far, so it's more a case of selling our product and not debating what to wear. Don't forget to mention the heirloom pumpkins coming up or—"

"The barley wine, I know," Abbie said. "I'm the one who makes it every year. Think I've done well enough so far . . ."

"Yep, you're doing something all right," Emmett said.

"I was planning on washing up and throwing a sweater over these jeans."

"No—" Ana and Emmett sputtered in unison. "You're representing the farm," said Emmett.

"And it's a good excuse to wear something from the back of your closet," Ana added.

"Fine, but you do realize I have to deliver all this and be back before six . . ."

"We can do the delivery, right, Emmett?" Ana asked, but he did not answer.

"I've got it," Abbie said. "I can go to dinner as is. It's not a big deal."

"We'll do it," Emmett said.

"Are you sure?"

"I said we'll do it."

Emmett and Abbie exchanged one of their looks that Ana still couldn't decipher. It wasn't in their nature to say so, but they'd always wanted each other to be happy. For Emmett, that meant moving on from the night he lost his love, and for Abbie it meant having the courage to find hers.

"You can drop it all off at the back entrance with someone from the event staff," said Abbie, opening the oven and pulling out two loaves of bread that filled the kitchen with the scent of sweet citrus and cloves.

"Fine."

"You won't see her; she rarely comes into the kitchen."

"Despite the business she's giving us, I still think those people are ruining this town, and if he steps one foot out of that house, so help me I will—"

"Emmett," said Abbie, resting the loaves on top of the stove. "He's not going to be there. She mentioned he's out of the country for a while, so just pull around to the back, knock on the side door, and hand off the boxes. Quick and easy. I'll invoice for everything later."

"Whatever you say."

"And take a deep breath. She probably doesn't want to see you either."

It was a quiet ride out of Garber Farm. Emmett accelerated down Crescent Lane, driving faster than usual, whipping the truck around the curve of the hill as they passed fewer and fewer glowing porches, the farmland giving way to the coast.

"Is that it?" Ana said, clinging to the window and straining her eyes to take in the sea.

"Sure is. Much better in the day—" He paused. "Have you not been out here yet?"

"Nope, cooped up on the farm or inside the hallowed halls of Hadley High, Boss. But holy wow, even just watching it whir by is outstanding."

Emmett suddenly pulled off the road and turned back around. The truck bounced up and down as he drove along a roughly paved path that soon gave way to sand.

"There it is," he said.

"It's . . . wow. It's endless."

"Why are you sitting in here? Get out there and dig your feet in for a minute."

Ana creaked open the van door and climbed down, landing on the soft sand. The beach stretched out for miles in either direction. It was a treacherous coast, she thought, the waves rolling in with a whoosh and a crash and exploding farther away against the walls of jagged cliffs.

"This is unreal."

"I know it's brisk tonight," Emmett said, "but when it's warm, there's nothing better than burying your toes in the sand."

"Do you come out here often?" she said, stepping back from the incoming waves.

"Used to all the time. I still drive by, but I haven't set foot in the sand in well over a year."

They stood there watching the waves roll in and out, the water shimmering in the moonlight in the distance.

"What happened to her?" Ana asked.

"Who?"

She hesitated. "Your wife. Josie."

Emmett put his hands in the pockets of his coat and looked up at the sky. "She left," he said, clearing his throat. "Nothing more or less—said she never figured out who she was and wanted to set herself free."

"Free from what?"

"Me, mostly."

"Had you been together a long time?"

"Yep. She was just out of high school—Abbie's year—I was already working the farm. We've all known one another since we were kids."

Ana didn't know if she should ask any more questions, but she wanted to know more.

"Man, we used to have fun out here," he continued. "Used to ride our trucks in the dunes, build big ol' bonfires near the cliffs, and just stay out here all night talking, laughing, being stupid. Thing is, I never thought there was anything wrong with all this. Thought our life was nice, simple. Hell, I thought we'd have kids and all that, but Josie never wanted them. I think she just didn't want me."

"No offense, but Josie sounds like an ungrateful jerk."

Emmett did his half laugh, half snort. "She's complicated."

"How much time do we have left?" Ana asked.

"Couple minutes, whenever you're ready."

Ana bent down and began unlacing her boots. She pulled off her socks and sank her feet into the cold sand. "Un-freaking-real," she said. She wriggled her toes in and out of the sand and walked farther down toward the waves, debating whether or not to stick a toe into the receding water.

"Water's cold," Emmett said, coming up to stand next to

her in his own bare feet. "But you might as well do it if you're here."

Ana took a few steps forward while Emmett stayed back. The water crashed away from her before another wave rolled in, and though she wanted to run, she forced herself to hold steady as the chill rolled right over her feet.

Darkness surrounded them, both from the edge of the forest on one side of the road and the expanse of ocean on the other. The truck rambled on before making a sharp turn down Tidal Road.

"I'll help you carry some of the boxes to the door," Emmett said with a stitch of concern unraveling the corners of his mouth, "but I'll leave you to do the knocking and conversing with whoever answers."

"Is there anything else?"

"Like what?"

"I don't want to presume, but it feels like there's something about this place that unhinges you."

"Unhinges?"

"Ruffles. Unnerves. Tears open. Makes you want to rip things apart. I don't know, you seem angry."

"It's nothing," Emmett mumbled. "Just look at this place."

They drove through heavy iron gates and up a one-lane road dappled with light from the house in the distance. As they got closer, the road brightened and gave way to a circular driveway fanning out like an upside-down smile in front of an enormous house ablaze in lights, its multiple chimneys pumping plumes of smoke into the night sky.

"Holy—I mean, it's . . ."

"A monstrosity," Emmett said as they passed the driveway

and turned down a smaller road around the back of the house. "No one needs a house this size."

"It's grotesque, but kind of in a compelling way," Ana said, staring up at the height, which she imagined must be three stories, wondering which window was Cole's.

There were several cars parked in an adjacent lot, but Emmett bypassed it and pulled in near a side entrance per Abbie's instructions.

"Let's make this quick," he said, jumping out of the truck.

Emmett stacked the heaviest boxes and crates on a wooden bench near the door while Ana kept the flower bundle and fruit box in hand, not wanting anything to crush them. He instructed her to wait to knock until he was back in the truck, so she did, watching as he pulled up the collar of his coat and switched on the stereo. She didn't expect the door to swing open as quickly as it did, a petite woman in a tight but tasteful dress standing there, her dark hair swept up and away from her face, presumably to show off crimson lips and ears dwarfed by diamonds.

"What are you doing out here?" she asked with a terse smile. "Come in immediately."

Ana turned to motion to Emmett, but only the back of his head was visible through the truck window, the sounds of Bruce Springsteen drowning out any chance of shouting for his attention. Ana followed the woman into a small room painted a seagull gray, rows of shoes and boots lining the floor, dozens of coats hanging along the wall above them. She couldn't help but notice the pairs of muddy racing boots and motocross gear that had been given its own dedicated corner.

"Right this way," the woman directed.

They made their way through a small hallway, Ana's

shoes squeaking along the shiny hardwood floors, until they reached the largest kitchen she'd ever seen. Aside from the high ceilings and chandelier—*a chandelier in a kitchen*—there were marble countertops, walls of cabinets, and multiple ovens currently being tended to by a bearded man dressed all in white.

"That's Pascal," the woman said, pointing to the man in the pristine apron and hat. "He'll set you up and get you out on the floor. We'll be serving soon, so if you can change immediately that would be wonderful."

"But I have the delivery from Garber Farm . . ."

"Excellent! So glad she finally dropped it off. Just set it down there and one of the kitchen staff can help you bring in the rest. Again, if you can change right there, please," she said, indicating one of several doors. "There are uniforms and a place for you to hang your clothes. You can start with a tray of canapés passed around to the guests in the study, please."

Ana watched as the woman breezed out one of the kitchen doors, the clicking of her pointy beige heels fading away along with a cloying perfume neither floral nor powdery, more an exotic blend of black musk. Ana set the box on the counter.

"Excuse me?" she said to the man in the hat, who put up a hand as if to say "Wait," his other hand pulling fresh rolls from the oven.

"Jonno," he said to a slender man using tweezers to place microgreens on small squares of a gelatinous substance. The man looked up at Ana, clinking the tweezers down on the marble.

"I'm here with a delivery from Garber Farm," she said. "But the woman said I'm supposed to get changed? I have no idea what she's talking about."

He rolled his eyes and leaned in. "Mrs. Brannan thinks everyone here is some sort of help," he said in an indeterminable accent while inspecting the box on the counter. "Ah, fantastic. Pascal! All is good," he said, turning to the man at the oven then back to her. "You have other boxes?"

"They're out the door."

"I get them in a minute. Can you take that box to the pantry for me on the way out?"

"Sure. Wait, who did she think I was?"

He shrugged his shoulders. "Waitstaff? Cleaning? Dog sitting? All of the above?"

He went back to his work, so Ana picked up the box and made her way out of the kitchen, mentally kicking herself for not changing out of her farm clothes before they left the house. She opened a door to head back down the way she came, but found herself in a different hallway altogether. Not wanting to bother anyone back inside the kitchen, she continued walking, figuring the pantry must be behind one of the several doors lining the hall. There was a humming noise coming from farther down, so she followed it to one of two doors, choosing the larger of the two, which she pushed open gently with her foot.

"That's the laundry room," said a voice behind her. "The kitchen is over—"

She turned around, startled. "Hi," she said, glass jars in the box wobbling.

"Hi," he responded with confusion.

"Why are you always sneaking up on me?"

"I'm not. This is my house. What are you doing here?"

"I'm making a delivery but got lost in your castle."

Cole's face broke into a faint smile, his eyes intense. An old soul, she thought.

"This is so weird . . . seeing you in my house. You haven't really spoken to me much at school."

"I know, it's even weirder for me. Your mom seems . . . in control of the party."

"You met my mom?"

Again his face shifted. Ana couldn't tell if it was amused horror or composed rage.

"I did," she said. "She asked me to put on a uniform."

"She *what?*"

It was definitely composed rage, Ana decided. Cole looked down the empty hallway and then walked past her and pushed open the door leading into the laundry room, holding it open for her to follow him in. For some reason, her feet shuffled forward, even though her head shouted that she needed to go, needed to get back to Emmett and the truck.

"Cole, I've got to—"

"Wait," he whispered before shutting the door, taking the box from her, and putting it up on a counter. They stood in the bright white room, a washing machine moaning between them, neither one of them saying anything. "My mother told you to put on a uniform?" he asked, his voice teetering on the edge of explosion.

"Um, yes."

"Okay, I'm confused, though as you can see, I'm also wearing a uniform."

She looked down to his striped tie and buttoned-up shirt tucked into tailored black trousers, his normally messy hair combed slightly to the side. It was the opposite of his dark jeans, gray T-shirt, and faded jacket look. Still, he wore it well.

"You dress like this at home?" she asked.

"Only on Thursdays—kidding—just when my mom is

having one of her cocktail parties, and usually only when I'm in trouble. Don't tell anyone at school I'm wearing this tie."

"Or what? You'll tell people your mom tried to hire me as your butler?"

Cole's hand reflexively floated up to his face, and his fingers, covered in scratches, squeezed his forehead. "I don't know what to say other than I'm sorry," he said, barely making eye contact, walking to the other side of the small room. "My mom is a lunatic."

"It's fine—"

"No, it's embarrassing and wrong and typical."

"It's an honest mistake."

"Is it, though? She has a way of putting everyone to work, so don't take it personally. But really, I'm just . . . I'm so sorry. I apologize on her behalf."

"It was worth it just to get to see this house, which is . . . well, it's resplendent. But I'm sure you know that. Where do you keep the dragons?"

"Tonight they'll be released into my mother's lair," he said, tilting his head down to meet her eyes. "Where have you been, Cortez?"

"Around."

"You've been avoiding me at school, and I haven't seen you in the enchanted forest."

"Enchanted?"

"I'm running with the theme here . . ."

"I told you," she said. "I'm not supposed to be back there."

"I kind of hoped you'd go anyway."

"Why?"

"Because I'm not supposed to go back there either, but I went," he said, taking a step closer, "hoping you had too."

It may have been the confined space or the size of the

washing machine spinning at full speed, but Ana had to remind herself to breathe.

"I thought we were maybe becoming friends," he continued.

"I have a friend, her name is Rye; you have a friend and his name is Jim. Do you see where I'm going with this?"

He sighed. "What did Rye tell you?"

"Nothing. But what's going on between you two? Seriously. And what's the deal between your family and the Garbers?"

"It's a long story . . . two different long stories. Minor tragedies, really."

"I want to hear them."

"If I tell you, you might not want to . . ."

"To what?"

He leaned over and pressed his lips to hers. She'd had no time to react, so she gave in. It was a soft kiss, both of them holding back and surprised by what was happening.

"Sorry, I had to," he said, pulling away.

"Stop apologizing," she whispered, pulling him back.

The door swung open, hitting the wall, grazing Ana's shoulder.

"What in heaven's name is going on in here?"

They both turned around, shocked at the sight of Nadine Brannan, eyes wide and mouth agape in a silent scream.

"Mom, don't freak out."

"Excuse me. What are you doing in here, young lady? I *specifically* asked you to change and head to the study. This is unprofessional and intolerable behavior. Please get your—"

"Mom, please. She's a friend of mine from school . . ."

"She's our employee for the evening, Cole. *You* I will deal with later."

"Ana!" Emmett called from down the hall. "Ana Cortez!"

Nadine backed out of the laundry room looking as if she'd seen a ghost.

"Emmett."

"Nadine."

"What are you doing here?" she asked, confused.

"Dropping off Abbie's delivery. Now I'm looking for Ana," Emmett said.

"Who's Ana?"

"My friend you just tried to put to work," Cole said.

"I'm here." Ana squeezed past Cole and Nadine into the hall.

"Where have you been?" Emmett asked.

"They've been in my laundry room," Nadine said.

"Hello, Mr. Garber." Cole extended his hand. "We've never met before, but I'm Cole Brannan; I think you already know my—"

"I know exactly who you are," Emmett said, softening his voice in a way Ana thought odd and brimming with unspoken meaning. Even though there was visible sweat pulsing at his temples, he took Cole's hand and shook it. "What's going on?" he said, turning to Ana.

"It's just a misunderstanding. I was making Abbie's delivery, and I think things got mixed up in the kitchen."

"Indeed," Nadine said, looking at Emmett. "Does she belong to you?"

"She works—she lives with us, yes. We need to get going, let you get back to the party. I hope all is . . . I hope you're doing well," he said, putting his baseball cap back on. Ana was amused to see he'd removed it, as if in a holy place. "Abbie sends her best. Ana, shall we?"

Ana followed Emmett, but paused in the hallway.

"It was nice to meet you, Mrs. Brannan," she said, even though Nadine continued to glare at Cole. "Your house is spectacular."

"Mm-hm" was the only reply.

"Again, *we* apologize," said Cole. "I'll walk you out." He started toward her, only to stop with the squeeze of his mother's manicured hand.

The washing machine buzzed.

"Bye."

"Bye."

Emmett remained silent on the way back to the farm. Bruce Springsteen filled the truck with a quiet lament. Ana couldn't figure out what was louder or more "on fire," The Boss or her boss. Impulsively, she turned down the music.

"I'm sorry for whatever I've done to make you mad. I didn't have a choice. When I walked in she—"

"This has nothing to do with that."

"If you're mad about Cole and the laundry room, I can explain—"

"No need. Nadine made it clear as will I. There will be no more of that. I asked you to make the delivery and come straight back to the truck—"

"But I got lost—"

"I know I'm not your parent, but you are our responsibility while you're staying with us. We will not tolerate that kind of behavior in our house, as I'm sure Nadine doesn't allow it in hers. I'm not sure what was going on and, frankly, don't care to, but I don't want you seeing that boy again."

"That'll be tough since I see him at school every day . . ."

"Ana," Emmett said, raising his voice and making no effort to tone it down. "I think you know what I mean."

She kept her mouth shut, staring out the window at the dark trees.

"*No retreat, baby,*" Bruce sang. "*No surrender.*"

CHAPTER FOURTEEN

It was a late-September morning, everything still covered in dew. Ana rubbed her hands together and angled her headlamp back up into the tree as she continued clumsily picking the figs off the lowest branches. She couldn't seem to find a rhythm like she did on other trees, her mind seesawing from her troubles catching up with schoolwork to being ignored by most of her fellow classmates. And try as she might to control it, her mind continually wandered to Cole Brannan, reliving the kiss over and over until she barely remembered the details. It had been too quick, she decided, as compared with the only other kiss she'd had more than a year ago in one of the group houses. She hadn't expected that one either, nor had she reciprocated.

She glanced at the watch Abbie lent her, squinting at its worn face.

"*He terminado*, I'm finished," she said, shaking the basket full of picked fruit, eager to get back to the house and get to school. She waved to Vic and Rolo, who were on a ladder working higher up in the tree, their usual conversation on mute. She walked across the fields to Manny, who waited at the sorting tables under the tent, his breath visible in the lone overhead light.

"How's that tree looking?" he asked as Ana heaved her basket up onto the table.

"Almost clean. I think they'll have it stripped within the hour."

"Good. How are your hands?"

"I'm surviving. I don't know why you guys think I can't handle it. It's not like it doesn't get chilly in Los Angeles sometimes and it isn't like this is an arctic tundra."

Manny gave her a look.

"Yes, my hands are fine," she said.

"How's school? You never talk to me anymore, always running here, running there. I know you're busy, but how's everything going?"

"Well, I think."

"And?"

"And what?"

"That's all you've got? I know there's more swimming around in there. Don't tell me you're keeping only Vic and Rolo in the loop."

"I'm doing what you all told me to do—diligently doing my work, going to school, paying attention, doing my homework, keeping my mouth shut, coming back to do more work, going to bed early—on repeat."

"Those boys still bothering you?"

"I told you, I've got it under control."

"And when are you having any fun?"

"Fun?" she gasped in mock dismay. "Fun isn't allowed

in the vicinity of Emmett Garber. You and I both know that."

"But you've made friends, no? I saw you and Rye Moon on Main Street the other day."

"Yes, she's pretty much it, along with this other kid Brady. Other than that, I'm just trying to figure out how everything works. High school's weird. It's a battlefield of contradictions."

"I can't say I remember. Never really finished."

"I'm just trying to stay out of trouble."

"You say that as if you're worried."

"Well, this is how it normally goes. . . . I start school, I go to class and try to avoid certain people, just kind of keep to myself and go to the library, and then something pisses me off or someone says something stupid and I just can't help myself."

"Is someone bothering you?"

"Not entirely."

"Is it something else then?"

"I don't know how to say this without its sounding complicated, but sometimes I'm homesick without ever really having had a home, you know? Not to dissolve into dramatics, but sometimes I see something or meet someone who reminds me of a person I used to know or a place I used to visit, and I remember feeling safe for a time. But that feeling eventually goes away, and there's nothing I can do about it. I remind myself that all I have is me; I remind myself of this every day because that's all I'll probably ever have. I'm never going to miraculously have some mom or dad worrying about my grades or getting into college or, just, you know, being concerned about my future. Not to diminish what I've experienced here so far, because it's been amazing, and you and Abbie have made me feel very welcome, but sometimes it just hits me that I'm going to be on my own soon. It's not like it hasn't felt that way all these years, but I'm going to really and truly be alone without any other net or system to catch me or fling me to some other house or home or correctional facility. And maybe that's where I'm going to end up anyway—jail. My life has certainly felt locked and chained sometimes. What if this all goes away tomorrow because of something I do to screw it up? I'm good at screwing things up right when they're getting good. Maybe going back there is where I'm supposed to be anyway. I ask myself this question the most when I start to get settled somewhere. It's my legacy, and it's not like I still don't have some ties back there waiting to initiate me into a different kind of family, if I want it, to load the safety of a weapon into my pocket or strap it under my belt. It's written on my spine where I'm supposed to belong, and I can't seem to erase the itch that's always lingering there."

Manny took a moment before responding. He couldn't tell if Ana was finished talking or looking out into the fields searching for more words. He had trouble finding his own.

"I can't begin to understand, and I won't pretend to know what you've gone through," he said, "but you put a lot of pressure on yourself."

"I know I sound crazy."

"You don't, at all. Some things are out of our control, *mija*, especially where we came from and what we left behind. But we can choose how we react and how we move forward. You're not alone here."

"I don't want to sound ungrateful or presume that this is going to last. It's only a job, right? But it's been—" She stopped herself and inhaled, holding her breath for a moment before letting it out again. "It's been one of the best experiences of my life, in a while at least. I don't want to sabotage it. My abuela wouldn't want me to."

"Then don't," Manny said. "Simple as that."

Ana glanced at her watch again. "I'm late. Gotta run. See you tomorrow, compadre."

"See you," he said.

She ran all the way back to the farmhouse, slicing through the incoming fog with Dolly chasing behind her. It felt good to push her heels into the damp dirt, to quicken her pace and outrun her thoughts, get the blood pumping it all out of her head. She kicked off her muddy shoes and banged them against the back steps while Dolly chased a roaming chicken back to its coop. She stepped into the kitchen in just her striped socks, glad for another hand-me-down, whomever's feet the socks had once warmed.

"We've got five minutes," she said to Abbie, who was sitting at the kitchen table sipping a cup of coffee and reading a food magazine, a pair of reading glasses clinging to the edge of her nose.

"Breakfast's on the table," Abbie said, not looking up.

Ana quickly laced up her boots and washed her hands before grabbing a waffle and taking a bite while standing against the counter.

"Have a seat," Abbie said.

"No time."

"Relax. Enjoy your breakfast."

Ana sat down at the table and spooned some yogurt, along with some of Abbie's honeyed figs, on top of her waffle. She didn't know if it was the chill in the air, her chat with

Manny, or her lingering thoughts, but her chest was tight and stomach hollow even after finishing a second waffle.

"What are you reading?" she asked Abbie, knowing Abbie would never talk about Will Carson being the reason she was suddenly reading so many food magazines or why she had started talking about the Slow Food movement at the dinner table. She'd even asked Ana about food blogs, something she'd never seemed interested in but assumed high school kids knew all about.

"Oh, these gourmet magazines," Abbie said. "It's good to be in the know—for the business, of course—but I'm tired of reading about shaved Brussels sprouts."

Abbie had taken to wearing her hair more loosely and naturally in the past few weeks, Ana noticed, the effect of which made her seem infinitely younger.

"Are you working on some new stuff for The Bracken?"

"They're hounding me for some sort of 'cider collaboration,' as Will calls it."

"That sounds fantastic! Not that I've tried your cider, but it's one of the most popular products, right?"

"I like to save it for special customers."

"But he is a special customer, right?"

Abbie looked over her glasses at Ana, who continued chewing with a giant smile. She put down her magazine.

"I liked the river drawing you were working on last night," Abbie said. "The one with the bits of music coming out of the water? I found it sparse and ethereal."

"It's still a work in progress, but we've been doing life drawing in class. I just finished a pen portrait of Brady with graffiti lettering underneath. I tried to make it look like a Renaissance painting. I think it's one of my best pieces."

"Sounds intriguing."

"His mom hates it, and Mrs. Darnell thought it was too ornate and literal. I thought it was clever."

"Trust your instincts, not the critics . . . I probably shouldn't say that," Abbie said.

There was a honking at the front of the house. Ana popped up and grabbed the lunch bag sitting on the edge of the counter, throwing it into her backpack along with her sketchbook. Abbie walked her to the door and waved to Rye.

"Be careful," she said, reaching out for Ana's shoulders but patting only the sides of her arms for a second. "I've triple-checked with Della that Rye is a good driver and she insists she is, but if you feel unsafe, call me immediately."

"Okay . . . thanks."

"And, listen, I haven't discussed this with you yet, but I have a phone meeting with Mrs. Saucedo tomorrow to discuss your progress. It's not a big deal, but I want us to sit down and talk."

"That sounds ominous."

There was another honk, this time long and sustained, Rye faking a yawn while looking at a nonexistent watch on her wrist.

"We'll talk after school," Abbie said. "I'll see you at The Bracken."

"Looking forward to hearing more about the joys of salsafry."

"Salsify?"

"Face it, my version sounds way better."

Rye cranked the stereo as they made their way out of the farm in her black VW Beetle. "Isn't this the sickest and sweetest car ever invented?"

"The answer to that question is a resounding yes," Ana said, meaning it because she'd never seen a car that actually looked like its given name nor one with a bumper covered in stickers with slogans like Not Your Average Angry Girls Club and The Radical Notion That Women Are People. Ana strapped herself in. "You must be the only person in Hadley with a convertible," she said.

"Used convertible, but I have no intention of taking the top down. I like subverting its purpose."

Ana drummed her fingers against her knees in rhythm to the music, watching the farmland roll by out the window. It was her first time hitching a ride with someone her age, let alone someone with her own car.

"Let's chat," Rye said, turning down the music. "In honor of fully embracing best friendship and doing the whole ride to school together thing, I think it's time we have the whole sharing of deepest, darkest secrets moment. We need to know right up front that we've got each other's backs."

"I don't really have anything to tell . . ." Ana said, her mind going over the words "best friendship."

"You're hilarious," Rye said. "I'll start. I work at my dad's store most days after school, as you know. It's punishment and the only way I'm able to have this car. In my time there, I may or may not have stolen something—one thing, maybe a few things—that I consider collateral for having my free time taken away from me."

"What did you take?"

"I'll save that for the next month of our friendship, something to look forward to. Now you . . ."

"Honestly, I don't have anything to share."

"Then I'll prompt you. Tell me something insane about

L.A. Do you even know how cool it is that you lived there? Tell me about one of your foster homes."

"It's not what you think it is."

"Go on . . ."

Ana took a moment before answering. It's not that she didn't want to, but more that she didn't know which story to reveal, which secret to tell.

"I don't have anywhere else to go, when I get back."

"Why?"

"Because I'm in the foster system."

"I know that . . ."

"The last place I lived ended up not working out in the most spectacular of ways. That's why I'm here. It's not just an internship. If everything goes well, I can emancipate myself when I finish the job on the farm, which means I have to get a real job and go to school, but maybe get to live in assisted housing, which is kind of like a halfway house. The alternative is I get placed in a group home, which is not where any sane person wants to be."

"Why don't you just stay here?"

"It's up to my caseworker to decide, or Abbie and Emmett, I guess."

"So, you get to live with Emmett and Abbie, work on the farm every day, and then you maybe get to go live wherever you want on your own in L.A.?"

"It's not as easy as that . . ."

"Not to say it isn't difficult, because I'm sure it is, but oh my God, you are the luckiest person I know! I work a job and go to school and have to live with my parents, who are infuriating, but I still have to graduate, go to college, and *then* be given my freedom, which is like a hundred years from now."

"That doesn't sound so bad."

"You don't know the half of it. So, you're really, truly going back to L.A., then?"

"I don't know . . ."

"Do you have any family there?"

"Not really."

"What happened to your parents? Let's get into it."

Rye pulled the car into a spot in the back of the lot and threw the clutch into park, turning toward Ana and folding her hands in her lap, raptly waiting for an answer.

"We need to get to class."

"You didn't answer my question."

Ana grabbed her backpack and opened the door to get out.

"Hey!" Rye shouted. "Can you at least tell me about your ink?"

"My what?"

"Just come back in here for a second," Rye pleaded. "It's five minutes until the bell. What's the tat on the back of your neck? I've seen it, so you can't hide from this question."

"It's nothing."

"I've noticed it peeking out of your shirt sometimes. I mean . . . it's illegal, right? To have one at our age? I did some research."

"It's nothing."

"I told you my secret, now you have to tell yours," Rye said.

Ana took a moment. She unzipped her jacket and pulled her sweater down, revealing the mark just below the nape of her neck.

"It kind of looks like a mathematical symbol, like a backward three or something. What does it mean?" Rye asked.

"It's . . . hard to explain. The short story is my parents were killed. It was a gang thing. They were shot to death when I was a kid. The long story is I got this as a result of it."

"But when did you get it done?"

"A long time ago. It wasn't my choice," she said, taking a breath. "I've never shown it to anyone before, at least not willingly."

Rye wanted to ask more questions, hating herself for spreading the gang rumor about Ana. "We'd better go."

They got out of the car as the bell rang out across the parking lot and looked at each other for a second before breaking into a sprint toward the entrance of the school, laughing themselves out of breath until they stopped just outside the doors.

"Hey," Ana said.

"What?"

"I've never met anyone who wanted to share anything like that with me, so thanks for letting me share right back."

"I guess this means we're officially BFFs or whatever," Rye said with an eye roll. "Do we need to take our shirts off and bump bras or something?"

"No, but we've got to find a better meaning for that acronym."

Though she'd successfully avoided Cole outside of class per Emmett's instruction, Ana and he continued to catch each other's eyes during English period. Rye would do the usual and rush out saying she had to stop in the yearbook room on the way to her next class. Ana knew it was because Cole was still sitting in his seat waiting to talk to her.

"This is the only way I can seem to get your attention," he said as Ana gathered her things. "I'm just going to sit here and refuse to move, regardless of whether someone else needs this seat for next period or I get detention for ditching gym. It'll all be on you."

"I'm not avoiding you . . ."

"Yes, you are."

"Okay, I am," she said, slinging her backpack onto her shoulder. "Can we talk while I walk to biology? Unlike you, I can't ditch."

He stood up and looked at her in the way that made her want to ditch the whole rest of the school day. "I like your sparrow sweater," he said.

"Thanks. Sparrows are good or bad luck, depending on what you believe."

"What do you believe?"

"That we shouldn't be talking."

He grabbed her hand and led her to the back doors, pushing them open.

"Cole, I can't be late," she warned.

"Then go back in."

They stood alone outside. Cole crossed his arms and waited for her to speak.

"Emmett said I can't see you anymore."

"So?"

"So, that's a rule I can't break. I don't get a slap of the hand by Mommy . . . I get sent back to L.A."

He shook his head. "I get that my mom made a small misunderstanding into a huge situation, but it's not like she or Emmett is going to come pry us apart at school."

"And when will we see each other? You eat lunch with your same crowd, and Rye and I have ours, not that you've ever tried to sit with us. We can see each other in English class," she said, wishing she hadn't said any of it.

The bell rang. Ana closed her eyes and shook her head.

"I'm sorry I made you late," he said, moving closer to her. "And since we're late for real, why don't we just stay late?"

"Look, until you're ready to tell me what's going on with you and Rye and what's up with your mom and the Garbers, I'm unavailable." She turned and headed back inside.

"Bad luck then, I guess," he said.

"Basics, ladies and gentlemen," Mrs. Darnell said, projecting to the class, "are often the trickiest to get right."

"Not unless you're already a boring basic," Rye whispered to Ana, who tried not to laugh.

"Part of my goal in this class is to free up your imaginations by first instilling the basic techniques. Once you have them down, you'll have more tools to choose from when we're doing free creation pieces. Today's assignment is simple: draw these objects exactly as you see them. You have thirty minutes starting now."

Ana began sketching with her pencil, drawing and shading quickly, seeing the objects in her memory. Rye looked back and forth at the objects repeatedly, sighing every time her pencil hit the paper.

"He waited for you, huh?" she said.

"Who?"

"Stop being so coy polloi," Rye said, erasing the bottom half of her sketch. "I know you two like each other."

Ana didn't say anything.

"You may avoid each other like the plague within the

confines of school, but don't pretend you don't make googly eyes at each other in class. And don't tell me it's a coincidence that he suddenly decided to sit in the bleachers near our lunch table either. You guys aren't fooling anyone."

"You know what?"

"What?"

"I'm not talking about this unless you give me some information," Ana said, employing the same technique she used with Cole. "Why do you two have a problem with each other?"

"Because aside from his nihilistic tendencies and love of pyrotechnics, he's a monumental ass. Let's not even get into his motocross obsession, which is as cliché as it effing gets in these parts."

"So what, maybe you're not into the same things. I don't think he's a terrible person." Ana didn't know why she felt the need to defend him. "You're always going on about how you wish people saw you differently. Maybe he feels the same."

"You don't know him as well as I do."

"How well do you two know each other?" Something about the thought of Rye and Cole knowing each other well made Ana nauseated all of a sudden.

"He was my sort of best friend before you."

"What?"

"Yeah. We hung out all the time, but not at school. We're into the same stuff, so we'd listen to music or chill by the beach sometimes. Then he went and told everyone I was quote unquote 'not into dudes' and everything changed. He was drunk at this bonfire party at his house, which isn't an excuse if you're truly someone's friend and they asked you to keep it a secret. Anyway, he told someone who told someone else and so on and so forth and now I'm a freaking piranha in this school."

"Pariah?"

"That's what I meant. But both work."

"Did he apologize?"

"Sort of—it was the end of the year, and then he went away. But let me tell ya, no one's forgotten. Jim Tilsen called me 'psych-dyke' in the hall the other day, and Kelsey Weaver has made more than a few comments in the girls' locker room."

"Time, class," Mrs. Darnell said, making her rounds.

"Rye Moon, I'm starting with you."

Rye handed Mrs. Darnell her simple line drawing of each of the three shapes.

"What is this?"

"It's minimalism, which is how I see them."

"Where is the shading? The shadows? You would do well to spend more time concentrating and less time talking. I'd like this done again. You can come in tomorrow at lunch. Your turn, Ms. Cortez."

Ana handed her a drawing of the objects as if they were floating on water, their reflections altered by ripples underneath.

"This is an interesting concept, but the exercise was to draw the objects in an exact manner to the best of your abilities. The objects are what they are; they don't exist on another plane or in another dimension."

"But I thought it was so much more interesting this way . . ."

"Know the rules before you break them," Mrs. Darnell said, handing the sketch back. "You will join Ms. Moon tomorrow for lunch and there will be no talking."

"Oops," Rye said when Mrs. Darnell walked away. "Guess we're officially jailbirds."

"Double bad luck," Ana said.

The Bracken was empty when Ana walked in. It was still early days for the restaurant, and though they were starting to have repeat customers for breakfast and lunch, the afternoon hours were slower, the café's imported espresso machine sitting quietly. Ana loved the feel of the place, the exposed brick and dark back wall, the found artwork and roughed-up bistro tables. She wasn't one for taxidermy, but Will insisted on keeping the deer head left by the previous restaurant, and Ana appreciated that he'd taken her advice and strung dried flowers through the antlers.

"Hey, there," Will said through the window to the kitchen. "I just let the boys have a break, so I'll be right out. What'll you have? Cappuccino? Snack?"

"Sure, what are you making?"

"Welsh rarebit."

"Not really a fan of rabbit."

He laughed. "You'll like this."

Ana sat down on one of the bar stools at the counter and fished her sketchbook out of her backpack. She flipped through her work—the new label she'd made for Abbie featured a silhouette of Vic, for a batch of spicy pickled carrots, and the other was an unfinished drawing of the creek back in the forest behind Garber Farm. Will switched the stereo on. The sound of screaming guitars filled the empty café. He sang along in the back, something about kick-starting his heart.

"You're the only customer who won't mind if I put this

on," Will said, sliding a plate over to her. "Heavy metal and cooking are loves too passionate for some people."

"What is this?" she asked.

"Welsh rarebit, better known as bubbling cheese on toast."

"You sure there's no rabbit in here?"

"Positive."

Ana took a bite as Will made the cappuccino. "Unexpected and so good," she said, still chewing. "Taking something basic and flipping it."

"It's how I approach my cooking, but this is a traditional recipe. I had to learn all the classics before I could rearrange them."

"I got in trouble for not doing that mere hours ago, even though my drawing was bomb."

"Bomb?"

"Explosively good. I'm not good at much else, so I might as well be proud of what I am. Still, my teacher is hardcore. I'm relatively sure she hates my work."

"You don't think you're hardcore? It's like you don't even see yourself sitting there in your wild hair and vintage leathers intimidating as all hell to probably every boy in school. Listen," he said, setting the cappuccino on the counter before dusting it with cocoa. "I was a little older than you when I started cooking, and it was cutthroat. Why do you think I have this tattoo?" He pointed to the butcher knife inked on the inside of his forearm. "I earned this," he said, "because I fought the worst parts of myself to get to someplace better on the other side. I had guys breathing down my neck, lived in the worst parts of town, no money, never slept; it was brutal. But look at this place. Think it was worth it?"

Ana nodded as she chewed.

"Believe in your work and listen to the people who know better than you do."

"And what am I supposed to do when I'm on my own?"

"Follow your instincts and kick some ass. You've got plenty of time, kid. Until then, listen to Abbie."

"But I've got only a few more months—"

The door of the café opened and shut. Will leaned back from the counter, his entire face and body erupting into a grin. "Speak of the devil," he said as Abbie walked in, taking off what Ana noticed were new sunglasses and sitting next to her at the counter.

"What did I miss?" she said, grinning back at Will.

"We're eating rabbit and listening to metal," he said with a wink. "Can I get you anything?"

"Just making a quick pit stop on the way home. Take your time, Ana," she said, heading for the restrooms across the café.

Ana took a gulp of her cappuccino.

"Wanna know a secret?" Will asked temptingly.

"Always."

"You know who else got me through those dark moments back in the day?"

"Who?"

He pointed toward the restrooms.

"But I thought you two only met this summer?"

"Oh, I met Abbie way before that, not that she knew I existed. I talked to her every night before bed. Just looking at her on my wall gave me something to fight for. She was my first crush, but don't tell her I said that."

"Ready?" Abbie said, emerging from the back, pulling her jacket over jeans and a T-shirt that Ana also noticed were tighter and lower cut than she normally wore them. "We've got to run, but we'll see you next week."

"Or sooner," Will said.

Ana couldn't figure out what he was talking about. She reached for the envelope of cash in her backpack.

"On the house, and the tip comes in the form of a *shhhh*," Will said, putting his finger to his lips. "Find someone to fight for."

CHAPTER FIFTEEN

If the summer produce season was lively, the annual Hadley Harvest Festival was an all-out riot. Residents worked year-round perfecting their seasonal goods for the sprawling October event. Though it was Abbie's favorite day of the year, it was always a hassle to Emmett, who preferred staying home to talking to customers. But Garber Farm's booth showcased such an abundance of products that they both hoped it would be even more profitable than in previous years.

Ana and Abbie stayed up the evening before the fair hand painting a Garber Farm sign to hang over the booth. Ana drew the lettering and surrounded it in flourishes of orange zinnias and squash blossoms that Abbie punctuated with color. And though Emmett scoffed at the amount of time they were spending perfecting their creation, he couldn't argue that the work wasn't an improvement over last year's booth.

As always, Garber Farm was awake early. Abbie, Ana,

and Manny helped Emmett load both his and Manny's trucks before the two of them went ahead with the bulk of the produce. In keeping with Abbie's yearly tradition, she and Ana drove over to the Moons' to help them with their load too, as well as to share in celebratory spiced doughnuts and mugs of cocoa.

"It's going to be a long day," Abbie warned. "Be prepared to get your ear talked off and your nerves stretched thin. We're also going to have a heck of a good time." She and Ana sat in the Moons' dimly lit living room next to a crackling morning fire.

"I don't know what is keeping that girl," Della said, pulling a shawl over her shoulders. "I'm sending you in, Ana. I think you'll have better luck than I will."

Ana headed upstairs and knocked on Rye's door.

"Wake up, sleepy," she said.

"Kill me now," she heard from the other side.

Ana opened the door and found Rye sitting on her bed, a blanket over her shoulders as if she had only just awakened.

"Rising from the dead?"

"I can't even handle this morning. My dad is forcing me to wear what I can describe only as *The Shining* meets corporate rodeo." Rye thrust her tiny hands through the blanket, tossing out something plaid and something denim, along with an apron advertising Moon Pharm General Store, complete with a yellow moon. She sat glaring at the pile, her damp hair slicked to the side.

"Can you believe this?" she croaked.

"Blasphemy," Ana said. "Come downstairs and have a doughnut."

Rye threw off the blanket and hopped off her bed. She headed to the mirror barefoot and dressed only in a tank top and boy shorts. "I could just go like this," she said, scrutinizing herself in the mirror. "My nonexistent everything will only further the Ryan rumors."

"Or you can put on the uniform and give it a Rye spin. Isn't western always in?"

"Somewhere, not here, aka not on this person." Ana shot Rye a look. "Fine. Should I accessorize with silver moon earrings or go full Pharm with my vintage *Valley of the Dolls* pin?"

"Moons all the way."

Abbie's excitement and Emmett's moans predicted the Garber Farm booth at the Hadley Harvest Festival would be one of the big tickets. Ana still couldn't believe the hordes of people swarming around their tented tables, eager hands grabbing pumpkins, jars of kumquat marmalade, as well as Abbie's new butternut squash empanadas. Behind the counter, Abbie kept a batch of hard cider, along with her bottles of barley wine, reserved for those in the know who either preordered or knew to ask for them. Ana bagged produce while sometimes answering questions about everything grown on the farm, surprising herself with her own knowledge of in-season vegetables. She gave more than a few shout-outs to her coworkers in the fields and was delighted to meet Manny's wife and two kids. Vic and Rolo stopped by, enjoying their day off, even bringing Joey, who said how much he missed the farm, along with them.

"Delicata, I presume?" Will Carson asked, catching Ana off guard as he was suddenly in front of her, inspecting the bounty of squash.

"Yep. We also have butternut, acorn, spaghetti squash, and kabocha, which is new to the farm this year."

"Well, well, look who's learning her *Cucurbitas.*"

"My *what-what-itas?*"

"Winter squash," Will said, his once-longish hair newly shorn and oiled to the side, his beard trimmed and speckled with threads of gray. Where Ana once thought he looked like a lonely pirate, battered and brooding, today he resembled a forlorn sailor in his navy blue overcoat and dark jeans, every bit of him groomed and smelling of cedar and tobacco. "I've been trying to get the lovely lady's attention, but she's always occupied with other customers," he said, looking over at Abbie, who had thrown a colorful scarf over her field jacket and jeans, her hair pulled up in a bun, her attention very deliberately focused on Ellery Jonas and Pearl Parnell, who were fawning over jars of marmalade.

"Is there something I can assist you with?"

"Don't go fully professional on me, kid. I know what's lurking under that tone. Barley wine and cider," he said with a wink. "She's been coy about sharing them with me, but I've heard she's a true brewmaster."

"I'm not allowed to touch those," Ana said, even though the cases of bottles were directly under the table at her feet and Abbie had already sold several. "She's been up every night perfecting them, so I'm sure they're abnormally good, like everything else she makes."

"Darling girl!" Ellery and Pearl sang as they scooted over to Ana and fussed over the swallow sweater and vintage jeans she had bought at their store.

"Isn't she just the most fascinating creature?" Ellery said, laying a hand on Will's forearm, her pillbox hat threatening to tumble into the mini pumpkins. "I just love how you've accessorized with that scarf in your hair. It's functional yet chic."

"Devastating, simply devastating," Pearl chimed in from behind enormous glasses, one hand clutching an oversize turquoise necklace weighting down her blouse. "With that hair and such an arresting profile, you're Klimt's *Portrait of a Young Woman*!"

The ladies moved on to another booth. Will promised to come back later when "the lady" wasn't so preoccupied. The day wore on and customer demand finally began to dissipate, so Abbie allowed Ana to help out at the Moon Pharm booth. On the way there, Ana wandered the grounds, breathing in the scents of cinnamon-dusted funnel cakes and smoked meats. Vendors were selling everything from home-baked pies to hand-loomed sweaters, and there were small crowds gathered around carnival games. Ana was drawn to the one booth sitting off by itself, constructed to look like a small house, the sign above it painted in whimsical lettering that spelled out THE HONEY POT. She approached and immediately recognized the proprietor, who sat in a rocking chair on the makeshift porch, hands holding on to the straps of his overalls while he stared off into the distance.

"Hello, Mr. Kinman," Ana said.

"Squirrely! Good to see ya. Want a taste?" He dipped a small sample spoon into a jar of honey, which Ana immediately popped into her mouth, letting the honey coat her tongue before she swallowed.

"Heavenly—smooth and completely different from the last batch I tried. What flavor is it?"

"That's a well-kept secret," the man said. "Tell me, how's tricks over in Garber country? Life unspooling in prosperous directions?"

"Yep. Working hard, trying to keep my grades up."

"You've got so much swirling around in there," he said

with a swish of his hand, indicating her whole person. "Let go sometimes, don't let it rule ya. I hear you've got a hell of a painterly hand. I'm assuming you're the one who painted the sign over the farm's booth?"

"Yes, sir."

"Town needs more artists and sundry creative folk like that man from the city and his Crackin'."

"You mean The Bracken?"

"That's the one. Fine fellow. Town's all up in shoulders thinking he's going to take over the saloon, but he's got his own thing going and is respectful to his neighbors. Yep, we need more outlaws in these parts. Place used to be full of 'em until gold and greed killed the grit and gumption. But I feel the tides changing."

"How's your bear?"

"Well, he's not as spry as he used to be and has taken to wandering the forests with the owls, but he comes back to chat from time to time."

"Tell him I said hi," Ana said.

"Will do."

She continued on to the Moons' booth, which was laid out with teas and tinctures concocted by Rye's parents as well as handwoven rugs, ceramics, and tribal art. Rye was hunkered down in the back of the booth staring into her phone, one leg nervously dangling over the other, when she saw Ana approach.

"Finally," Rye said, pulling her apron off and throwing her fuzzy black sweater over the plaid shirt and jeans. "Let's blow this joint."

"Rye—" Charlie Moon said with a grim nod.

"Come on in, Ana," Della interrupted, ushering Ana behind the booth.

"You win for booth beautification," Ana said. "Hands-down favorite next to Alder Kinman's honey."

"Potty break," Rye announced, causing her father to add a sigh to his nod. "We're taking a fairgrounds walk, a pit stop, and then we're going to check out the fireworks later, okay?"

"That's fine," Della said. "Just make sure you let Abbie and Emmett know where you are and be back right after the show."

Rye and Ana made their way across the grounds, avoiding recognizable faces from school, most of whom eyed the twosome as if they were either something to mock or be wholly frightened of—Ana couldn't tell. They stopped at the Lawson Dairy booth where Brady appeared to be holding court in an oversize suit, jabbering on to chuckling customers.

"Grade-A chocolate milk—best in town, folks!" he shouted.

"Looking good, little man," said Rye as she and Ana sidled up to the counter.

"Where have you been?" Ana asked. "You haven't had lunch with us in a week."

"Taking care of business, as you can see. Oh, and I've been devoted to Hessie Wakefield. She's tall for her age, but we're both in FFA together."

"Sounds scintillating," Ana said.

"On the house, ladies," Brady said, sliding over two small cups of chocolate milk before resuming his sales pitch to the constant crowd.

Ana and Rye continued to stroll with their milk, sipping and making fun of various members of the football team paying to arm wrestle a burly-looking logger. The sun dipped down behind the tree-covered hills, the air nipping at their rolled-up sleeves. They avoided Jim, Kelsey, and the rest of Cole's group of friends, who were laughing over by the rides. Though Ana didn't want Rye to notice, she kept her eye out for Cole.

"We need something stronger than milk," Rye said, "especially for the fireworks. I figure we've got about an hour before we head up to the graveyard on the hill. It's the best view in town."

"What do you have in mind?"

"Oh, you know, maybe something to *enhance* the multi-colored brilliance in the sky."

"I'm not following . . ."

"Can be found in the forest? Sometimes you have them in soup?"

Ana continued to blink at Rye.

"They're *magic*ally delicious?" Rye said before sighing. "'Shrooms. I know a couple of people who get them in the forest and sell them during the fair specifically for this purpose."

"Oh," Ana said. "Yeah, I can't."

"But they're from the earth; it's not like we'll be dousing our tongues in acid or sticking needles in our arms or anything."

Ana took a breath. "Sorry, not into it, have to say no."

"For someone who's spent time on the mean streets of an urban metropolis, I'm surprised you have no game when it comes to having fun sometimes. It's so not a big deal. People at school have done them."

"I can't jeopardize my place here. They'd send me back if they found out. Plus, I don't want to. But you're more than welcome."

"No buts, I get it. I'm going to the ladies. Do you need to?"

"I was going to head over to the food trucks," Ana said, lying, hoping she'd run into Cole.

"Why don't I meet you back at my parents' booth? We can grab a bite on the way to getting our fireworks on. The best spot is all the way up that hill behind the church on the other side of Main. We'll have to walk a ways, but it's worth it for the view. I'll stop and tell Abbie and Emmett you're going with us before making my way back."

Rye took off toward the restrooms behind Hadley High's football field. Ana wandered back toward the carnival games, curious to check out the tarot card woman sitting cross-legged on a Persian rug in front of a sawed-off tree stump. There was a line, just like at every other booth, so Ana turned back around to return to the Moons'.

"Hey," Cole said.

"Hey," she answered, doing her best to act as though she weren't happy to see him.

"How are you?" he said, doing the same.

"Fine. But then again, you see me in class every day."

"And yet you still haven't spoken to me since the last time we talked, so . . ."

"Turkey legs."

"What?"

Ana told her brain to tell her mouth to stop making a fool of herself. "Are you in line for a turkey leg? Because the entire concept seems surreal to me."

"I was just walking up to the graveyard," he said, putting his hands in his jacket. "Where are you headed?"

"Same place, apparently. What a coincidence."

"Indeed, you might say. But then again, the tarot lady probably just foretold this moment."

They stood there catching eyes catching them standing

in close proximity. Ana suddenly couldn't remember if she was supposed to meet Rye back at the Garbers' or the Moons' booth or if they were meeting up on the hill. There were whispers shooting up around them.

"C'mon," Ana said, grabbing his arm, surprising herself and Cole and everyone else pretending not to watch or listen.

They walked side by side through the crowd, weaving through the fair toward Main Street, dodging curious looks from students and townspeople alike. Cole grabbed her pinky finger, and she let him.

"Did you work today?" he asked.

"Yep," she said, ignoring Alder Kinman's thumbs-up as they passed. "I'm guessing you did not. Do you ever?"

"Well, racing is like a job, or used to be. I'm not really on the circuit this year. But to answer your question, yes, my family has a wine booth at the fair. My mom's doing tastings from some new vineyard my dad bought."

"Your dad bought a whole vineyard?"

"His second one. I'm pretty sure he bought it as a guilt gift for my mom. And she doesn't care as long as it makes her more money. But, yes, I do have to work."

"Is your dad helping out?"

"My dad helps out by staying away."

They crossed through the carnival games area, bypassing a group of fellow classmates huddled around a table in front of the ice cream truck. Ana noticed Kelsey Weaver noticing them, her head dipping down behind a group of girls.

"I have an idea," Cole said, grabbing her hand and leading her in the opposite direction. They dashed through a mass of people carrying plates full of fair food. He squeezed her hand and she squeezed back before they ducked behind

Minerva Shaw's booth, which was dripping in dangling butterfly paraphernalia.

"I can't go in here," Ana said.

"Why? She's giving away free masks to the kids. Grab two and we'll go incognito the rest of the way. I need to get something from our booth. Be right back."

Ana peeked between booths and saw that the Brannans' stand was just across the pathway. Nadine Brannan was pouring wine to multiple middle-aged sippers, her pencil skirt and heels still in place. Minerva's table was busy too, with parents ushering their children in for last-minute face paint or butterfly masks.

Ana positioned herself at the corner of the booth, hoping to grab a few masks without Minerva noticing. But Minerva Shaw noticed everything.

"Well, hello, *Ana* Cortez. Or should I say, *'Hola'*?"

Ana forced herself to smile. "Hello, Mrs. Shaw."

"Call me Minerva, dear. Are you enjoying the fair?"

"Immensely," Ana said. She turned to look for Cole but didn't see him.

"Well, I'm sure the Garbers are selling out of everything as usual, what with all of the local fans like that Will Carson. Tell me," she said, taking a moment. "Did you happen to receive the little present I left for you on Abbie's counter?"

"I did. It was a surprise, a good surprise."

Ana didn't want to seem rude, but she couldn't help but remember what Minerva said to her that day at the mansion.

"I'm glad. It was not my intention to overreact, and certainly not to such a spirited young person new to town. I hope you can forgive my ignorance. I hope we can start over again."

Minerva clapped her hands and grabbed the cheeks of a little boy whose mother she seemed to know.

"Lookee here, Charles Watson, this is Ana Cortez," Minerva said, gesturing toward Ana as if she were part of a puppet show. "She comes all the way from Los Angeles. Isn't that exciting? Her ancestors come all the way from the great land of Mexico. That's pronounced 'Meh-hee-co' in Spanish. Can you say 'Meh-hee-co'?"

The little boy laughed and pointed to the butterfly masks. Ana grabbed one and handed it to him.

"*Mariposa*," Ana said. "That's 'butterfly' in Spanish."

The little boy laughed and ran with the mask, his mother close behind.

"You're certainly good with the little ones," Minerva said.

"I've had a few foster siblings."

Minerva gave her a warm smile, genuine and apologetic. "Looks like your friends are waiting for you," she said. "My, my, is that Cole Brannan?"

Ana turned to see Cole and who she assumed was his younger sister approaching.

"Do you mind if I take a few masks, Mrs. Sh—Minerva?"

"Take what you need, dear."

Ana grabbed them and met Cole halfway.

"Hey, this is my sister, Camille," he said. "She wouldn't let me walk away without meeting you."

"Hi," Camille said with a quick wave of the hand. She looked to be about thirteen, petite with long dark hair and a dress Ana was certain her mother had forced her to wear. "I like your sweater."

"Thanks," Ana said. "I like your dress."

"It's hidge," Camille said.

"Aka hideous," Cole said. "This one would much rather

be slashing around on her dirt bike right now than handing out winery brochures."

"Truth," Camille said.

"I don't know if this is your thing, but do you want one of these butterfly masks?"

"Totally!" Camille took it and put it on. "Now I can come with you guys and Mom won't notice."

"No can do. We're heading out, but I'll see you later, okay?" Cole said.

"You're seriously going to leave me behind?"

He nodded.

"You do and I'll tell Mom you have wine hidden in your coat."

"You do and I'll tell Mom you went off trail last week."

Camille gave Cole a dirty look and walked away.

"What are you doing?" Ana whispered.

"Having fun," he responded. "Let's get lost."

"I don't think it's a good idea . . ." Ana didn't want to get caught for stealing wine, especially from Cole's mother.

"Believe me, she'll never know it's gone. She has cases of this stuff at home."

He put on his mask and grinned. She shook her head and put on the mask as they wound their way toward the exit of the grounds. Ana kept an eye out for Rye, who was nowhere to be found, not even at the Moons' booth.

"Don't worry, she'll be there," Cole said. "Everyone will."

They kept walking down a deserted Main Street as the streetlights flickered on.

"Bold move, Brannan," Ana said, pulling off her mask. "So, are you going to share what you have stuffed in your pockets?"

He smiled and pulled out two mini cans of sparkling wine.

"Honestly, they look and taste like soda. Pack a pretty weak punch."

They popped the small cans open and continued strolling past the bookstore.

"So, where are you taking me?" Ana asked.

He took her hand again as they cut across Main Street. They passed Monarch Mansion and a few houses before heading into a children's playground near the stone church, tossing their cans and watching a group of people making their way up the hill in the distance. Cole walked over to the swings. He grabbed the chains and pushed off from the ground. Ana kicked off in the swing next to him. They swung back and forth in silence, higher and higher, watching the sky bleed pink over the town. Ana remembered being on a swing set once. There was a sudden gasp in her throat and a feeling like she wanted to jump. She dragged her feet in the dirt and came to a stop.

"What's the matter?" he said.

"Long time since I've been on a swing set."

"Me too."

"Playgrounds were never that fun for me as a kid."

"We can go somewhere else," Cole said, worried.

"No, I like it here." She wanted to add "with you" but didn't.

"My mom left me on a playground swing once," Ana continued. "I don't know why I remember this, but I was so little, and she just left me there for hours, I think."

Cole put his head down, his hair falling into his eyes. "I don't know what to say to that."

"It's insane?"

"I was going to say 'cruel,' but yes. My dad slapped me across the face once. I lost a race on purpose, and he slapped me. I think it surprised him more than me. He never did it again."

Cole couldn't believe he'd just compared his situation to Ana's.

"It's always the thought of why they did it that stings the most, right?" Ana said.

"Exactly. Like how for a split second, while their reflexes were making the decision, you didn't factor into their action at all."

They both sat there for a moment before slowly swinging again.

"If you don't mind my asking, where's your dad?"

"Oh, he's out and about tending to his priorities." Cole didn't feel like it was his place to talk about the circumstances of his father's departure, especially when the Garbers clearly hadn't told Ana about it.

"It's weird, but there was a time when I went with it— everything—without much care," he continued. "I kind of wish I was still like that now."

"I know what you mean."

"I was in with the groups at school, went to the house parties, kind of walked through it all in a numb daze. It was a break from the racing. It's a lifestyle more than just a sport, something my dad and I have been doing since I was a kid, you know? And I was just burned out. He was always pushing me to ride. I would hold the weight of the bike over these jumps, my adrenaline choking every part of me. One day, I kind of snapped out of it and asked myself why I was doing it. Was it for me or him? I thought it was for us both, but then he started going out of town more and not being available. He didn't even notice that Camille wanted to race more than I did."

"Are you okay with your dad now?"

"I don't see him that often because he's always off with—with work. It's civil," he said in a way that Ana couldn't tell was sad or resolute.

"We should find Rye," Ana said, but noticed Cole's disappointment at the mention of Rye's name. "She told me about what happened, you know."

"What did she say?"

"That you outed her at some party. She's hurt by it."

Cole took a breath and stopped swinging. "Yeah, I screwed that up masterfully."

"You know she's still dealing with it, right? People at school are taunting her and saying things. It's not right."

"It was an accident, a stupid one. I trusted the wrong people, drank more than I should have—not that that's an excuse. I've apologized, gone over there, sent her letters over the summer . . . she won't forgive me."

"Can you blame her?"

They both continued swaying lightly on the swings as it grew darker. There were audible voices up on the hill cheering for the fireworks to begin.

Cole bumped his swing into Ana's. "Shall we get going?"

"Sure," she said, bumping him back.

He pushed his swing over to her as far as it would go. "Are you going to help me out here?"

She pushed her swing out to meet him.

Though they both hesitated for a moment, knowing what was coming, someone leaned in first and they kissed. It was a real first kiss this time, quiet and deep. And if there were fireworks, neither one of them noticed.

"Yo, Cole!" someone shouted. "Put it away, dude!"

They parted.

"My friends are here," Cole said with a sigh.

A group of guys and girls approached, Jim and Kelsey among them. Every single person eyed Ana with curiosity.

"Ana, this is everyone," he said. "Everyone, this is Ana."

"We've got beer, dude, and so much more," a guy in a sweat-shirt said. "Let's crack it all open before the show starts."

A couple of guys jumped around on the merry-go-round pretending to surf at high speed while the group of girls unfurled a blanket in the grass.

"We don't have to hang out with them," Cole whispered, though she knew he probably wanted to stay.

"I'm going to go find Rye," she said, getting up from the swing.

"You looking for your little friend?" Kelsey approached, her hair swinging from side to side behind her. "She's up on the hill near the cemetery tripping balls. Bought a double portion from Dillon and took twice the amount we did. Maybe she'll do us all a favor and fall into an open grave."

Ana refrained from saying or doing anything that might get her sent back, no matter how much she wanted to punch Kelsey Weaver right in the mouth. Manny's voice popped into her head, telling her it wasn't worth it. Instead, she started running and didn't stop until she made it out of the play-ground and past the church, the sounds of laughter trailing behind. She took a breath at the base of the stone steps leading up to the cemetery and then ran up them, two at a time, as a loud boom rang out overhead, bright lights guiding her way. She passed shadows of people on benches in and around the old gravestones, but she kept climbing, knowing Rye must be up there. There were rows of people clustered across the top viewing area so she kept heading up. Just before reaching the top, Ana peered down to take in the

graveyard, which cascaded down the hill. The fireworks illuminated the gravestones and the various people, making
it an eerily wondrous sight.

"More," she heard someone say up ahead. "Glitter. Stars.
And more, please. I'd like some mo', please!"

All by herself, on a long and empty bench, was Rye Moon
stretched out like a contented cat. There was another loud
boom and another before pops and crackles across the sky.

"Rye?" Ana called out, running to the bench. "It's me.
Are you okay?"

"Well, look who it is—it's my old pal come to rescue me
on the wings of a Pegasus." She was calm, a faint smile on
her face.

"Can you stand? I'm going to take you back down the
hill."

"I can walk, silly. I'm not trapped inside my brain. Whoa.
Wait. Did you see that over there?"

"Over where?"

"The man sitting on the grave," she said, her voice going
quiet. "I think we've summoned him from the dead, like a
séance. I think he has something to tell us."

"It's just a man, a real man, watching the fireworks with
his girlfriend."

Ana reached down and scooped her up, throwing Rye's
arm around her shoulder, walking her across the cheering
crowd to the top of the stairs.

"I thought you forgot about me," Rye said. "Electric flowers! Do you see them? Magical mysteries igniting the sky
like comets of gold from heaven!"

"We all see them, they're just fireworks."

"We must sit," Rye said, her legs buckling as she oozed to
the ground.

"I've got you," Ana said. "We're going to take this step by step."

"I got me, you got you."

Rye stood up and took a few steps but stopped, transfixed by the sky and then by a nearby gravestone, which she reached out to touch.

"Rye, can you tell me what you took?"

"Silly string bin."

"Did you take mushrooms?"

"That's what I just said. I took the mushrooms, introduced them to my mouth and then swallowed. How we got to this stone planet is beyond my comprehension, but isn't it grand?"

The fireworks exploded again overhead, massive starbursts igniting the valley and trees below. Ana put her arm around Rye, remembering someone telling her once that it was important to make someone in an altered state feel taken care of and in a safe place. "I'm here," Ana said, to which Rye burst into laughter.

"I love you," Rye answered, trying to catch her breath. "Really, really mean that. We are joined here together on Planet Fate. Let us pray."

"Ana!" Cole shouted from the bottom of the stairs. He bounded up before she had time to tell him to stay where he was.

"It's you," Rye said. "A real American hero. Have you come to take me back to my home planet? Let's all stay on this one."

Ana gave Cole a look that said, "Yes, it's that bad."

"Wait. I'm detecting vibes. He's *your* hero, not mine," Rye said to Ana. "He's taking you and leaving me, and there's no water on this planet!"

Cole bent down and hoisted Rye up into his arms. She

gave a squeal before letting her head fall on his chest and again erupting into a fit of giggles. They made their way down step by step, fireworks still bursting overhead.

"About what happened back there—"

"Let's not," Ana said.

"Kelsey's kind of jealous and had no right to say that."

"Kelsey is a wretched person. Why you went out with her is beyond me."

"How did you know I went out with her?"

"We did a séance," Rye said. "The dead have risen. She is one of them."

As they got closer and closer to the bottom, Ana spotted the same group of Cole's friends running around and screaming in the playground. "Is there a way we can avoid them?" she asked.

"We'll have to go backward to go forward, but it's only two blocks out of the way."

"Where are you guys taking me?" Rye asked. "Let's go to Disneyland! Ana? Can you fly us there on your back?"

Cole struggled to hold Rye. She wriggled to the ground at the bottom of the stairs and remained still for a moment. The last of the fireworks rained down from all sides, and Rye suddenly burst into a sprint. She ran for half a block before stopping in the middle of the street and opening her arms to the sky.

"Stay where you are!" Ana shouted as she and Cole ran to catch up.

"Rye? How much did you take?"

"Little baggie," she said, sitting down on the curb. "I can't go home like this. I don't even have my helmet for the journey, and there are elephants in the sky."

Ana and Cole sat down on either side of her, neither one of them knowing what to do.

"I think we should go back to the booth," Ana said.

"I don't think that's a good idea."

"It's you," Rye mumbled. "It's *you*," she repeated, looking from one to the other. "Everything makes sense now!" She attempted to stand up again, but sat back down grabbing her head as if she were trying to make sense of her thoughts. "You and you are two," she continued before doubling over in guttural giggles. "Like father, like son, right, Coley? I'm supposed to hate you, but I don't. I miss you. Why did you fly away? Wait. Shhhh. You guys, I need to fly away. Someone has to fly me home. *Now*."

"C'mon," Cole said, keeping his calm. "We're all going to walk back together."

They started walking down Main Street toward the fair, each of them holding one of Rye's hands. The street was still empty, people beginning to trickle in through the side streets up ahead. Ana glanced at Cole. He gave her an "everything will be fine" look.

"I'm going to be murdered tonight," Rye said. "Did you know that?"

"Shhhh, you're fine," Ana said, putting her arm around Rye's shoulders.

"I have to hide. My dad's going to murder me. My mom's going to give me a life sentence. I have to go. I have to go!"

"We have to do something," Ana said as Cole stopped Rye from breaking into another run. "I can't be late. We're both supposed to be back right after the fireworks."

"What do you suggest we do? Take her to her parents?"

"No!" Ana and Rye said simultaneously.

"There," Ana said, pointing up ahead. "We're going to The Bracken."

They walked Rye to the café. The light was on, but the door was locked. Ana jiggled it before knocking on the window.

"Are we getting sandwiches?" Rye asked.

Will peeked out from the window of the kitchen and immediately came out, followed by Abbie. They made their way to the front door.

"No, no, no," Rye said. "No Abbie!"

"Keep calm," Ana said.

"What's going on?" Will said unlocking the door. "Come inside. Is everything all right?"

"Ana? Are you okay?" Abbie asked. "I was about to head back to the fair. I'm . . . I'm glad you found me on the way." She looked just as guilty of something as Ana did, both of them acknowledging they weren't where they were supposed to be.

"Rye's not feeling well," Ana said, both terrified and relieved by Abbie's presence.

"What's going on," Abbie said confrontationally, her anger directed at Cole.

"Whoa," Rye said. "That dead deer is dancing under a halo of flowers up there. This planet is way better."

Will tried to suppress a smile.

Abbie looked from Ana to Cole before turning to Rye. "Hey there, lovely girl," she said, softening her voice. "How you doing?"

"Are you going to murder me?"

"Of course not, sweetie, we're here to spend some time with you. Doesn't that sound fun?" She put her hand on Rye's back and rubbed it. "We're just going to chill in that booth over here, drink some tea, and listen to some music. How does that sound?"

"That sounds nice."

She walked Rye over to the booth and sat her down, sliding over a small vase full of flowers for her to look at, then walked back to Ana and Cole at the counter.

"Mushrooms or LSD?" she asked.

"Mushrooms. A small bag's worth," Cole said.

"We didn't know what to do or where to take her," Ana said.

"And you? Are you on anything?" Abbie took a moment to scrutinize both Ana's and Cole's eyes.

"No," Ana said. "We're trying to help."

"I'll make some tea," Will said and headed back to the kitchen.

"My parents are going to murder me," Rye said from the booth.

"Cole, would you mind pulling the shades over the windows? The street is about to fill up again." Abbie turned to Ana. "What happened? I want a full explanation."

"I lost Rye at the fair but ran into Cole. So, we walked to the cemetery because that's where Rye said we were supposed to go anyway. We found her like this."

"Were you drinking?"

"What? No."

Abbie took a long look at Ana, who forced herself to remain calm despite the lie, worried that this would certainly be her last night in Hadley. "Go have a seat," Abbie continued. "Be very encouraging and soothing with her. Keep it light and positive."

"Here's the tea," Will said, setting it down next to Abbie. "I'd let it cool a bit first."

"Abbie?" Rye said. "You can't tell my parents. Please, please don't get my parents."

"Music," Abbie commanded. "Something soothing or melodic and complex. No heavy metal."

Will nodded and went back into the kitchen.

Ana was floored by Abbie's all-knowing confidence. She seemed to know exactly what to do, giving orders while keeping her focus on Rye the whole time.

"Cole, I think it's a good idea if you head home now," Abbie said, the sounds of the café's regular bluesy soul music floating out of the kitchen. "We can take it from here."

"I want to help," he said.

"I know you do, hon," Abbie said. "But I think it's best if we handle it."

Cole nodded and glanced at Ana, giving her a wave.

"Thanks for your help," Ana called out, watching him walk out the door.

"Here's how it's going to go," Abbie said. "You're going to stay here with Rye and Will. I'm going to handle Emmett and the Moons. Rye will sleep at our house tonight. Do not let her wander, but if she wants to eat, that would be helpful."

"Am I in trouble?" Ana asked

"That's yet to be determined."

"You guys," Rye said, leaning over the top of the booth. "It's like we're floating in parallel universes."

CHAPTER SIXTEEN

No one slept well at Garber Farm that night. Ana awoke later than usual. There was no farmers' market the day after the festival, so Abbie had suggested she sleep in. They'd been up with Rye for part of the night, most of which involved Rye begging Abbie not to call her mother. They'd listened to music for a while before Rye fell asleep on the couch. Ana had tossed and turned all night, playing the day's events over and over again in her mind.

When she woke up, she showered quickly and changed before heading downstairs. It was dark all over the house, including the kitchen. Abbie wasn't there and Rye wasn't on the couch. She flipped on the light, lit the flame under the teakettle, and sat at the table and waited. She tried to focus on reading a homework assignment, but her mind kept wandering to Cole, Rye, the fireworks, and the way it all ended, awkward and confusing, her stomach still sick with worry. There was a light rain falling outside. She heard the van pull up. Abbie came through the back door, shaking her wet coat out and then sitting down at the table. Her eyes were red, as if she hadn't slept.

"Morning," she said.

"Good morning—or not so good," Ana said. "Where's Rye?"

"At home. Begged me the whole way not to say anything, so I just dropped her off at the door." Abbie ran her hands through her hair and stood up to make some tea. "Not telling my best friends that their daughter was at my house coming down from a mushroom trip is not one of my finest moments. Nor is this situation something you should be involved in. We have a scheduled call with Mrs. Saucedo this evening and, to be honest, I have no idea what to say."

"Maybe we shouldn't say anything, like Rye said."

Abbie sighed. "This is so not what I planned," she said. Ana wondered if she should substitute "you" for "this" because she felt somewhat to blame. "I want to discuss last night through with you step by step. Now that I know about you and Cole—or can assume I know enough—why don't we start with that."

"There's nothing going on," Ana said.

"You and I both know that's a lie."

Ana's mind zigzagged. Though she'd been up for most of the night rehashing what she might say to Abbie, especially because she and Rye had been separated in the farmhouse and hadn't been able to go over their stories, her mind drew a blank as to what she should say next. She stared at the placemat, concentrating on the colors, telling herself over and over not to run outside or back upstairs.

"You're right. I'm sorry," she finally said. "I should have told you that Rye and I were with Cole for the fireworks."

"From what I've heard it was just the two of you."

Again, Ana remained silent.

"I heard from Minerva Shaw that you and Cole made quite the pair at her booth."

"She gave us masks. I think we even came to an understanding about the whole Coke situation . . ."

"Regardless, Rye told me you two were supposed to meet but you disappeared. She said she looked for you and later found you with Cole. How she ended up taking psychedelic drugs remains a mystery that neither one of you has been able to answer. I'd like you to fill in the blanks, please."

Ana didn't know whether she should be honest about Rye's offering the mushroom experience to her first, and that she had declined. She didn't know how much she should emphasize she had nothing to do with Rye's choosing to do what she did. And she certainly didn't know Rye would tell Abbie about her and Cole.

"Yes, I was with him," Ana said, in a low voice. "We're friends, which doesn't seem like a crime to me. I lost Rye, ran into him, and when we couldn't find her, we went up to the hill where we were planning on meeting her anyway."

"She said you were gone a long time."

"I guess we lost track of time talking."

"That's why I gave you my watch."

Ana ran her fingers up and down the placemat, the tops of her bitten fingernails snagging the woven threads.

"This still doesn't explain the mushrooms," Abbie continued. "Where did they come from?"

"I don't know."

"Ana, I want you to be honest with me and tell me where they came from."

"I heard one of the kids say someone named Dillon, but I wasn't there when she got them."

"What about Cole?"

"He wasn't there either."

Abbie's face was flushed. She took a sip of her tea and rubbed her eyes. "Everything was going well until last night. I thought we had an agreement. I thought you and I were on the same page. I don't know what happened, or whose fault it was, or if there were two or three of you, but I do know this . . . you are not allowed to sneak around with Cole again. I realize I have no control over you at school, but Emmett and I have discussed it, and we think it's best to limit your social activities at this point."

"What does this have to do with Cole?"

"It's complicated, and I don't want to get into it right now, but he is not a positive influence for someone in your situation. You will continue to do your work, go to school, and to follow our rules. Do I make myself clear?"

Ana squeezed her eyes shut. She refused to look up as much as she forced her mouth to remain shut. Abbie seemed far away, the farmhouse too, as if it had transformed into every other foster home she'd been to.

"Think what you will, but I'm not interested in drugs," Ana said flatly. "Never have been, never will. My mother and father did them and dealt them. Did you know that? And then they were both shot for them. I was right there on the floor holding on to my mother's hand, trying to shake her awake. I stayed like that for an entire day. When I say I don't know what happened with Rye, I don't. I never meant to make you upset. I never meant to be in that situation. I take full responsibility for my actions, but Cole and I did nothing wrong."

Ana had spent most of the day upstairs, and to Abbie that was worrying. Ana had refused to come down for lunch or to answer her door. Abbie remained downstairs and got on with her chores. Had she been too harsh? Should she have called Della and Charlie anyway? Abbie paced across the kitchen, just as she had as a teenager.

She knew a bit about Ana's past from correspondence and conversations with Mrs. Saucedo, and they both agreed not to dwell on what was in Ana's file. Knowing what she now knew about Ana's parents, though, she wondered if she would have still said yes to Ana's coming to the farm. "What am I thinking? I absolutely would," she said to the kitchen sink as she scrubbed it. "Over and over again."

"Hi," Ana said sheepishly, walking into the kitchen.

"Did you get some rest?" Abbie asked, putting down the sponge.

"I did some sketching."

"May I fix you something to eat?"

"I'm not hungry, thanks."

Abbie thought she should say something about Ana's parents. Should she apologize for Ana's loss or tell her she was there if Ana ever wanted to talk?

"I need some fresh air," Ana said. "Do I still have permission to take Dolly for a walk?"

"Of course," Abbie said without hesitation, not knowing what else to say.

Ana walked out the back door, and Abbie watched her cross the garden path. The phone rang. Abbie continued to watch as Ana put the leash on Dolly. She listened to Della say that Rye had told her everything about the night before. She was no longer allowed to spend time with Ana. "I understand," Abbie said, continuing to stare out the window as Ana smiled and whispered something into Dolly's ear. She wondered how to break the news as she listened to the

rest of what Della had to say. "I understand," she said again,
then hung up. Abbie wasn't allowed to come over anymore
either.

Ana leaned against the rock at the side of the creek waiting
for Dolly to finish drinking. "Why does nothing ever go the
way it's supposed to?" she asked to the dog, frustrated she
hadn't brought her sketchbook or snacks. She waited, paying
attention to the time on her watch, hoping Cole had thought
of the same thing. After twenty minutes, she decided to
forge on. She led Dolly through the creek before joining the
path again, traversing steep inclines until there were signs
of the sunset up in the distance. They stopped for a moment,
just listening, the sound of whooshes and roars up ahead.
"That's where we're headed, Miss D," Ana said, rubbing
Dolly behind the ears. "We're going to catch the last of the
light in the sky and bring it back with us."

They walked on until the trees began to thin out, giving
way to a grassy hill. The ground underfoot became sparse
and sandy, and the roars grew louder up ahead. She wrapped
the leash tight around her wrist and the two galloped toward
the water in the distance, the sun a dull round spotlight
hanging just above the waves.

"Un-freaking-believable," she said to Dolly, to herself, to
the beach down below as they stood at the edge of a small
cliff, the ground dropping off and giving way to miles and
miles of ocean. They were close to the spot Emmett had
taken her to. She led Dolly down the side of the hill, steep
in parts and slippery, but they made their way carefully
before jumping down into the soft sand. The flatness of the
beige beach stretched out on either side of them; there was

nothing and no one as far as Ana could see, just choppy waves and the lapping of water in and around the rocky cliffs of the coast. She unleashed Dolly, who then unleashed herself, bounding into the edges of the water before running up and down the beach with incredible speed, her bark announcing the pair's triumphant arrival. Ana plopped down, removed her shoes, and sank her toes into the sand. She didn't care that it was cold or that she'd forgotten a scarf. She took deep breaths and watched the waves.

The memories began to roll back, like they hadn't in weeks. She thought about the concrete building she'd lived in as a child, the one with the shattered windows, and about the lone hand hanging off the edge of the couch, its fingernails chipped red against the floor. She fast-forwarded to her abuela's kitchen, her onetime home, to the unwrapping of caramel candies, the scent of burned tortillas coated in butter and cinnamon waiting at the end of a school-day afternoon. She instinctively reached behind and scratched the base of her neck. "The mark of them," she thought to herself.

How much longer could she last in Hadley? What was left in L.A.? Was she always condemned to return?

There were barks followed by a roar in the distance, this time not from the waves but from a dirt bike riding along the ridge. She called Dolly, who refused to budge, transfixed as she was by the buzzing up above, the bike jumping up and over small boulders close to the edge. The bike stopped and the biker stood still for a moment before he kicked it back to life and made his way closer. Ana grabbed Dolly and put the leash back on, watching and waiting as Cole parked the bike before heading down to the shore.

"Hey," he said.

"Hey," she responded.

She threw her arms around his neck and willed him to hold on to her. He tightened his arms around her waist and kissed her lightly on the neck.

"Don't let go," she said.

"Wasn't planning on it."

They held on to each other for a moment longer, Dolly barking in circles.

"You're shaking," he said. "Come sit closer to the rocks."

They walked farther in and sat down in the crevice of the cliffs away from the wind; Dolly stretched out at their feet.

"How did it go?"

"I'm not sure, actually. I haven't seen or heard from Rye. I'm not supposed to see you anymore either. Again."

"Figured as much."

He reached over and took her hand.

"I think this is my fault," Cole said. Everyone else in Hadley was aware of all of his mistakes except for Ana, he thought. She looked at him without seeing his family or his history, and in turn he did the same. "How are we supposed to stop right when we're getting started?"

"Maybe it's like you said, or like your buddy Jack typed; maybe there's beauty in the ending."

"I'm good at those."

"Me too."

He pulled her close. They watched the waves.

"Rye and I used to be friends, good friends," he said, wanting to tell her everything. "We used to hang out in the forest near the creek. I don't want you to feel weird about this, because it's in the past, but I had the biggest crush on her. I used to follow her around all the time, probably too much."

"No surprise there. It's one of your most annoying characteristics."

"Ha. Yeah. So. We were close, like we hung out together every day, went to the movies together, liked the same music . . . You already know she's the only other person in our school who's remotely interesting. Anyway, we became close friends—the closest thing to a best friend, I guess—and she tolerated my feelings for her. She also tolerated my trying to kiss her one night, which was terrible and awkward, and then we had this intense talk."

"About what?"

"Rye never spoke to you about this? I thought you were the new me?"

"We're relatively new best friends, and I'm still coming to terms with that concept."

"She's conflicted, you know? About her sexuality, about a lot of things. It was hard coming out to her parents, but they took it well from what she said."

"Rye's not very Hadley," Ana said with a laugh. "Not that it has anything to do with who she wants to make out with."

"Nope, but she's stuck here like the rest of us. I think it affects her differently from how it affects you and me. She's tough but super fragile too, not that she'd show anyone that side of herself. But she showed me, and then I went and . . . I didn't mean for what happened to happen. Like I told you, I got drunk at my own party, which was typical last year. One of my friends started bothering me about Rye, pestering if we were doing it, etcetera, and he just wouldn't shut up. So I told him that it wasn't like that, that she wasn't like that. I don't even remember exactly what I said, but word got around school, as things do around here. I didn't know how to make them stop."

"Uh, you tell them they're being horrible and stand up for your friend. That's a start."

"I know," he said. "But it didn't work out that way. I wouldn't have even taken my own apology."

Ana was quiet.

"I've got to go," she said.

"Now I feel like I've messed this up too."

"You and I are both good at making messes," she said, kissing him lightly on the lips before taking Dolly's leash. "But we need to get better about cleaning them up."

"Do you want to get out of here?" he said. "Like forever?"

"Forever's a long time," she said, standing up.

"Where are you going?"

"I need to get home."

CHAPTER SEVENTEEN

It was a silent ride to school but for the sound of the stereo. Abbie had been strangely quiet since the night before. When Ana returned from the beach ready to talk, to be open, to do all the things Mrs. Saucedo said she should do to make her situation better, she stepped into the empty kitchen and found a plate of food next to a note that said, "Had to run out, please eat without me." It had been strange too that Abbie hadn't returned by bedtime, so Ana set her alarm and tried to stay awake as late as she could. When there was still no Abbie early in the morning, she fixed herself a bowl of cereal and met Manny out in the fields for her chores before returning to find the van idling and waiting to take her to school.

They passed the Moons' house. Ana saw Rye's car in the distance, but Abbie remained focused on the road. Ana thought it strange she hadn't heard from Rye or that Abbie hadn't received word from Della. Maybe all turned out well, she hoped, and Rye kept the whole mess of Saturday night a secret. Still, something didn't feel right and she couldn't dismiss whatever it was hanging in the air of the front seat. "Clean it up," she reminded herself as she watched the fog hovering over the trees.

"What are we listening to?" Ana asked.

"Some mixtape I've had forever."

"Who's the singer?"

"Bonnie Tyler, I think."

"She sounds emphatic, don't you think?"

"*I need a hero, I'm holding out for a hero 'til the end of the night. . . .*"

"I don't know, wasn't paying attention, hon."

"Why doesn't she just be her own hero? I mean, why is she waiting for some knight on a steed when she could get a steed herself?"

"It's just a song."

"I've been thinking since, you know, everything that happened on Saturday, that I need to maybe be more open with you and Em—"

"We're here," Abbie said, pulling into the school parking lot. "Look, hon, I haven't known how to tell you this, but things didn't go well with the Moons yesterday." She parked the van and turned toward Ana. "I don't know what was said, but Della isn't happy with the situation and we need some time for everything to blow over."

"What do you mean?"

"She wants you two to spend some time apart."

"But I didn't do anything. I mean, I probably should have looked in more places to find her, but . . . I don't know what I did wrong." She couldn't hold it in. The tears were there, so she let them come, wiping at her cheeks.

"We'll talk about it after school, but I need some time to sit down with Della and figure this all out. I'm trying to understand what happened too."

"But I told you what happened!" Ana said, the tears coming faster, harder. "I'm trying—I'm trying to fix it! What more do you want me to do?"

The bell rang loud and low. There was laughter and rushing around outside the door of the van.

"We'll talk after school. I'll see you at The Bracken."

Ana opened the door and slammed it shut. She walked across the parking lot as she wiped her face, taking deep breaths to calm herself before going inside. She cleaned herself up at her locker and made her way to homeroom, going over what she would say when she saw Rye. When she got to class, Rye's seat was empty, so she sat down and opened her sketchbook.

"Guess my wish came true." Ana looked up as Kelsey Weaver slid into the seat in front of her. "Guess *Ry*an did meet the grave."

"Why are you calling her that?"

"What? Ryan? It's just a joke—lighten up."

"Actually, why don't you shut it."

"What did you say?"

"Did I stutter? I told you to *shut it*."

Ana wasn't sure how loud she'd said it, but the entire room went quiet.

"Girls, is there a problem?" Ms. Gregg asked, concerned. "Ana?"

"No, ma'am, not unless you call small-minded ignorance and a deploringly awful sense of humor a problem."

The bell rang for first period. Ana continued sketching

in her notebook and watching the door for Cole, but he never arrived. She drifted in and out of her classes. At lunch, there was still no sign of Rye or Cole. She waved to Brady in the cafeteria at his new lunch table and made her way to the art studio.

"Do you have a makeup assignment, Miss Cortez?" Mrs. Darnell peered at Ana from behind a canvas on an easel.

"No, I was just hoping to come in early to work on my midterm project. May I?"

"By all means."

Ana went to her assigned drawer and pulled out the large piece of drawing paper nearly filled with color. The assignment had been what Mrs. Darnell called a "free creation" piece. The theme, which was still written on the chalkboard, was WHERE I COME FROM.

Ana set the paper down on the table, took out her colored pencils, and got to work. She pressed the colors in one by one, working fast as she shaded and rounded the edges, softening the people and place. She was so lost in the work she didn't notice Mrs. Darnell standing over her.

"May I have a look?"

Ana leaned back, not saying anything.

Mrs. Darnell's eyes roamed over the piece, taking in a woman in a floral dress floating in a creek, her braids and fingernails and toes tethered to the shore as if held there by veins, an open hole where her stomach should be, the water flowing pink. There were trees casting dark shadows, music lyrics written in cursive lettering floating up and out of her into the breeze.

"Who is the woman?"

"My abuela . . . my grandma."

"Her face is very beautiful. Can you tell me more about it?"

Ana swallowed and cleared her throat. "She's resting, in the river, alone, but the water is cleansing her."

"And the lyrics? They're in Spanish?"

"Yes, in English they say, 'Take me to the river, cover me with your shawl, because I'm dying of cold.'"

"What's the symbolism behind all of the black doves watching from the trees?"

"They represent different elements . . . my mother and father, other people from where I grew up." She sat up and wiped her face and nose.

"It's just extraordinary, Ana, absolutely stunning. I know you're not entirely finished, but you should feel very proud of this work, very proud of sticking to what flows from you."

The bell rang. Mrs. Darnell placed her hand on Ana's shoulder and walked back to the front of the classroom. She continued working, oblivious to the other students coming in until a book slammed down on the table.

"I'm so relieved to see you," Ana said, careful not to push. "I . . . I hope you're feeling better."

"I'm grounded until graduation, and I'm not allowed to talk to you, so . . ."

"Abbie told me. That's not going to stop me from being concerned about you, though."

"What's the point when I know you'd rather hang out with Cole anyway?" Rye sat down and rummaged through her bag.

"That's not true and you know it. Yes, we're interested in each other, but he's interested in you too. I know he wants to make things right and go back to being friends."

"What, did he tell you all about his sappy apologies? Did he lure you in with his bad-boy-gone-good lies? Has he been cast in his own teen soap opera yet?"

"He told me how much your friendship means to him."

"He told you what you wanted to hear to get into your pants. You know he told Jim about me—*Jim* of all people. Friends don't do that to one another. Friends protect one another and wait for one another and don't go running off with the first cute boy they meet."

"Rye . . ."

"You have no idea what kind of pressure I get from home to be the smiling little girl in the picture all the time. You have no idea what it's like for your parents to look at you like you're about to break."

"No, you're right. I don't know what it's like."

"I can't do the wrong thing, okay? And I can't handle their suddenly being hands off with me, like I've got some sort of disease they're sympathetic to but don't know how to treat."

The bell rang and everyone began making their way to their seats, projects in hand. Rye got up, went to her drawer, and came back with her sewing kit and the large piece of fabric she'd been tailoring. The class began to work, quiet chatter reverberating around the room. Rye threaded her needle; Ana went back to her drawing.

"I told them it was your idea."

"What was?" Ana said, looking up.

"I told my parents you were the one who wanted to take the mushrooms, that I felt pressured. I don't know why I said it, but I did."

Ana rose from the table and walked out of the room.

There were more people than Ana imagined there would be walking down Main Street at this time in the afternoon.

She ducked into Bungle Records, which, thankfully, was empty, and began perusing the back rows of vinyl records, hoping she wouldn't be spotted. She hadn't intended to walk out of art class and continue walking all the way out of school, ditching her last period entirely. She flipped through the records in the punk section while listening to the owner hum along to a live album for some jam band. She checked her watch and figured she could kill time looking at records for another hour.

She flipped through cover after cover, wondering if she'd have to explain everything to Abbie.

Had the Moons' told Abbie that it had been Ana's fault too? Had Abbie believed them? Is this why she'd left last night and had been so quiet earlier that morning?

"Looking for anything in particular?" the owner inquired, eyeing her as if she were a thief.

"Yeah, where's the heavy metal section?" she asked. He pointed her to the row behind where she was standing. She began sorting through the records again, passing photo after photo of men with big hair and illustrations of demonic skeletons. She wanted to move on to another section, but also needed to kill time, so she decided to keep flipping through until she got to the end. "Hair, skeleton, hair, horns," her mind said. "Hair, hair, Abbie."

She couldn't help gasping.

"Find what you were looking for?" the man said, fearing something was wrong.

"No, sir . . . I mean, yes, sir."

She pulled the record out and looked at it closely. The band was called Nightshade and the album was titled *Midnight Angel*. It was glossy black except for the photo of a much younger Abbie in a somewhat revealing white dress

on the front of it, her hands in the prayer position as she
floated up to the sky.

"How much is this?" she asked.

"Twenty-five. It's a collector's item."

Ana fished for the bus ticket money she'd always kept at
the bottom of her backpack, just in case, and paid for it.

She was in such a daze from ditching school and finding
the album that she didn't realize she was early when she
entered The Bracken. There were a few people inside at
various tables, so Ana had a seat at the counter.

"Food, coffee, or both?" asked the new waiter behind
the bar.

"Nothing. Actually, I'm looking for Will. Is he around?"

The waiter headed to the kitchen. Ana swiveled in her
seat. The café was becoming more crowded, she noticed: a
few people having coffee in the corner, a man enjoying a
bowl of soup. It was sunny outside despite the dropping
temperatures, a golden tint to the afternoon light. Ana felt
a longing to know what it must feel like to belong to a place,
and hoped that if she continued to make things right, that
maybe she would. Maybe this would be her place.

"Aren't you early?" Will said, drying his hands.

"History midterms. I finished early."

"Want something while you wait for Abbie?"

"No, thanks," she said. "But I brought something for
you." She reached into her backpack, pulled out the brown
paper bag, and handed it over to him.

"What's this?" Will said, sliding the album out of the
bag, his eyes going wide. "No! Where did you find it?"

"At Bungle across the street. She's been there all along."

He laid it on the counter and stared at it.

"It's her, isn't it?" Ana said.

"It is," he said, picking it up and holding it in front of him. "Still slays me right through the heart."

Will flipped it over and they both read the song names, laughing at the titles and the photo of the band, who featured the requisite amount of hair and black leather pants.

"What are you two so engrossed in?" Abbie said, coming in and sitting down at the counter.

They both looked up, startled.

"What is that?" Abbie said, leaning in before going completely rigid. "Whose is this?" she demanded, her face flushed.

"I . . ."

"It's mine," Will said. "Guilty as charged."

"Get your things, Ana."

"But—"

"*Now.*"

She marched out of the restaurant. Ana grabbed her backpack and turned to Will, who shook his head and shrugged his shoulders as if he didn't know what had happened either.

Abbie drove faster than normal. She whipped the van around and rolled down her window, the cold air streaming in.

"Was that some kind of joke?" she said.

"It wasn't meant to be."

"Why on earth would he have that? I bet he's had it the whole time! I told him I never wanted to see that thing again."

"I bought it for him."

"You what?"

"I found it in the record shop, and I knew it was something Will might like, so . . ."

"*How* would you know that it would be something he would like?"

"Because he likes you."

They rounded the black oak tree and pulled into the driveway. A white Mercedes was parked along the fence. "Who is this?" Abbie said before both she and Ana saw Nadine Brannan standing on the front porch with Emmett. "Here we go," Abbie said. "As if this day couldn't get any more absurd. Let me do the talking."

They got out of the van and walked toward the front door. Emmett was pacing back and forth while Nadine stood still, one hand resting on her hip. "Hello, Nadine," Abbie said, approaching.

"I hope you're happy with yourself," Nadine said to Ana.

"What's going on?" Abbie said.

"Why don't we all go inside," Emmett said. "Ana, please wait on the porch."

"No, she should hear this," Nadine continued. "My son has had a tremendously difficult time," she said, turning to Abbie. "I'm sure you're aware of our family situation. It's been difficult on my kids—Cole especially. All was going well after all that business last year. I'm sure you heard about the bonfire from the paper and, well, you know the rest. He's finally back in school, getting his grades up, back together with all of his friends, and then in the last few weeks—I couldn't put my finger on it—but something shifted. And then my mind went back to that night in our laundry room . . ."

"What night?" Abbie interrupted.

"That's when it all began, the two of them. And now my son is sneaking out to ride his bike, listening to all of this loud music, locked up in his room. He came home last night telling me all about this girl, this Ana, and how he wants to make everything right at home, as if that is going to fix all our problems. . . ."

"I'm not sure what we're getting at here, Nadine," Emmett said.

"Well, I've made some inquiries and discovered quite a lot about Miss Cortez."

"Ana, go back to the van, please," Abbie said, but Ana remained standing at the foot of the front steps.

"I know the two of them have been meeting out in the woods. Cole is forbidden back there, and we signed papers with you and with Mr. Kinman that forbid anyone from cutting through our property to the cliffs."

"Wait a minute," Emmett said. "Let's not go accusing—"

"Did you not walk to the cliffs yesterday?" Nadine said accusingly, turning toward Ana.

"Yes and no . . ."

"Which one is it?" Emmett asked.

"I ran into Cole in the forest a long time ago. We had a brief conversation before I headed back. I also ran into him yesterday when I took Dolly for a walk. . . ."

"I never gave you permission to walk all the way to the beach," Emmett said.

"You see," Nadine said. "She is not to be trusted."

"Hey now," Abbie said.

"Look, you have no idea about the money we have spent rehabilitating our son this summer. He had a bit of a hiccup last year, but we sent him away and fixed the problem. He's a happier kid, and my daughter is happy to have her brother back. I don't expect either of you to understand the gravity of a situation such as this, but when my son confided in my daughter what he's been up to and she dutifully divulged all of this to me, including the fact that the other night he was drinking with her—" Nadine pointed to Ana. "I had to come over here and set things straight. I understand you are the sort of charitable people who feel comfortable opening up your home to someone like this, but I cannot and will not allow my son to be taken back down that road again."

"And which road do you think that is?" Abbie asked.

"Not the road my husband took, getting involved with someone like . . ."

"Someone like what?" Abbie pressed.

"I would think that you of all people would understand, Emmett," Nadine said.

That was all it took. One sentence, one look from Nadine Brannan, and Emmett allowed all the pent-up rage to spill out onto the porch.

"Get off our property *right* now," Emmett said, taking a step toward her. "I said get in your goddamned car and leave!"

Nadine walked down the stairs as Ana watched, dumbfounded at what just took place, trying to understand what she did to cause this much of a commotion. Abbie walked over to Emmett and tried to put her hand on his shoulder, but he pulled away.

"I can't handle this," Emmett said, speaking to himself. "I can't handle this anymore."

He made his way to the barn as Nadine sped out of the driveway and back down the road.

"I don't understand what's happening," Ana said.

"Let's go inside," Abbie said softly. "This isn't your fault. I need to explain a few things."

She held open the door, but Ana couldn't move. She'd been here before, been in the corner, under the table, behind the couch. There was always an accusation followed by yelling. There'd be a conversation, an explanation, and then she'd be asked to leave.

"I need to tell you about Emmett and Josie," Abbie said. "It will all hopefully make more sense. This has nothing to do with you."

"If it's okay, I'd like to be alone for a while." Ana walked past Abbie into the dark house, crossing through the parlor, knowing which furniture to dodge, which paintings on the wall not to knock into. She made her way upstairs and fell into the bed. She stayed there, giving in to the heaviness, waiting for Abbie to knock. The house remained quiet and still.

She wasn't sure how long she'd been asleep, but it was dark when she woke up. She turned on the light and sat up, propping her sketchbook on her knees. She thought she heard a rumble outside. The light was off in the hallway, so she went to the window and pushed back the curtain. There was a single light fixed on the road, someone on a motorcycle. She turned off the lamp and turned it back on again, then turned it off and on again one more time. The figure in the road flashed a headlight in the same way.

Ana put on her jacket and opened the window.

CHAPTER EIGHTEEN

She was surprised they made it down the farm's dirt road without being caught. They pushed the motorcycle down the hill together. It was just a quick joyride, Cole had said. He handed her a helmet and she hesitated before jumping onto the back behind him, her arms encircling his waist. He kicked the machine to life, and they sped down Crescent Lane, away from the farm and toward the beach.

Cole continued on the road for several miles. The motorcycle roared underneath her, the wind shushing against her helmet. Ana wondered if Abbie had knocked on the bedroom door by now. She closed her eyes and held on tight. When she opened them, she and Cole were speeding through the redwoods, flashes of green and brown and red illuminated by a single headlight. Cole slowed down and pulled off the road, edging them up to a metal sign advertising a campground. They sat there for a moment before he eased them both off the leather seat.

"Here seems good," he said.

Ana glanced from side to side. The sky was a ghost gray. Nothing but trees surrounded them. "Where are we?"

"There's a campground through the trees," Cole said. "I dirt biked all over these woods with my dad when I was a kid, so I know exactly where we're going. I thought we could watch the sunrise."

"But what are we doing?" she mumbled to Cole and to herself.

"Getting lost," he answered.

She nodded, still unsure. "Fine. Just for a little while, and then you can take me back, okay?

Cole grabbed his backpack from the rear of the motorcycle. He led them down a path and into the woods with a flashlight. The air was clean and pungent, the trees still dripping from a recent rain. There was a chill in the air. Ana was glad she'd worn her sneakers and jacket. She zipped up the jacket over Emmett's Tom Petty T-shirt.

They arrived at the camping area, which was completely empty. There were signs that read NO TRESPASSING.

"Technically the grounds aren't open," Cole said. "But that's never stopped me before."

Ana pulled a blanket out of the backpack and threw it around her shoulders. She wandered over to a nearby picnic table to watch Cole make a fire.

"Rye told me you were a pyro," she said. "I believe the word 'nihilistic' was also thrown in."

"My bonfires are legendary. But trust me, I know what I'm doing."

He got the fire going as she spread the blanket out on the ground. They sat down next to each other and watched the fire crackle and burn.

"What?" she said.

"Nothing." He wanted to tell her that even when she scrunched her face, he never wanted to stop staring at it. "You scare me, that's all."

"I scare you?"

"Yeah. I don't know how to explain it, but you have this look that's one part 'I could kill you' and one part 'Rescue me.'"

"Is that what you're doing? Rescuing me? Because I can rescue myself."

It was the first time anyone had come to her rescue, though, she thought—besides the time Abbie helped her get into art class, and the time Mrs. Saucedo got her a job on a farm, or earlier in the day when Will had lied on her behalf.

"That's not what I meant." Cole couldn't read Ana's mood, but it had shifted since they'd entered the woods.

"I think I need to get back," she said, remembering what Manny had told her about going with her gut.

"What's the rush? It's not as late as you think, and if they've already discovered you're gone, what's one more hour?"

Cole was right. It wasn't as if Abbie and Emmett cared in the way she thought they did anyway. It was almost November. They'd probably be sending her back soon. After the incident with Rye, ditching class, Nadine accusing her of being an alcoholic influence on Cole, and now this, she figured she might as well enjoy what might be the last good night for a while.

"So, about my mom coming to visit the Garbers earlier," Cole started to say.

"Can we not?" Ana said. "I don't want to relive it for both our sakes."

He walked over to the fire and pushed the logs around, making the flames leap higher.

"When I asked you if you wanted to get lost with me for-ever, I sort of meant it," he said.

"Where are we going to get lost to?"

"I don't know, Portland? There's so much good music, and I hear they have killer doughnuts."

"Are you serious?"

"Kind of, not really. It was just a thought." But Cole was serious. The thought of going back to a fractured household seemed worse. He was sick of his mother's constant worry, sick of her blaming his father for everything, even though he agreed with her.

"But you have a family. They'd be devastated if you left. Your mom can't even handle you talking to a girl in the laundry room of your own house."

"Actually, it's me she can't handle. I just feel it would be better for everyone if I weren't there all the time. It's like my mom sees my dad's face in mine or something, like I'm a constant reminder of what he did to her, to us."

"She loves you, you know; even if it means attacking other people, she does it to protect you. She said some crazy things to me, and I can still tell you that she did it because she wants nothing but the best for you. I think you're luck-ier than you think."

Cole shook his head and exhaled toward the sky. "Hon-estly, I don't know what to say when people go on about how perfect they think my life is just because I live in that stupid house."

"That's not why I said it . . . but please, lump me into a stereotype."

"That wasn't what I was doing. Sorry. I'm just sick of the whole situation at home. I'm tired of hearing my sister cry all the time."

Ana didn't press him.

"Are you cold?" he asked. "Hungry?"

"All of the above, I think."

He reached into the bag and pulled out several small wrapped packages. He slid one over to her. "What is it?" she asked.

"Leftovers pilfered from our kitchen."

Ana unwrapped a wedge of cheese. There were crackers, nuts, olives, fruits, and chips along with half a loaf of bread, cookies, and plastic utensils. He reached back into the bag and pulled out a thermos.

"Courtesy of Nathaniel Brannan," he said, raising the thermos to the sky. "What is promised to be an extraordinary pinot noir."

"Did you pilfer the family vineyard too?"

"Yep, got it right here in my pack."

They snacked and sipped, periodically stoking the fire, trying not to laugh at each other when there were moments of silence. It was easier to study him in class when Ana was a row behind and he wasn't looking. She liked that he sometimes rested his hand on his neck, an absentminded reflex as if he were trying to reach out and hold onto himself. Ana never knew that he'd always imagined reaching for her.

"What?" she said.

"Nothing," he answered. "You just . . . I don't know. I want to kiss you all the time. Not gonna lie."

"I think I just got wine up my nose." She laughed, doubling over.

"What's that?" he asked, reaching over and touching the nape of her neck.

"A tattoo." She pulled up the collar on her jacket.

"I know it's a tattoo. May I see it?"

"It's getting cold . . . right?"

He reached over and grabbed her hand, touching each finger, pressing his thumb into her palm. She didn't understand how every logical thought seemed to evaporate with even his lightest touch.

"Why don't you want to talk about it? We've got a whole fireside chat going on here."

"Because it's hard to . . . because I hate it."

His hand went to her neck again, brushing her hair away and resting on her back. "It's interesting, though, and it's obviously something you chose—"

"It's not, and I didn't," Ana said, pulling away and staring into the fire. "I was six years old, they held me down, I screamed the whole time."

"You had that done when you were *six*?"

"It happens sometimes, but they usually do it in a more hidden place until you're old enough to get one that's visible."

"Who did this?"

"Some people my parents were involved with. . . ." She didn't want to come right out and say it was a gang. She didn't want to name them or give them any more attention than they'd given her. "More of an organized crime group— drug dealing, guns, that sort of thing. Both of my parents were a part of it."

"And these people did this to you? Why?"

"Because my parents were taken, and my grandma."

"What do you mean?"

"They were killed by a rival gang." She stopped, not believing that she was saying it. In all the years Mrs. Saucedo had tried to get her to open up even the slightest about both the first and second times she'd been brought in to child services, Ana had never spoken a word. She took a breath and continued. "My parents were shot while I was in the house. My grandma got hit a year later on the sidewalk in the middle of the day. When my grandma was killed, this woman took me in right off the street. She knew my parents, was part of their crew, I guess. Her husband and son too. Anyway, they were the ones who did it. It isn't completely uncommon. But it marks me as theirs. Forever. It's part protection, part possession. That's how it works."

His hand lingered on her neck. "No wonder you don't want to go back there . . ."

"I'm tired," she said, resting her head on his shoulder.

He slid his hand down her back, pulling her closer to him. She rested her lips on the edge of his ear.

"I want to kiss you all the time too," she whispered.

They watched the fire die down, the forest growing louder, both of them knowing they should get up and go.

"Just five more minutes," she said.

"Okay," he answered.

They laid back on the blanket. Ana rested her head on Cole's chest. They both looked up at the moon.

CHAPTER NINETEEN

Against her better judgment, Abbie did as Ana asked and left her alone for the night. She peeked out of her bedroom door a few times, but the light in Ana's room remained dark. She didn't know what to say to her or how to explain Emmett's temper and the long saga behind it. She didn't know how to talk to Emmett either, so she decided to give in to her routine.

She headed downstairs to start breakfast. Eggs, toast, homemade jam, and a cup of blackberry tea were Ana's favorites. She busied herself and waited to hear the footsteps upstairs. Still, she heard nothing. By the time the food was ready and she checked the time, she knew something was wrong. She hadn't heard the alarm clock go off either, so her mind began jumping to conclusions. She ran through the back door and out to the barn. Emmett's lights were on, so she knocked on the door.

"Hello," he grumbled in the doorway, his face hanging, his eyes barely open, the smell of scotch on his breath.

"I don't want to talk about last night," Abbie said. "Just come with me."

"Why?"

"Because Ana hasn't come downstairs and I'm worried."

"Probably overslept. Has a tendency to do so . . ."

"Just come with me."

He reluctantly followed, shushing Dolly's barking. They crossed through the garden—Abbie quickly, Emmett struggling to keep up—and into the house.

"Listen," Emmett said, leaning against the counter. "I don't know what happened yesterday but . . ."

"Not now."

Abbie continued up the stairs and to Ana's door, knocking on it once and then twice, but there was no answer. She slowly turned the knob and pushed the door open. The early morning light was dim, but it was enough to see that Ana's bed was made and she wasn't in it. "Oh my God," Abbie said. She pushed the door open all the way and went inside. "Oh no."

"What is it?" Emmett asked, making his way into the room and sobering up at the implications.

Abbie began systematically checking under the bed, in the armoire, and behind the curtains as if Ana were playing a cruel game of hide-and-seek.

"She's gone," Emmett said.

"No, she's not." Abbie darted to the bathroom, checking behind the shower curtain. She ran to her own bedroom and checked in every possible place including out the window before running downstairs.

"She's gone," Emmett said at the top of the stairs as Abbie

shuffled around the living room making a frantic mess, her hands holding on to the sides of her face. "She's gone," he said again, the words drifting away and then sinking back in.

He walked over to Ana's bed, picked up her sketchbook, and began flipping through it. He stopped at a detailed drawing of a house—Garber Farm—with Abbie standing in front surrounded by a lush garden sprouting wildflowers and vines of pickles. There were empty jars of marmalade rooted to the ground and a chicken pecking at a shriveled tomato. On the porch, seated in a rocking chair, was Emmett, Dolly seated dutifully by his side. Upstairs, in the window, watching over it all, was a solitary shadow barely shaded in. At the bottom of the paper, written in needlepoint print, was the word "sweet," with blank lines on either side of it, as if waiting to be stitched together to read "Home sweet home."

"You're going through her things at a time like this?" Abbie shouted frantically from the doorway.

"Look at this," Emmett said. He turned the page to another drawing. It was a pencil sketch of two interlocking women's bras—one small and black with messy triangles, the other sturdy and straightforward but covered in a pattern of what looked like backward threes. It was an odd drawing, Emmett thought, even if it was astonishing in its skill. At the bottom of the page, written out in graffiti, were the letters *BFF*.

"We've shattered her heart," Abbie said, on the verge of tears.

Emmett closed the notebook. "Honestly? She either snuck out to see Rye or, if my hunch is correct, Cole Brannan. Either way, I'm calling the police."

Emmett headed downstairs to the phone. Abbie paced in Ana's room. She opened up the armoire and sitting on the

Frida Kahlo book at the bottom of it was a map of Hadley and surrounding areas. She grabbed it and ran downstairs.

Emmett hung up the phone, his hand lingering on the receiver. He took a deep breath, trying to both compose himself and keep from passing out. "Cole's gone too," he said as Abbie leaned against the counter in semirelief. "His mother called last night and reported him missing. Said he'd taken his father's motorcycle. The police haven't started a search because they figured it was just a teen boy doing what teen boys do, only he's doing it with, well . . . our Ana."

Abbie held up the map.

"I think she's gone for good."

It was midmorning when Alder Kinman showed up at the front door of Garber Farm with a paper bag in his hand. Abbie ushered him into the kitchen where Emmett and Manny were talking to the sheriff and two policemen. "Heard what happened, gentlemen," he said. "Brought some honey and some news."

Abbie rested her hand on his arm and whispered, "Not now."

"We've already searched the woods behind the house but still have a few of our guys doing a final sweep," the sheriff said. "There's not much more we can do since it hasn't been twenty-four hours and, technically, it looks as though both parties left willingly like most kids in love do, like a few others I know have done in the past," he said, clearing his throat and nodding knowingly at Emmett.

"We need to find her," Emmett said.

"I understand that, but usually in cases like this, the kids come back and apologize and continue doing what kids do in the parking lot of Hadley High. I wouldn't worry."

"But she's our responsibility. What are we supposed to do?" Abbie asked.

"Wait. If she's not back by tomorrow, give us a call."

The officers shook Emmett and Abbie's hands and headed out the front door. Emmett paced back and forth, shaking his head. "This isn't enough," he said. "We have to do more."

"Got honey, got news," Alder Kinman repeated.

"Kind of you to bring it by," Abbie said. "We're just in the middle of a crisis at the moment."

"Heard all about it, whole town's talking."

"We're just trying to figure out what to do," Abbie said, Emmett still pacing across the room, Manny sipping a cup of coffee at the kitchen table. "But we appreciate your concern."

"I'm concerned all right, especially with that storm coming. It's set to hit hard this afternoon. Worried about those two kids being up north."

"What are you talking about?" Emmett asked.

"They went up north to the state park."

"How do you know that?"

"Eli told me."

"Who's Eli?" Abbie asked.

"A friend."

"Where is this friend and how does he know where Ana is?" Emmett said, raising his voice.

"Emmett," Abbie said, gesturing for him to calm down.

"Well, he lives in the forest and makes it his business to patrol the areas up north. I saw him this morning and he said they're up there."

"Did he see them?" Abbie asked.

"No telling. He has a strong intuition."

"Where is this man?" Emmett said. "I want to talk to him myself."

"Well, that's going to be difficult because he's got other things to do this afternoon. He lives by his own credo, as most bears do."

"Are you telling me that Eli is a bear?" Emmett asked.

"Yeah, boy."

Emmett ran his hands through his hair and went out the back door.

"Can you tell me more about what Eli said?" Abbie asked Alder politely. Manny raised his eyebrows.

"Well, he said they were up somewhere near King's Pass. I say we gather all the folks we can and get a search going before the rain hits."

Abbie looked at Manny, who looked back at her.

"Emmett!" she shouted.

It was a quick drive to the Moons' house down the road, but to Abbie it felt like an eternity. She bit the side of her cheek, not caring that she was chewing a hole through it, and went over everything she'd handled poorly. As far as she was concerned, this was entirely their fault. Ana was the reason she and Emmett were getting along again. She was the reason the workers stayed and seemed to enjoy coming to work more than ever before. And though he was unable to see it and would never admit to it, she was the reason Emmett was breaking his wicked spell.

Abbie parked in the Moons' driveway. She walked across the gravel and thought of Ana out in the woods somewhere, hopeful that she was smart enough to know that she was wanted, that she was loved, and that there were people coming to get her.

"Come in," Della said, opening the door, her face uncharacteristically tense.

"Thank you," Abbie said, holding back a wave of tears. "I have something for Rye. I thought she might be of help— that is, if she wants to be involved. Ana has run away."

"We heard."

"Della . . . I don't know what to say other than I'm sorry. I should have called you the other night, I should have told you what happened yesterday morning when I brought Rye back. I . . . I'm not good at this."

"I accept your apology," Della said, opening her arms, the two old friends embracing. "That girl has been beating herself up all morning and is still grounded." Della walked to the foot of the stairs and called up to Rye, who was already on her way down. "What do you have to say to Abbie?"

"I'm sorry for what I put you through the other night."

"It's quite all right."

"And I'm sorry for lying about Ana."

"What do you mean?"

Rye looked to her mother, who nodded back. "I lied to my parents and told them Ana forced me to take the mushrooms, but she didn't. She wanted nothing to do with it. But I think that's why she ran away."

"Well, we can't do anything about that now." She handed the BFF drawing to Rye and watched her face as it lifted and fell.

"I'm going to kill her when we find her," she said. "I mean that in a good way."

They decided to form teams with Emmett as the lead and head contact. One group fanned out along the southern border of the park, while another headed farther up north to the park's main entrance. Will Carson joined Abbie and the Moons. Manny rounded up the boys to accompany Emmett, with Rolo in particular wanting to get started as soon as possible. Alder Kinman suggested they check local campgrounds too. "Something tells me that's where you'll find them."

Manny drove with Emmett in the passenger seat of the truck. He'd known his boss for a very long time, had learned to gauge the ever-shifting moods. But in all the years, through all the circumstances and heartbreak, he'd never seen Emmett this thoroughly unsettled.

"I know what you're thinking," Manny said. "We'll find her."

CHAPTER TWENTY

She woke up and wondered where she was. It was damp outside, thick clouds swelling overhead, the fresh air mingling with morning drizzle. Her nose was cold and there was someone wedged in next to her. Ana turned her face and there was Cole, looking serene with his eyes closed. She sat up and realized they'd fallen asleep.

"Oh my God," she said. "Oh. My. God. Wake up!"

She gently shook Cole, who barely stirred.

"It's the next day!" she shouted, frantic. "Get up!"

Cole opened his eyes as Ana got up and began pacing around the campground. There was a rustling out in the forest, possibly a deer or fox. She glanced at the watch, being reminded of its previous owner, whose spirit still ticked along with it.

Cole finally came to, the realization of their predicament sinking in. As he woke up, the drizzle turned into steady drops of real rain, and the branches began swaying overhead.

Cole jumped up and folded the blanket. They both picked up
the remnants of their late-night feast, surprised they hadn't
been attacked by some wild animal for a morsel of cheese.

"I'm going to be in so much trouble," Ana said.

"So am I."

"They're probably already buying my return ticket to L.A."

"I may have to join you. . . . Is this the way we came in?"
Cole asked. There were several clearings in the trees, none
of them marked.

"I don't remember, didn't notice. Haven't you been here
before?" Ana joked.

"I have, but now there's a trail over there," he said, pointing in the opposite direction, "and one over there too." Turning toward a wider path on the opposite side of the grounds,
he said, "I should have checked the perimeter last night."

"This is a problem," Ana said.

"I think it's the wider one. The trail most people use is
always the widest one, right?"

"I'm going to say yes and hope we're right."

They headed down the wider trail into the trees. It was
flat and smooth as they wound in and around the massive
trunks keeping them dry under the branches. The path nar-
rowed up ahead, and Ana wondered if Cole noticed it too. It
seemed as if they'd been walking longer than they had the
night before, but Cole soldiered on, grabbing her hand to
help her over a fallen tree crossing the pathway.

"I don't remember this tree," she said.

"Maybe it fell over in the night."

"You really don't know where we're going, do you? I can
tell by your expression that you think we're going the wrong
way too," Ana said.

"This feels like the right way."

"Except that it's not. It's raining and I don't think it's safe to ride on a slick highway if the weather gets worse."

"Ana. I've been riding since I was a kid. We have all the time in the world to get to where we're going."

"No, we don't," she said, feeling out of breath. "I'm doing it again."

"What?"

"Screwing it all up."

"We just fell asleep; it's not a big deal. Just tell them the truth when you see them."

"I don't get yelled at or grounded, okay? I get sent to live in a group home with a bunch of other people like me who have had the worst of the worst. I've done it twice before, and I'd rather stay here and live off the land than go back to that."

"Hey," Cole said, worried. The Ana he'd always seen was calm and in control. This Ana was losing it. "Let's head back the other way, okay?"

"It won't change the fact that we're late and that I'm completely done here. That everything—the farm, the Garbers, Rye, you—all of it is going to go away."

"You don't know that's going to happen," he said, reaching for her hand. "There's no sense stressing about it now when there's nothing you can do."

"But there's something I could have done," Ana said, moving her hand away. "I could have avoided you just like Emmett told me to."

"Why are you freaking out?"

"Because this is serious to me, okay? This is it for me. I don't have a family to go back to. I don't have another chance."

"Why don't we calm down for a minute . . ."

"Don't tell me to calm down. Why aren't *you* freaking out? You have two parents and a sister who love you. They're probably sick with worry. I can't believe that I'm worried about people who probably don't even care about me, and you have people who actually do and you could care less."

"Whoa, wait. Where is this coming from all of a sudden?"

"I just . . . I just don't think you know how great you have it."

"Oh, so it's great that my mom cries every night and drinks herself to sleep because she's devastated by my dad. It's great, as you say, that my younger sister purposefully crashed her dirt bike—twice—just to get their attention. I grew up in a big house, yes, and with two parents, but they've fought every day of my life. They've put us in the middle of their battles and pitted us against each other. Yeah, I may have done some acting out last year, but the fact that their punishment was to send me away and then lock me down for the entire summer was awful. I'll never forget how happy they looked to leave me in the middle of the wilderness with a bunch of people who actually have serious problems. The only thing they've agreed on in as long as I can remember is getting rid of me."

"They spent tons of money on you to hike in Yosemite for a couple of months. I'm sorry, but that doesn't sound too terrible."

They both stood there in the middle of the forest, the rain pelting down and the wind picking up and whirring through the trees.

"I think your parents' marriage falling apart has nothing to do with you. You have a place to live and people to take care of you—a family—that's something I'll never have. Have you ever thought about what that's worth?"

"Do you not think you have anything that's worth something?"

"I have a file," she said. "It tells several sad stories, all of which are written down so nobody will forget, especially me. When I hear people talk about their 'home' or their 'family,' I always want to tell them that even their ability to use those words is all I've ever wanted. Try being locked in a house for days while your parents go off somewhere to get high or forget about you altogether in the backseat of their car. Try getting a dog as a kid only to watch it get beaten and then eaten alive by other dogs. I watched that happen, in our backyard, and I've had to learn how to live a different version of that story so it doesn't haunt me at night. Try hearing gunshots across the street, next door, in your own house, and then finding your mother on the couch covered in her own blood. Try going to live with your grandma afterward, who loves and cares for you, who is the family and the home you've always wanted, only to have her gunned down by the same hands that killed your mother and stole your father and all because she walked down the wrong street. I've been shuffled from house to house, stranger to stranger, no one ever wanting me or believing in me or having faith in me. And I carry those people, that backwards three on the back of my neck, every day wishing, however terrible it all was, for them to come back."

Cole stepped closer and put his arms around her, even though she didn't embrace him back. "I'm not in your file," he whispered. "Neither is Rye. Abbie and Emmett are a new chapter."

"Ana!" Abbie shouted.

"Ana! Cole!" Will echoed behind her.

"This is pointless," Abbie said, stopping in the middle of the trail.

"We're not giving up," Will said. "If she's out here, we'll find her."

"She took off before we had a chance to explain. This is all my fault," Abbie said, shaking her head, and starting to walk faster. "I can't believe I got so upset about that stupid album cover."

"I can't either. I used to pray to that woman."

"Now you'll probably shout at the devil."

"Did you just make a heavy metal joke in the middle of a crisis?" Will asked, putting his hand on her arm.

"I'm delirious," Abbie said. "Don't read too much into it. But . . . well, I think it's flattering that you're my only fan."

"I told Ana about how I worshipped that album. I think she found it randomly, sort of like you found her."

Abbie stopped and took a breath.

"She's more mature than you give her credit for," Will said.

"She reminds me of me at that age, which is ironic considering I did this exact same thing to my father," Abbie said. "Only when I ran I didn't come back until there was significant crash and burn . . . and an album to prove it."

Rye and Della caught up with them, Della clearing the thicket with her walking stick. "A fierce spirit always finds her way back—and she will."

"Seriously, Mom, she's been making out all night with a hot dude on an ironic motorcycle on the open road. They're probably holed up in some diner making eyes at each other over a plate of waffles," Rye said, sauntering past them and continuing to call out into the trees.

"I can't seem to shake this ominous feeling," Abbie said. "I can't seem to stop shaking."

"Are you sure this is the way?" Ana said.

"We've tried every other path; this is the only one left," Cole said, taking her hand.

They continued walking down the muddy trail, the rain lighter and dripping from the trees.

"So, are you finally going to enlighten me about what's going on between the Brannans and the Garbers?" she asked, stopping in the middle of the trail. "I've earned this story."

"It's not easy for me to talk about."

"If I get shipped back to L.A. without hearing about what caused the rift, I don't know what I'm capable of doing. And please don't say it's solely about land."

"Emmett should be the one to tell you."

"Well, he's not here, so go for it."

"The land was an issue at first—"

Ana put her hands over her ears.

"Which is how my dad met Josie."

Ana's hands shifted to her mouth. "No."

"Yes. They ran off together a little more than a year ago. They left us all handwritten notes, of course, because it's only polite, right? Ours was left on the fridge—have no idea where Emmett found his. But they took off to the Bahamas, then to New York, then back to San Francisco, where he bought her an apartment, apparently, and moved in without looking back, except for when his wife refused a divorce, and then he moved to Keyserville. Now, he splits his time in between. My mom still refuses to divorce him, so she started throwing parties with his money instead."

"Hardcore."

"I think that's also why she's purposely been ordering catering from Abbie."

"Double hardcore."

"My sister's begging and pleading didn't bring him back, nor did my bonfire party or stint in Yosemite. He still sends money in his absence, but I refuse to touch a cent."

"Why not?" Ana said, skipping up ahead. "We could have flown to Portland."

She waited for his laugh, or a snarky comment, but when she turned around, she froze.

A makeshift command center had been set up near the entrance to Kenyon Park. Emmett's and Manny's trucks were parked along with those of various townsfolk who had joined the hunt. Abbie and the others were surprised to see a few police cars in the mix, including the sheriff's.

"I thought you said they didn't want to do a big search," Della said.

"They didn't. But it's not like they have anything else better to do," Abbie said.

The sheriff emerged from behind his car with a distraught Nadine Brannan behind him. Two other police officers stood nearby taking notes.

"But that's his motorcycle!" she yelled.

"I know it is, ma'am, and that's why we've got our guys out on the trail searching. They're in here somewhere. My guess is they got lost, which happens all the time up in these parts."

"He left his credit card and his cell phone on the kitchen counter in plain sight for me to see. If that doesn't scream suicide note, I don't know what else does."

"Mrs. Brannan, we have all the evidence to believe that your son left of his own volition. We're trying to rule out something happened to these kids in the forest. We lose hikers out here all the time with this kind of weather. We're doing the best we can."

Abbie watched as Nadine's face dropped. It wasn't because she wasn't in control or that the police were unwilling to make her son a priority; Abbie realized that she was suffering as a mother, and no one was noticing that. Abbie walked over as Nadine stood there, her face blank.

"How are you holding up?" Abbie asked.

"Not well. If these idiots would actually get out there and do their jobs properly, maybe we'd have found my son by now. There's no telling where he could be, and they're losing time by limiting the search to right here because of some crazy beekeeper's bear theory. It's the most ludicrous thing I've ever heard of! I could kill my husband for moving us to this place."

Abbie refrained from saying anything she'd regret, especially the part where Alder Kinman found Cole's motorcycle near the entrance to the park. She chose to respect Nadine's pain as a mother even if she didn't understand the woman's undermining platitudes. "I can empathize with how worried you must feel."

"And how is that?"

"I'm only measuring it with what I'm feeling about Ana, and my fears and worries for her well-being. I can only imagine how difficult this must be for you."

"How can you begin to relate when you're not a mother

and you've never had children of your own? You don't have
the slightest inkling of what this feels like; so spare me the
empathetic concern." Nadine stopped herself. "I'm . . . I'm
sorry," she said, taking a moment. "I had no right to say
that. It's . . . it's been a long night and a tough year."

Despite her desire to walk the other way, Abbie put her
arm around Nadine's shoulders.

"I know," she said. "We'll find them"

They both stood completely still. There was a crunching of
sticks before Ana felt hot breath on her hand. It crept into
Ana's peripheral vision first, just a few feet to her left,
before making its way over to where Cole was standing. She
couldn't move. Cole gave her a look that said, "Stay calm."
The mountain lion eyed her and moaned, a long guttural
moan from the back of its throat as it licked its lips and low-
ered its head, its whiskers sniffing in Cole's direction.

It paced behind them, growling, before coming into full
view.

Something told them both not to scream or run. They
kept their eyes locked on each other, as flashes of burnt
yellow slunk in and out of the trees around them. Ana was
angled in a way that she had a clear view of the lion as it got
close enough to touch. Her legs began to tremble. She moved
her foot slightly, catching the cat's attention.

"It's coming," she mouthed to Cole as the cat moved forward and then back again. It hunkered down and growled.

Cole moved his body, positioning himself to take the full
weight of the attack if the cat should pounce. "Look at me,"
he mouthed to Ana.

The cat moved forward again before it stopped abruptly

just a few feet away. Ana looked back and forth from Cole to the cat as its entire body angled to jump.

There was a rustling in the trees.

The cat stepped back, then snapped its head to the right. It leaped and disappeared into the brush. Just as they were about to take a breath, a massive black bear ambled into the clearing. It stopped and seemed to make eye contact with Ana before continuing in the direction of the mountain lion.

"That's Eli," Ana said.

"Eli?" said Cole, still afraid to move.

"Yeah. I think I know that bear."

The sheriff and volunteer police officers headed back to Hadley, a few others joining them. Abbie approached Emmett, who was staring at a park map like it held the secrets of the universe.

"How's it going?" she asked him.

"Not well. We need to get back out there before it gets dark. I don't understand why people are leaving."

"Because they have jobs and families to tend to. But we can appreciate their help."

"I'm going back out there," Emmett said.

"Maybe's she's back at the farm already . . ."

"Minerva would have called by now," he said. "Your friend, the chef guy—"

"Will."

"Yes, Will. He just called and said he made it back to the restaurant. He rallied everyone on Main Street, so everyone's looking down there too, apparently."

"I'm amazed and not surprised," Abbie said.

"He's, uh, he seems like a good guy. Looks like Dad's

nightmare, of course, just like all the rest of them. But I give you my approval."

"Your approval? Do I still need that, big bro?"

"Always."

"At some point, we need to think about calling Mrs. Saucedo." Abbie sighed.

"I don't want to do that yet," Emmett said, taking control of the situation. It had been a long time since Abbie had seen her brother focused on something other than the farm. "I've been thinking, what if they're on their way to San Fran or up north and they crashed on that kid's bike? We are responsible for her well-being, Abbs. I don't understand why she left, why she didn't think to call or tell us when she's coming back."

"I don't think she wants to come back."

"She does," Manny said, approaching and tossing a couple of flares into Emmett's backpack. "I talk to her. But she worries. She puts pressure on herself. She's concerned about pleasing you both, but doesn't know how to do that and also be her own person. You have to trust that she has good instincts, especially for her age. She's very strong, not unlike two other people I know."

Della and Rye Moon ran to Charlie Moon's car, which pulled into the small parking area, and grabbed a box of flashlights to pass out to everyone. Nora and Brady Lawson arrived straight from the school run, a trunk full of milk and cookies from their dairy to hand out to the search party. Vic and Rolo huddled around Manny's truck with Joey, the three of them discussing Ana's disappearance and if she'd ever return, Joey vowing to return with her. Nadine Brannan stayed by her car, her ear glued to a phone, continuing her one-woman assault, allowing no one to intervene.

Everyone gathered with flashlights, water bottles, whistles, and even a bullhorn, waiting for Emmett's instructions as to how to divide into groups and which directions to go. That's when they heard the shouts. Way down the road, walking out of the trees and onto the edge of the road, was Alder Kinman, followed by Ana and Cole.

Without thinking, Abbie Garber ran down the road and met them halfway. Emmett watched as she threw her arms around Ana and held her there, not letting her go. Ana wrapped her arms around Abbie, the tears coming fast and quick, a relief in the heaving. Rye ran all the way too, embracing both Ana and Abbie, shaking them, smiles erupting. Emmett watched his sister put her arm around Ana again, her mouth saying, "You're okay. You're here. You're with us."

"You gave us one hell of a scare," he said as he approached.

"Even more than the day you saw me sitting at the airport?" Ana said.

"Much more than that." He patted her shoulder and pulled his hand away again. She hugged him anyway.

"Where were you?" Manny asked impatiently as he approached. "We've been so worried."

"We went for a ride and then we fell asleep. I'm . . . I'm sorry. I wasn't thinking when I left."

"Neither was I," Cole said, hoping if he chimed in as much as possible that maybe Ana wouldn't be sent away. He scanned the side of the road where all the cars were parked. He wasn't surprised that he didn't see his mother.

"We ran into some trouble," Ana said.

"Trouble?" said Emmett.

"They brushed up against a mountain lion," Alder Kinman explained, leaning against Emmett's truck with his thumbs hooked in his belt loops.

"If it wasn't for Eli," Cole said.

"Eli?" Emmett said, turning around.

"Eli . . . the bear, saved us," Ana said. "Scared the mountain lion away."

Alder nodded his head. "Yep. Just like I told ya, Eli's a good man."

The hugs continued all around. No one asked questions about what went on between Ana and Cole or why they'd run away. Nadine Brannan finally came running from her car, shouting to someone on the phone before tossing it into her handbag. She crossed the clearing, past the cars, making a beeline for her son as Cole walked up to meet her. Ana watched her run, waiting for her to embrace him, as Ana knew she would; she watched Cole waiting for the same thing. But once Nadine got there, tears running down her cheeks, she stopped and kept her distance.

"What in the hell were you doing? I've been on the phone with your father, who is outraged; your sister is a mess. And, in total, you have worried us to death with this selfishness. Was she worth it?"

"I'm fine, Mom. It's great to see you too. Thank you for the warm welcome. Glad you were able to reach Dad, wherever he is."

"What were you thinking? Did she put you up to this?"

Cole took a breath, realizing everyone was listening even though they were pretending not to.

"Do you realize what could have happened? And after all the progress you've made? I am utterly embarrassed, your father is furious . . ."

Cole glanced over at Ana, who looked back.

"Mom," he said, lowering his voice. "I'm sorry if I worried you."

"I can't handle this anymore, Cole, I just can't—"

He embraced his mother without giving her a moment to step back.

She was quiet before letting go. She reached up and embraced him back. "I can't stay here," she said. "Everything's falling apart. All of these people, this place . . . I don't know what to do anymore."

"I know," Cole said.

He looked over his mother's shoulder at Ana, who was looking over Abbie's shoulder. She smiled at him. It was a strange feeling, he thought, having your heart ripped in two. He knew the decision needed to be made, and he was the one who'd have to make it.

"We can leave here," Cole said to his mother. "If that will make it better."

Ana waved as the Moons drove away. She laughed as Rye thrust herself out of the back window of the car, both of them saluting each other, hands over breasts. Abbie was on the phone updating both Will and Minerva about the rescue. Emmett and Manny were talking with Joey, who said he wanted to return to Garber Farm. Ana leaned up against the back of the pickup truck. If she'd had her sketchbook, she thought, she wouldn't have wanted to capture this scene. Sometimes it was much better just to live it.

There was a flashing of headlights. Ana waited as Cole crossed the small parking area. She walked toward him and he toward her.

"You have to go?" she asked.

"We do," he nodded. "You have to stay?"

"Indeed."

Ana bit her bottom lip, holding it all in. She had never been pulled in two different directions before, but she knew which way she was going. She nodded her head and swallowed the tears. They held each other for a moment.

"See ya, Cortez," he said.

"See ya, Brannan."

She held out her hand and he took it.

"To beautiful endings."

EPILOGUE

It was the same wooden chair she was used to sitting in. It belonged to her now, or so she liked to think. There were papers on the table, more so than usual. Mrs. Lupe Saucedo sat opposite and adjusted her glasses.

Ana ran her hands along her kneecaps, smoothing down her new dress, adjusting herself to the fit. She remembered the first time she tried it on for Ellery Jonas and Pearl Parnell, who suggested she pair it with the new-old boots she purchased so many months ago.

"When something old fits like it was tailor-made," they said, "you can't let it go."

But she did let the dress go that day, a regret she kept in the back of her memory, never suspecting the fine ladies of Ellery Pearl Salon and Vintage would take it off the rack and hold it for her until the day it was meant to be hers.

"New dress for the occasion?" Lupe asked.

"Is this the first time you've seen me in a dress?"

"Yes, but it's perfect."

Ana crossed her legs, bobbing the top one up and down as Lupe finished going through the papers. "You ready?" she asked.

"I think so."

"I've been waiting for this day," she said.

"Me too."

Lupe handed the papers over along with a pen, indicating where Ana needed to sign. Ana squiggled the pen on page after page until she got to the last one, when she paused for a moment before signing her name in full.

"Welcome home," Mrs. Lupe Saucedo said, standing up, walking around the kitchen table, and giving Ana a hug. "Let's go tell them it's official."

Lupe and Ana walked out onto the front porch. Emmett let Dolly go, and she ran and barked her usual circles.

"There's no getting rid of me now," Ana said, hugging Abbie and Emmett. She made her way around to everyone— Manny and the boys, the Moons, her best friend, Rye.

"Killer dress, I told you you'd like it," Rye whispered.

"Roar."

"Roar."

It was a bright spring day, Hadley's ever-present clouds ducking in and out of the farm's redwood trees as the gathered group all sat around the picnic table sharing tea and cake.

"I hate to finalize an adoption and run," Lupe said, "but I've got a plane to catch."

Ana ran over to her and threw another hug around her neck. "Don't forget to say hi to the kiddos for me."

"Don't forget to call or come visit," Lupe said. "I want to

know how you're doing. Please tell Abbie thank you for the pickles and marmalade."

"I will," Ana said. She walked Lupe to the rental car.

Ana watched as Lupe drove out of Garber Farm, taking the file with the photograph of the girl in the pink puffy coat with her.

"Is it time?" she asked.

"Let's do this," Abbie answered.

They ran upstairs to grab their suitcases. Ana threw hers in the back of the van along with Abbie's, careful not to disturb the boxes of Garber Farm Artisanal products, which included Abbie's Brew and Moon Pharm Tea.

"Will you miss us or do you have activities to keep yourself occupied?" Abbie asked Emmett.

"Doll and I will manage just fine," he said.

Ana hopped into the passenger seat and studied how Abbie shifted the van into gear.

"I promise to let you practice once we're out on the road," Abbie said, "but only if you promise not to crash."

They made their way into town and pulled up to their usual spot outside The Bracken.

"Making progress," Abbie said, taking in the side wall of the building. "When do you expect to finish?"

"Next month, if I paint every weekend," Ana said.

"I won't be a minute." Abbie jumped out of the van and ran inside.

Ana stayed for a moment to take in her mural. The wild forest scene was nearly complete. She'd already finished the trees and ferns, but she still had a long way to go with the animals. She crossed the street and peered in at the crowd inside the restaurant. She watched as Abbie slipped behind the counter to grab the to-go bag, leaning into the window to shout something to Will, who waved a gloved hand.

"Yo!" Rye said, peeking out the front door. "Are you coming in or what?"

"Aren't you working?"

"Yeah, but that doesn't mean I can't share gravy fries with you at the bar every time I walk by with a tray of something you'll probably get to watch me drop."

"We're on when I get back. Abbie said we have to get on the road."

"Okay . . . well, have fun and bring back something—or someone," Rye said with a wink.

The drive to San Francisco was just under four hours, but Ana and Abbie didn't mind. In between bites of Will's sweet potato tots, they held marathon-long singing sessions with Stevie as well as Ana's addition of the Hex, who were slowly growing on Abbie. It was Abbie and Ana's first official trip together, and the first time Ana had ever done something fun for spring break.

"As you know, I'll be running from restaurant to restaurant this afternoon," Abbie said. "I'll come back and get you in a couple of hours. Then we'll go for the best burrito of your life."

"I'll believe it when I taste it."

"Please be careful and wait for me where I told you. Does he live nearby?"

"I told you, they're in Marin. It's just coffee."

"Okay. But don't go making another break for it."

Ana stepped out of the van and ran her fingers through her hair. She looked up and down the street before taking a deep breath.

"You look incredible," Abbie said through the window. "Don't do anything you've already probably done."

Ana waved good-bye and made her way down Valencia Street. She passed shops and bookstores and stopped at a stenciled painting of Frida Kahlo on the sidewalk.

The coffee shop was a few doors down. Her chest leaped as she picked up the pace.

It was bustling as she walked through the door of the shop. Every table was taken with people chatting, studying, or sipping alone. She scanned the room looking for the right table. She continued along all the way to the back, and just when she thought she might be out of luck, he appeared.

"Hi," she said.

"Hi," he answered.

THE STORY OF PENGUIN CLASSICS

Before 1946 . . . "Classics" are mainly the domain of academics and students; readable editions for everyone else are almost unheard of. This all changes when a little-known classicist, E. V. Rieu, presents Penguin founder Allen Lane with the translation of Homer's *Odyssey* that he has been working on in his spare time.

1946 Penguin Classics debuts with *The Odyssey*, which promptly sells three million copies. Suddenly, classics are no longer for the privileged few.

1950s Rieu, now series editor, turns to professional writers for the best modern, readable translations, including Dorothy L. Sayers's *Inferno* and Robert Graves's unexpurgated *Twelve Caesars*.

1960s The Classics are given the distinctive black covers that have remained a constant throughout the life of the series. Rieu retires in 1964, hailing the Penguin Classics list as "the greatest educative force of the twentieth century."

1970s A new generation of translators swells the Penguin Classics ranks, introducing readers of English to classics of world literature from more than twenty languages. The list grows to encompass more history, philosophy, science, religion, and politics.

1980s The Penguin American Library launches with titles such as *Uncle Tom's Cabin* and joins forces with Penguin Classics to provide the most comprehensive library of world literature available from any paperback publisher.

1990s The launch of Penguin Audiobooks brings the classics to a listening audience for the first time, and in 1999 the worldwide launch of the Penguin Classics Web site extends their reach to the global online community.

The 21st Century Penguin Classics are completely redesigned for the first time in nearly twenty years. This world-famous series now consists of more than 1,300 titles, making the widest range of the best books ever written available to millions—and constantly redefining what makes a "classic."

The Odyssey continues . . .

The best books ever written

PENGUIN CLASSICS

SINCE 1946

Find out more at www.penguinclassics.com

Visit www.vpbookclub.com